# PRAISE FOR THE BESTSELLING NOVELS OF IRIS JOHANSEN

## THE FACE OF DECEPTION

"One of her best . . . a fast-paced, nonstop, clever plot in which Johansen mixes political intrigue, murder, and suspense." —*USA Today*

"The book's twists and turns manage to hold the reader hostage until the denouement, a sure crowd pleaser." —*Publishers Weekly*

## AND THEN YOU DIE

"Iris Johansen keeps the reader intrigued with complex characters and plenty of plot twists. The story moves so fast, you'll be reading the epilogue before you notice." —*People*

"Fans of Mary Higgins Clark will enjoy Iris Johansen's latest, a supercharged thriller. There's peril, romance, and suspense aplenty as the good guys face the clock to stop the villains."
—*Alfred Hitchcock Mystery Magazine*

"A well-crafted romance thriller." —*Kirkus Reviews*

# THE KILLING GAME

## IRIS JOHANSEN

**BANTAM BOOKS**

NEW YORK   TORONTO   LONDON

SYDNEY   AUCKLAND

Excerpt taken from *Flight to Arras* by Antoine de Saint-Exupéry.
Translated from the French by Lewis Galantière.
Harcourt Brace & Company, 1942.

This edition contains the complete text
of the original hardcover edition.
NOT ONE WORD HAS BEEN OMITTED.

THE KILLING GAME
A Bantam Book

PUBLISHING HISTORY
Bantam hardcover edition published September 1999
Bantam paperback edition / May 2000

ISBN 0-553-58155-4

*Published simultaneously in the United States and Canada*

Bantam Books are published by Bantam Books, a division of Random
House, Inc. Its trademark, consisting of the words "Bantam Books" and
the portrayal of a rooster, is Registered in U.S. Patent and Trademark
Office and in other countries. Marca Registrada. Bantam Books, 1540
Broadway, New York, New York 10036.

My sincere appreciation once again to N. Eileen Barrow with the FACES Laboratory at Louisiana State University. She always meets my bizarre questions with courtesy, warmth, and a sense of humor.

Also my deepest thanks to Engineer Jarod Carson with the Cobb County Fire and Emergency Services for giving so generously of his time and help.

# CHAPTER
# ONE

*Talladega Falls, Georgia*
*January 20*
*6:35 A.M.*

The skeleton had been in the ground for a long time. Joe Quinn had seen enough of them to recognize that. But how long?

He turned to Sheriff Bosworth. "Who found it?"

"Two hikers. They stumbled on it late last night. Those rains the past few days washed it out of the ground. Hell, that storm slid half the mountain into the falls. A real gully washer." His gaze narrowed on Joe's face. "You must have hotfooted up here from Atlanta as soon as you heard about it."

"Yes."

"You think it's connected to one of the Atlanta PD's cases?"

"Maybe." He paused. "No. This is an adult."

"You're looking for a kid?"

"Yes." Every day. Every night. Always. He shrugged. "The initial report didn't say whether it was an adult or a child."

Bosworth bristled. "So? I never have to make reports like this. We're pretty crime free here. Not like Atlanta."

"You knew enough to recognize possible knife wounds to the skeleton's rib cage. But I do admit our problems are a little different. What's your population?"

"Don't come up here and slam me, Quinn. We've got a strong law enforcement body. We don't need any city cops messing around our jurisdiction."

He'd made a mistake, Joe thought wearily. He hadn't slept in nearly twenty-four hours, but that was no excuse. It was always an error to criticize local police even when they were taking potshots at you. Bosworth was probably a good cop, and he'd been polite until Joe cast aspersions on how he did his job. "I'm sorry. No offense."

"I do take offense. You have no idea what our problems are here. Do you know how many tourists we have every year? And how many get lost or hurt in these mountains? We may not have murderers or drug dealers, but we take care of every one of our citizens besides those tenderfeet who come up from Atlanta and camp in our parks and fall down in gorges and mess up—"

"Okay, okay." Joe held up his hand in surrender. "I said I was sorry. I didn't mean to downplay your problems. I guess I'm a little jealous." His gaze wandered out over the mountains and the falls. Even with Bosworth's men climbing all over, taping and scouring the area, it was still unbelievably beautiful. "I'd like to live here. It would be nice to wake up every morning to all this peace."

Bosworth was slightly appeased. "It's God's country. The Indians used to call the falls 'the place of tumbling moonlight.' " He scowled. "And we don't find skeletons like this. This must be one of yours. Our people don't kill each other and toss the bodies into the ground."

"Perhaps. It's a long way to transport a body. But in this wilderness, it would be quite a while before a corpse is discovered."

Bosworth nodded. "Hell, if it hadn't been for the

rains and the mud slide, we might not have found it for twenty, thirty years."

"Who knows? It might be that long already. I'll get out of your way. I'm sure your medical examiner will want to get at the bones and examine them."

"We have a coroner. He's the local undertaker." Bosworth added quickly, "But Pauley's always willing to ask for help when he needs it."

"He'll need it. If I were you, I'd make a formal request to our pathology department. They're usually willing to cooperate."

"Could you do it for us?"

"I can't. I'll be glad to put in a word, but I'm here in an unofficial capacity."

Bosworth frowned. "You didn't say that. You just flashed your badge and started asking me questions." His eyes suddenly widened. "My God, you're Quinn."

"It's no secret. I told you that."

"But I didn't make the connection. I've been hearing about you for years. The skeleton man. Three years ago you were over in Coweta County checking out two skeletons found there. Then there was that body found in the swamps near Valdosta. You were down there too. And that skeleton up near Chattanooga that you—"

"Word does get around, doesn't it?" Joe smiled sardonically. "I'd think you'd have better things to talk about. So? Do the stories make me some kind of urban legend?"

"No, just a curiosity. You're looking for those kids, aren't you? The ones Fraser killed and then refused to tell where he'd buried them." He frowned. "That was almost ten years ago. I'd think you'd give up."

"Their parents haven't given up. They want their children home for proper burial." He looked down at the skeleton. "Most victims belong to someone somewhere."

"Yeah." Bosworth shook his head. "Kids. I never understand why anyone would kill a kid. It makes me sick."

"Me too."

"I've got three kids. I guess I'd feel the same way those parents do. God, I hope I never find out." Bosworth was silent a moment. "Those cases must have been closed when Fraser was executed. It's mighty decent of you to keep trying to find those children on your own time."

One child. Eve's child. "It's not decent. It's just something I've got to do." He turned away. "Thanks for putting up with me, Sheriff. Call me if I can act as liaison between your coroner and the Atlanta PD."

"I'd appreciate that."

He started down the cliff and then stopped. To hell with not offending another law officer. The sheriff was clearly out of his depth, and by the time someone knowledgeable came on the scene, it might be too late to save the evidence. "Could I make a couple of suggestions?"

Bosworth stared at him warily.

"Get someone out here to photograph the body and entire crime scene."

"I was going to do that."

"Do it now. I know your guys are doing their best to locate evidence, but they're probably destroying more than they're finding. A metal detector should be used in case there's any evidence covered by the mud. And get a forensic archaeologist to excavate the skeleton and an entomologist to examine any dead insects or larvae. It's probably too late for the entomologist, but you can never tell."

"We don't have any of those people on our staff."

"You can hire them from a university. It may save you from having egg on your face later."

Bosworth thought about it and then said slowly, "Maybe I'll do that."

"It's up to you." Joe continued down the hill toward his car parked on the gravel road below.

Another blank; it had been a long shot anyway. But he'd had to check it out. He had to check them all out. Someday he'd get lucky and find Bonnie. He had to find her. He had no choice.

BOSWORTH STARED AFTER Quinn as he walked down the hill. Not a bad guy. A little too cool and contained, but maybe that went with dealing with those scumbags in the city. Thank God, he didn't have any weirdos out here. Just good people trying to lead a good life.

The skeleton man. He hadn't told the truth. Quinn was more of a legend than a curiosity. He had once been an FBI agent but had quit the Bureau after Fraser was executed. He was now a detective with the Atlanta PD and supposedly a good cop. Tough as nails and squeaky clean. These days it was hard for city cops not to give in to temptation. That was one of the reasons Bosworth stayed in Rabun County. He never wanted to experience the cynicism and disillusionment he had seen in Quinn's face. He couldn't be forty yet, but he looked as if he had gone to hell and back.

Bosworth glanced down at the skeleton. This was the kind of thing Quinn faced on a daily basis. Hell, he even went looking for it. Well, let him have it. Bosworth would be glad to get rid of the skeleton. It wasn't fair for his people to be drawn into this nasty—

His walkie-talkie buzzed and he pressed the button. "Bosworth."

"QUINN!"

Joe looked over his shoulder at Bosworth at the top of the cliff. "What?"

"Come back up here. My deputy just radioed me that my men on the far ridge have found more bodies." He paused. "Well, skeletons."

Joe tensed. "How many?"

Bosworth's plump face had paled in the early morning light, and he looked dazed. "Eight, so far. He thinks one of them is a little kid."

THEY HAD FOUND the Talladega bodies.

Dom turned off the television set and leaned back in his chair to consider the ramifications.

As far as he knew, this was the first time any of his kills had been discovered. He had always been very careful and methodical, always going the extra mile. In this case many extra miles. Those had all been Atlanta kills and he had transported the bodies to what had been his favorite graveyard then.

Now they had been found, not through diligent search but by an accident of nature.

Or an act of God?

Any religious fanatic would say that God's hand had uncovered those bodies to bring him to justice.

He smiled. Screw all those holier-than-thou fanatics. If there was a God, he looked forward to taking him on. It might be the challenge he needed just then.

The Talladega skeletons were little threat. By the time of those murders, he had learned enough not to leave a hint of evidence. If there had been any mistakes, the rain and mud had probably erased them.

He hadn't been as careful in the early days. The thrill had been too intense, the fear too vivid. He'd even picked his victims at random to make the kill more uncertain. He was long past such foolishness. But he'd been so methodical lately that the excitement was dwindling. If the excitement went away, then so did his reason for living.

He quickly blocked the thought. He'd gone through this before. He just had to remember that the satisfaction came from the kill itself. Everything else was a plus. If he needed a challenge he'd choose someone harder, someone with ties, someone who was loved and would be missed.

As for the discovery at Talladega, he must look on it only as an interesting development, something to watch with amusement and curiosity as the law struggled to put together the pieces.

Who had been the kills at Talladega? He vaguely remembered a blond prostitute, a homeless black man, a teenager selling his body on the streets . . . and the little girl.

Funny, but until that moment he'd completely forgotten about the little girl.

*Pathology Department*
*Atlanta*
*Five days later*

"The child was seven or eight, female, and probably Caucasian." Ned Basil, the medical examiner, read from the report on his desk, which had come from Dr. Phil Comden, a forensic anthropologist at Georgia State. "That's all we know, Quinn."

"How long had she been in the ground?"

"Uncertain. Possibly between eight and twelve years."

"Then we have to find out more."

"Look, it's not our problem. The skeletons were found in Rabun County. The chief stretched a point to even get a forensic anthropologist to examine these bones."

"I want you to recommend facial reconstruction."

Basil had known that was coming. The moment they'd brought in the kid's skeleton, it was a given. "It's not our problem."

"I'm making it our problem. Nine bodies were found in Talladega. I'm asking for reconstruction on only one."

"Look, Chief Maxwell doesn't want to be drawn into this mess. She'd only turn me down. She allowed you to bring the child's body here because she knew that all the missing-children groups would be on her ass if she didn't make the token effort."

"I need more than a token effort. I need to know who this child is."

"Didn't you hear me? It's not going to happen. Why don't you give up?"

"I need to know who she is."

Jesus, Quinn was relentless. Basil had run into him a few times before, and the detective had always interested him. On the surface he appeared quiet, easy, almost lazy, but Basil had always been aware of his razor-sharp intelligence and alertness. He'd heard somewhere that Quinn was an ex-SEAL, and he could believe it. "No recommendation, Quinn."

"Change your mind."

He shook his head.

"Have you ever done anything wrong, Basil?" Quinn asked softly. "Something you wouldn't want anyone to know?"

"What are you getting at?"

"If you have, I'll dig until I find it."

"Are you threatening me?"

"Yes. I'd offer you money, but I don't think you'd take it. You're pretty honest . . . as far as I know. But everyone has something to hide. I'll find it and I'll use it."

"You son of a bitch."

"Just make the recommendation, Basil."

"I haven't done anything that—"

"Lied on your income tax? Let an important report slide by because you were overworked?"

Dammit, everyone lied on their income tax form. But municipal employees could be booted out on their ass for that. How could Quinn find out about—

He'd find out. Basil's lips tightened. "I suppose you want me to recommend the forensic sculptor too?"

"Yes."

"Eve Duncan."

"You bet."

"There's no betting about it. Everyone in the department knows it's her kid you've been looking for all these years. The chief won't go for that either. Duncan's too high-profile after that political cover-up case she worked on. Reporters would be climbing all over the place if she was brought in."

"It's been over a year. That makes Eve old news. I'd work it out."

"Isn't she somewhere in the South Pacific now?"

"She'd come back."

Basil knew Eve Duncan would come back. Everyone at the Atlanta PD was familiar with her story. A young girl who had borne an illegitimate child and then fought her way out of the slums against enormous odds. She was nearly finished with college and was on her way to a decent life, when she had been struck by the cruelest blow. Her daughter, Bonnie, had been murdered by a serial killer and her body had never been found. Fraser, her killer, had been executed without revealing the location of any of the bodies of the twelve children he'd confessed to killing. Since that time Eve had dedicated herself to finding other lost children, alive and dead. She had gone back to school, gotten a degree in fine arts from Georgia State, and become a top forensic sculptor. She had qualified in age progression and superimposition, earning a superior reputation in both.

"Why are you hesitating?" Quinn asked. "You know damn well she's the best."

Basil couldn't deny that. She had helped the department out on many occasions. "She carries a hell of a lot of baggage. The media will go—"

"I said I'd take care of it. Recommend her."

"I'll think about it."

Quinn shook his head. "Now."

"The department won't pay to fly her back."

"I'll do it. Just put through the recommendation."

"You're pushing, Quinn."

"It's one of my finest talents." His lips lifted in a sardonic smile. "But you won't even feel the bruise."

He wasn't so sure. "It's a waste of my time. Chief Maxwell will never go for it."

"She'll go for it. I'll tell her that I'll release your recommendation to the press if she doesn't. It will be a question of letting Eve work on the skull in privacy or have the media asking the chief why she's not doing everything possible to solve the little girl's murder."

"She'll can your ass."

"I'll risk it."

It was clear he'd risk anything to get his way in this matter. Basil shrugged. "Okay, I'll do it. It will be a pleasure to see you kicked out on your ear."

"Good." Quinn headed for the door. "I'll be back in an hour to pick up the recommendation."

"I'm going to lunch. Make it two hours." A minor victory, but he'd take anything he could get. "You think it's the Duncan kid, don't you?"

"I don't know. Maybe."

"And you want her mother to work on the skull? You bastard. What if it is Bonnie Duncan? What the hell do you think that will do to her mother?"

The only answer was the door closing behind Quinn.


*An island south of Tahiti*
*Three days later*


He was coming.

Her heart was beating hard, fast. She was too excited. Eve Duncan drew a deep breath as she watched the helicopter settle on the tarmac. Good heavens, you'd think she was waiting for the angel Gabriel. It was only Joe.

Only? Her friend, her companion through the nightmare that had almost torn her apart, one of the anchors of her life. And she hadn't seen him in over a year. Dammit, she had a right to be excited.

The door was opening and he was getting out of the aircraft. God, he looked tired. His face was almost always without expression and, to anyone unfamiliar with it, impossible to read. But she knew that face. From a thousand different situations she had memorized every glance, every tightening of the mouth, the little secret signs that told so much. There were new deep lines graven on either side of his mouth, and his square face was a little pale.

Yet his eyes were the same.

And the smile that lit his face when he saw her . . .

"Joe . . ." She ran into his arms. Safety. Familiarity. Togetherness. All was right with the world.

He held her tightly for a minute and then pushed her back and dusted a kiss over the bridge of her nose. "You have a few freckles. Have you been using your sunscreen?"

Protective. Bossy. Caring. Two minutes, and they were back where they were when she'd left him all those months before. She grinned up at him as she adjusted her wire-rimmed glasses. "Of course, but it's hard not to get a little sun here."

He studied her up and down. "You look like a beachcomber in those shorts." He tilted his head. "And relaxed. Not totally relaxed but not wound up tight as you were the last time I saw you. Logan's been taking good care of you."

She nodded. "He's been very kind to me."

"And what else?"

"Don't be so nosy. It's none of your business."

"That means you're sleeping with him."

"I didn't say that. But what if I am?"

He shrugged. "Nothing. You were in pretty bad shape after what you went through with that last reconstruction. It's entirely natural for you to have drawn close to Logan. A billionaire who whisked you away from the media to his own island in the South Pacific? I'd be surprised if you hadn't fallen into his bed and even more surprised if he hadn't made sure you would."

"I don't fall into anyone's bed. I make a choice." She shook her head. "Now, stop picking on Logan. You always were like pit bulls with each other." She led him toward the Jeep. "And he's going to be your host while you're here, so you might as well be civil."

"Maybe."

"Joe."

He smiled. "I'll try."

She breathed a sigh of relief. "Did you see Mom before you left?"

"Yes, she sent you her best. She misses you."

Eve wrinkled her nose. "Not much. She's too involved with Ron. Did she tell you they're going to be married in a few months?"

He nodded. "How do you feel about that?"

"How do you expect me to feel? I couldn't be happier for her. Ron's a nice guy and Mom deserves a good relationship. She's had a rough life." That was an understatement. Her mother had grown up in the slums, been addicted to crack for years, and when she was fifteen had brought Eve into the same nightmare world. "It's good she has someone. She's always needed people, and I've always been too busy to give her the attention she should have."

"You did your best. You were always more like a mother than a daughter to her."

"For a long time I was too bitter to do her much good. It was only after Bonnie came that we managed to bridge the gulf." Bonnie. When her daughter had been born, she had changed everything, transformed Eve's whole world and everyone in it. "It will be better for Mom now."

"And what about you? She's all you have."

Eve started the Jeep. "I have my work." She smiled at him. "And I have you, when you're not yelling at me."

"I notice you didn't say Logan. Good."

"Were you trying to trap me? I care very much for Logan."

"But he hasn't got you sealed and delivered." Joe nodded with satisfaction. "I didn't think he could do it."

"If you don't stop talking about Logan, I'll dump you beside the road and let you hitchhike back to Tahiti."

"I'd have a tough time. No boats land on this island."

"Exactly."

"Okay. Since you have me at a disadvantage."

Yeah, sure. Joe at a disadvantage was a rare phenomenon. "How's Diane?"

"Fine." He paused. "I haven't seen much of her lately."

"A cop's wife has a hell of a life. Another rough case?"

"The roughest." He gazed out at the sea. "But I wouldn't have seen her anyway. Our divorce was final three months ago."

"What?" Shock rippled through Eve. "Why didn't you tell me?"

"There wasn't much to tell. Diane never really became accustomed to being a cop's wife. She'll be happier now."

"Why didn't Mom say anything to me?"

"I asked her not to worry you. You were supposed to be relaxing."

"Oh, God, I'm sorry, Joe." She was silent a moment. "Was it my fault?"

"How could it be your fault?"

"You were my friend, you helped me. For God's sake,

I got you shot. You were almost killed. I know she was angry with me."

He didn't deny it. "It would have happened anyway. We should never have gotten married. It was a mistake." He changed the subject. "What kind of work have you been doing since you've been here?"

She looked at him in frustration. The divorce must have hurt him, and she wanted to help. But he had always edged away from talking about his marriage. Maybe she could get something out of him later. "I haven't had much work. Principally superimpositions and age progressions. A few reconstruction cases the LAPD sent me." She made a face. "I soon discovered that most agencies prefer a forensic sculptor on the same continent. I'm pretty inaccessible here. I've actually done some regular sculpting to keep myself busy."

"Satisfying?"

"In a way."

"Not a good way?"

"It feels . . . strange."

"Most people would say that working on skulls is a little strange. What does Logan say?"

"Logan thinks regular sculpting is healthy for me. He's probably right."

"Does it feel healthy?"

"No, there's something . . . missing."

"Purpose."

She was not surprised Joe understood. He understood everything about her. "It's the lost ones. I could be doing more to help the lost ones come home. Logan says I need to distance myself. He thinks I should walk away, that it's the worst possible career for me to have."

"And what do you say to him?"

"To mind his own business." She grimaced. "Just like I tell you. I wish you'd both realize I'm going to do what I want to do regardless of what either of you think."

Joe laughed. "I never had any doubt about that. I

don't think Logan does either. Are you going to let me see your work? I've never seen you sculpt anything but skulls."

"Later maybe." She gave him a hard stare. "If you're decent to Logan." She turned into the driveway leading up to the large white plantation house. "He's been terrific to me. I won't have you abusing his hospitality."

"Nice house. Where do you work?"

"Logan had a lab built for me on the beach beside the house. Stop trying to change the subject. Are you going to be nice to Logan?"

"You're very defensive. As I remember, Logan can take care of himself."

"I always defend my friends."

"Just friends?" His gaze narrowed on her face. "Not lovers?"

She looked away from him. "Lovers can be friends. Stop probing, Joe."

"Does it make you uneasy? Or are you already uneasy? Is he pushing too hard?"

"No, *you're* pushing too hard." She parked in front of the house and jumped out. "Back off."

"No problem. I think I've got my answer." He took his suitcase out of the backseat. "I'll be much less abrasive once I have a shower. Do you want me to face Logan now, or do you want to show me where to lay my weary head?"

Less abrasive was definitely better. "You can join us later for dinner."

"If I'm supposed to dress for dinner, you'll have to send me to the kitchen. I brought only this one suitcase."

"Are you nuts? You know I don't live like that. I change a couple of times a day only because it's so hot here."

"You never know. You're running in fast company these days."

"Logan isn't fast company. Well, not here on the island. We live as casually as I did in Atlanta."

"Very smart of Logan."

"He works hard too. He does as much here as he did when he was in the States. He likes to relax when he gets the chance." She stopped at the front door. "Why have you come, Joe? Are you on vacation?"

"No, not exactly."

"What do you mean?"

"Well, the department does owe me a few weeks. I've worked a lot of overtime while you've been here basking in tropical bliss."

"Then why do you say you're not 'exactly' here on vacation? Why did you come, Joe?"

"To see you."

"No, why now?"

He smiled. "To bring you home, Eve."

LOGAN TURNED AWAY from the window as she came into the study. "Where is he?"

"I showed him to his room. You'll see him at dinner." She wrinkled her nose. "I know you can hardly wait."

"Bastard."

She sighed. Having to strike a balance between these two men she cared about was irritating. "I could have met him in Tahiti. You promised you'd be nice to him."

"As nice as he is to me." Logan held out his hand to her. "Come here, I need to touch you."

She moved across the room and took his hand. "Why?"

He didn't answer. "We both know why he's here. Has he talked to you yet?"

"He said only that he came to bring me home."

He cursed. "And what did you answer?"

"I didn't."

"You can't go, dammit. You'll just fall back into that dark hole where I found you."

"It wasn't so dark. I had work. I had purpose. You never understood that, Logan."

"I understand that I'm going to lose you." His hand tightened on hers. "You've been happy here, haven't you? Happy with me?"

"Yes."

"Then don't let it happen. Don't listen to that damn Pied Piper."

She stared at him helplessly. Dear heaven, she didn't want to hurt him. Tough, smart, charismatic John Logan, corporate giant and businessman extraordinaire. She'd never dreamed he'd be this vulnerable. "My staying here wasn't supposed to be a permanent arrangement."

"I want it permanent. I never intended anything else."

"You never told me."

"Because I had to walk on eggshells or you'd have run away. I'm telling you now."

She wished he hadn't. It made her decision more difficult. "We'll talk about it later."

"You've already made up your mind."

"No." She had grown accustomed to this lovely, tranquil place. She had grown used to Logan. These had been days of tenderness, affection, and peace. If she also felt restlessness, wouldn't it eventually go away? "I'm not sure."

"He's going to try to make you sure."

"I make my own decisions. He won't pressure me."

"No, he's too smart. He knows you too well. That doesn't mean he won't use everything he can to make you go back. Don't listen to him."

"I have to listen to him. He's my best friend."

"Is he?" He gently touched her cheek. "Then why is he drawing you into a world that could destroy you? How long can you deal with skulls and murder without having a breakdown?"

"Someone has to do it. I can bring closure to a lot of parents who are still searching for their children."

"Then let someone else do it. You're too close."

"Because of Bonnie? She only makes me better at what I do. She makes me work harder for those other parents who also want to bring their children home."

"It makes you a damn workaholic."

She grimaced. "Not on this island. I don't have enough to do."

"Is that the problem? We can go back to the States. We'll go to my place in Monterey."

"We'll talk about it later," she repeated.

"Okay." He kissed her hard and sweet. "I just wanted to get in my innings before Quinn. You have options. If you don't like the ones I've given you, we'll find others."

She hugged him. "I'll see you at dinner."

"Think about it, Eve."

She nodded and left the room. How could she not think about it? She cared about Logan. Did she love him? What was love? she wondered. She didn't know much about man-woman love. Eve had thought she loved Bonnie's father, but she'd been only fifteen; later she'd recognized her feelings for him as passion and a need for comfort in a rough world. She'd had a few other encounters, but they'd been unimportant, fading immediately into the shadow of her work. Logan was not unimportant, and he'd fight being overshadowed by anyone or anything. He could rouse her to passion and he was kind and caring. She would be sad if he disappeared from her life. Surely that could be love.

She didn't want to analyze anything now. After she talked to Joe would be soon enough. She'd go down to her lab and work for a while on that age-progression photo of Libby Crandall, who'd been kidnapped at age eight by her father.

Eve moved down the hallway toward the French doors that led to her lab. Sunny. Everything was sunny and bright and clean on this island. That's how Logan wanted to keep her life, always in sunlight, away from the darkness. Why not let him? Let the pain fade. Let the memory of Bonnie slip away. Let someone else help all the other children who were lost out there.

Not possible. Never. Bonnie and the lost ones were woven into the fabric of her life and her dreams. They were a big part of who she was, maybe the best part.

Logan knew her so well, it seemed impossible he'd never accepted the truth about her.

That she belonged in the darkness.


*Phoenix, Arizona*


Darkness.

Dom had always liked the night. Not because it was concealing but because of the excitement of the unknown. Nothing appeared the same at night, and yet for him everything became so much clearer. Wasn't there something by Saint-Exupéry about that?

Oh, yes, he remembered . . .

*When the destructive analysis of day is done, and all that is truly important becomes whole and sound again. When man reassembles his fragmentary self and grows with the calm of a tree.*

He was never fragmented, but night did make him feel calm and strong. Soon the calmness would be gone, but the strength would sing through him like a thousand-voice choir.

Choir. He smiled as he realized how one thought led to another.

He straightened in the driver's seat. She was coming out of the house. He had chosen her carefully for difficulty; he was sure she would be more stimulating than his last kill. Debby Jordan, blond, thirty-one, married, mother of two. She was treasurer of the PTA, had a nice soprano voice, and belonged to the Hill Street Methodist Church choir. She was going to choir practice now. She would never get there.

# CHAPTER
# TWO

Joe and Logan were polite during dinner, but Eve could sense the antagonism between them.

She *hated* it. She liked everything honest and clear. Watching them was like watching two icebergs drift toward each other and never knowing when they would collide because there was so much hidden beneath the surface.

She couldn't stand it. To hell with dessert.

She jumped to her feet. "Come on, Joe. Let's go for a walk."

"I'm not invited?" Logan murmured. "How rude, and we haven't finished dinner."

"I'm finished." Joe stood up and threw down his napkin. "And, no, you're not invited."

"Oh, well, I'd only be bored. I think I've guessed what you're going to say to Eve." He leaned back in his chair. "Go ahead. Do what you came to do. I'll talk to her when she gets back."

"You wouldn't be bored." Joe strode toward the door. "Hell, you're scared shitless."

Eve hurried after him into the hall. "Dammit, did you have to say that?"

"Yes." He smiled. "It had to come out. I've been too nice all evening. It was giving me indigestion."

"You're in his house."

"That gives me a bellyache too." He headed for the French doors. "Let's go walk on the beach."

She would be glad to get out of the house too. The tension was so thick, she couldn't breathe.

She kicked off her shoes as soon as they reached the terrace and watched Joe take off his shoes and socks and roll up his pant legs. It reminded her of the last time she'd seen him on his speedboat, bare-chested, khakis rolled up to his calves, laughing over his shoulder at Eve and Diane as he weaved the boat across the lake. "Do you still have the lake cottage?"

He nodded. "But I gave the Buckhead house to Diane as part of the settlement."

"Where do you live now?"

"An apartment near the precinct." He followed her down the path toward the beach. "It's fine. I'm not there much anyway."

"I can tell." Her feet sank into the cool, soft sand. This was better. The sound of the surf was calming, and being alone with Joe was soothing too. They knew each other so well, it was almost like being by herself. Well, not really. Joe never let her forget who and what he was. It was just that they . . . meshed. "You're not taking care of yourself. You look tired."

"It's been a rough week." He fell into step with her and walked in silence for a few moments. "Did your mother tell you about Talladega?"

"What?"

"I didn't think she would. It's all over the newspapers but she wouldn't want to tell you anything that might jar you away from here."

She stiffened. "What's happened?"

"Nine skeletons were found on the bluff near the falls. One of them is a little girl. Caucasian."

"How . . . little?"

"Seven or eight."

She drew a deep breath. "How long has she been buried?"

"The first estimate is between eight and twelve years." He paused. "It may not be Bonnie, Eve. The other skeletons are adults, and as far as we know, Fraser killed only children."

"As far as we know. He wouldn't tell us anything." Her voice was uneven. "The bastard only smiled and wouldn't tell us anything. He told us he buried her and then wouldn't tell us a damn—"

"Easy." Joe took her hand and gently squeezed it. "Take it easy, Eve."

"Don't tell me to take it easy. Bonnie might have been found and you expect me to be calm about it?"

"I don't want you to get your hopes up. The kid might be older. The time she was in the ground might be longer or shorter."

"It might be her."

"It's a possibility."

She closed her eyes. Bonnie.

"And it might not."

"I could bring her home," she whispered. "I could bring my baby home."

"Eve, you're not listening. It's far from a sure thing."

"I'm listening. I know that." But she was closer than she'd come all these years. It could be Bonnie. "Can we check dental records?"

He shook his head. "No teeth in any of the skulls."

"What?"

"We think the killer pulled the teeth to prevent identification."

She flinched. Smart move. Brutal but smart. Fraser had been smart. "There's still DNA. Could you get enough samples for tests?"

"We got some from the bone marrow. The lab's processing it. But you know the results could take a while."

"What about using the same private lab we used last time?"

"Teller's not doing DNA profiling any longer. He wasn't pleased with all the publicity his lab got on the job he did for us."

"Then how long?"

"Four weeks minimum."

"No. I'd go crazy. I have to know." She drew a deep breath. "Will they let me reconstruct her face?"

"Are you sure you want to?"

"Of course I want to." Seeing Bonnie's face come to life beneath her hands . . .

"It's going to be traumatic for you."

"I don't care."

"I do," he said roughly. "I don't like to see you bleed."

"I won't bleed."

"The hell you won't. You're bleeding now."

"I have to do it, Joe."

"I know." He looked out at the sea. "That's why I came."

"Can you get them to let me do it?"

"I've already set it up."

"Thank God."

"It could be the biggest mistake I've ever made."

"No, it's the right thing, the kind thing."

"Bullshit." He started back for the house. "It's probably the single most selfish thing I've done in my life."

"What do you know about the killings?"

"I'll fill you in on the details on the plane. I have tickets for both of us on a flight tomorrow afternoon from Tahiti. Is that too soon?"

"No." Logan. She had to tell Logan. "I'll pack tonight."

"After you tell Logan."

"Yes."

"I could tell him."

"Don't be stupid. Logan deserves to hear it from me."

"Sorry. You're a little overwrought. I only meant to—"

"What a puny word. Southern belles are overwrought. Scarlett O'Hara might be overwrought. *I'm* not overwrought."

He smiled. "Well, you're better than you were a few minutes ago."

Was she? The dread of facing Logan and telling him she was leaving had superseded other emotions, but as soon as the job was done and she was alone, the pain would come flooding back.

Then face it. Let the pain come. She had faced it for years. She could face it again. She could face anything now.

She had a chance to bring Bonnie home.

### Phoenix, Arizona

Dom placed the candle in Debby Jordan's hand and rolled her into the grave he'd dug for her.

He had hurt her. He'd thought he'd evolved beyond the primitive need for the victim's pain. But in the middle of the kill he'd suddenly realized he wasn't feeling enough and he'd panicked. He'd pierced and torn in a frenzy of frustration. If the pleasure of the kill disappeared, what was left for him? How could he go on living?

Smother the panic. It would be all right. He had always known this day would come, and the problem was not unsolvable. He just had to find a way to bring freshness and challenge back to the kill.

Debby Jordan was not a portent of the ultimate boredom and deadness he feared most. It didn't matter that he had hurt her.

DAMMIT, SHE HAD hurt him.

Eve gazed out at the surf gently rushing against the

shore. She'd run out to the beach after she'd spoken to Logan hours ago, and she'd been sitting there ever since, trying to regain her composure.

There was already so much pain inflicted by strangers in this world; why did she have to hurt someone she cared about?

"You told him?"

She turned her head to see Joe standing a few yards away. "Yes."

"What did he say?"

"Not much. Not after I told him it might be Bonnie." She smiled sadly. "He said you'd played the one card he couldn't top."

"He's right." Joe sat down beside her. "Bonnie's always the indisputable factor in all our lives."

"Only in mine. You never knew her, Joe."

"I know her. You've told me so much about her that I feel as if she's my child."

"Really? Did I tell you how much she loved life? Every morning she'd come and jump on my bed and ask me what we were going to do, what we were going to see that day. She radiated love. I grew up choking on bitterness and poverty and I used to wonder why I was given a child like Bonnie. I didn't deserve her."

"You deserved her."

"After she came I tried to deserve her." Eve forced a smile. "I'm sorry, you're right. I shouldn't burden you with this."

"It's no burden."

"Sure it is. It should be only my albatross."

"Not possible. When you're hurting, everyone around you feels it." He picked up a handful of sand and let it slowly sift through his fingers. "Bonnie's still here. For all of us."

"You, Joe?"

"Sure, could it be any different? You and I have been together for a long time."

Since that nightmare time after Bonnie had disappeared. He had been an agent with the FBI then, younger, less cynical, capable of being shocked and horrified. He had tried to comfort her, but there had been no comfort in the world during that hideous period. Yet he had somehow managed to pull her back single-handedly from a nearly fatal depression until she could function on her own. She grimaced. "I don't know why you stick around. I'm a lousy friend. I never think about anything but my work. I'm selfish as hell or I would have known you and Diane were having trouble. Why do you put up with me?"

"I wonder sometimes." He tilted his head, as if considering. "I suppose I'm used to you. It's too much trouble to make new friends, so I guess I'll have to keep you."

"Thank God." She drew up her knees and linked her arms around them. "I hurt him, Joe."

"Logan's tough. He'll get over it. He knew you weren't going to be a sure thing when he lured you here."

"He didn't lure me here. He was trying to help."

Joe shrugged. "Maybe." He stood up and pulled her to her feet. "Come on, I'll walk you back to the house. You've been out here long enough."

"How do you know?"

"I saw you run out. I've been waiting on the terrace."

"All this time?"

He smiled. "I didn't have any other pressing engagements. I figured you needed the time alone, but now you should go to bed."

He had stood there in the darkness, silent, strong, waiting patiently until he could help her. She suddenly felt stronger herself, more optimistic. "I'm not going back to the house but you can walk me back to the lab. I have some work to do and then I have to pack."

"Do you need help?"

She shook her head. "I can manage." She headed toward the small house a hundred yards away. "I've just been putting it off."

"Second thoughts?"

"You know better." She opened the door of the lab and turned on the light. "But sad thoughts. Regretful thoughts." She moved toward the computer on the desk. "Go away. I have to finish this age progression. It's been a long time for Libby's mother. She's almost given up hope."

"Nice place." Joe's gaze was wandering around the room, from the beige couch heaped with orange and gold pillows to the framed pictures on the bookcase. "You've made it yours. Where's the sculpture you've been working on?"

She nodded at the pedestal beside the large picture window. "Your bust is a work in progress. But there's a finished one of Mom in the armoire beside the door."

"My bust?" He stared at it. "Good God, it *is* me."

"Don't be flattered. I didn't have any models, and I know your face almost as well as I do my own."

"Jesus, I can see you do." He touched the bridge of the nose. "I never realized anyone noticed that little bump. I broke it playing football."

"You should have had it taken care of at the time."

He grinned. "But then I would have been too perfect." He paused. "I'd have thought you'd do one of Bonnie."

"I tried. I couldn't do it. I just found myself staring at the clay." She adjusted her glasses and brought up the picture of Libby on the monitor. "Maybe later."

"But you think you can reconstruct the little girl's skull?"

He was being very careful not to refer to it as Bonnie's skull, she noticed. "I have to do it. I can do whatever I have to do. Go away, Joe. I have to work now."

He strolled toward the door. "Try to get some sleep."

"After I finish the progression." She pulled up the photographs of Libby's mother and maternal grandmother. Study them. Don't think about Bonnie. Don't think about Logan. Libby deserved her entire attention. She had to age the eight-year-old girl to fifteen. It wasn't going to be easy. Block everything else out.

Don't think about Bonnie.

*"TOO BAD YOU don't have time to finish Joe,"* Bonnie said.

*Eve turned over on the couch and saw Bonnie standing staring up at Joe's bust. She looked as she always did when she came to Eve: blue jeans, T-shirt, red hair a riot of curls. But she appeared smaller than usual next to the pedestal.*

*"I have more important work to do now."*

*Bonnie wrinkled her nose as she glanced at Eve over her shoulder.*

*"Yeah, you think you've found me. I keep telling you I'm not there anymore. It's just a bunch of bones."*

*"Your bones?"*

*"How do I know? I don't remember any of that anymore. You wouldn't want me to remember."*

*"God, no." She paused. "But I think you know where he buried you. Why won't you tell me? I just want to bring you home."*

*"Because I want you to forget the way I died." Bonnie moved over to the window and gazed out at the sea. "I only want you to remember me when I was with you and how I am now."*

*"A dream."*

*"A ghost," Bonnie corrected. "Someday I'm going to convince you."*

*"And then they'll lock me up in the nuthouse."*

*Bonnie giggled. "No way. Joe wouldn't let them."*

*Eve smiled and nodded. "He'd cause a ruckus. I'd rather avoid the entire scenario if you don't mind."*

"I don't mind. It's probably better that you don't tell anyone about me." She tilted her head. "It's kinda nice having these times all to ourselves. Like a very special secret. Remember the secrets we used to have? The time we surprised Grandma on her birthday with that trip to Callaway Gardens. We made her get in the car and then we took off. The flowers were so pretty that spring. Have you gone there since?"

Bonnie running around Callaway Gardens, her face alight with joy and excitement . . . "No."

"Stop that." Bonnie frowned. "The flowers are still beautiful, the sky is still blue. Enjoy them."

"Yes, ma'am."

"You say it, but you don't mean it." She gazed back out at the sea. "You're glad to be leaving the island, aren't you?"

"I have a job to do."

"You'd have left the island soon anyway."

"Not necessarily. It's been very peaceful here. I like the sunlight and the tranquillity."

"And you like Logan and didn't want to hurt him."

"I did hurt him."

"He'll be sorry to see you go, but he'll be okay." She paused. "I knew Joe would come for you, but I didn't know—I don't like this, Mama."

"You've never liked the idea of me searching for you."

"No, I mean . . . I have a feeling . . . there's a darkness."

"You're afraid I won't be able to survive working on your skull."

"It's going to be bad for you, but that's not what . . ." She shrugged. "You'll go anyway. You're so stubborn." She leaned against the wall. "Go back to sleep. You have all that packing to do. You did the age progression very well, by the way."

"Thank you," she said mockingly. "Talk about self-praise."

"I can't compliment you about anything," Bonnie said plaintively. "You think you're doing it yourself."

"Since you're a dream, that's the logical conclusion." She was silent a moment. "Libby's father was supposed to be a violent man. He took her as a revenge kidnapping. Is Libby still alive? She's not with you?"

Bonnie lifted her brows. "In your dreams or the other side? You can't have it both ways, Mama."

"Forget it."

A smile illuminated Bonnie's face. "She's not here with me. You have a chance of bringing her home."

"I knew that." Eve turned over on her side and closed her eyes. "I wouldn't have done all that work if I hadn't known there was a good chance."

"A logical supposition?"

"Exactly."

"Not instinct?"

"Sorry, I hate to pop your bubble, but these dreams of you are the only foolishness I'll lay claim to." She paused. "Are you coming with me?"

"I'm always with you." A silence and then haltingly, "But it may be difficult for me to get through. The darkness . . ."

"Is that skeleton you, baby?" Eve whispered. "Please. Tell me."

"I'm not sure. I can't tell if the darkness is for you or for me. . . ."

WHEN EVE WOKE, the palest glimmer lightened the horizon. She stayed in bed for another twenty minutes, watching the dawn creep over the ocean. Strange, she didn't feel as rested as she usually did after dreaming of Bonnie. She was a little uneasy. A psychiatrist would say the dreams were a catharsis, a way of handling her loss without going insane—and he'd probably be right. The dreams had started about a year after Fraser was executed, and their effect was positive. So she'd be damned if she'd go to some shrink to try to rid herself of them. A memory of love never did anyone any harm.

She swung her legs to the floor. Time to stop brooding and get moving. She had to pack and meet Joe at the house at eight.

And say a final good-bye to Logan.

"YOU LOOK LIKE you're visiting a dying friend." Logan was coming down the stairs when she reached the hall. "Are you ready to go?"

She braced herself. "Yes."

"Where's Quinn?"

"Waiting in the Jeep. Logan, I never—"

"I know." He waved dismissively. "Come on, let's get going."

"You're coming with us?"

"Don't look so wary. Only as far as the heliport." He took her elbow and nudged her toward the door. "I won't be left here like a forlorn lover. That's bullshit. I'm hereby kicking you off my island. Don't ever come back." He smiled crookedly. "Unless it's tomorrow, or next month or next year. Come to think of it, I might accept you if you hurry back in the next decade. Otherwise, forget it."

She smiled with relief. "Thanks, Logan."

"For making it easy for you? Hell, there's no way I'd taint your memory of our time here. We were too good together." He opened the front door. "You're a special woman, Eve. I don't want to lose you. If you don't want me as a lover, I'll be your friend. It will take a little while for me to adjust, but it will happen. I'll make it happen."

She reached up and kissed his cheek. "You're already my friend. I was a mess when I came here with you. No one could have been more generous or done more for me than you during this last year."

He looked down at her and smiled. "I haven't given

up, you know. I want a hell of a lot more. This is just the first stage of a sneak attack."

"You never give up. That's one of the things that's so wonderful about you."

"See, you're already appreciative of my sterling qualities. I intend to capitalize on that and move forward." He pushed her toward the Jeep, where Joe waited. "Come on, you'll miss your helicopter."

THE HELICOPTER WAS already sitting on the tarmac when Joe pulled into the heliport.

"May I speak to you a moment, Quinn?" Logan asked politely.

Joe had been expecting it. "Get on board and buckle up, Eve. I'll be right with you."

She gave them both a wary glance but didn't interfere.

When she was in the helicopter Logan asked, "It's not Bonnie, is it?"

"It could be."

"You son of a *bitch*."

Joe didn't respond.

"Do you know how much this is going to hurt her?"

"Yes."

"But you don't care. You wanted her to come back and you used Bonnie to do it."

"She wouldn't have thanked me if I hadn't told her about the skeleton."

"I could break your neck."

"I know. But it wouldn't be the intelligent thing to do. You've done a good job of making Eve grateful as well as sad. The last thing you want is for her to leave on a sour note. That would make it much more difficult to draw her back."

Logan drew a deep breath. "I'll be coming back to my office in Monterey next week."

"I thought that would be the next move."

"I'm keeping an eye on you. You won't be able to blink without me knowing it. If this reconstruction does any damage to Eve, I'll decimate you."

"Fine. Are you finished now?"

He started the Jeep. "I'm just beginning."

Joe watched him drive away. Logan was a tough bastard, but he genuinely cared about Eve. He had many qualities Joe admired—intelligence, fairness, loyalty. If things were different, if he weren't an obstacle, Joe might have liked him.

Too bad.

He was an obstacle and Joe had learned when he was in the SEALs that there were three things you could do about an obstacle. You could jump over it. You could go around it.

Or you could pound it into the ground until it didn't exist.

THE PLANE FROM Tahiti had scarcely reached optimum altitude when Eve asked Joe about Talladega. "I want to know everything." She grimaced. "And don't tell me I'm overwrought again, or I'll sock you."

"No, I believe I'll avoid that word in the future," Joe murmured.

"You said she was the only child?"

"Unless they've found more bodies while I've been gone. But I doubt it. They scoured the area pretty thoroughly."

She shuddered. Nine lives gone. Nine human beings buried in the earth and abandoned. "Have you been able to identify any of them?"

"Not yet. We don't even know if they're native to Rabun County. We're combing missing persons records statewide. Then we'll see if any of the DNA profiles on our possibles match our skeletons. It's doubtful that they were all buried at the same time. It looks like someone was using the bluff as his own private cemetery."

"Fraser," she whispered.

"Eight adults, one child," he reminded her. "Fraser confessed to killing twelve children. He never mentioned any adults, and he had nothing to lose after he was convicted."

"That doesn't mean anything. Who the hell knows what he did? He would never tell us anything that might help the parents find those children. He wanted us to suffer. He wanted the whole world to suffer."

"It's a long shot. You've got to be prepared to find out this is another killer."

"I'm prepared. No clues?"

"The rib cages of three victims showed signs the deaths were probably caused by knife wounds. We're not sure about the others. But the killer might have left a signature. There was wax residue in the right hands of all the skeletons."

"Wax? What kind of wax?"

He shrugged. "They're analyzing it."

"They should be done by now. Why are they moving so slowly?"

"Politics. The mayor doesn't want another serial killer to make Atlanta look bad and Chief Maxwell doesn't want to take the flak. The city's already had Wayne Williams and Fraser. The chief would just as soon keep this case in Rabun County. Unfortunately, Rabun doesn't have our facilities and she's having to offer limited assistance. The FBI Behavioral Science Unit is also lending a hand. They're already at Talladega to examine the site and the skeletons."

"Then how did you get permission for me to do the reconstruction?"

"Well, actually, I had to twist a few arms. The chief's afraid there'll be a media circus if they find out you've been brought in."

"God, I hope not." She had fled thousands of miles to escape the publicity, and now she was confronted with it again.

"We'll keep them away. I've set up a lab for you at the lake house."

"They'll still find us. There are always leaks."

He smiled. "I have a few ideas on how to circumvent them. Trust me."

She couldn't do anything else. She leaned back in the seat and tried to relax. It was going to be a long flight, and she had to rest to be ready for the work that lay ahead.

A child's skull to bring to life.

Bonnie?

"COME ON." JOE grabbed her arm after they'd cleared Customs. "We can't go out in the waiting area. There's a mob of reporters out there." He smiled at the red-coated customer service representative beside him. "Right, Don?"

"Enough to cause you a big problem. This way." He led them toward an emergency exit. "A skycap will bring the bags."

"Where are we going?" Eve asked as they went down a stairway.

"Employees entrance leading outside the North Terminal," Joe answered. "I thought there would be a leak and called Don to help us." Don ushered them through a long hall and out into the street in front of the terminal. "Thanks, Don."

"No problem." Don waved over the skycap who had just come out the door. "I owed you a favor, Joe."

Eve watched Don disappear back into the terminal. "Okay, now that we're away from—What are you doing?"

Joe was in the middle of the street. "Hailing your own personal cab."

A gray Oldsmobile pulled to a stop beside them. A woman was at the wheel.

"Mom?"

Sandra Duncan smiled. "I feel like an undercover agent or something. Were there reporters at Customs?"

"So I was told," Joe said as he and the skycap loaded the luggage into the trunk.

"I thought there would be when I saw the newspaper this morning."

Joe tipped the skycap. Eve jumped in the front seat and Joe got in the back. A few seconds later her mother was driving down the street toward the airport exit.

"Joe called you?" Eve asked.

"Somebody had to do it." Sandra grinned at her. "Since my own daughter didn't see fit to let me know."

"I would have called you once we were settled."

"But now I have you to myself until we get to Joe's place." She gave her an appraising glance. "You look good. You may have put on a pound or two."

"Maybe."

"And you have freckles."

"That's what Joe said."

"You should have worn your sunscreen."

"Joe said that too."

"Joe has good sense."

"You look wonderful." It was true. Her mother looked young, chic, and glowing with health and vitality. "How's Ron?"

"As good as can be expected." Her eyes were twinkling. "He says I exhaust him. I do lead him a pretty strenuous dance. But what the hell. Life's too short not to enjoy it."

"How's your job?"

"Fine."

"This is a weekday. Am I making you miss work?"

"Yep, but they were glad I didn't come in. After the

story in the paper this morning, they knew reporters would be all over the courthouse if I showed up."

"I'm sorry, Mom."

"It doesn't matter. I'm the best court reporter they have, and they know it. All this uproar will die down again just like it did the last time." She glanced over her shoulder at Joe. "I'm heading up north toward your cottage. Do you want to stop anywhere?"

Joe shook his head. "No, but I want you to drive around the city a little to make sure we're not followed."

"Right." Sandra glanced at Eve, her expression sobering. "Joe says the chances aren't good, Eve. It may not be Bonnie."

"A lousy chance is better than none at all." She smiled. "And stop fretting, Mom. It's going to be okay. Whatever happens, I can handle it."

"You know I don't approve of this. You've got to let her go before you tear yourself apart. I loved Bonnie too, but I had to come to terms with reality."

What Sandra had done was come to terms with her view of reality, and it was obviously bringing her happiness. Well, more power to her. Eve ignored the tiny flicker of envy and said, "I'm not avoiding reality. I'm just trying to find my daughter and put her to rest."

Sandra sighed. "Okay, do what you have to do. Call me if I can help."

"You know I will." Sandra was frowning, so Eve reached over and affectionately squeezed her arm. "It's not going to be that bad. The reconstruction will take only a few days, and then I'll know."

Sandra grimaced. "A few days can sometimes seem like a century."


EVE DUNCAN.

Dom studied her photograph in the newspaper. Curly red-brown hair framed a face that was more fascinating than pretty. Hazel eyes gazed at the world from behind round gold-rimmed glasses. He remembered seeing this picture in the paper last year and thinking how she had changed from that desperate woman at the Fraser trial. The older Eve Duncan looked stronger, more confident. A woman whose determination could move mountains and topple governments.

And now she was turning that determination in his direction. Of course, she didn't know it was his direction. She wanted only to find her child—which made her just as vulnerable as she had been all those years before.

He had actually considered her as a kill back then but had dismissed the idea almost immediately because of the notoriety of the Fraser trial. She had been too visible and there were enough satisfying, less risky kills.

But the satisfaction was waning.

He could correct that problem now, he thought with relief. Eve Duncan was strong enough to challenge and purge him. He would tread carefully with her, inject each moment with every possible drop of emotion, build slowly so the final explosion would be strong enough to clear away all the deadness and debris inside him.

He had a strong belief in fate and was beginning to think Eve Duncan had been put at this place and time just for him. It was lucky he had ignored temptation when she first passed through his life. Then she would have been only an ordinary kill, no more important than any other.

Now she could be his salvation.

"Nice." Sandra's gaze traveled over the cottage and then down to the boat dock. "I like this, Joe."

"Then why didn't you come here all the times I invited you?" Joe started unloading luggage from the trunk.

"You know I'm city born and bred." Sandra drew a deep breath. "But I could tolerate this. Eve should have told me about that beautiful view of the lake."

"I did," Eve said. "You wouldn't have any of it."

"Well, it is pretty isolated. Aren't there any other houses on the lake?"

"No, Joe bought the lake and surrounding acreage and won't sell any of it."

Sandra grinned at Joe. "How unfriendly of you."

"I like privacy when I'm up here." He closed the trunk. "I get enough of people when I'm in the city. I kept the title in the name of my trust and no one knows I own this place. Not even the department." He smiled at Eve. "Except a few chosen friends."

"Well, at least the cottage looks nice and friendly," Sandra said.

Eve had always liked the A-frame. It was small and cozy and had plenty of windows that welcomed the sun and the outdoors. "Come on in and see the inside."

"I have to get back to the city. Ron worries when I don't show up for dinner."

"You could call him."

Sandra shook her head. "Hey, I'm not stupid. I don't want him getting used to eating alone. I'll call you tomorrow and we'll talk then." She gave Eve a long hug. "Welcome home, baby. I've missed you." She stepped back and looked at Joe. "Do you need a lift back to town?"

"I have a Jeep up here. I'll use that. Thanks, Sandra."

"No problem." Sandra got back in the driver's seat and started the car. "See you soon."

Eve watched the car disappear down the gravel road, then helped Joe carry the luggage up the porch steps.

"You know, I don't get it." He shook his head. "You two haven't seen each other for over a year, and she goes off to dinner with her boyfriend and it's okay with you?"

"You don't have to get it. We understand each other." No one who had not been there during her hellish childhood would be able to empathize. The scars were still there and they would never go away, but she and Sandra had built on them and forged a bond they could live with. "Mom has never had a stable relationship before. She has a right to protect it. She's really hooked, isn't she?"

"Yep." He unlocked the door. "But she doesn't appear to mind."

"No." Eve paused. "It will seem strange not to have Diane here."

"Why? You came here before I was married. Diane never really liked this place. She preferred civilization."

She glanced around and remembered how Joe's retriever had always bounded up to greet her. "Where's George? Is he in the city apartment?"

"No, Diane has him. I'm never home. He's better off with her."

"That must have been hard."

"Yeah, it was. I love that dog." He opened the door and gestured to a corner of the room.

"Good God." Video cameras, a computer, a worktable and pedestal. "Where did you get all this?"

"I raided your lab in town and brought out all the equipment the insurance company replaced after it was trashed last year. I think I got everything."

"I think you did too." She went inside. "You seem to have met all my needs."

"My goal in life," he said lightly. "I stocked the house with food too. It's chilly in here." He crossed to the fireplace and knelt before the logs. "I'll light the fire before I leave."

"You're not staying?"

He shook his head. "Reporters are looking for you. It will be hard to trace the cabin but not impossible. I have to find a way to cast out a few red herrings." He paused. "And I'm going to tell Sandra not to come up here until you've finished the job. She might be followed. If you want to catch up on everything, do it on the telephone. Okay?"

"Okay." He had mentioned everything except what was most important. "And when do I get the skull?"

"Tomorrow. It's still at Georgia State with Dr. Comden, the anthropologist who did the report. I'll get a release from the department, pick it up tomorrow morning, and bring the skull with me in the afternoon. If there's any change of plan, I'll call you." He moved toward the door. "In the meantime, try to get some sleep. You didn't doze more than an hour on the flight over."

"Okay." She added deliberately, "But first I'm going to call Logan and tell him we've arrived safely."

"He won't expect it."

"But he'll appreciate it. I'm not going to shut him out

of my life just because we're not together anymore. He deserves more than that."

Joe shrugged. "I'm not going to argue with you. Just don't let him upset you. You need to rest."

"I'll rest."

"I mean it. Neither one of us knows how you're going to react when you see that kid's skull. Exhaustion won't help. I don't want you going to pieces."

"I won't go to pieces."

"Get some sleep," he repeated. The door shut behind him.

She went to the window and watched him stride around the cottage toward the garage, where he kept the Jeep. A few minutes later it appeared in the driveway and then disappeared from view down the road.

She was alone.

The sunlight suddenly seemed weaker, colder, as it touched the lake. On the far bank, pine trees cast shadows that blended and formed a dark blanket. She shivered, then moved over to the blazing fire and held out her hands. The warmth was welcome, chasing away the chill that had attacked her.

Imagination. Everything was as it was before Mom and Joe had left. Eve just wasn't accustomed to being alone any longer. On the island she had seldom been by herself. Even when she was working, Logan was never more than five minutes away.

Face it. The chill hadn't come from loneliness but from dread and nervousness. She was no more sure than Joe of how she would react to having that skull in her hands. If she would be able to close out the horror and be totally professional.

Of course she would. She owed it to Bonnie.

Or whoever the little girl might be. She mustn't think of her as Bonnie, or her hands and mind might play tricks on her. She had to view the skull with total detachment.

But when had she ever been able to do that? she wondered ruefully. Every reconstruction concerning a lost child was heart-wrenching, leaving her emotionally drained by the time she finished. But she had to control all emotion this time. It was absolutely necessary not to let herself fall into that dark pit.

Keep busy. Don't think about what awaited her. She reached for the telephone and dialed Logan's digital number. No answer. The call went to his voice mail.

"Hi, Logan, just calling to tell you that I'm at Joe's cottage. I'm fine and I'm going to get the skull tomorrow. I hope everything's well with you. Take care." She hung up.

Not being able to touch base with Logan made her feel even more isolated. That safe, sane life with Logan seemed so far away already and was growing more distant with every second.

For God's sake, snap out of it. She'd go for a walk along the lake and tire herself so that she'd sleep.

All the clothes in her suitcases were tropical, so she went into Joe's bedroom and found jeans and a flannel shirt. She put on her own tennis shoes and grabbed Joe's windbreaker. A moment later she was out the door and going down the steps.

SHE WAS ALONE.

Dom watched Eve Duncan stride briskly down the path to the lake. Her hands were in the jacket pockets and there was a faint frown on her face.

She was taller than he remembered but appeared very fragile in the oversize jacket. She wasn't fragile. He could see that in the way she moved, the set of her chin. Strength was often more of the spirit than the body. He'd had kills that should have succumbed immediately but had fought ferociously. She would be such a one.

All that subterfuge at the airport had been interesting, but he had been a stalker too long to be taken in by it. He had learned a long time ago that you had to keep one step ahead if you were going to reap your reward.

And that reward was almost in his grasp. Now that he knew Eve Duncan's whereabouts, he could put the game in play.

### Georgia State University

"Good morning, Joe. Could I talk to you a minute?"

Joe stiffened as he recognized the tall man straightening away from a wall of the Science Building. "I'm not answering any questions, Mark."

Mark Grunard smiled engagingly. "I said talk, not question. Though if you really feel you need to open up and—"

"What are you doing here?"

"It wasn't difficult to figure out that you'd come here to pick up the skull. I'm only glad my fellow journalists are too busy trying to track down Eve Duncan. Now I have you all to myself."

Joe silently cursed the Atlanta PD for releasing the whereabouts of the skeleton. "The hell you do. No story, Mark."

"Do you mind if I walk you down the hall to Dr. Comden's office? I'll take off the minute we reach the lab. I have a proposition for you."

"What are you up to, Mark?"

"Something beneficial to both of us." He fell into step with Joe. "Will you listen?"

Joe studied him. Mark Grunard had always impressed him as being both honest and smart. "I'll listen."

"YOU CAME FOR the kid?" Dr. Phil Comden rose to his feet and shook Joe's hand. "Sorry I didn't have much on my report." He moved toward the door at the end of the corridor. "I read that Eve Duncan is doing the reconstruction."

"Yes."

"You know facial reconstruction won't stand up in a court of law. You should wait for the DNA."

"It's going to take too long."

"I guess so." He led Joe into the lab toward a bank of drawers similar to ones used in morgues. "You just want the skull?"

"Yes, you can return the rest of the skeleton to the Pathology Department."

"She thinks this is her kid?"

"She thinks there's a possibility."

"Bummer." He reached for the drawer handle and pulled it open. "You know when you're working on one of these kids you can't help but think about how they— shit!"

Joe pushed him aside and looked down into the drawer.

EVE ANSWERED THE phone on the first ring.

"It's gone," Joe said harshly.

"What?"

"The skeleton's gone."

She went rigid with shock. "How could that be?"

"How the hell do I know? Dr. Comden says the skeleton was in the drawer last night when he left the lab. It wasn't there at noon today."

She tried to think. "Could the Pathology Department have picked it up?"

"Dr. Comden would have had to sign the release."

"Maybe there was some foul-up and they picked it up without getting—"

"I called Basil. No one was authorized to pick up the skeleton."

She was dazed. "Someone has to—"

"I'm trying to find out where the snafu is. I just didn't

want you to wait around for me to bring it to you. I'll call you when I know something."

"She's . . . lost again?"

"I'll find her." He paused. "It could be a macabre joke. You know how college kids can be."

"You think one of the students stole the skeleton?"

"That's what Dr. Comden's guessing."

She closed her eyes. "Oh, my God."

"We'll get it back, Eve. I'm questioning everyone who was near the lab last night and today."

"Okay," she said numbly.

"I'll call you when I know something," he repeated, then hung up.

Eve put down the receiver. She mustn't get upset. Joe would find the skeleton. Dr. Comden was probably right. It must be some kid who thought it hilarious to pull such a prank and—

The phone rang. Joe again?

"Hello."

"She was a pretty little girl, wasn't she?"

"What?"

"You must have been very proud of your Bonnie."

She froze. "Who is this?"

"I had trouble remembering her. There have been so many. But I should have remembered her. She was special. She fought for her life. Do you know that children very seldom struggle? They just accept. That's why I seldom choose them anymore. It's like killing a bird."

"Who is this?"

"They flutter and then go quiet. Bonnie wasn't like that."

"You lying son of a bitch," she said hoarsely. "What kind of sicko are you?"

"Not the usual kind, I assure you. Not like Fraser. Though I do have an ego, I never take credit for someone else's kills."

She felt as if she'd been punched in the stomach. "Fraser did kill my daughter."

"Did he? Then why didn't he tell you where her body was? Where all the bodies were?"

"Because he was cruel."

"Because he didn't know."

"He knew. He just wanted to make us suffer."

"That's true. But he also wanted to increase his notoriety by confessing to kills he had no business claiming. At first I was irritated, and then amused. I even spoke to him in jail. I'd left a message saying I was a newspaper reporter and he wasn't going to let that chance go by. When he called me back, I gave him a few more details to feed the police."

"He was caught in the act of killing Teddy Simes."

"I didn't say he was totally blameless. Actually, he had legitimate claim to the Simes boy and four others. But the rest were mine." He paused. "Including little Bonnie Duncan."

Eve was shaking so badly, she could scarcely hold the receiver. She had to control herself. It was a crank call. Some pervert who wanted to hurt her. She'd gotten a few similar calls during Fraser's trial. But this man sounded so calm, so sure, almost indifferent. Make him talk. Make him prove he was lying. "You said you don't like to kill children."

"I was experimenting at that point. I was trying to see if they were worthwhile pursuing on a regular basis. Bonnie almost convinced me of it, but the next two were a terrible disappointment."

"Why—are you—calling me?"

"Because we have a bond, don't we? We have Bonnie."

"You lying bastard."

"Or, rather, I have Bonnie. I'm looking at her right now. She was much prettier when I put her in the ground. It's sad that we all end up as a collection of bones."

"You're . . . looking at her?"

"I remember her walking toward me across the park at the school picnic. She was eating a strawberry ice-cream cone and her red hair was shining in the sunlight. There was so much life in her. I couldn't resist."

Darkness. Don't faint.

"You have that same spark. I can tell. Only you're so much stronger."

"I'm going to hang up now."

"Yes, you sound a bit under the weather. Shock can do that. But I'm sure you'll recover soon. I'll be in touch."

"Damn you. *Why?*"

He was silent for a moment. "Because it's necessary, Eve. After this little chat, I'm even more convinced than I was before. I need you. I can feel your emotion like a tidal wave. It's . . . exhilarating."

"I won't answer the phone."

"Yes, you will. Because there's always a chance you might get her back."

"You're lying. If you killed those other children, why did you bury only Bonnie with all those adults?"

"I'm sure I must have buried more than they found. I vaguely recall at least two other children. Let's see . . . two boys. Older than Bonnie. Ten or twelve."

"Only one child's skeleton was found."

"Then they missed the others. Tell them to try in the gorge itself. The mud slide must have washed them over."

The line went dead.

Eve slid down the wall to the floor. Cold. Ice cold.

Oh, God. Oh, God.

She had to do something. She couldn't just sit there in horror.

Joe. She could call Joe.

She dialed his digital number with a shaking hand.

"Come back," she said when he answered. "Come back."

"Eve?"

"Come—back, Joe."

"What the hell's wrong?"

There was something else she should tell him. "Talladega. Tell them—to look in the gorge—itself. Two—little boys." She hung up and leaned against the wall. Don't think about it. Wrap the numbness around you until Joe gets here.

Don't faint. Don't let out the scream building inside you.

Just wait until Joe comes.

SHE WAS STILL sitting on the floor when Joe arrived an hour later.

He was across the room in four strides, kneeling beside her. "Are you hurt?"

"No."

"Then why the hell did you scare me to death?" he said roughly. He carried her to the couch. "I nearly had a heart attack. Christ, you're cold."

"Shock. He said—I was in shock."

He was rubbing her left hand, warming it. "Who said you were in shock?"

"Phone call. I thought it was a crank. Like one of those calls I got after Bonnie—" She had to stop for a minute. "But it wasn't a crank. Did you call Talladega?"

"Yes." He took her other hand and began massaging it. "Talk to me."

"He said he had Bonnie's bones." The numbness was wearing off and she was beginning to shake. "He said she wasn't as pretty as when he—"

"Take it easy." Joe grabbed the throw from a chair and tucked it around her. He crossed to the kitchenette and began making instant coffee. "Just take deep breaths. Okay?"

"Okay." She closed her eyes. Breathe deep. Ride out the pain. Ride out the horror. In. Out. Let it go or it will rip you open.

"Open your eyes." Joe was sitting on the couch beside her. "Drink this."

Coffee. Hot. Too sweet.

He watched her drink half the cup. "Better?"

She nodded jerkily.

"Now talk to me. Slowly. Don't force it. If you have to stop, do it."

She had to stop three times before she finished. When she finally fell silent, he just sat there for a moment. "Is that all? Have you told me everything?"

"Isn't that enough?" she asked unevenly.

"Hell, yes." He nodded at the cup. "Drink the rest."

"It's cold."

"I'll get you another." He got up and strode back to the kitchenette.

"He killed Bonnie, Joe."

"It could have been a crank call."

She shook her head. "He killed her."

"You're not yourself. Give yourself some time to think it over."

"I don't need time. He knew about the ice cream."

He looked up at her. "The ice cream?"

"He said she was eating a strawberry ice-cream cone that day in the park."

"That detail has never been released to the press," Joe murmured.

"Fraser knew it. He told the police that Bonnie had been eating a strawberry ice-cream cone."

"He also described what she was wearing."

"He could have found that out by reading the papers."

"He knew about the birthmark on her back."

Eve rubbed her aching temples. Joe was right. That was why they had been so sure that Fraser had killed her. Why had she been so sure? "He said he tricked Fraser into calling him back by saying he was a newspaper reporter and then fed him details. Is that possible?"

Joe thought about it. "It's possible. Fraser was giving interviews to anyone who would listen. It drove his defense attorney crazy. And no one would have known the substance of their conversation since Georgia has a law against taping without permission. Why would they have even tried to tape it? Fraser had already confessed to the murders. It was going to be an open-and-shut case."

"None of the bodies he'd said he'd buried had been found."

"That wasn't as important to them as it was to you."

God, she knew that. It had been like beating her head against a wall to get them to keep on searching after the confession. "It should have been."

Joe nodded. "But they had enough to send Fraser to the electric chair. Open and shut."

"And the ice cream . . ."

"A lot of time has passed. The vendor might have told any number of people."

"The police told him not to discuss it."

Joe shrugged. "For some people the case was closed when Fraser was executed."

"Okay, the vendor could have told someone. But what if he didn't? What if Fraser didn't kill her?"

"Eve . . ."

"What if that bastard who called me killed her? He stole her from the lab. Why would he do that, unless he—"

"Shh." Joe brought her the fresh cup of coffee and sat down beside her again. "I don't know the answer to any of those questions. I'm just playing devil's advocate so we can strike a sane balance."

"Why should we be sane? That son of a bitch who killed her can't be sane. You should have heard him. He loved hurting me. He kept hammering away at me until he drew blood."

"Okay, let's talk about him. What about his voice? Young? Old?"

"I couldn't tell. He sounded like he was talking from the bottom of a well."

"Mechanical distorter," Joe said. "What about phrasing? Accent? Vocabulary? Slang?"

She tried to remember. It was difficult to separate the manner from the words that had caused her so much pain. "No accent. He seemed . . . well spoken. I think he's educated." She shook her head wearily. "I don't know. I wasn't trying to analyze anything from the moment he mentioned Bonnie. I'll try to do better next time."

"If there is a next time."

"There will be. He was exhilarated. He said so. Why would he call me once and just leave it at that?" She started to take a sip of coffee, then stopped. "You have an unlisted number here. How did he get it?"

Joe shook his head. "I'm more concerned that he found you."

"Guesswork?"

"Possibly." He paused. "We have to consider that he still may be some kid at the university playing a nasty joke on you."

She shook her head.

"Okay, then there's the possibility that he was the murderer of those people at Talladega. But he didn't kill Bonnie and wants to take credit for it as he accused Fraser of doing."

"He knew about the ice cream."

"Or he's one of those people who confess to every murder and had nothing to do with any of them."

"We'll know soon enough about that one," Eve whispered. "If they find those boys at Talladega."

"They're searching now. I called Robert Spiro the minute I hung up with you."

"Who's Robert Spiro?"

"An agent with the FBI Behavioral Science Unit. He's part of the team handling Talladega. Good man."

"You know him?"

"He was at the Bureau when I was there. He moved to the Profiling Unit a year after I resigned. He'll call me if they find anything."

"No." She set down her cup and tossed the throw aside. "I need to go to Talladega."

"You need to rest."

"Bullshit. If they missed those bodies before, I'm not going to let them make the mistake again." She stood up. Jesus, her legs felt weak. They'd get better. Walk. "Can I take the Jeep?"

"If you take me with it." Joe put on his jacket. "And if you wait until I make enough coffee to fill a thermos. It's cold outside. This isn't Tahiti."

"And you're afraid I'm still in shock."

He headed for the kitchenette. "No, you're almost back to normal."

She didn't feel normal. She was still shaking inside and felt as if her every nerve was exposed and raw. Joe probably knew it and was tactfully ignoring it. She had to ignore it too. Just do one thing at a time. First, find out if that bastard had told her lies about Talladega. If he had lied about Talladega, then he could have lied about Bonnie.

But what if he was telling the truth?

THEY REACHED TALLADEGA Falls after midnight, but the searchlights and lanterns dotting the surrounding cliffs made it seem like day.

"Want to wait here?" Joe asked as he got out of the Jeep.

She was staring up at a cliff. "Is that where they found them?"

"The first skeleton was discovered on the next ridge, the rest up there. The child was found nearest the gorge." He didn't look at her. "It's just a hole in the ground. There's nothing there now."

But a little girl had been buried at that spot all these years. A little girl who might be Bonnie. "I have to see it."

"I thought you would."

"Then why did you ask if I wanted to wait here?" She got out of the car and started walking.

"My protective instinct." He turned on his flashlight and followed her. "I should know better."

"Yes." There had been a frost earlier in the evening, and the earth crunched beneath her feet. Was she walking in the footsteps of the murderer as he carried his victims to their graves?

She could hear the roar of the falls. Then, as she reached the top, she saw it pouring in a long, silver stream across the gorge. Brace yourself. Don't turn your head. Not yet.

"To your left," Joe said quietly.

She drew a deep breath and tore her gaze from the falls. She saw yellow tape and then . . . the grave.

Small. So small.

"Okay?" Joe was holding her elbow.

No, she wasn't okay. "She was buried here?"

"We think so. This is where she was found, and we're pretty certain the mud slide just uncovered her."

"She was here all along. All this time . . ."

"It may not be Bonnie."

"I know that," she said dully. "Stop reminding me, Joe."

"I have to remind you. You have to remind yourself."

The pain was too strong. Block it out. "It's beautiful here."

"Very beautiful. The sheriff says the Indians called the falls 'the place of tumbling moonlight.'"

"But he didn't bury them in this place because it's beautiful," she said shakily. "He wanted to hide them where they'd never be found and brought home to the people who loved them."

"Don't you think you've been here long enough?"

"Give me a minute more."

"Whatever you need."

"God, I hope he didn't hurt her," she whispered. "I hope it was over quickly."

"That's enough." Joe turned her away from the grave. "Sorry, I thought I could stand it, but I can't. I've got to take you away from—"

"Stop right where you are and don't move a muscle."

A tall, thin man was walking toward them along the edge of the cliff. He was holding a flashlight in one hand and a revolver in the other. "Identify yourself."

"Spiro?" Joe stepped in front of Eve. "Joe Quinn."

"What are you doing up here?" Robert Spiro demanded. "It's a good way to get shot. We've got this area staked out."

"The FBI? I thought you were here in an advisory capacity."

"We were, but we've taken over the investigation. Sheriff Bosworth didn't argue. He wanted out."

"You think the murderer is going to come back? Is that why you're staking out the graves?" Eve asked.

Spiro glanced at her. "And who are you?"

"Eve Duncan, this is Agent Robert Spiro," Joe said.

"Oh, how do you do, Ms. Duncan." Spiro shoved the gun in his underarm holster and lifted the lantern higher to look at her. "Sorry to scare you, but Quinn should have let me know you were coming."

Spiro was in his late forties with deep-set dark eyes

and brown hair that sharply receded from a broad fore-head. Lines bracketed both sides of his mouth, and the expression on his face was more world-weary than any-thing Eve had ever seen. She repeated, "You think he's going to come back? I know it's not uncommon for a serial murderer to return to the graves of his victims."

"Yeah, even the very smart ones can't resist that last thrill." He turned to Joe. "We haven't found anything yet. You're sure this is a solid tip?"

"It's solid," Joe said. "Are you stopping to wait until daylight?"

"No. Sheriff Bosworth said his men know the gorge like the backs of their hands." He looked at Eve. "It's cold near these falls. You need to get out of here."

"I'll wait until you find the boys."

He shrugged. "Suit yourself. It may be a long time." To Joe he said, "I need to talk to you about that 'solid' tip. Care to take a walk?"

"I won't leave Eve alone."

"Charlie!" Spiro called over his shoulder, and a man with a flashlight appeared. "Joe Quinn, Eve Duncan, this is Agent Charles Cather. Take Ms. Duncan to her car and stay with her until Quinn comes back, Charlie."

Charles Cather nodded. "Come with me, Ms. Duncan."

"I won't be long, Eve." Joe turned to Spiro. "If we're going to walk, let's go to the command center."

"Whatever." Spiro started back along the cliff edge.

Eve watched them. They were closing her out and she was tempted to go after them.

"Ms. Duncan?" Charles Cather said politely. "You'll be more comfortable in your car. You must be cold."

She looked down at the grave. Yes, she was cold. Cold and tired and empty. The sight of that grave had nearly torn her apart, and she needed a little time to recover. Besides, Joe would not let her be closed out for long.

She started down the cliff. "Come on, I have some hot coffee in the Jeep."

"COULD I HAVE another cup?" Charlie Cather leaned back in the passenger seat. "I'm really feeling this cold. Spiro says I need to toughen up, but I tell him it's from living in South Georgia all my life."

She poured him more coffee. "Where in South Georgia?"

"Valdosta. Do you know it?"

"I've never been through there, but I've heard about the university. Have you ever gone to Pensacola? I used to take my daughter there on vacation."

"Every spring break. Nice beach."

"Yes. Where's Agent Spiro from?"

"New Jersey, I think. He doesn't talk much." He grimaced. "Well, not to me. I'm new at the Bureau, and Spiro's been there forever."

"Joe seems to respect him."

"Oh, so do I. Spiro's a great agent."

"But you don't like him?"

"I didn't say that." He hesitated. "Spiro's done profiling for nearly a decade. It does something to a man."

"What?"

"It . . . burns him out. Profilers usually socialize only with other profilers. I guess when you're a man who stares at monsters every day, it's hard to talk to someone who doesn't do that too."

"You're not a profiler?"

He shook his head. "Not yet. They just accepted me into the unit and I'm still training. I'm here to tote and fetch for Spiro." He took a sip of coffee and then said quietly, "I've seen your picture in the paper."

"Have you?"

"I'm sorry if that's your little girl they found up there."

"I've known for a long time that there was no hope. I just want to bring Bonnie home so I can lay her to rest."

He nodded. "My dad was MIA in Vietnam and they've never found the body. Even when I was a kid I used to worry about where he was. It didn't seem right that he was lost there."

"No, it doesn't." She glanced away from him. "And my daughter wasn't in a war."

"No? Seems like there are wars everywhere. You can't even send a kid to school without worrying if one of his classmates has an attack rifle. Somebody has to stop it. That's why I joined the FBI."

She smiled. "Charlie, I do believe you're one of the good guys."

He made a face. "I sounded pretty hokey, didn't I? Sorry. I know I'm green as grass compared to Spiro. Sometimes I get the feeling he thinks I'm still in kinder-garten. Demoralizing as hell."

Eve could see how it would be. She supposed a person aged quickly in a job like Spiro's. "Are you married, Charlie?"

He nodded. "Last year. Martha Ann." A sudden smile illuminated his face. "She's pregnant."

"Congratulations."

"We should have been sensible and waited. But we both wanted kids. We'll make out."

"I'm sure you will." She was feeling better. Life wasn't all graves and monsters. There were people like Charlie and Martha Ann and the baby on its way. "Want some more coffee?"

"I've almost emptied your thermos. I'd better not—"

"Open the window." It was Joe, his face pressed against the fogged glass.

She rolled down the window.

"They found them," Joe said. "At least they found bones. They're bringing them up to the command cen-ter now."

She got out of the Jeep. "Children?"

"I don't know."

"Two?"

"There are two skulls."

"Intact?"

Joe nodded.

"Then I'll be able to tell. Take me there."

"Can I talk you out of it?"

She was already climbing the cliff. "Take me there."

THE STRETCHER WAS rigged on a pulley and Eve watched as it was hoisted up slowly. On the stretcher were two blanket-wrapped bundles.

"You're trying to keep the bodies separated?" she asked Spiro.

"As best as we can. I wouldn't bet on the bones not being mixed up. It looked like the mud slide washed them down."

The stretcher reached the top of the cliff and was settled on the ground. Spiro knelt beside it and opened one blanket. "What do you think?"

"Give me some more light." She knelt next to him. So many bones. Splintered. Broken. Like the bones of an animal after carnivores had—

Get a grip. Do your job. The skull.

She took it in her hands and examined it. No teeth. Joe had told her the other skulls didn't have teeth. Ignore the horrifying image of the murderer pulling them. Concentrate. "It's a child. Preteen male. Caucasian."

"You're sure?" Spiro asked.

"No. Anthropology isn't my specialty, but I'd bet on it. I've done hundreds of reconstructions on children this age." She gently put the skull down and opened the other blanket. It held fewer bones and the skull was staring up at her.

*Bring me home.*

*Lost. So many lost ones.*

"Anything wrong?" Spiro asked.

"Leave her alone, Spiro," Joe said.

Could anything be more wrong than a world that could destroy children? "No, nothing's wrong. I was just studying it." She picked up the skull. "Another male. Preteen Caucasian. Maybe a little older than the other." She put the skull down and got to her feet. "You'll have to get a forensic anthropologist to confirm." She turned to Joe. "I'm ready to leave now."

"Hallelujah."

"Wait," Spiro said. "Joe told me about the telephone call. I need to talk to you."

"Then come to my cottage to see her." Joe was already pushing Eve down the cliff. "We're out of here."

"I want to see her now."

Joe looked back over his shoulder. "Don't push it," he said softly. "I won't have it, Spiro."

Spiro hesitated and then shrugged. "I guess it can wait. God knows, I have enough to do here."

EVE SETTLED INTO the passenger seat. "You didn't have to make an issue of it. I could have talked to him."

"Yeah, I know." He stomped on the accelerator. "And you could have stayed up on that ridge, staring at those bones. Or gone back to look at that little girl's grave. How about leaping over tall buildings in a single bound? You don't need any more punishment to prove you're Superwoman."

She leaned back on the headrest. God, she felt tired. "I'm not trying to prove anything."

He was silent a moment. "I know. It would be easier if you were."

"He told me the truth. There were two other children up there. He could have been telling the truth about Bonnie."

"One truth doesn't guarantee another."

"But it makes what he told me more plausible."

Another silence. "Yes."

"And if it's true, then he's been out there all along. Walking, breathing, enjoying life. When Fraser was executed, at least I had the comfort of knowing Bonnie's murderer had been punished. But it was all a lie."

"You're jumping to conclusions."

But she had a terrible feeling she wasn't. "There were two preteen boys Fraser admitted to killing. John Devon and Billy Thompkins."

"Yes, I remember."

"We have to identify only one of them to form a link between Fraser and the caller. I want you to persuade Spiro to give me one of those skulls to reconstruct."

"There may be some red tape. The FBI has their own way of doing things."

"You know Spiro. You were in the FBI. You can get him to cut through the tape."

"I'll try."

"Do it." She smiled mirthlessly. "Or you'll find another skeleton missing. If I can't have Bonnie, I *will* have one of those boys."

"You're already thinking of her as Bonnie."

"I have to call her something."

"There was another missing girl of about the same age on Fraser's kill list."

"Doreen Parker." She closed her eyes. "Damn you, Joe."

"You want it too much. I won't have you taking that kind of fall if it's not true."

"Just get me a skull."

He muttered a frustrated curse. "I'll get it for you. Spiro should be grateful for any help on this case."

"Then let him be grateful. We're going to need him. He knows about monsters."

"So do you."

Only one monster. The one who had dominated her life since Bonnie had disappeared. She had called the monster Fraser and now she found that might not even be its name. "I don't know enough. But I'm going to have to learn."

"You're so sure he's going to contact you again?"

"He'll call me." Eve smiled bitterly. "As he said, we have a bond."

"Go to bed," Joe said as they stepped inside the cottage. "I'll call Spiro and put in a request for a skull."

Eve glanced at her watch. It was almost four in the morning. "He won't be in a very accommodating mood if you wake him up."

"I doubt he's asleep. He doesn't sleep much when he's on a case. He's pretty driven."

"Good." She headed for her bedroom. "I believe in driven."

"Tell me something I don't know." He reached for the phone on the table. "Go on, get some rest. I'll get your skull for you."

"Thanks, Joe." She closed the door behind her and moved toward the bathroom. Shower and go to bed. Don't think of Bonnie. Don't think of those two little boys. Don't try to draw conclusions. All that could wait until she was rested and able to conquer the horror and the shock. Tomorrow when she woke she would try to put the pieces together.

"YOU LOOK LIKE hell," Joe told Eve. "Couldn't you sleep?"

"A few hours. My mind wouldn't turn off. Is Spiro going to give me a skull?"

"He wouldn't commit. He said he'd discuss it when he finished talking to you."

"He's coming here?"

"He'll be here by three this afternoon." He checked his watch. "Another thirty minutes. You have time for breakfast or lunch. Which do you want?"

"Just a sandwich." She headed for the refrigerator. "I can't seem to get warm. I borrowed another one of your flannel shirts."

"I noticed. It looks better on you." He sat down at the bar and watched her build a ham and cheese sandwich. "I don't mind sharing with you. I've become accustomed to it over the years. It's kind of comfortable."

She nodded in perfect understanding. Being with Joe was as comfortable as feeling his soft shirt against her body.

"I have something to tell you." Joe shook his head when she looked up in alarm. "It's not that bad, but you have to know."

"Know what?"

"Mark Grunard's found out where you are."

She frowned. "Mark Grunard?"

"TV journalist. He must have spent days digging into records to find this cottage. I had to make a deal. You've heard of him?"

She nodded slowly. "He's on Channel Three. Investigative reporting. I remember him from Fraser's trial." She grimaced. "As well as I can remember anyone or anything except Fraser."

"I told you I had to find a way to draw reporters away from here. I couldn't do it by myself, so I had to make a deal."

"What kind of deal?"

"Mark Grunard's spot on the six o'clock news last night was about the search for you. He showed a shot of this cottage and expressed his disappointment that this wasn't the hideaway. However, he had been given a tip about a houseboat off the coast of Florida. After the broadcast he hopped a plane to Jacksonville, and I'd bet half the reporters in the city did too."

"And what did you have to promise him?"

"An exclusive. He keeps quiet until we're ready to release. But you'll have to meet with him here a couple of times."

"When?"

"The first one fairly soon. He's already paid his first installment on the deal. He'll want something in return. Do you have an objection to Grunard?"

She tried to remember Mark Grunard more clearly. Older, graying at the temples, with Peter Jennings's warmth. "No, I guess not." She smiled. "What would you have done if I'd told you I couldn't stand him?"

"Ditched him." He grinned. "But it makes my life easier that I don't have to go back on my word. Finish your sandwich."

"I'm eating." She took another bite. "What made you choose Grunard? Do you know him well?"

"Well enough. We have an occasional drink together at Manuel's. But he really chose me. He was camped out at Georgia State yesterday morning when I went to pick up the skull and made me an offer I couldn't refuse."

"And you can trust him?"

"We don't have to trust him. As long as he thinks he's going to get a payoff, I guarantee he'll lay those red herrings all over the South."

"I guess we can't expect more than—"

A knock on the door.

"Spiro." Joe started across the room. "You should have finished your sandwich, dammit."

"Dictator." She pushed the plate away as Joe let Robert Spiro in. He nodded politely. "Ms. Duncan." He turned to Joe. "I've been fending off the media all morning. They want to know how I knew there were two more skeletons in that gorge."

"And what did you tell them?"

"That it was profiler instinct," he said sourly. "Why not? After all we've done to debunk it, they still believe there's something spooky about our unit anyway." Spiro turned to Eve. "Is there anything you have to add to what Joe told me?"

Eve looked at Joe.

He shook his head. "I told him everything."

"Then there's nothing else," Eve said. "Except that he's going to call again."

"Maybe."

"He'll call. And I want you to be ready for him. Can you bug the phone?"

"Hasn't Joe arranged that yet?"

"I was a little busy last night," Joe said dryly. "Besides, getting my department to do the bug will require finesse, because the Atlanta PD is fighting becoming involved."

"Then they're fighting a losing battle if those two boys are who you think they are."

"Let me find out," Eve said. "Give me a skull."

Spiro was silent.

"Give it to me."

"It could be dangerous to involve you any more."

"I couldn't be more involved."

"Yes, you could be, if this man who called you is really the murderer of those people at Talladega. Right now he's looking at you as a passive victim and feeling a wonderful sense of power. That might even be enough for him. But the minute you take aggressive action, he could become angry and desperate to reassert himself."

"It won't be enough for him." She stared him in the eye. "And I won't be a passive victim. That son of a bitch has Bonnie—that little girl's bones. He killed her."

"Possibly."

"Probably. He knew about those boys. Can you get enough DNA for an analysis?"

"We're trying. The bones are pretty shattered and—"

"And then there will be another delay while the samples are analyzed. Give me a skull."

Spiro raised his brows and glanced at Joe. "Obstinate."

"You don't know the half of it. Better give her a skull."

"Are you going to be responsible, Quinn? I'm not kidding about any initiative raising the ante."

"I'm the only one responsible for me," Eve said. "Give me a skull."

He smiled faintly. "I'd be tempted to do it if I didn't know what a—"

The phone rang.

Joe started toward the phone by the door.

"Wait." Spiro nodded at Eve. "Pick it up. Is there another extension?"

The phone rang again.

"Kitchen," Joe said.

Spiro ran to the kitchen, and Eve picked up the receiver at his signal. "Hello."

"Listen carefully." The voice was unmistakable. "I know you probably have this phone bugged by now, and I'm not going to stay on the line long. From now on I'll call you on your digital phone." He chuckled. "Did you enjoy your trip to Talladega? Cold night, wasn't it?"

He hung up.

She slowly hung up and turned to Spiro.

"He's using a mechanical voice distorter," Spiro said. "Is that how he sounded before?"

"Yes."

"Interesting."

"He knew about my trip to Talladega. He must have followed us."

"Or he's bluffing."

She shivered. "I don't think he's bluffing."

"Neither do I." He shrugged. "I'll give you your skull. It's not going to make any difference. He's going to play out his scenario no matter what we do."

"How can you tell?" Joe asked.

"There are two kinds of serial killers. The disorganized and the organized. A disorganized killer is spontaneous, random, and sloppy. Talladega has some of the marks of an organized killer. Bodies hidden and transported. Weapon and evidence absent. We'll probably find other signs as we go along. Your caller's being very careful not to be recognized. There's nothing sloppy about this man, which fits the usual pattern."

"What's the usual pattern?" Eve asked.

"Average to above-average intelligence, aware of police procedures and may even associate with the police. Owns a car in good condition, travels frequently, usually commits crimes out of his area of residence. He's socially adept, has verbal skills that he uses to—"

"That's enough." Eve shook her head. "You argued with me but you believed this man is the Talladega monster all along, didn't you?"

"My job is to take the supposed truth apart and look at it every way possible." He headed for the door. "When he calls again, write down everything he says the moment you hang up. Digital calls are tough to trace, but I'll arrange for a bug on the house phone. He might decide to call on that line if he can't reach you on your digital."

"How does he even know I have a digital? How will he get my number? It's private. For that matter, Joe's number here is unlisted too."

"There are ways if you're determined enough and smart enough. As I said, one of the characteristics of the organized serial killer is average to above-average intelligence. But you're right. One of the first things I'll do is run a check on the phone companies and see if there's been any detected infiltration into their computer banks." He stopped at the door. "I have a skull in my car. Come out and get it, Joe."

"And what are you going to tell Joe that you don't want me to hear?"

He hesitated and then shrugged. "That I'm sending Charlie down to guard the cottage while you're working on the skull. I have to go back to Talladega to meet with Spalding from the Child Abduction Serial Killer Unit and explain why I'm stepping on his toes by giving you a skull. CASKU might have their own forensic sculptor on tap."

"I don't need Charlie. Joe is here."

"A little more protection won't hurt. A hell of a lot more protection wouldn't be bad. I'll try to arrange it as soon as possible. One of the other marks of the organized killer is that he targets his victim." He frowned. "Though the victim is almost always a stranger. It makes me uneasy that he wants to establish an intimate link with you."

"I'm sure he's sorry to upset your profile," she said ironically. "It could be he's not going to play by your rules."

Spiro's lips tightened grimly. "You'd better hope he does. It may be our only way of catching him."

"When will Charlie be here?"

"A couple of hours. Why?"

"I want Joe to go back to Atlanta and get me photographs of those boys. I'll need to verify after I do the reconstruction."

"Joe should stay here," Spiro said. "I'll have the Bureau fax me the photographs to Talladega and I'll bring them to you myself."

"Thank you."

"Don't thank me. I should tell you to leave this place and go to the city. You're too isolated here."

"I need the isolation to work on that skull."

"And I need to get my hands on that killer." He

shrugged. "So I guess I'm willing to risk your neck to get him."

"Nice," Joe said.

"Don't give me that." Spiro suddenly whirled on him. "I warned you both of the danger of working on a skull, and you wouldn't listen. Well, don't blame me for doing anything I can to get that asshole. I've just spent a week staring at those nine graves. God knows how many more he's killed. Can you guess how many serial killers are out there? We probably catch only one in thirty. The dumb ones. The ones who make mistakes. The smart ones walk away and kill and kill again. This is one of the smart ones. But this time we have a chance. I don't know why, but he's giving us a shot at him, and I'm damn well going to take it."

"Okay. Okay." Joe lifted his hands in surrender. "But don't expect me to let you use Eve as bait."

"Sorry." Spiro struggled for control. "I didn't mean to—Maybe I need a vacation."

"It wouldn't surprise me," Joe said.

"Hell, I'm in good shape. Half the profilers in my department need therapy. Just be careful. I don't like this. There's something . . ." He shook his head. "Come on and get your damned skull."

Eve crossed to the window and watched Spiro open his trunk, pull out a small cloth-wrapped bundle, and give it to Joe. He lifted his head as if feeling her gaze on him and smiled sardonically at her. He raised his hand in farewell and slammed the trunk shut.

What had Charlie said about him?

*A man who stares at monsters.*

She knew how close to the edge that could push you. She'd been there.

Joe came into the cottage and shut the door. "Well, you've got it. I suppose you're going to want to start right away?"

She nodded. "Put it on the pedestal. Be careful. I don't know how much damage it's already sustained."

He unwrapped the cloth and placed the skull on the pedestal.

"It's the younger boy," she said. "What's his name?"

"John Devon. *If* he is one of Fraser's vic—"

"Don't give me ifs right now, Joe. I know what you're trying to do, but it's just getting in my way." She stepped closer to the pedestal and stared at the small, fragile skull. Poor child. Lost child. "John Devon," she whispered.

*Bring me home.*

God, I'll try, John.

She straightened her glasses and turned to the worktable. "It's getting dark. Will you turn on the lights? I've got to start measuring."

SPIRO CAME TO the cottage the next morning shortly before noon. He waved the manila envelope in his hand. "Got the photos. Do you want to see them?"

"No." Eve wiped her hands on a towel. "I never look at the photos until I'm finished. They might influence me."

He studied the skull. "Neither of those kids looked like that. Those little sticks sticking out all over make him look like a torture victim from the Spanish Inquisition. What are they?"

"Tissue-depth markers. I measure the skull and cut each marker to the proper depth and then glue it on its specific point on the face. There are more than twenty points of the skull for which there are known tissue depths."

"Then what?"

"I take strips of plasticine and apply them between the markers and build up to all of the tissue-depth points. When that's done, I start the smoothing and filling-in process."

"It's incredible that you can come as close as you do with just measurements."

"Measurements go only so far. Then technique and instinct have to take over."

He smiled. "I'm sure they do." He turned to her. "Have you gotten any more calls?"

"No."

He glanced around the cottage. "Where's Quinn?"

"Outside somewhere."

"He shouldn't have left you alone."

"He hasn't left me alone more than five minutes in the past twenty-four hours. I told him to go take a walk."

"He shouldn't have listened to you. It's not—"

"Where's Charlie?" she interrupted. "Joe's been trying to reach him since last night. He called Talladega and was told he'd left there, but he didn't show up here."

"Sorry if you were nervous. I knew Quinn was guarding you and I had a car patrolling the area. I sent Charlie to take a report on Talladega to Quantico. He'll be here tonight."

"I was too busy to be nervous. It was Joe who was anxious. But I'd think you'd make the reports yourself."

"There are some advantages to being a senior agent. I try to avoid Quantico. I'd rather be in the field." He smiled. "And Quinn is usually more than adequate. The Bureau was very sorry to lose him." His gaze shifted back to the skull. "When will you be finished?"

"Tomorrow, maybe. I don't know."

"You look tired."

"I'm okay." She took off her glasses and rubbed her eyes. "My eyes sting a little. That's always the worst of it."

"It won't be before tomorrow?"

She looked at him in surprise. "What difference does it make? I had to persuade you to even let me do the reconstruction."

"I want to know. If it is John Devon, it will give me somewhere to start. That's more than I have now." He paused. "This is a real nasty can of worms," he muttered. "And I've got a feeling . . ."

She smiled. "One of those 'spooky' profiler instincts?"

"So I get hunches occasionally. Nothing spooky about that."

"I guess not."

He walked over to the window and gazed out. "I'm worried about this killer. Those bodies were buried years ago and he was very careful even then. What's he been doing since that time? What did he do before Talladega? How long has it gone on?"

She shook her head.

"You know, I've often wondered what killers become if they're permitted to go on for a long time. Do they change? How often can you kill before you change from monster to super monster?"

"Super monster? It sounds like something out of a comic book."

"I don't think you'll find him funny if you ever have to confront him."

"You mean a killer becomes smarter over the years."

"Smarter, more experienced, more arrogant, more determined, more calloused."

"Have you ever dealt with one of these super monsters?"

"Not that I know about." He turned to look at her. "But then, wouldn't a super monster take on the coloration of everything around him? You'd pass him on the street and never suspect him. If he'd been allowed to go on long enough, Bundy might have become a super monster. He had the fundamentals but he was too reckless."

"How can you be this clinical?"

"If you let in emotion, you're at an immediate disadvantage. The man who called you wouldn't allow himself to become emotional if it got in his way. But he'd prey on your every emotion. It's part of the power trip." He shook his head. "Don't let him feel your fear. He'll feed on it."

"I'm not afraid of him."

He studied her. "I believe you're telling the truth. Why aren't you afraid? You should be. Everyone's afraid to die."

She didn't answer.

"But maybe you're not," he said slowly.

"I have the same sense of self-preservation everyone does."

"I hope you do." His lips tightened. "Listen to me, don't underestimate this man. He knows too much. He could be anyone. He could be a clerk who works for the phone company or the cop who stops you for speeding or a lawyer with access to court records. Remember, he's been at this a long time."

"How could I forget?" Her gaze shifted to the skull. "I have to go back to work now."

"I guess that's my exit cue." Spiro headed for the door. "Let me know when you finish."

"I will." She had already closed him out as she began to join the markers.

JOE QUINN WAS waiting beside Spiro's car. "Come on, I want to show you something."

"I didn't think you'd go very far." Spiro followed him around the house. "You shouldn't have left her alone."

"I didn't leave her alone. I was never out of sight of the cottage." He left the driveway and moved into the shrubs. He knelt down. "See these marks? Someone was here."

"That's not a foot imprint."

"No, he cleaned the area. But the grass is bent. He tried to comb it, but he was in a hurry."

"Very good." Spiro should have known Quinn would

pick up on any anomaly. He was sharp, and his SEAL training made him particularly formidable. "You think it was our man?"

"I don't know anyone else who would try to disguise his being here."

"He's watching her?"

Quinn raised his head, his gaze on the woods. "Not now. No one's out there."

"You'd sense it?" Spiro said mockingly. "ESP?"

"Something like that." He smiled crookedly. "Maybe it's my Cherokee blood. My grandfather was a half-breed."

And maybe it was that SEAL training again. Search and destroy. "You must have expected to find this or you wouldn't have gone looking."

"He was ugly to her. He wanted to hurt her. I thought he might want to see her pain." He stood up and moved back a step. "Or maybe he wanted to make sure he knew where she was. Either way, he'd come. Get a forensic team out here to see if they can collect any evidence."

"Listen, we've got our hands full at Talladega. Get your own people to do it."

"They won't do anything until they're sure they have to be involved, and they won't know that until Eve finishes the reconstruction. They won't dare not jump in at that point because of Eve's reputation."

"But until then I guess you have to rely on me. In which case, it would behoove you to ask instead of order."

"Please," Joe bit out.

Spiro smiled. "You gave in too easily. I would have had a team out here anyway."

"Bastard."

"You needed taking down a notch." He turned away. "Charlie will be here by dark. I understand you've been worried."

Joe's gaze narrowed on his face. "You wanted me to worry. When I couldn't reach Cather, I called you. When you didn't answer your digital, I phoned the command site and Sheriff Bosworth said you were too busy to take the call."

"He was right. It turned out that no aerial shots had been taken of the grave sites to determine if there's a pattern. It kept me pretty busy coordinating the photography."

"Too busy for a two-minute phone call? You wanted to make me sweat."

"Worry keeps a man sharp. You're going to need to be sharp."

"And I'm not sure Cather's the agent to guard Eve. He doesn't impress me."

"He's not standard FBI, if that's what you mean. He's not cynical and he's eager instead of methodical. I had a hell of a time getting him approved for the unit, but that doesn't mean he's not fully qualified. And a fresh eye sees things a jaded one doesn't. He'll do a good job. Besides, I've given orders for three other agents to do sentry duty and patrol the woods around the cottage. They'll report to Charlie. Satisfied?"

"Hell, no."

"No, you want a battalion."

"The fewer the guards, the more likely that maniac will come calling."

Spiro looked him directly in the eye. "That's right. I'll supply enough men to keep her safe, but I don't want to discourage him."

"You'd rather she run the risk?"

"Don't be ridiculous. She's valuable. She may be our only lead."

"Answer me."

"I have to catch this one, Quinn. I can't take a chance on him slipping away. You can laugh, but after these days at Talladega, staring at those graves, I sometimes feel—" He stopped and then shrugged. "He's mine."

"And Eve?"

"She's only one woman. There's no telling how many more people he'll kill if we don't get him now."

"You bastard."

"Yes, but if you want that killer, I'm your best bet. I'll keep on going until I have him." He started to walk away but stopped. "You know, I don't like Eve Duncan's attitude."

"Too bad. She's working her butt off to get an identification on that skull."

"No, that's not what I—" A frown creased Spiro's forehead. "She's not afraid of him. He's not going to like that. It will make him angry and more determined to break her. If he can't reach her, he'll try for someone close to her."

"I twisted a few arms over the phone last night and got a twenty-four-hour guard on her mother."

"Good."

"But I didn't tell Eve and I'm not going to tell her about anyone watching the cottage. So make sure your forensic guys don't plod around here like elephants. She's working so hard, I doubt she'd notice if they did, but she's got enough to worry about."

"You're very protective."

"You'd better believe it. You might think about that, Spiro. Because if that asshole gets to her and it's your fault, she won't be the only victim."

CHARLIE CATHER ARRIVED at the cottage four hours later. "Sorry to be late." He grimaced. "I meant to get here an hour ago, but I got a late start from Quantico. I hoped I'd get the analysis before I left, but they hadn't finished."

Eve glanced up from the skull. "What analysis?"

"From VICAP. Violent Criminal Apprehension Program. It's a nationwide database that allows us to type in all the facts of a violent crime and then does a search for similar modi operandi on reported crimes during a given period."

"I didn't know Spiro had authorized one," Joe said.

"Oh, he did, and we've been giving VICAP the reports on the bodies to narrow their search. They've been waiting for the last report, but it got lost in a damn paper shuffle. I found it only right before I left Talladega, so I took it myself to Quantico."

"And what given period did you tell the computer?" Eve asked.

"Thirty years. Just to be safe."

She stared at him, stunned. Thirty years?

Charlie turned to Joe. "I told them to call me here with the results. I'll be outside in my car. Will you tell me when it comes?"

"Why not wait here?" Eve asked.

Charlie shook his head. "Spiro told me to be on guard duty outside. He wouldn't appreciate having me warming my tush inside." He grinned. "I could have told them to call me on my digital, but I thought it wouldn't hurt to use the phone call to get me inside to defrost." He walked over to the pedestal. "You've made a lot of progress, haven't you? How much longer?"

She shrugged. "It depends on how it goes."

"They do a lot of computer imaging and stuff at Quantico, but this is kind of . . . personal."

"Yes."

"He looks so fragile. Poor little kid. God, it makes me sad. I don't know how you take it."

"The same way you stand what you do. It's my job."

"It makes you scared to bring a kid into this world, doesn't it? You know, some of the guys at the unit won't let their kids out of their sight. They've seen too much of what goes on to ever feel safe. I'll probably feel the same way after my baby is—"

"I'll let you know when you get your call," Joe interrupted. "Eve has to get back to work now."

The dismissal was pointed. Charlie's words had been thoughtless and Joe was stepping between her and possible hurt, Eve realized.

"Yeah, sure." Charlie headed out the door. "I'd appreciate it. See you later."

"You didn't have to toss him out," Eve told Joe. "He didn't mean any harm."

"He talks too much."

"He's just young. I like him." She turned back to the pedestal. "They probably won't find anything through the VICAP search. They haven't caught the bastard in over ten years."

"Then it's time they did."

Joe sat on the couch and picked up his book. "I'll give you another hour and then you stop to eat. No arguments."

"We'll see."

"No arguments."

She glanced at him. He was giving off the aura of the quintessential immovable object.

What the hell. An immovable object could be very comforting in this volatile world. "Okay. No arguments."

LOGAN CALLED WHILE Eve was at dinner. "I got your two messages. I was running around the island, closing up shop. I'm flying out to Monterey tomorrow."

"You didn't tell me you were leaving the island."

"It's not the same now. Time to get back to the real world." He paused. "Are you working on the skull?"

"Not the little girl. A boy we found."

"You said you were going to work on—Why the hell are you still there?"

"Things happened."

"You're not telling me everything. Hell, you're not telling me anything."

She knew darn well if she told him what had been happening he would be on his way immediately. "I'm going to get the little girl's skull. I have to work on this one first."

Silence.

"I don't like it. There's too much you're not saying. I'm going to fly out to Monterey tonight instead of tomorrow. I'll call you as soon as I arrive."

"Logan, it's wonderful of you to want to help, but you can't do anything this time."

"We'll see." He hung up.

"He's coming here?" Joe asked.

"Not if I can help it. I don't want him near that killer."

He frowned. "You're being a little more protective than I'd like."

"Too bad. Logan's a great guy and my friend. You feel protective toward your friends." She deliberately met his gaze. "Don't you, Joe?"

He grimaced. "Okay, you got me." He changed the subject. "Want some dessert? We've got Rocky Road ice cream."

ANOTHER CALL CAME on Eve's digital phone at eight that evening.

Eve tensed. Her phone, not the cottage phone. It could be her mother. It could be Logan again. It didn't have to be that monster.

Joe picked up her phone, which she'd laid on the coffee table after she'd talked to Logan. "Do you want me to answer?"

She shook her head. "Give it to me." She punched the button. "Hello."

"Bonnie's waiting for you to come and get her."

Her hand tightened on the phone. "Bullshit."

"After all these years of searching for her, you've come so close. It's a pity you're going to fail now. Have you finished with the boy's skull yet?"

"How do you know I'm doing—"

"Oh, I'm keeping close watch over you. After all, I do have a vested interest. Haven't you sensed me standing behind you, looking over your shoulder as you work on the skull?"

"No."

"You should. You will. Which boy is it?"

"Why should I tell you?"

"It doesn't really matter. I only vaguely remember them. They were just two of those frightened little birds. Not like your Bonnie. She was never—"

"You bastard. You probably don't have the guts to kill anyone. You creep around, making anonymous phone calls, threatening and trying to—"

"Anonymous? Is that annoying you? You can call me Dom if you like. But what's in a name? A rose by any other name would smell as—"

"The only thing that annoys me is that you think you can terrify me with these pitiful tricks."

"And now you're trying to annoy me." He laughed in delight. "And I believe you're succeeding. How refreshing. It only proves how right I was to choose you."

"Did you harass those other poor people at Talladega before you killed them?"

"No, that would have been reckless, and I wasn't at that point yet."

"But you are now?"

"I'm at the point where I'm willing to take a few chances to make life interesting. It was bound to happen sometime."

"Why me?"

"Because I need something to cleanse me. The moment I saw your photograph in the paper I knew you were the one. I looked at your face and I could see all the emotion and torment that's building inside you. It's only a question of making that emotion soar until it breaks through." He paused. "Can you imagine what an explosion that will be for both of us?"

"You're insane."

"Quite possibly. By your standards. Science has made such a study of the mind of the murderer. The causes, the early signs, the way we justify killing."

"How do you justify it?"

"I don't. Pleasure is justification enough. I recently heard that recreational homicide went up twenty-five percent in the last ten years. I started long before that. It seems that society is finally catching up to me, doesn't it? Maybe you're all going mad too, Eve."

"Bullshit."

"Then why let me go on killing? Have you ever considered that perhaps we've never really lost our cave instincts? The bloodlust, the search for power through that final act of violence. Perhaps in your heart of hearts you all wish you could be like me. Haven't you ever wanted to hunt, to prey?"

"No."

"You will. Ask Quinn how it feels. He's a hunter. He has the instinct. Ask him if his heart beats faster when he nears the kill."

"Joe's not like you. No one is like you."

"Thank you. I regard that as a compliment. I believe it's time to hang up now. I just wanted to touch base with you. It's important that we get to know each other. You're not one to fear the unknown."

"I'm not afraid of you."

"You will be. But it's clear I'll have to work at it a little harder. No problem. I wouldn't have it any other way." He paused. "Bonnie misses you. You should really be together." He hung up.

Pain tore through her. Damn him. He'd had to throw that last jab. She pressed the off button and looked at

Joe. "He just wanted to touch base with me. The bastard wants me to be afraid of him."

"Then pretend to be afraid. Don't challenge him."

"Screw that."

Joe smiled faintly. "I thought I'd try. Did you find out anything we can use?"

"He said his name is Dom. He's been killing for more than ten years and does it purely for pleasure. He's analytical about himself and the world in general. He's as smart as we thought he was." She turned back to the pedestal. "Will you write all that down and call it in to Spiro? I have to get back to work."

"It wouldn't hurt for you to take a break."

"Yes, it would," she said fiercely. "I won't let that bastard disturb my concentration. He wants to control me, and I'll be damned if I let him. I won't give him anything he wants."

She stood before the skull. Her hands were shaking a little. Steady them. It was time for the final stage. Nothing must interfere with the sculpting. She had to be cool and detached.

*Haven't you sensed me standing behind you, looking over your shoulder as you work on the skull?*

She restrained the impulse to turn her head. No one was staring at her back or over her shoulder. No one was behind her but Joe.

If she let Dom influence her by sparking her imagination, then it would be a victory for him. Close him out. Think of the little boy, not of the monster who had killed him.

Bring him home.

With slow, certain strokes she began to mold the child's face.

SHE WAS STRONGER than Dom had thought.

A surge of excitement tingled through him. She was

going to stretch him, make him work for every ounce of emotion he drew from her.

It was no real surprise. He had been prepared for it. He welcomed it. It would force him to dig deep to find a way to jar her.

He already had an idea how to do it.

He started the car, backed out of the convenience store parking lot, and headed back to Atlanta.

**5:40 A.M.**

Finished except for the eyes.

She reached for her eye case on the worktable.

Brown was the most prevalent eye color, and she almost always used brown eyes when reconstructing. She placed the glass eyeballs in the sockets and stepped back.

Is it you, John Devon? Did I do a good enough job to bring you home?

"Do you want the photo now?" Joe asked quietly.

She'd been vaguely aware that he'd been sitting on the couch all through the night, waiting. "Yes."

He stood up and opened the large envelope on the coffee table. He discarded one photo and carried the other to her. "I think this is the one you want."

She stared at the photo without touching it. He was wrong, she didn't want it.

Take it. Bring him home.

She reached out and took the photo. She should have put in blue eyes, she realized dully. Everything else was a match. "It's him. It's John Devon."

"Yes." He took the photo and tossed it on the workbench. "I'll call Spiro right after I get you to bed."

"I'll call him."

"Shut up." He was pulling her across the room and down the hall. "I said I'd do it. You've done your part."

Yes, she'd done her part. John Devon had been found and that meant—

"Stop thinking," Joe said roughly as he pushed her down on the bed. "I knew it would start eating at you the minute you finished. But, dammit, you've got to rest now." He disappeared into the bathroom and came back with a damp washcloth. He sat down beside her and began wiping the clay from her hands.

"I should take a shower."

"When you wake up." He tossed the washcloth on the nightstand, made her lie down, and covered her with a quilt.

"I was afraid it was going to be him," she whispered. "Half of me wanted it to be John Devon, but I was afraid too."

"I know." He turned out the bathroom light, sat down beside her, and took both her hands in his. "But you wouldn't give up, would you?"

"I couldn't. You know I couldn't."

The slight tightening of his grasp was his only answer.

"Since it was John Devon, that means that monster might have been telling the truth. Fraser might not have killed Bonnie."

"He could still have been the one who killed her. Because Dom killed one of the children Fraser confessed to murdering doesn't mean he killed all of them."

"But the chances are better now that Dom killed her."

"I don't know, Eve," he said wearily. "I just don't know."

"And he might still have her. That little girl could be my Bonnie. It wasn't enough that he killed her; he's keeping her like some kind of trophy."

"He's keeping her as bait."

"I hate the idea of that monster with her. I hate it."

"Shh. Don't think about it."

"And how am I supposed to stop?"

"Hell, how do I know? Just do it." He paused. "This is what he wants from you. Control. Wouldn't he love the idea of you lying here suffering because of something he'd done? Go to sleep and cheat the son of a bitch."

He was right, she was doing exactly what Dom wanted her to do. "I'm sorry. I didn't mean to fall apart. I must be tired."

"Now, I wonder why?"

"I'm confused. It's difficult not to—I wanted to bring her home but not like—"

"Face it after you've slept for a while."

"You have to call Spiro."

"It will wait. I'll stay here until you go to sleep."

"You haven't slept either."

"How do you know? I doubt you were aware I was on the planet while you were working on that boy."

"That's not true."

"Isn't it?"

"I always know you're there. It's like—" It was hard to explain. "It's like having an old oak tree in your garden. Even if you don't pay attention to it, you never really forget it's there."

"I believe I've been insulted. A tree? Are you trying to call me a knothead?"

No, if he was like a tree, it was because he gave shelter and strength and endurance. "Smart man. I should have known I couldn't fool you."

"And I'm not *that* old."

"Old enough." She was smiling, she realized. A moment before she had been in pain, but she felt better now. Joe always made it better. "I'm okay. You don't have to stay with me."

"I'll stick around. You've got to be hysterical if you're

calling me an oak tree. The only way you'll get rid of me is by going to sleep."

She was already getting drowsy. It was safe to let everything go for now. Joe was there, holding back the darkness. "This reminds me of when we were on Cumberland Island after Fraser was executed. Remember? You held my hands like this and made me talk and talk. . . ."

"Now I'm trying to shut you up. Go to sleep."

She was silent a moment. "He's beginning to scare me, Joe."

"There's nothing to be scared about. I won't let anything happen to you."

"I didn't think I'd be afraid. I was only angry at first, but he's smart, and killing me isn't his main priority. He has to make me feel . . . he has to hurt me. He needs it."

"Yes."

A sudden thought exploded through her. "Mom."

"She's under guard. I made sure he can't touch her."

Relief surged through her. "You did?"

"It was the logical move. Not bad for a knothead."

"Not too bad." If Mom was safe, a prime weapon was taken away from Dom. He couldn't hurt Eve through someone she loved.

The hell he couldn't. He still had Bonnie.

But Bonnie was dead. Eve might be sick with horror at the thought of him having Bonnie, but he could no longer hurt her daughter. Eve was the only one who could be hurt, and she would hide that hurt from him.

"It's okay. I told you, your mom's safe," Joe said. "There's no reason to be uneasy."

She was uneasy. Trust Joe to sense it. Not about her mother. If Joe said she was safe, she was safe. She was just . . .

Forget about it. Go to sleep and when she woke they would find a way to catch the bastard and bring Bonnie home. He wasn't invincible. He had made a mistake when he contacted Eve. There wasn't any way he could really hurt her.

She had no reason to be uneasy.

HER NAME WAS Jane MacGuire and she was ten years old.

Dom had seen her a few days before when he was cruising the public housing developments on the south side. He had first been attracted by her red hair and then by her air of independence and defiance. She walked down the street as if daring the world to get in her way. No docile little bird here.

Too defiant to appeal to Eve Duncan? Her own daughter had been completely different. But then, Bonnie Duncan had not been brought up in four foster homes like Jane MacGuire. She'd had no need to learn to be streetwise.

He cruised slowly behind the kid. She was going somewhere. She had a purpose.

She suddenly darted into an alley. Should he go after her and risk having her see him? The danger wasn't that great. As usual when he was on the hunt, he'd taken the precaution of a disguise.

He parked the car and got out. She was too good a prospect. He had to make sure.

SON OF A bitch. The creep was following her again.

Well, let him, Jane thought crossly. He was just another dirty old man like the ones who hung out at the school yard and drove away fast if Jane screamed for the teacher. She knew this alley and could run faster than him if she needed to get away. She had noticed him following her yesterday and kept to the public streets.

She couldn't do that today.

"I'm here, Jane."

She saw Mike crouched inside a big cardboard box

against the brick wall. He looked cold. He'd probably slept in the box last night. He usually did when his father came home. Bad luck the bastard had decided to wander back in January, when it was so cold.

She reached into a jacket pocket and handed him the sandwich she'd stolen from Fay's refrigerator that morning. "Breakfast. It's pretty stale. I couldn't get anything else."

She watched him gobble down the food, then shot a glance behind her.

The creep had ducked into the shadows of a garbage dump. Good place for him.

"Come on. Time to go to school," she told Mike.

"I ain't going."

"Sure you are. You want to grow up stupid like your father?"

"I ain't going."

She played her trump card. "It's warm there."

Mike thought about it and then got to his feet. "Maybe I'll go just today."

She'd thought he would. The cold and an empty belly were enemies. She'd spent a lot of nights in alleys herself when she'd been staying with the Carbonis. That was the foster home before Fay's and it was there she'd learned that if she caused enough trouble, not even the welfare money would make foster parents keep her. Welfare was always ready to give them another kid if one didn't work out.

Fay was much better. She was always tired and often crabby, but sometimes Jane thought she might grow to like her . . . if she stayed long enough.

She glanced back at the creep. Still hiding behind the dump. "I think maybe you should find another place to sleep tonight. There's a place near the Union Mission. I'll show you."

"Okay. You goin' to school now?" Mike asked. "Maybe I could walk along with you."

He was lonely. He was only six and hadn't learned how to ignore the emptiness yet. "Sure. Why not?"

She smiled at him.

DOM HADN'T BEEN sure until he'd seen her smile.

The smile was warm and sweet. All the more appealing because of the kid's usual air of wariness and toughness. Without that streak of softness he wouldn't have been sure. But now he was convinced.

Little Jane MacGuire was perfect.

"YOU'RE SURE HE'S the Devon boy?" Spiro asked when Joe opened the door later that afternoon.

"It's close enough." Joe gestured to the pedestal. "The picture's on the worktable. See for yourself."

"I'll do that." He crossed the room. "Where's Ms. Duncan?"

"Still sleeping."

"Wake her up. I need to talk to her."

"Screw you. She's exhausted. Talk to me."

"I have to—" He gave a low whistle as he compared the reconstruction with the photo. "Damn, she's good."

"Yes."

He tossed the photo back on the worktable. "I almost wish it wasn't him. You realize what this means?"

"Yes, and so does Eve."

"I'm going to have to use her, Quinn."

"No one uses Eve."

"Unless she wants to be used," Eve said from the doorway. She came toward them. She'd obviously just gotten out of bed; her hair was tousled, her clothing rumpled. "And the fact that he's John Devon doesn't make that much difference to you, Spiro. You would have tried to use me anyway."

Spiro glanced back at the skull. "He could be telling the truth about Fraser taking credit for his kills."

"Some of his kills," Joe corrected Spiro. "All we have are the two boys."

"Aren't they enough?" Spiro turned to Eve. "Are you going to help me?"

"No, I'm going to help me. You and Joe keep my mom safe and I'll let you use me as bait."

"The hell you will," Joe said.

She ignored him and asked Spiro, "He's been watching me, hasn't he?"

"Quinn told you?"

"No, but Dom knew about our trip to Talladega." She glanced at Joe. "What else?"

"Someone's been keeping an eye on the cottage. I had Spiro send a forensic team yesterday to go through the bushes where he'd been standing, watching."

"Thanks for telling me."

"I'm telling you now. You were a little busy before." He smiled. "I don't think he'll be back with Charlie and those other guards patrolling outside and me inside."

"Don't be too sure. He's bored or he wouldn't have taken so many chances."

His smile faded. "You think he's that unbalanced?"

"I believe he's desperate for some reason. But I don't think he'll try to kill me yet. Not until he gets what he wants."

"And when he does, we'll be here," Spiro said.

"Will you?" she said wearily. "Why would he attack if he knows there's a chance he'll be caught? If he's as smart as you believe, he'd find a way to get to me and elude you. Did your team find any evidence in the stuff they collected yesterday?"

"We're still sifting through—" Spiro shook his head. "We don't think so."

She shrugged. "I rest my case."

"And what do you suggest?"

"That we go after him, not wait for him to come after me."

"It's much safer for you to—"

A knock on the door.

Charlie smiled apologetically. "Sorry to bother you, but I wondered if my call had come through. It's taken a lot longer than I thought it would."

"No call," Joe said.

"Why not ask me?" Spiro said dryly. "Did it occur to you that as your superior, I'm the one they would contact?"

Charlie eyed him warily. "Did they?"

"Last night. They're faxing the full report to me at Talladega. They were surprised I knew nothing about your request that they call you directly."

Charlie grimaced. "Sorry. I guess I was being a hot dog."

"Well, eagerness is better than apathy."

"Did they find any cases that matched?" Joe asked.

"Two possibles. Two skeletons were found three months ago in San Luz, a suburb of Phoenix. No teeth. Wax sediment in the right hands."

"Children?" Eve asked.

Spiro shook his head. "Adults. One man. One woman."

"Arizona," Joe repeated. "That's a long way."

"Who says Dom is a local boy?" Spiro said.

"He was here ten years ago," Eve said. "He's here now."

"It's a mobile society, and organized serial killers are known to be particularly mobile." Spiro turned toward the door. "At any rate, I'll send a man to Phoenix to see if he can find out anything more from the local PD. We'll probably have to organize an interstate task force now."

"Could I go?" Charlie asked.

"No, you may not," Spiro said. "You stay here and guard Ms. Duncan. I don't want you out of sight of the cabin, and you make sure those other perimeter guards are on their toes."

"Eve," she said dryly. "Formality is pretty silly under the circumstances."

"Eve." Spiro smiled. "I suppose you're right. We all may become more intimate than we'd like before this is over. Good-bye. I'll let you know if I find out anything else." He paused at the door. "Stay inside, Eve. I evidently have more faith in my guys and your friend Quinn than you do."

As soon as the door closed behind Spiro, Charlie grinned. "I'd better get outside. I could see Spiro wasn't pleased with me for going over his head. It will take a little groveling and strict obedience for me to redeem myself."

She smiled back, then returned to her bedroom to shower.

Phoenix, Arizona. Two bodies.

Eleven at Talladega. Two in Phoenix. How many more had Dom killed? How could a man murder that many people and remain human?

Was he human? How much evil could he commit without his soul becoming twisted and—

She was cold and starting to shake. Stop it. It didn't matter what manner of monster Dom had become. All that was important was that they catch him and keep him from murdering again.

The hot water poured out of the showerhead onto her body.

But it didn't banish the chill.

"FOR HEAVEN'S SAKE, stop prowling, Joe," Eve said. "It's after midnight. Why don't you go to bed?"

"You go to bed. I'm a little tense, okay?"

"You don't have to bite my head off."

"Yes, I do. It's one of the few things that I'm allowed. There's damn few of them that I can—" He stopped.

"Sorry. Maybe I'm getting cabin fever waiting for something to happen."

So was she, and she didn't feel like being sweet and generous about Joe's nerves. "If you won't go to bed, make yourself useful and go out and give Charlie a cup of coffee."

"Maybe I will."

She drew a deep breath as the front door shut behind him a few minutes later. She had never seen Joe this explosive. Ever since that afternoon he'd been—

Her phone rang.

"Did I wake you?" Dom asked.

Her heart was pounding. "No, I wasn't asleep."

"Oh, yes, you must have slept after you finished working on little Johnny Devon. It was him, wasn't it?"

"I told you I wouldn't tell you anything."

"Defiant. That means I guessed right. I knew you'd do a fine job. You take great pride in your work."

"Why are you calling me?"

"It's important that I stay in touch with you, that we get to know each other better. I'm sure that's what Agent Spiro told you. Draw the bastard out. Find out everything you can for the FBI profile. Isn't that right?"

"Something like that."

"I'll cooperate. But you have to give me something too. I want a profile on you, Eve."

"You already seem to know a great deal about me."

"Not enough. For instance, do you believe in reincarnation?"

"What?"

"Reincarnation. Millions of people do, you know. Such a comforting belief." He chuckled. "As long as you don't come back as a cockroach."

"What are you talking about?"

"But I don't think God would let your Bonnie come back as a cockroach, do you?"

"Shut up."

"That hurt, didn't it? I could almost feel it myself. Pretty little Bonnie . . ."

It had hurt. The bizarre idea had stabbed her. Stupid to let him hurt her. Even stupider to let him know he'd hurt her. "It didn't bother me. Why should it? I don't believe in reincarnation."

"You should consider it. As I said, it could be very comforting. I've been thinking a lot about it lately. Are you familiar with the Bible?"

"Some."

"It's not my favorite tome, but there are some unique ideas in it. I found one particularly amusing. Genesis 2:22."

"I don't know what that is."

"I'll tell you. But first go to the front door and get my present."

"Present?"

"It's on the left edge of the porch. I couldn't just come up to the front door and leave it with that FBI agent watching you so closely."

She moistened her lips. "What kind of present?"

"Go get it, Eve. I'll hang on."

"I'd be dumb to go outside just because you tell me to. You could be waiting for me."

"You know better. You know I'm not going to hurt you yet." He paused. "But I won't promise not to hurt Quinn if you call him. This is just between us. Go get the present."

She moved toward the door.

"Are you doing it?"

"Yes."

"Good. Now, let's see. They say that the souls of victims of violence are troubled and return to earth as soon as possible. So Bonnie would have been reincarnated immediately."

"Bull."

"I killed her ten years ago, didn't I? That means we're

looking for a ten-year-old child. Either a boy or a girl."
He chuckled. "Since we've ruled out cockroaches. Are
you at the front door yet?"

"Yes."

"Check the window and you'll probably see your stalwart guard sitting in his car by the lake. That's where he
was when I left your package a few hours ago."

She glanced out the window. Charlie wasn't in the
car, he was standing by the front fender, talking to Joe.

"Are you on the porch yet?"

"No."

"Are you afraid of me, Eve? Don't you want to know
what's in the package?"

"I'm not afraid of you." She opened the door. She was
wearing only an old T-shirt, and the cold wind struck
her bare legs. "I'm on the porch. Where's the damn
package?"

"You'll see it."

She did see it, a small brown cardboard box on the
very left edge of the porch.

"Quinn would say you're foolish to go near it. It might
be a bomb or maybe I put some kind of gas or poison in
the box. But you know I don't want you injured or
dead."

She did know it. She moved toward the box.

"Or maybe I do. I could be waiting in the shadow of
the porch right now. Do you see any suspicious shadows, Eve?"

"No, where are you?"

"But it's so dark on the porch you can't see shadows,
can you?"

She stopped in front of the box.

"Eve?" Joe had turned away from Charlie and had
seen her.

"Or I might be in my car, miles away. Which do you
think is true?"

She knelt beside the box.

"Eve!"

She opened the box.

Something hard and white gleamed inside.

Dom's voice was soft in her ear. " 'And the rib, which the Lord God had taken from the man, made he a woman, and brought her unto the man.' Genesis 2:22."

"What the hell are you doing?" Joe was beside her, trying to draw her away from the box.

She shoved him. "Leave me alone."

"God and I have a lot in common. If you believe in reincarnation, then by killing your Bonnie I, like God, created a brand-new human being. Though I didn't actually create her from Bonnie's rib, I thought you'd appreciate the symbolism." He paused. "By the way, her name is Jane." He hung up.

The phone dropped from her hand. She stared down into the box.

"Don't touch it," Joe said.

"I'll call Spiro and get a team down here to check it out." Charlie ran down the steps toward his car.

"Dom?" Joe asked.

She nodded.

"Did he tell you what this is?"

She nodded again.

So small . . .

She reached down and touched it with one finger. Smooth . . .

Tears began to run down her cheeks.

"Eve."

"It's Bonnie. It's Bonnie's rib."

"*Shit.*" Joe picked her up and carried her inside. "Son of a bitch. Bastard."

"Bonnie."

"Shh." He sat down on the couch and rocked her. "Dammit, why didn't you call me?"

"Bonnie's rib."

"It could be an animal bone. He could have lied to you."

She shook her head. "Bonnie."

"Listen to me. He wanted to hurt you."

And he had succeeded. God, how he had succeeded. Pain was searing through her. She had told herself only last night that he had no real weapon against her, that she could control—Dammit, she couldn't stop crying.

And she couldn't stop thinking of that little fragment of Bonnie in that box.

"Go bring it in."

"What?"

"It's . . . cold out there."

"Eve," Joe said gently. "It's evidence. We can't move—"

"Do you think he'd leave any evidence? Go get it."

"Even if it's Bonnie, she can't feel—"

"I know I'm not being reasonable. I just don't want her out in the cold if I can help it. It . . . hurts me. Bring her in."

Joe muttered a curse and got to his feet. A moment later he came back with the box. "You're not looking at it again." He crossed the room and slid the box into a drawer of her worktable. "And it's going to the lab for analysis."

"Okay."

"And stop crying, dammit."

She nodded.

"Oh, shit." He dropped down beside her and gathered her in his arms. "You're killing me. Please. Stop crying."

"I'm sorry. I'm trying. It was the shock. I didn't expect—" She swallowed. "He got the response he wanted from me, didn't he?"

"What did he say?"

She shook her head. "Not now. Give me a minute."

His arms tightened around her. "Take all the time you

need. I'll give you ten years if you need them. Why not? Hell, I've already given you one decade."

What was he talking about? She didn't have a decade. She might not have any time at all. She buried her head in his shoulder, trying to get past the horror of the box and face an even greater horror. "He said that—" She couldn't go on. Not yet.

*Her name is Jane.*

"IT'S ALL BULLSHIT," Joe said flatly. "Reincarnation?"

"Did he sound as if he believed in it?" Spiro asked Eve.

"Not really."

"Then he could have been manipulating you."

"He'd like me to believe it." She smiled bitterly. "That could make it very entertaining for him."

"He knows you're too intelligent to fall for that crap," Joe said.

"He also knows I care about children." Her hands clenched on her lap. "And bones aren't enough for him. What if he's chosen his next victim? What if he can make me a part of the kill, make me the cause of it?"

"Clever," Spiro murmured.

"It's nice to be so detached," Eve said unevenly. "I'm not finding much to admire in the bastard."

"I'm not admiring him, merely assessing his capabilities. And this is all supposition on your part."

"He went to a great deal of trouble to bring me that box."

"And it gave you a great deal of pain. He may regard that as enough return."

She shook her head. "It's just the opening gambit. He hit me with Bonnie. He hit me with the threat to another little girl. And he tried to tie the two together in my mind."

"And did he succeed?" Spiro asked.

"Of course not."

Spiro's gaze narrowed on her face. "Not even a little?"

She looked down. "I wouldn't let him do that to me."

"I hope not."

"We have to find her. We have to find that little girl."

"She may not even exist," Joe said.

"She exists."

"If she did exist, he may already have killed her."

She shook her head. She wouldn't believe that. "I don't think so."

Spiro said, "I'll rush the analysis of the contents of that box and get back to you." He turned to Joe. "I want to know how Dom got that close to the house."

"Don't you think I've asked myself the same question a million times? It shouldn't have happened. But it did. Eve needs more guards."

"This lake curves around like a snake. There's nothing to stop anyone from taking a canoe into one of the inlets and making his way to the cabin. I'd have to set up a two-mile chain of agents to monitor all that lakefront."

"At least get a truckload of equipment out here and trace his calls to Eve."

"I don't know how much good it will do," Spiro said. "But I agree that—"

"No," Eve said.

They both looked at her.

"If he finds out we're trying to trace the calls, he may not call again. I have to talk to him."

Joe muttered a curse.

"You know I have to do it, Joe."

"Oh, yes, he's got you, dammit."

"And what if he doesn't call you?" Spiro asked.

"He'll call again. Soon." She lifted her head. "He wants me to know who the girl is."

"You know who she is. He already told you her name and her age."

"That was just a tease. Enough to make me worry but not enough for me to find her. We *have* to find her."

"Then it's your responsibility to convince Dom to tell you more," Spiro said.

Her responsibility. That was what Dom wanted, for her to be responsible for the life of that child. For her to try to save a little girl she didn't even know.

*Her name is Jane.*

And she was only ten years old. Too young to know how to fight the monster stalking her.

Just a little girl. She'd be helpless. . . .

JANE'S FIST LANDED squarely on Chang's nose and blood spurted. "Give it back."

Chang screamed and clutched his nose. "Fay, Janie hit me. I didn't do nothing and Janie hit me."

"Jane, stop it," Fay called from the kitchen. "And, Chang, quit tattling."

"Give it back," Jane said through gritted teeth.

"Thief. Crook." Chang backed away. "I'm going to tell Fay and she'll have you put in jail."

"Give—it—back." She punched him in the stomach and then grabbed the apple that dropped from his hand. She was halfway across the room when Fay said, "Stop right there, Jane."

Sighing, she stopped in her tracks. Bad luck. A few seconds more and she would have been out the front door.

"She stole an apple from the fridge. She's been stealing stuff for the last two days." Chang smiled maliciously. "You gonna have her arrested, Fay?"

"What kind of stuff?" Fay asked.

"Food. I saw her put a sandwich in her schoolbag yesterday."

"Is that true, Jane?"

Jane didn't answer.

"And she punched me."

"Be quiet, Chang. For heaven's sake, you're two inches taller than she is."

"You said I shouldn't fight," he said, sulking.

"I also said you shouldn't tattle, but you do it." Fay dug into her pocket and handed him a tissue. "Go on. You'll be late for school."

Chang wiped his nose. "Jane was late yesterday."

"Jane's never late for school."

"She was late yest—" He met Jane's warning gaze and backed toward the door. "Ask her." He bolted out of the house.

Fay crossed her arms over her chest. "So I'm asking you."

"I was late."

"Why?"

"I had something to do."

"What?"

Jane was silent.

"Have you been stealing food?"

"Not much."

"You know I have a tough time stretching the food budget for the three of you."

"I won't eat tomorrow."

"You don't eat enough now. It's Chang and Raoul who are always hungry. Which brings me to ask why you stole food, when half the time I can't get you to eat my dinners."

Jane didn't answer.

"When I was in the fourth grade there was a bully who made me give him my lunch every day. I'd understand if you—"

"No one made me do it."

Fay smiled faintly. "And if they tried, you'd punch them in the nose."

Jane nodded.

"If you have a problem, it might help if you talk to me."

"I don't have a problem."

"And you wouldn't tell me if you did. Why do I even try?" Fay wearily brushed a strand of hair back from her forehead. "Go on. You'll be late."

Jane hesitated. It would be harder to get food now. Could she trust Fay? "May I keep the apple?"

"If you tell me why."

"Someone needs it."

"Who?"

"He can't go home right now. His father's there."

"Who?"

"Could I bring him here?"

"A child? Jane, you know I can't accept any more children. But if he's having trouble at home, we can call Family Services and see if they can intercede with his parents."

She should have known Fay wouldn't understand. "They won't help. They'll go see them and then they'll leave and make a report. It would make it worse for him."

"Who is this? Tell me."

Jane started for the door.

"Jane, I want to help you. Trust me. You're going to get into trouble."

"I'll be okay. I won't be late for school again."

"That's not what I mean." Fay was looking helplessly at her. "I want to be your friend. Why can't I get through to you? Why do you keep everything bottled up inside?"

"Could I have the apple?"

"I shouldn't let you—Oh, go ahead, take it. But I don't want you punching Chang again."

"Okay." Jane opened the door and ran down the steps. That she had made Fay unhappy made her feel bad. For a moment she had thought Fay would understand and help her, but she should have known better.

You couldn't count on anyone to help you. You had to do it yourself.

At least Fay had not made her give up the apple the way some grown-ups would have. But there would be no more food for Mike from Fay's refrigerator. She would have to find it somewhere else.

Her forehead creased in a frown as she began to consider how she would do it.

# CHAPTER
# SIX

Dom made Eve wait over forty-eight hours before he called again.

"Did you like my gift?" he asked.

"I hated it. You knew I would."

"But how could you hate your own flesh and blood? Oops, slip of the tongue. No flesh, no blood, just bone."

"Who is she?"

"I told you, it's your Bonnie."

"No, you know who I mean. Who is this Jane?"

"Well, she may be your Bonnie too. Have you thought about the possibility of—"

"What's her last name?"

"She's not as pretty but she has the same red hair. Unfortunately, she's had a rougher time this go-around than when she was your Bonnie. Four foster homes." He clucked regretfully. "So sad."

"Where is she?"

"You'd recognize the place."

She felt a sudden chill. A grave? "Is she alive?"

"Of course."

"Do you have her?"

"No, so far I've only been observing her. I find her very interesting. You will too, Eve."

"Tell me her last name. Dammit, I know you want me to know."

"But you have to earn it. It's part of the game. Don't try to bring the police into it or I'll be very unhappy. I'm sure your maternal instincts will lead you to little Jane. Find her, Eve. Before I become impatient." He hung up.

She punched the end button.

"No luck?" Joe asked.

She stood up. "We're going to Atlanta."

"What the hell?"

"He said I'd recognize the place where she can be found. I know Atlanta better than any other place. Do you have contacts with child welfare?"

He shook his head.

"Do you know anyone else who can help us? He said she'd been in four foster homes. There have to be records."

"We can try Mark Grunard. I don't know anyone who's better at digging out information, and he has contacts everywhere."

"Will you call him?"

"Look, the Atlanta PD will help now. They have no choice, not after the Devon ID."

"He doesn't want me to bring in the police. He wants me to find her. It's like some kind of game to him."

"Will you stay here and let me go and look for her?"

"I told you, that's not what he wants. He wants me to search for her. It has to be me."

"Then don't give the bastard what he wants."

"And have him send me her head in a box?" she asked unevenly. "I can't risk that. I have to find her and find her quick."

"Okay, but I'm going with you." He reached for the phone. "Go pack a toothbrush and a change of clothes. I'll call Mark and tell him what we need so he can get started on it."

"Set up a meeting with him. Dom's got to see me making the effort to find her. He'll be watching me."

"That's no problem. I told you I'd promised Mark you'd see him as soon as possible. I'll have him meet us at my apartment in the city."

JOE'S APARTMENT WAS in a luxury high-rise across the street from Piedmont Park. He drove down into the secured gated parking garage and they took the elevator to the seventh floor.

"It's about time, Joe. I've been waiting almost an hour." Mark Grunard grinned at them. "Don't you realize I'm an important man in this town?" He extended his hand to Eve. "I'm glad to see you again, Ms. Duncan. Though I'm sorry it's in these circumstances."

"So am I." She shook his hand. He appeared almost the same as she remembered him—tall, fit, with a charming smile. Perhaps in his early fifties, he showed the years with a few more laugh lines around his blue eyes. "But I'm glad you've agreed to help us."

"I'd be an idiot otherwise. This is big stuff. It's not often I get a chance at an exclusive that could net me an Emmy."

"What about your fellow reporters?" Joe asked. "Are we going to be safe here?"

"I think so. I laid a false trail to Daytona Beach in the newscast last night. Just don't be stupid." He frowned. "I contacted Barbara Eisley about our problem. She's head of Child and Family Services. It's not going to be easy. She says all files are private."

Red tape, Eve thought with frustration. A child could be murdered while they dithered about blasted rules. "Can't you persuade her?"

"Barbara Eisley's a tough nut. She'd make a great drill sergeant. Can you get a court order?"

Joe shook his head. "We can't go through the system. Eve's afraid Dom will move on the little girl if we do."

"Barbara Eisley has *got* to help," Eve said.

"I said it's not going to be easy, I didn't say impossible," Grunard said. "We just have to use a little persuasion."

"Could I see Ms. Eisley?"

Grunard nodded. "I thought you'd feel like that. We're taking her to dinner tonight." He held up his hand as Joe opened his mouth to protest. "I know, Eve can't go where she'll be recognized. I have a friend who owns an Italian restaurant on the Chattahoochee just outside the city. He'll give us good pasta and complete privacy. Okay?"

"Okay." Joe unlocked his apartment door. "Pick us up across the street, inside the park, at six."

"I'll be there."

Eve watched Grunard walk toward the elevators before she followed Joe into the apartment. "He appears very"—she searched for the word—"solid."

"That's why he's so popular." He locked the door and Eve looked around the apartment.

"Good God, you could have done better than this, Joe. It looks like a hotel room."

He shrugged. "I told you I didn't do much more than sleep here." He headed for the kitchen. "I'll make coffee and sandwiches. I doubt if we're going to eat much at that dinner with Barbara Eisley."

She followed him into the kitchen. She doubted she could eat much now either, but she'd have to. She needed all her strength. "I think I may have met Eisley before."

"When?"

"Years ago. When I was a kid. There was one caseworker . . ." She shook her head. "Maybe not."

"You don't remember?"

"I've blocked a lot of that time out of my memory." She made a face. "It wasn't a very pleasant period. Mom and I were moving from place to place and every month the welfare department was threatening to take me away from Mom and put me in a foster home if she didn't get off the crack." She opened the refrigerator door. "Everything in here is spoiled, Joe."

"Then I'll make toast."

"If the bread's not moldy."

"Don't be pessimistic." He opened the bread box. "It's just a little stale." He popped bread into the toaster on the counter. "Considering what you went through as a kid, you might have been better off in a foster home."

"Maybe. But I didn't want to go. Back then there were times I hated her, but she was my mother. To a child, family always seems better than strangers." She got the butter from the refrigerator. "That's why it's so difficult to take abused children from their parents. They want to believe everything's going to be all right."

"And sometimes it's not."

"Evidently, it wasn't for this Jane. Not if she's been in four foster homes." She went to the window and looked down into the street. "You don't realize how rough it is out there for kids, Joe."

"I realize. I'm a cop. I've seen it."

"But you haven't been there." She smiled at him over her shoulder. "Rich boy."

"Don't be snooty. I couldn't help it. I tried to get my parents to abandon me, but they wouldn't do it. They sent me to Harvard instead." He plugged in the coffeemaker. "It could have been worse; they were thinking about sending me to Oxford."

"Terrible fate." She looked back out the window. "You never talk about your parents. They died when you were in college, didn't they?"

He nodded. "Boating accident off Newport."

"Why don't you talk about them?"

"Nothing to talk about."

She turned to him. "Dammit, Joe, you didn't spring fully grown in Atlanta. I've tried dozens of times to get

you to tell me about your folks and the way you grew
up. Why do you keep dodging?"

"It's not important."

"It's as important as the way I grew up."

He smiled. "Not to me."

"You're only fifty percent of this friendship. You know
everything about me. Stop shutting me out."

"I don't believe in living in the past."

"How the hell can I really know you if you won't talk
to me?"

"Don't be crazy. You know me." He chuckled. "For
God's sake, we've been together more than ten years."

He was dodging again. "Joe."

He shrugged. "You want to know about my parents? I
didn't know them very well. They stopped being interested in me about the time I stopped being a cute little
tyke." He got down cups from the cabinet. "Can't blame
them. I was never an easy kid. Too demanding."

"I can't imagine you demanding anything. You're too
self-reliant."

"Imagine it. Accept it." He poured coffee into the
cups. "I'm still demanding as hell. I've just learned ways
of camouflaging it. Sit down and eat your toast."

"You never demand anything of me."

"I demand your friendship. I demand your company.
Most of all, I demand that you stay alive."

"Those are the most unselfish demands I've ever
heard."

"Don't you believe it. I'm probably the most selfish
man you've ever met."

She smiled as she shook her head. "No way."

"I'm glad I've got you fooled. But someday you'll find
out how I've deceived you all these years. You slum
brats just can't trust us rich kids."

"You've switched the conversation around to me
again. Why do you keep doing that?"

"I'm bored with me." He yawned. "In case you haven't noticed, I'm a very dull fellow."

"The hell you are."

"Well, I have to agree that I'm witty and supremely intelligent, but my background's pretty mundane." He sat down opposite Eve. "Now, what about Barbara Eisley? What do you remember?"

Stubborn bastard, he'd told her as much as he was going to. She gave up as she had so many times before. "I told you, I'm not sure I knew her. There were so many caseworkers and, hey, they never stayed long in the job. Can't blame them. Techwood wasn't the safest neighborhood."

"Think."

"Bully." Okay, stop avoiding thinking about that hell-hole where she had grown up. She let the memory flow back to her. Dirt. Hunger. Rats. The smell of fear and sex and drugs. "She might have been one of the caseworkers. I remember one woman in her late thirties. I thought she was old. She came to one of the houses on Market Street. I think I was nine or ten. . . ."

"Sympathetic?"

"I think so. Maybe. I was too defensive to judge. I was angry at Mom and the whole world."

"Then you may have trouble bonding with her tonight."

"I don't have to bond with her. I just have to convince her to open those files and help us find that child. There's no *time*."

"Easy." His hand covered hers on the table. "One way or the other, we'll get the records tonight."

She tried to smile. "I suppose if she won't help, you'll pull a Watergate at the welfare office?"

"Possibly."

He meant it. Her smile faded. "No, Joe. I don't want you to get into trouble."

"Hey, if you're good, you don't get caught. You don't get caught, you're not in trouble."

"Simplistic."

"The whole world should be so simple. I'd say the life of a kid is worth a little risk. If you're persuasive enough, it may not be necessary for me to turn burglar. Who knows, Barbara Eisley may not be as tough as Mark claims. She could be a pussycat."

"HELL, NO," Barbara Eisley said. "I don't open those records for anyone. I'm up for my pension next year and I'm not taking any chances."

Barbara Eisley was definitely no pussycat, Eve thought in discouragement. From the moment Grunard had introduced them, she'd avoided talking about the files. When Joe finally pinned her down after dessert, she responded with the bluntness of a hammer blow.

"Now, Barbara." Grunard smiled at her. "You know that no one is going to jerk your pension for a little infringement involving a child's life. Besides, you've been with the department too long."

"Bull. I'm not diplomatic enough for the mayor or city council. They're just waiting for a reason to bounce me out of my job. The only reason I've lasted this long is that I know where a couple of political bodies are buried." She stared accusingly at Mark. "And you quoted me on that child abuse case two years ago. It made my department look negligent."

"But it caused extensive reform. That's what you wanted."

"And put my ass in hot water. I should have kept my mouth shut. I don't take risks like that anymore. I do everything by the book. I help you do this today, and tomorrow they find a way to use it against me. I'm not going to end up without a pension. I've visited too many old people in public housing trying to survive. That's not going to be me."

"Then why did you accept Mark's invitation?" Joe asked.

"Free dinner." She shrugged. "And I was curious." She turned to Eve. "I've read about you, but the media is sometimes full of hot air. I wanted to see for myself how you'd turned out. Do you remember me?"

"I think so. But you've changed."

"So have you." She studied Eve's face. "You were a tough little kid. I remember I tried to talk to you once and you just stared at me. I thought you'd be hooking or dealing by the time you were fourteen. I would have liked to have made another try with you, but I had too many cases." She added wearily, "There are always too many cases. Too many kids. And most of the time we can't help them. We take them away and the court gives them right back to their parents."

"But you try."

"Because I'm too stupid to give up hope. You'd think after all these years I'd learn, wouldn't you? You turned out all right, but it was nothing I did."

"You must make a difference sometimes."

"I guess so."

"You could make a difference this time. You could save a little girl."

"Get a court order. If it's that important, there should be no problem."

"We can't do that. I've told you I can't go through channels."

Barbara Eisley was silent.

"Okay, you won't give us the records, but maybe you remember something about this child," Joe said.

An undefinable expression crossed her face. "I don't handle casework any longer. I have too much paperwork."

Eve leaned forward. "But you do remember something."

Eisley was silent a moment. "I had to authorize taking

a little girl out of a foster home two years ago. The couple who was caring for her claimed she was disruptive and disobedient. I had to bring the child in and interview her. She wouldn't talk to me, but she was covered with bruises. I checked her medical record and she'd been taken to Grady Hospital twice with broken bones during the last year. I gave permission for her to be removed from the home. I also removed the foster parents from our rolls." She smiled. "I remember thinking she must have been a gutsy little kid. She kept on giving those bastards hell."

"What's her name?"

She ignored Eve's question. "She was a smart kid. High IQ, did well in school. She probably figured they'd give her up as a meal ticket if she caused enough trouble."

"You placed her with another family?"

"We had no choice. Most of our foster parents aren't abusive. Sometimes we make mistakes. We can only do our best."

"Tell me her name."

Eisley shook her head. "Not without a court order. What if I was wrong?"

"What if you were right? She could die, dammit."

"I've spent my entire life trying to help kids. Now I've got to think of myself."

"Please."

She shook her head again. "I've worked too hard. I still work hard." She paused. "You'd think in my position I wouldn't have to take work home." She nodded at her briefcase beside her chair. "But I had some old files on a computer disk to review, so here I go again."

Hope flared inside Eve. "That's too bad."

"It goes with the territory." She stood up. "It's been an interesting evening. Sorry I can't help you." She smiled. "I believe I have to go to the rest room. I suppose you'll be gone when I come back. I hope you find the little girl." Her gaze narrowed on Eve. "I just remembered, the kid reminded me a little of you. She stared at me with those big eyes and I thought she'd go on the attack any minute. Same tough little—Something wrong?"

Eve shook her head.

Barbara Eisley turned to Mark. "Thanks for dinner. But I still haven't forgiven you for quoting me in that story." She turned and made her way through the tables toward the rest room.

"Thank God." Eve reached for the briefcase. It was unlocked and there was only one disk in the leather pocket on the side. Bless Barbara Eisley. She tucked it in her purse. "She wants us to take it."

"You mean steal it," Joe murmured as he threw some bills down on the table.

"Which puts her in the clear." Eve turned to Mark. "Do you have a laptop with you?"

"In the trunk of my car. I always keep it there. We can check the disk as soon as we reach the parking lot."

"Good. You'll have to drop into Barbara Eisley's office tomorrow and leave the disk on her desk. I don't want to get her into trouble." She stood up. "Let's go. We need to be out of here before she comes back. She might change her mind."

"Not likely," Joe said. "It's pretty clear you impressed her when you were a kid."

"Or Jane did." She started for the door. "Or maybe she's just a woman trying to do the right thing in a wrong world."

THERE WERE TWENTY-SEVEN records on the disk. It took Mark twenty minutes to scan the first sixteen.

"Jane MacGuire," Mark read from the computer screen. "The age is right. Four foster homes. Physical description checks out. Red hair, hazel eyes."

"Can you print it out?"

Mark plugged a small Kodak printer into the laptop. "She's living right now with a Fay Sugarton who's also foster parent to two other children. Chang Ito, twelve, and Raoul Jones, thirteen."

"The address?"

"Twelve forty-eight Luther." He tore off the printout and handed it to her. "Do you want me to get out my street map?"

Eve shook her head. "I know where it is." Dom had said she would recognize the place. "It's in my old neighborhood. Let's go."

"You want to go see her tonight?" Joe asked. "It's almost midnight. I doubt if this Fay Sugarton will take kindly to being awakened by strangers."

"I don't care how she takes it. I don't want—"

"And what are you going to say when you do see her?"

"What do you think? I'm going to tell her about Dom and ask her to let us keep Jane until the danger is over."

"It will take some persuasion to make her do that if she cares anything about the kid."

"Then you'll have to help me. We can't leave her in a place where—"

"You're going to need Fay Sugarton's cooperation," Joe said quietly. "You don't want to get off on the wrong foot."

Okay, be sensible. Dom had set up the elaborate ploy because he wanted her to make contact with Jane Mac-Guire. He probably wouldn't make a move until she'd—

Probably? God, was she risking a child's life on probabilities? He could be at that house on Luther Street right then. "I want to go tonight."

"It would be better—" Mark began.

She cut him off. "I just want to make sure everything's okay there. I won't go inside and wake everyone up."

Mark shrugged and started the car. "Whatever you say."

• • •

THE HOUSE ON Luther Street was small and gray paint was peeling from the porch steps. But the rest of the house appeared neat and well cared for. Cheerful fake greenery hung from plastic baskets on the porch.

"Satisfied?" Mark asked.

The street was deserted. No cars cruising, no one stirring. Eve wasn't satisfied, but she felt a little better. "I guess so."

"Good. Then I'll drive you and Joe to his apartment and come back to watch the house."

"No. I'll stay here."

"I was expecting that." Joe reached for his phone. "I'll call for an unmarked car to park out here tonight and have the officer go in immediately if he sees anything out of the ordinary. Okay?"

"I'll stay here too," Mark said.

She looked at the two of them, undecided. And then she opened the car door. "Okay. If you hear or see anything, you call us."

"You're going to walk? Let me run you home."

"We'll get a taxi."

"In this neighborhood?"

"So we'll walk until we get to where we can find one. I don't want you leaving here."

Mark looked at Joe. "Will you please tell her she shouldn't be wandering this neighborhood? It's too dangerous."

"Jane MacGuire wanders around this neighborhood every day of her life," Eve pointed out. "She manages to survive." Just as Eve had survived all those years ago. Jesus, it was all coming back to her.

"The car will be here in five minutes." Joe had finished his call and he and Eve got out of the car. "Don't worry, I'll take care of Eve," he told Mark. "Or maybe I'll let her take care of me. This is her turf."

"We'll be back at eight in the morning." Eve started

down the street. Nothing really changed around here. The grass growing in the cracks in the sidewalk, the dirty words chalked on the pavement.

"And how do we get back to civilization from here?" Joe asked as he fell in beside her.

"This is civilization, rich boy," Eve said. "The real wilds are four blocks south. You'll notice I'm heading north."

"And where did you live?"

"South. You're a cop. You must be familiar with this area."

"Not on foot. They shoot at cops in this part of town . . . when they're not killing each other."

" 'They.' The mysterious 'they.' We're not all criminals down here. We have to live and survive just like anyone else. Why the hell do you—"

"Hold it. You know damn well who I was talking about. Why are you jumping on me?"

He was right. "Sorry. Forget it."

"I don't think we'd better forget it. You were talking as if you were still living in one of those houses on Luther Street."

"I was never lucky enough to live on Luther Street. I told you, this is uptown."

"You know what I mean."

She did know. "I haven't been down here since we moved out after Bonnie was born. I didn't think I'd react like this."

"Like what?"

"I was feeling like the kid I was all those years ago." She smiled ruefully. "I was on the attack."

"That's how Barbara Eisley described Jane Mac-Guire."

"Maybe she has a right to want to strike first."

"I don't doubt she has every right. I'm merely suggesting that you analyze what being back here has done to you. It's you against the world again." He added deliberately, "Or maybe you and Jane MacGuire against the world."

"Nonsense. I've never even met the child."

"Maybe you shouldn't meet her. Why don't you let me go see her alone in the morning."

She turned to face him. "What are you saying?"

"Why did Dom choose someone from this neighborhood? Why did he bring you back here? Think about it."

She walked in silence for a moment. "He wants me to identify with her," she whispered. Christ, she was already identifying with the little girl. She and Jane had walked the same streets, suffered abandonment and hardship, fought their way through loneliness and hurt. "He's setting me up. First talking to me about reincarnation and then choosing Jane MacGuire. He's not satisfied with killing a child and laying the guilt on my doorstep. He wants me emotionally involved with her."

"That's the way I figure it."

Bastard. "He wants me to feel as if he's killing my daughter all over again." Her hands clenched into fists at her sides. "He wants to kill Bonnie again."

"And that's why you shouldn't go near Jane MacGuire. You're already forming an attachment and you've not even met her."

"I can keep her at a distance."

"Sure."

"It won't be that difficult, Joe. Not if she's like me at that age. I wasn't exactly approachable."

"I would have approached you."

"And I would have spit in your eye."

"It's not a good idea for you to see her."

"I have to do it."

"I know," Joe said grimly. "He hasn't left you any way out."

No way out.

Of course there would be a way out. She had fought her way out of this neighborhood. She had fought her way back to sanity after Bonnie had been killed. She wouldn't let that son of a bitch trap her now. Joe was wrong. She loved kids, but she was no bleeding heart. She could save Jane MacGuire's life and beat that monster. All she had to do was keep at a distance a little girl she didn't even know.

But Dom wouldn't keep Jane at a distance. His shadow was already looming over her.

Don't think about it. Tomorrow she and Joe would talk to Fay Sugarton. Tonight Jane MacGuire was under guard and sleeping peacefully.

The little girl would be safe tonight.

Maybe.

"I'VE BEEN LOOKING for you, Mike. I told you to go to the alley near the mission." Jane sat down near the big cardboard box. "It's not good here."

"I like it," Mike said.

"It's safer where there are people."

"This is closer to home." Mike eagerly reached for the paper bag she held out to him. "Hamburgers?"

"Spaghetti."

"I like hamburgers better."

"I have to take what I can get." What she could steal, really. Well, it wasn't exactly stealing, was it? Cusanelli's gave its leftovers to Meals on Wheels or the Salvation Army instead of throwing them out. "Eat it and then go over to the mission."

He was already eating the spaghetti. "Why did you come so late?"

"I had to wait until the restaurant closed." She stood up. "I've got to get back."

"Now?" He was disappointed.

"If you'd been at the mission, I could have stayed a few minutes. It's too late now."

"You said Fay slept hard and wouldn't wake up."

Maybe. "I have to go climb in the kitchen window.

Chang and Raoul have the room next door to the kitchen."

"I don't want to get you in trouble."

But he was lonely and wanted her to stay. She sighed and sat back down. "Just until you finish." She leaned against the brick wall. "But you got to go to the mission alley. It's not good to be alone. There are all kinds of creeps around who could hurt you."

"I always run away like you told me."

"But there's no one to hear you if you call out."

"I'm okay. I ain't scared."

She knew she couldn't make him understand. Fear was where his father lived. Everywhere else was safe in comparison. Maybe it would be okay tonight. She hadn't seen that creep for a couple of days. "How long does your father usually stay when he comes back?"

"A week, maybe two."

"It's already been a week. Maybe he's gone."

Mike shook his head. "I checked after school yesterday. He was on the porch with Mom. But he didn't see me."

"Did your mom?"

"I think so, but she looked away real quick." He stared down at the spaghetti. "It ain't her fault. She's scared too."

"Yeah."

"It will be just fine once he goes away again."

It wouldn't be fine. Mike's mom was one of the hookers who worked Peachtree, and she was gone more than she was home, but he still defended her. It always surprised Jane how kids could never see their parents the way they really were. "Are you finished with that spaghetti?"

"Not yet."

He had a bite left, but he wasn't eating because he wanted her to stay.

"Tell me about the stars again."

"You could find out for yourself if you learn to read. It's all in that book of legends in the school library. You got to learn to read, Mike, and you can't learn if you don't go to school."

"I only skipped once this week. Tell me about that guy on the horse."

She should go now. She would have only a few hours' sleep before Fay woke her to go to school. Mr. Brett had yelled at her for falling asleep in third period yesterday.

Mike nestled closer.

He was lonely and maybe more scared than he'd said. Oh, well, while she was there she could make sure no creep snuck up on him. "Just a little longer. If you promise me you won't come here anymore."

"I promise."

She tilted her head back. She liked the stars as much as Mike did. She had never noticed them until she'd gone to stay with the Carbonis. She could remember staring out the window and trying to close out the fear by seeing pictures in the sky. When she'd found the book in the library, it had helped even more. Books and stars. They had helped her; maybe they would help Mike.

Tonight was clear and the stars seemed brighter than usual. Bright and clean and far away from this alley off Luther Street.

"The guy on the horse is Sagittarius, but he's not really on a horse. He's half horse, half man. You see that string of stars? That's the string of his bow as he draws it back to . . ."

# C H A P T E R
# SEVEN

"I beg your pardon?" Fay Sugarton stared at her three visitors. "Jane?"

"She's in danger," Eve said, seated on the sofa with Joe and Mark. "Please believe me."

"Why? Because she's the right age, has red hair, and was in four foster homes before coming here? You admit you practically pulled her name from a hat."

"She matched the profile," Joe said.

"Did you check county records as well as city records?"

"We believe Dom would choose a child from this area."

"Maybe, maybe not. There could be other children in the county who match the profile. You didn't search in depth." Fay crossed her arms over her breasts. "And you don't even know if this guy who's calling you isn't some sicko practical joker."

"He knew about the two boys at Talladega," Eve said.

"That doesn't mean he's after Jane."

"Do you want to take the chance?"

"Of course I don't." She stared at Eve. "But I don't intend to let you jerk Jane away from me unless I'm convinced there's a need for it. She's been tossed from one home to another since she was two. I'm responsible for her now. I won't have her torn from another home and frightened out of her wits."

"We're not the ones who will frighten her."

"Bring me proof; show me how you'll protect her and I'll let her go."

Eve drew a deep breath. "Proof may come too late."

"You don't realize how damaged this child is. I want a chance at earning her trust." She turned to Mark Grunard. "And if you try to put me or any of this on TV, I'll sue the station."

He held up his hands. "I'm just an observer." He paused. "But I'd listen if I were you. No one is trying to victimize the child but this Dom. We're trying to save her, Ms. Sugarton."

Fay hesitated and then shook her head. "Bring me proof and I'll let you take her."

"You're putting the child at risk," Eve said.

Fay gave her a shrewd glance. "I don't imagine you'll let her become a victim. I'd bet you'll have a guard on her."

"That may not be enough. She needs to be hidden away."

"I don't see you hiding."

"That's my choice. A child has no choice."

Fay grimaced. "You don't know Jane."

"She's a *child*, dammit."

"A child who's been abused and neglected most of her life. She doesn't think much of grown-ups already, and you want me to tell her someone's trying to kill her just for the hell of it?"

"What kind of proof do you want?" Joe asked.

"It sounds like you found Jane too easily. I want the welfare people to go through *all* their records, both city and county, and make sure Jane is the only one who fits the profile. And have that FBI agent, Spiro, come by and talk to me. I trust the FBI." She glanced at Joe. "No offense, but my kids have had problems with the local police and I don't like you showing up with this TV man."

Eve looked at Joe. If Dom didn't want the police involved, he wouldn't be pleased at seeing the FBI there.

He shrugged. "I don't like it either, but we *have* located the little girl. He can't move on her without our knowing it now."

Eve turned back to Fay. "Then it's settled. You'll talk to Robert Spiro. Please listen to him. We've told you what a problem we're having with Family Services."

"I promise to listen. No more than that." She stood up. "Now, if you'll excuse me, I have housework to do and then I have to go to the grocery store." She said to Eve, "Sorry, but I have to be sure. Jane's a tough proposition. This may blow any chance I have of reaching her."

"For God's sake, help us."

"I'll do what I can. Right now she's at Crawford Middle School on Thirteenth Street." Fay walked to the chest across the room, rummaged through the top drawer, and handed a photograph to Eve. "That's her school picture from last year. She gets out at three and walks home. It's only four blocks. Keep an eye on her, but I don't want you talking to her." Her lips firmed. "If you scare her, I'll scalp you."

"Thank you." Eve thrust the photo into her purse. "But you're making a mistake."

Fay shrugged. "I've made a lot of them, but I can only do my best. I've had twelve foster children in the past six years and I think most of them are better for being with me." She moved to the door and opened it. "Goodbye. Give me proof and we'll work something out."

Mark Grunard said as they reached the street, "Tough lady. Evidently, she isn't easily impressed by my fame and sparkling personality."

"I like her." Eve scowled. "Though I'd like to break her neck. Why wouldn't she listen?"

"She believes she's doing what's best for the kid," Joe said. "And she's not about to take anyone's word without thinking it over first."

"So what do we do now?" Mark asked.

"You go home and get some sleep. You were up all night," Joe said. "As soon as we get to the car, we'll call Spiro and ask him to come down and talk to Fay Sugarton." He looked at Eve. "And then I assume this afternoon we watch the school and make sure the kid gets home all right?"

She started toward the car. "That's the plan."

"I'M TIED UP here. I can't come right now," Spiro said.

"It can't be that important. We need you," Eve told him.

"It's important enough." He paused. "We found another body on the bank across the falls. They're digging up the entire area to see if there are any more."

"God." That made twelve bodies. How many more?

"But I'll try to break away tonight and drive down. I won't be able to stay long."

"When can you get here?" Eve asked.

"I'll be there before nine, and we'll go to see the lady together," he said wearily. "Is that all right?"

"It will have to be if you can't get here before that."

Joe took the phone from her. "We're not going back to the cottage tonight. Send Charlie down here in case I have to leave Eve for any length of time." He listened. "No, we don't want Charlie to talk to Fay Sugarton. He has about as much presence and authority as one of her foster kids. We need you to impress her. What about Spalding from CASKU? Okay, if he's gone back to Quantico, you get down here yourself. I don't care if it sounds like an order. It *is* an order." He hung up.

"You didn't handle him very diplomatically," Eve said. "He's trying to help us."

"As long as it means catching Dom."

"It's his job to catch killers."

"Not quite. He's a profiler. He's supposed to analyze and report, not join in the chase." His lips tightened. "But now he wants that bastard almost as much as we do."

"We should be grateful for that."

"I'm grateful." Joe scowled. "Sometimes. When he doesn't put Bureau business in front of protecting—"

"Shut up, Joe."

He made a face. "Okay, Spiro's only doing his job. I suppose I'm a little uptight."

He wasn't the only one. Eve's nerves were strung taut.

Joe started the car. "Come on, I'll buy you a hamburger at the Varsity and then we'll go on to the school."

"MY GOD, I'D forgotten how fast kids can move when they get out of school." Joe chuckled. "They're like a herd of buffalo heading for water. Did you go to this school?"

"No, it wasn't here when I was growing up." Her gaze searched the crowd of children. "I don't see any redheads. Where is she?"

"You have a photograph." He paused. "I've been wondering why you haven't looked at it since you got it."

"I didn't think of it."

"Sure?"

She glanced at him. "Of course I'm sure. Stop reading significance into a simple oversight."

"There's nothing simple about you. It's time to look at the photograph, Eve."

"I was going to do that." She pulled the picture out of her purse. It's only a little girl. She has nothing to do with Bonnie.

Relief rushed through her. "Not very pretty, is she?" The child in the photo was not smiling and had short red hair curling around a thin, triangular face. The only attractive feature she could claim were large hazel eyes, and even they were glaring out of the photograph. "She obviously didn't want her picture taken."

"Then she must have character. I never wanted my picture taken either."

Joe's gaze shifted to her face. "You're relieved. You were afraid she'd look like Bonnie."

"It seems Dom has a bad eye. She and Bonnie are nothing alike. Hell, maybe he's lying about everything. Maybe he never saw Bonnie."

"If he was around here then, he would have seen at least a photo of her. The media plastered her face all over."

Because she was pretty and sweet and loved life so much, she touched everyone who saw her, Eve thought. Not like Jane MacGuire, who was prone to strike out. "That Dom thinks I'd identify with her only proves how crazy he is. You didn't need to worry, Joe."

"That's nice. Maybe." He straightened in the driver's seat. "There she is. She just came out of the front entrance."

Jane MacGuire was small for ten, dressed in jeans, T-shirt, and tennis shoes. She wore a green book bag on her back and strode straight ahead without looking to either side.

No dawdling. No stopping to talk with friends as Bonnie had done. Bonnie had so many friends . . .

She wasn't being fair. Bonnie had always been surrounded by love and trust. Jane MacGuire had a right to be wary. But, God, she was glad the child was nothing like Bonnie. "She's reached the street. Start the car."

THE CREEP HAD a different car. Bigger. Newer. Gray instead of blue.

Or it could be another creep, Jane thought. The world was full of them.

She broke into a trot and darted around the corner.

She waited.

The gray car coasted slowly around the corner.

She tensed. Was it following her?

A man and woman? Maybe they're not creeps.

Or maybe they were. Better not take any chances. She climbed over the chain-link fence, ran across the yard, then scrambled over the far fence.

Out the gate that led to the alley.

She glanced over her shoulder.

No car.

Keep running.

Her heart was beating too hard.

Stop it. Don't ever let the creeps scare you. That's what they wanted. Scare you. Hurt you. Don't let them do it.

It was going to be okay.

Two more blocks and she'd be at Fay's house. Maybe she'd tell Fay about the creeps. Fay was like the teachers at school. As long as she understood the danger, she'd do what she could to help. It was only when she didn't understand that she—

Jane ran out of the alley into the street. The house was right ahead. Half a block.

She looked back over her shoulder, and her heart leaped into her throat.

Gray car. Turning the corner.

She hadn't lost them.

She flew down the street toward Fay's house.

Fay would keep her safe. She would call the cops and maybe they would care enough to come.

If they didn't, at least she wouldn't be alone. Fay would be there.

She ran up the steps, threw open the door, and slammed it closed behind her.

Safe. She was safe.

Maybe she was stupid to be scared. Maybe she wouldn't tell Fay.

That would be really stupid. She'd tell her. "Fay!"

No answer.

The house was silent.

Fay must be in the kitchen. She always made sure she was home when Jane and the boys returned from school.

Yes, Fay was in the kitchen. Jane was sure she heard the loose board near the sink creak.

But why hadn't she answered?

She slowly started across the living room toward the kitchen.

"Fay?"


"FAY SUGARTON ISN'T going to like this." Joe parked in front of the house. "She doesn't want us talking to the kid."

"Too bad. Dammit, we scared her. I'm not going to let her have nightmares about this." Eve opened the car door. "Fine tail you are. I told you not to let her know we were following."

"She's sharp." Joe got out of the car. "It's almost as if she was expecting it."

Eve glanced at him. "You think she knows she's being watched?"

"It seems we're going to have the opportunity to ask her." Joe climbed the steps and rang the doorbell. "If we can get Fay Sugarton to let us in the front door."

"She has no choice. She cares about the girl. It's not as if we're going to tell Jane about— Why isn't she answering the door?"

Joe rang the bell again. "She said she was going to the grocery store. Maybe she's not home and the kid's too scared to answer."

"She's had hours to get home from the store." She tried the door. "It's locked."

"The kid." He thought about it. "Then again, maybe not. What the hell." He put his shoulder against the door and broke through it. "Illegal is better than—Shit!" He crumpled to the floor as a baseball bat struck his kneecaps.

Jane whirled on Eve and struck her in the rib cage with the bat. Pain seared through Eve. She was barely able to dodge as the girl swung the bat at her head.

"Creep." Tears were running down her face. "Fucking creep." She swung the bat again. "I'll kill you, you dirty—"

Joe dove from his knees and brought Jane down.

"Don't hurt her," Eve gasped.

"Don't hurt her? I may have to have a knee replacement." He straddled the struggling child. "And she tried to knock your brains out."

"She's scared. We broke into the house. She thought—" Blood. The little girl was covered in blood. Her cheeks, lips, hands . . . "Oh, my God, she's hurt, Joe. He hurt her." She fell to her knees beside the girl and brushed the hair away from her cheek.

Jane sank her teeth into Eve's hand.

Joe pried her teeth apart and jerked Eve's hand away. "Careful." He cupped Jane's jaw and held it shut while he stared down into her eyes. "We're not going to hurt you, dammit. We're here to help. Now, where's Ms. Sugarton?"

Jane glared up at him.

"Police. Detective Quinn." He reached into his pocket and showed her his badge. He repeated, "We're here to help."

The child relaxed a little.

"Where are you hurt?" Eve asked.

Jane was still glaring at Joe. "Get off me."

"Get off her, Joe."

"This could be a mistake." Joe stood up and grabbed the bat.

Jane slowly sat up. "Lousy cop. Why weren't you here before?" Tears were running down her cheeks again. "Never here when anyone needs you. Lousy cop. Lousy cop . . ."

"I'm here now. Where are you hurt?"

"Not hurt. *She's* hurt."

Eve stiffened. "Ms. Sugarton?"

"Fay." Jane looked toward the kitchen. "Fay."

"Jesus." Eve jumped to her feet and ran toward the kitchen.

BLOOD.

And more blood.

On the Formica table.

On the overturned kitchen chair.

On the tile floor where Fay Sugarton lay slumped, eyes staring at them across the room, throat gaping where it had been slashed.

"Don't move." Joe was standing beside her. "There could be tracks. We don't want to disturb them."

"She's dead," Eve said dully.

"Yes." He turned her around and gave her a push toward the living room. "Go back and take care of the kid while I call this in. See if she saw anyone."

She couldn't tear her gaze from those staring dead eyes. "Dom," she whispered. "It has to be Dom."

"Go."

She nodded and moved slowly from the kitchen.

Jane was sitting huddled against a wall, her knees drawn up to her chest. "She's dead, isn't she?"

"Yes." She dropped down on the floor beside her. "Did you see anyone?"

"I tried to help her. She was bleeding. I tried to stop the bleeding . . . but I couldn't. I couldn't stop it. My health teacher said if we ever have an accident, we should always stop the bleeding first. I couldn't do it. I couldn't stop it."

Eve wanted to reach out and draw Jane close, but she could almost see the wall the child had built around herself. "It wasn't your fault. I'm sure she was already dead."

"Maybe not. Maybe I could have helped her if I'd been smarter. I didn't pay much attention to what my teacher said. I didn't think—I didn't know—"

Eve couldn't stand it. She reached out and tentatively touched the child's shoulder.

Jane jerked away. "Who are you?" she said fiercely. "Are you a cop too? Why weren't you here? Why did you let this happen?"

"I'm not police, but I have to know what happened. Did you see—" To hell with it. The child was in no shape to answer questions. "What do you say we go on the porch and wait for the police to get here?"

At first she didn't think the girl would agree, but then Jane rose to her feet and strode out of the house. She sat down on the top porch step.

Eve sat down beside her. "My name is Eve Duncan. The detective inside is Joe Quinn."

The girl stared straight ahead.

"You're Jane MacGuire?"

The girl didn't answer.

"If you don't want to talk, that's fine. I know you must have cared very much for Ms. Sugarton."

"I didn't care anything about her. I just lived with her."

"I don't think that's true, but we won't talk about it now. We won't talk at all. I just thought it would make you feel better if we weren't strangers."

"Talking doesn't mean anything. You're still a stranger."

And the child was going to make sure she stayed that way, Eve thought. The tears were gone, but her back was straight and rigid and the wall of distrust was higher than ever. Who could blame her? Any other child would have been in hysterics. It might have been a healthier reaction than withdrawal. "I don't feel much like talking either. We'll just sit here and wait. Okay?"

Jane didn't look at her. "Okay."

The child was still covered with blood, Eve realized suddenly. She should do something about it.

Not now. Neither of them was in any shape to do anything but sit there. She leaned her head against the newel post next to her. She couldn't get the memory of dead eyes out of her mind. Fay Sugarton had been a good woman, trying to do her best. She didn't deserve—

"I lied." Jane was still looking straight ahead. "I think . . . I liked her."

"So did I."

Jane fell silent again.

BARBARA EISLEY PULLED up at the curb at the same time as the first police squad car.

The officers poured into the house, but Barbara Eisley stopped before Jane. Her expression was amazingly gentle as she spoke to the child. "Do you remember me, Jane? I'm Ms. Eisley."

Jane stared at her without expression. "I remember you."

"You can't stay here any longer."

"I know."

"I've come to take you away. Where are Chang and Raoul?"

"School. Basketball practice."

"I'll send someone for them." She held out her hand. "Come with me. We'll get you cleaned up and then we'll talk."

"I don't want to talk." Jane stood and walked to the car at the curb.

"Where are you taking her?" Eve asked.

"The Child and Family Services holding facility."

"How safe is it?"

"It has security and she'll be surrounded by other children."

"I think you should let us take—"

"Bullshit." Barbara Eisley whirled on her, her tone as hard now as it had been gentle before. "She's my responsibility and none of you are going to touch her. I should never have become involved in this mess. The newspapers and politicians are going to come down on me like a ton of bricks."

"We have to keep her safe. Ms. Sugarton wasn't the target. She probably just got in the way."

"And you weren't able to help her, were you?" Barbara Eisley's eyes bored into her. "Fay Sugarton was a decent woman, an extraordinary woman who helped dozens of kids. She shouldn't have died. She might be alive now if I hadn't given you that—"

"And Jane might be dead."

"I should have kept out of it and that's what I'm doing from now on. Stay clear of me and stay away from Jane MacGuire." She turned on her heel and walked to the car.

Eve watched helplessly as it pulled away from the curb. Jane was sitting up straight in the passenger seat, but she looked terribly small and fragile.

"It was the only thing to do."

She turned to see Joe standing in the doorway. "I was hoping we could get her away before anyone showed up from Family Services."

He shook his head. "I called Eisley."

Her eyes widened. "What?"

"Child and Family Services always has to be involved

in cases like this. They serve to protect the children from the media and police interrogation. They'll take the heat off Jane."

"We could have protected her."

"Would she have let us? We're strangers to her. At the welfare facility she'll be surrounded by kids and staff. She'll be much safer, and we can still keep an eye on her."

Eve was still uneasy. "I wish you hadn't . . ."

"She may be a material witness in a murder case, Eve. Did she talk to you?"

Eve shook her head.

"Then I'll have to see her later tonight."

"Can't you leave her—" Of course he couldn't leave Jane alone. She might have seen something. "Barbara Eisley may not let you talk to her. She's not pleased with us."

"Sometimes it helps to have a badge." He pulled her to her feet. "Come on. I'll drive you home. Forensics will be here any minute. I'll have to come back, but you don't need to be here."

"I'll wait for you."

"No, you won't. I may be here hours and the media will be right behind the forensic team." He nudged her down the steps. "I called Charlie. He's at the lobby of my apartment building now and will keep an eye on you until I get there." He opened the car door for her. "As soon as you're inside the apartment, call Spiro and Mark and tell them what happened."

She nodded. "And maybe I'll call Barbara Eisley and see if I can talk her into seeing me again."

"Give it a rest, Eve. Let her cool off."

She shook her head. She couldn't forget her last glimpse of Jane MacGuire, sitting ramrod straight, afraid she'd break if she lowered her defenses.

Dom could break her and butcher her. How close had Jane come to Dom in the kitchen?

Panic rose inside Eve at the thought. Smother it. The immediate danger to Jane was over.

The hell it was. "I'm calling Barbara Eisley as soon as I get to the apartment."

"NO," BARBARA EISLEY said coldly. "Don't make me repeat myself again, Ms. Duncan. Jane stays in our custody. Come near her and I'll have you tossed in jail."

"You don't understand. Dom killed Fay Sugarton in broad daylight. He managed to get inside her house and then he cut her throat right in her own kitchen. What's to stop him from doing the same thing to Jane at the welfare house?"

"The fact that every day we deal with abusive parents and mothers on crack and heroin who want their children back. We know what we're doing. The location of the holding facility is confidential. And even if he found out where it is, no one's going to get past our security."

"You've never had to deal with—"

"Good-bye, Ms. Duncan."

"Wait. How is she?"

"Not good. But she'll get better. I'll send her to the therapist tomorrow morning." She hung up.

Eve remembered those therapists. Sitting there probing with their questions and then trying to hide their resentment when they couldn't get through to her. Jane would chew them up and spit them out just as Eve had when she was a child.

"No luck?"

She turned to Charlie, who was sitting across the room. "No luck. I'll try again tomorrow morning."

"You're persistent."

"Persistence is the only weapon I have with Eisley. Sometimes it works. Sometimes it doesn't." Dear God, she hoped it worked this time. "Have you heard anything from the agent Spiro sent to Phoenix?"

"Not much, only that their PD is cooperating. I wish

Spiro had let me go." He smiled. "Not that I'm not enjoying the company. It's just that I joined the FBI for more challenging work than guard duty. Although the subject does have me running all over Georgia to keep her under surveillance."

"Sorry. Coffee? I'm afraid there's no food in the refrigerator."

"I saw a Thai restaurant around the corner that delivers." Charlie pulled out his phone. "What do you want?"

She wasn't hungry, but she supposed she should eat something. "Anything with noodles, I guess. And get something to put in the refrigerator for Joe. He never stops to eat."

"Okay."

She picked up her purse and headed for the bedroom. "I need to call Spiro."

"No, you don't. I already did that after Joe phoned me. He swore like a trooper and said he's on his way."

She closed the bedroom door and leaned back against it.

She should call Mark, but she needed a little time to recover. She still felt sick about Fay Sugarton. Barbara Eisley couldn't be blamed for being angry.

She went to the window and looked down at the park across the street. It was dark now and the street lamps cast pools of light on the trees. The night shadows seemed threatening.

Are you down there, Dom? Are you watching, you bastard?

Her digital phone rang.

Joe? Spiro?

Her phone rang again.

She pulled it out of her purse. "Hello."

"How are you getting along with little Janie?"

"You son of a bitch."

"I was sorry I couldn't stay around to see your meeting, but the timing was a little tight. I didn't even get a chance to see the kid at close quarters."

"So you killed Fay Sugarton instead."

"You make me sound like a blunderer. There was no 'instead' about it. I had no intention of killing the child yet. Fay Sugarton was the target."

"For God's sake, why?"

"You and Jane couldn't bond while Sugarton was around. So she had to be taken out of the way. How do you like our little girl?"

"I don't. She tried to brain me with a baseball bat."

"That wouldn't deter you. You probably admire her spirit. I don't think I could have chosen better."

"You made a lousy choice. She's nothing like Bonnie."

"She'll begin to grow on you."

"She won't have the chance. It won't work. She's not with me."

"I know. We'll have to take care of that, won't we? It's not what I had in mind at all. Go get her from welfare, Eve."

"It's impossible."

"She has to be with you. You'll have to find a way to make that happen."

"You're not listening. They'll toss me in jail if I even go near her."

A silence. "Perhaps I'm not making myself clear. Either get her out of that welfare house or I'll go in after her. I'll give you twenty-four hours."

Panic soared through Eve. "I don't even know where she is."

"Find out. Think about it. You have contacts. There's always a way. I'd find a way."

"There's security. You'd never get near her. They'd catch you."

"I'd get near her. All it would take is one careless moment, one bored or disgruntled employee."

"I don't care anything about that child. I could never feel the slightest affection for—"

"Yes, you could. You just have to get to know her. You've spent years trying to protect and find children you never knew. Now I've given you one of your own. The potential is mind-boggling."

"I'm calling the police as soon as I hang up."

"And seal Jane's fate? It would, you know. I'd never stop trying. If I can't find a way to do it right now, I'll wait. A week, a month, a year. It's amazing how the passing of time makes everything easier for me. People forget, people lower their guard . . . and you wouldn't be close enough to her to stop me. Twenty-four hours, Eve." He hung up.

He was crazy, Eve thought. Eisley had said no one could get into that welfare facility.

But Eve herself had doubted it.

*All it would take is one careless moment, one bored or disgruntled employee.*

Wasn't that what Eve had been afraid of all along? Wasn't that why she had been urging Eisley to let her take Jane?

Her throat tightened as fear raced through her. He would do it. Christ, he would find a way to kill Jane if she didn't get her out of the facility.

She only had twenty-four hours.

Joe. She had to call Joe.

She was halfway through his number when she hung up. What was she doing? Was she really going to ask him to compromise his job by kidnapping a child from under the nose of welfare?

But she *needed* him.

So what? Stop being a selfish bitch and do what has to be done yourself.

How? She didn't even know where Jane was.

*You have contacts. There's always a way. I'd find a way.*

She started punching a phone number.

Mark Grunard answered on the second ring. He wasn't pleased. "Nice of you to let me know about Fay Sugarton. I got to her house along with half the newsmen in the city."

"I meant to call you. Things happened."

"That wasn't our agreement."

"It won't happen again."

"You're damn right it won't. I'm bailing out. You and Joe should have—"

"I need your help. Dom called again."

Silence. "And?"

"Welfare is keeping the kid at their holding facility. He wants her with me. He gave me twenty-four hours to get her."

"What happens if you don't?"

"What do you think happens? She's dead, dammit."

"It would be difficult to get to her at—"

"He'll do it. I can't take a chance."

"What does Joe say?"

"Nothing. I'm not telling him. Joe's out of it."

He gave a low whistle. "He's not going to like that."

"He's done enough. I won't have Joe crucified for helping me."

"But since you're calling me, I take it you're willing to sacrifice my humble self?"

"You have less to lose and more to gain."

"What kind of help do you want from me?"

"I need to know where she is. Do you have any idea?"

"Maybe."

"What do you mean, maybe?"

"Look, the location of that facility is a bigger secret than Level 4 of the CDC."

"But you know where it is?"

"Well, I followed Eisley once when she took a kid there during a big court case."

Then Dom could have followed Eisley too.

"It's a big old house on Delaney Street that used to be a convalescent home. The location could have changed though. That was over two years ago."

"We'll try it. Eisley said there's a guard."

"A security guard who patrols the grounds. I suppose you want me to distract him."

"Yes."

"And then? Once you've got her where are you going to take her?"

"I don't know. I'll find a place. Will you help me?"

"You're putting my ass on the line."

"I'll make it worth your while."

"Yes, you will." His tone hardened. "Because I'm going to be with you every step of the way."

"I can't do—" She drew a deep breath. "Okay, we'll work something out. Come and get me. I'll meet you across the street at the park."

"Not before midnight."

"Mark, it's only five-thirty now. I want to get her out of there."

"Okay, eleven. But if you want to go any earlier, you'll have to go by yourself. It's bad enough we have to run the risk of the security guard. I want everyone in that house asleep before I go near it."

Five and a half hours. How could she wait that long? She was already a nervous wreck. Okay, chill out. Dom had given her twenty-four hours. "All right. I'll eat dinner and then tell Charlie I'm going to bed. The kitchen door leads to a laundry room that opens to the hall. I can slip out and meet you at the park at eleven."

"Right."

She hung up. Done. Mark Grunard had been tougher than she had thought. Not that she could blame him. She was asking a great deal and not many people would give without wanting something in return.

Except Joe.

Don't think about Joe. She couldn't have him with her.

"Come on out," Charlie called from outside the bedroom door. "Food's here."

She braced herself. Just get through dinner and hope to slip out before Joe comes home.

# CHAPTER
# EIGHT

"Would you like to talk?"

"No." Jane stared straight ahead. Let her just go *away*. The house mother looked like a plump gray bird perched on the sofa and her cooing voice was driving Jane crazy. Maybe she was trying to be nice, but Jane had had enough. "I want to go to bed, Mrs.—" What was her name? "Mrs. Morse."

"You'll sleep better if you talk about it."

Talk about blood. Talk about Fay. Why did grown-ups always think it was better to talk everything over? She didn't want to think about Fay. She never wanted to think about Fay again. She just wanted to close the door to all the pain. No, there was one thing she had to know first. "Who killed her?"

"You're safe here, dear," Mrs. Morse said gently.

That wasn't what she had asked, and Mrs. Morse was lying. No one was safe anywhere. "Who killed Fay?"

"We're not sure."

"The cops have to have some idea. Fay never hurt anyone. Was it one of the gangs? Was anything stolen?"

"It's better if you don't think about it right now. We'll talk about it tomorrow." She reached out to stroke Jane's hair. "But we really should discuss how you're feeling."

She leaned away before the woman could touch her. "I don't feel anything. I don't care that Fay died. I wouldn't care if you died either. Just leave me alone."

"I understand."

Jane gritted her teeth. What could she say to make the woman leave her alone? She didn't understand. No one understood.

Except maybe Eve. Eve hadn't tried to talk. She had sat silently with Jane, but Jane had somehow felt—

Stupid. They had been together only a matter of minutes. If Jane got to know her, she'd see that Eve was the same as all the others.

"Is there anything I can do for you?" Mrs. Morse asked.

Let me out of here.

She knew better than to say it. She had been in this place before. She was being protected until they could find another home for her.

But Mike wasn't being protected. He was out there in the dark and he didn't know that there would be no food and no one to keep an eye on him.

And she was going to be locked up and not be able to help him.

Blood.

Fay's eyes staring up at her as she tried to stop the blood.

Bad. So much badness out there.

Mike.

"You're trembling," Mrs. Morse said. "My poor child, why won't you—"

"I'm not trembling," Jane said fiercely. She stood up. "I'm cold. You keep it too cold in this son-of-a-bitchin' place."

"We don't use language like that here, dear."

"Then throw me out, you old cow." She glared at her. "I hate it here. I hate you. I'm going to sneak into your room and cut your throat like that bastard cut Fay's."

The woman stood and backed away as Jane had known she would. These days threats of violence were treated cautiously by welfare personnel even when uttered by a kid like Jane.

"That wasn't necessary," Mrs. Morse said. "Go on to bed, dear. We'll discuss your problem in the morning."

Jane ran out of the living room, up the stairs, past the policeman posted outside her room, and slammed the door behind her. They'd given the tiny room to her alone this time, although she'd probably have to share once they decided she'd gotten over the shock of Fay's death. Most of the time each room was occupied by three, maybe four children.

And they'd never before posted a guard outside her door either. It must have something to do with what had happened to Fay.

She couldn't breathe. She moved over to the window and looked down at the yard below. Those rosebushes should be cut back. Fay had Jane prune her roses in the fall. She'd said that they'd come back fuller and more beautiful in the spring. Jane hadn't believed her, but she'd been willing to wait and see if—

Fay.

Don't think of her. She's gone. There's nothing you can do about her. Shut the door.

Think about Mike instead and the streets and the creeps who could hurt him. She could help Mike.

But not if she stayed here.

THE TWO-STORY BRICK building on Delaney Street was set back and surrounded by patchy lawns and poorly kept gardens. It had been built in the twenties and looked every one of its years.

"May I ask what you're doing to do?" Mark asked politely as he parked the car on a side street. "It's almost midnight and I'm sure the place is locked up tight as a drum. Providing you can find her in the first place, I'd be interested to know how you're going to get inside and then get the kid out without being shot by the security guard. He makes regular rounds."

I'd be interested to know too, Eve thought. "Do you have any idea where they'd keep her?"

"Well, they kept the boy in that court case on the upper floor. A room on the south side. First window facing the back."

"By himself?"

Mark nodded. "He was a special case."

Would Jane also be a special case? She'd just have to cross her fingers and pray she'd get lucky.

"I'm going around back and see if there's any way I can get in from there." She got out of the car. "You cover the other side, and if you run into the guard, distract him."

"Piece of cake," Mark said sarcastically. "Why don't you give me something hard to do? It's not—"

"Duck." She dove back into the car and pulled Mark down on the seat. "Patrol car."

The Atlanta PD car cruised slowly by the welfare house, shining its lights on the front of the building and grounds as it passed.

Eve held her breath, half expecting the car to stop. Had they been seen?

The police car drove on and turned the corner.

"I think it's safe now." Mark raised his head. "I suppose we should have expected welfare to request additional security."

"We've got to hope the guard is still the only one on the grounds." Eve got out of the car. "And that the police car doesn't come back anytime soon. Hurry." She was already skirting the walk and crossing the grass. Don't think. Just move fast and pray.

She arrived at the back of the building and looked up at the second floor. First window on the south side.

The room was dark and the window closed.

Great.

A rusty drainpipe clung to the side of the building, but it was at least a yard from the window.

What the hell was she going—

What was that?

She looked over her shoulder.

A sound?

Someone standing in the shadows?

No, there was nothing. It must have been her imagination.

She turned back to the house. First she had to find a way to get up to the second floor. Then she'd have to get inside the room without scaring Jane. The more she considered the situation, the more helpless she felt. She'd do better figuring out how to get into the ground floor and then—

The window was opening.

Eve tensed.

Jane stuck her head out and looked down at her. Could she tell who Eve was? Yes, the moonlight was bright enough for recognition. But that didn't guarantee anything. Everyone must seem like a threat to Jane right now.

She stared at Eve for a long while. Then she touched her forefinger to her lips as if to hush her.

The gesture was conspiratorial; the two of them against the world. Eve didn't know why she'd gotten lucky, but she'd take it. God, yes, she'd take it.

Jane tossed a knotted sheet out the window. It ended twelve feet above Eve's head. Jane started climbing down it like a monkey; how was she supposed to—

"Catch me," Jane ordered.

"It's not that easy. If I miss, you'll break—"

"Don't miss." She let go of the sheet and fell into Eve's arms. The child's weight knocked them both to the ground.

"Get *off* me," Jane whispered.

Eve rolled to the left and managed to sit up. "Sorry. You nearly broke my ribs."

Jane was on her feet and racing around the building.

"Shit." Eve jumped up and ran after her.

"Lose something?" Mark was holding Jane in a hammerlock. She kicked backward and connected with his shin. "Ouch. Stop fighting me or I'll break your neck, you little demon."

"Don't hurt her." Eve knelt down in front of the child. "We're trying to help you, Jane. Don't be afraid."

"I'm not afraid. And I don't need your help."

"You needed me to catch you."

"It was a long drop. I didn't want to break my legs."

Eve made a face. "You'd rather break my ribs."

Jane stared calmly into her eyes. "Why not? I don't care anything about you."

"But you must not think I'm a danger to you, since you didn't scream when you saw me."

"I needed someone. I knew the sheet wouldn't reach the ground."

"But you do believe I'm no danger to you?"

"Maybe. I don't know." She scowled. "Why are you here?"

Eve hesitated. She didn't want to scare the kid, but she sensed that Jane would see through a lie. "I was afraid for you."

"Why?"

"I'll tell you later. We don't have time now."

Jane looked over her shoulder. "This isn't the cop."

"No, he's Mark Grunard, a reporter."

"He wants to write stories about Fay."

"Yes."

"We should get out of here, Eve." Mark's voice was impatient. "I didn't run into the guard, but he's bound to come around soon. And who knows when that patrol car will come back."

She was as eager to leave as he was, but she wasn't

about to drag Jane kicking and screaming. "Will you come with us, Jane?" Eve asked. "Believe me, we just want you to be safe."

Jane didn't answer.

"You were leaving anyway. I promise we'll locate a place where they won't find you."

"Let me go."

Mark shook his head. "And have you run out on—"

"Let her go, Mark. It has to be her decision."

Mark's hold loosened and Jane quickly slipped out of his grip.

Jane gazed at Eve for a few seconds and then said, "I'll go with you. Where's your car?"


THEY HAD DRIVEN no more than four blocks when Jane said to Mark, "You're going the wrong way."

"Wrong way?"

"I want to go to Luther Street."

Fay's house. "You can't go back there," Eve said gently. "Fay's not there anymore, Jane."

"I know that. Do you think I'm stupid? She's dead. They'd take her to the morgue. I still have to go to Luther Street."

"Did you leave something there?"

"Yes."

"The police are at the house. They won't let you in and they'll take you back to welfare."

"Just take me to Luther Street. Okay?"

"Jane, listen to me. The house is under—"

"I don't want to go to the house. Just let me off at the alley two blocks away."

"The alley you ducked down this afternoon when you spotted our car?"

Jane nodded.

"Why?"

"I want to go."

"You left something in the alley?" Mark asked from the driver's seat.

"Why do you want to know? So you can put it on TV?" Jane asked fiercely. "It's none of your business."

"You are my business at the moment," Mark said. "Eve promised me a story if I helped her spring you. Do you know what the penalty is for kidnapping minors? I'll get thrown in jail and my career will go down the drain. I'm risking a hell of a lot and I don't need your sass, little girl."

Jane ignored him and turned to Eve. "Jail? Then why did you do it?"

"I was worried about you. I thought you might be in danger."

"Like Fay?"

Christ, what could she say now? The truth. "Like Fay."

"You know who did it?"

Eve nodded.

"Who?"

"I'm not sure of his real name. He calls himself Dom."

"Why did he do it? Fay never hurt anyone."

"He's not sane. He likes to hurt people. I know that's terrible, but there are people out there who don't care about anything but doing harm."

"I know that. The creeps. There are lots of them around."

Eve stiffened. "Are there?" She paused. "Have you seen any of them around lately?"

"Maybe." Jane glanced at Mark. "I watch the news on TV. They always show the creeps."

Mark shrugged. "It's my job."

"Have you seen anyone who scared you lately?" Eve persisted.

"He didn't scare me. He was just like those others who hang around the school yard."

"Did he follow you?"

"Sometimes."

"For God's sake, why didn't you tell someone?"

Jane looked out the window. "I want to go to Luther Street. Now."

"What did he look like?" Mark asked.

"Big. Quick. I didn't really see him. Just another creep. Take me to Luther Street or let me out of the car."

Mark glanced at Eve with raised brows. "Well?"

"Take us to the alley but use the Market Street entrance. We can't chance anyone seeing us from the house."

"You mean Quinn." Mark took a left at the next corner.

"Yes." Unless Joe had already gone back to the apartment and discovered she was gone.

"He's going to raise hell about this."

"I know." She leaned back in the seat. "I couldn't do anything else."

"I'm not complaining. If you weren't trying to protect Quinn, you wouldn't have felt it necessary to have my help. He's not above jettisoning me if he thought it better for you."

"*Hurry,*" Jane said.

There was such tension in her voice that Eve glanced at her in surprise. Jane was sitting straight up in the seat, her hands clenched into fists at her sides. "We'll be there soon, Jane."

"Just what did you leave in that alley?" Mark asked softly.

Jane didn't answer, but Eve could see her fists tightening into her palms and felt a sudden chill. "Speed it up, Mark."

"I'm doing the limit."

"Then go over it."

"Considering what we've just done, it's not smart to risk—"

"Do it."

He shrugged and pressed the accelerator.

"Thanks." Jane didn't look at Eve as she spoke the word grudgingly.

"What's in that alley, Jane?"

"Mike," Jane whispered. "The creep saw him. I told him to go over by the Union Mission, but he's probably back on Luther. It's closer to his mom."

"Who's Mike?"

"He's too little. I tried to keep him— Kids are dumb when they're that little. They don't know . . ."

"About creeps, Jane?"

"His father's a creep but not like—" Jane drew a deep breath. "You think that creep who's been following me is this Dom, who killed Fay, don't you?"

"I'm not sure."

"But you think he did."

"I believe he might have done it."

"Son of a bitch." Jane's eyes were glittering with tears. "Dirty son of a bitch."

"Yes."

"I should have told her. I thought he was just one of those creeps who went after kids. There are lots of them around. I didn't know he'd hurt—"

"It wasn't your fault."

"I should have told her. She wanted me to tell her things. I should have—"

"Jane, it wasn't your fault."

She shook her head. "I should have told her."

"Okay, maybe you should have told her. We all do things we regret. But you couldn't know he'd hurt her."

Jane closed her eyes. "I should have told her."

Eve gave up arguing. She'd had her own share of guilt and regrets after Bonnie had been taken from her. But Jane was only ten. Children shouldn't have to bear such heavy burdens. But since when was life fair? "How old is Mike?"

"Six."

Eve felt sick. Jane was the target, not this little boy. But would Dom care? Another life would mean nothing to him.

"Fay wouldn't let me bring him home with me. She wanted to call the welfare people about him. But I knew they'd just send him back to his father. Mike's afraid of him. I couldn't let her call." Her eyes opened. "I tried to keep him safe."

"I'm sure you did."

"But the creep saw me with him. He knows Mike's alone."

"He may be safe." Eve touched her shoulder. Jane was stiff as a board, but at least she didn't move away. "We'll find him, Jane. I'm sure Dom isn't anywhere near Luther. There are police all over the neighborhood."

"You said he was crazy."

"Not about his own safety. I'm sure Mike will be all right until we get to him." She hoped she was telling the truth. "And after that I'll make sure he stays safe."

"He can't go back to his father."

"I'll make sure he's safe," Eve repeated.

"You promise?"

Good God, what was she getting herself into? One kidnapping wasn't enough? "I promise." She paused. "But you've got to promise me that you'll do as I tell you so I can keep *you* safe."

"I'm not like Mike. I can take care of myself."

"A promise for a promise, Jane."

She shrugged. "Okay, if you're not stupid about it."

Eve breathed a sigh of relief. "I'll try not to be stupid. I'm sure you'll tell me if I am."

"You bet I will."

Mark pulled off the street and stopped just inside the alley.

"Turn off your lights," Jane hissed. "Do you want to scare him?" She scrambled out of the car and ran down the alley.

"Jane!" Eve jumped out and followed her into the darkness.

The digital phone in her handbag rang.

She ignored it. She couldn't deal with either Joe or Dom just then.

But she might have to deal with Dom in the flesh, she thought suddenly. He might have known that Jane would come to the alley.

He might be waiting ahead in the darkness.

NO ANSWER.

Joe's stomach clenched as he hung up. She should have answered; she always had the digital phone on. If she were asleep, the ringing would have woken her up. But she'd been so upset, he doubted she'd fallen asleep.

And where the hell was Charlie Cather?

He called the apartment phone.

Charlie answered drowsily on the second ring.

"Everything okay?" Joe asked.

"Fine. Locked up tight. Ms. Duncan went to bed a couple of hours ago."

He still didn't like it. Why hadn't she answered her digital? "She's okay?"

"Fine. She was a little quiet, but that's not unusual, is it? She's concerned about the kid."

"Yes."

"Did Agent Spiro arrive?"

"He's at the crime scene. I'm back at the precinct, but I have these damn reports to type up."

"I hear you. God, I hate paperwork."

She should have answered the digital, Joe kept thinking. "Go check on her."

"What?"

"Dammit, go check on her."

"Wake her up?"

"If you have to wake her, do it. Check on her."

"She won't thank me if I— Okay, I'll check."

Joe waited.

She was probably fine. It was unlikely Dom would try to get to her at the apartment. Besides, that wasn't in his game plan. It would be too simple. He was using Jane MacGuire to bait the net.

And one woman had already been caught in that net. All afternoon and night Joe had been dealing with her murder. When he'd looked at Fay Sugarton, all he could think about was Eve. But when wasn't he thinking of Eve?

"She's gone."

Joe closed his eyes. God, he'd known it.

"I swear, no one got into the apartment, Joe. I've been here all the time, and I checked the doors after Eve went to bed."

"Did she get any phone calls?"

"Not on the apartment phone. And I didn't hear her digital ring."

"You might not have heard it if she was in another room."

"She didn't mention a call."

Dom had called her. Joe knew it in his gut. Dom had called and she had left the apartment.

To meet him?

She wouldn't have done that. It would have been stupid, and Eve was never stupid.

No, to lure her out of the apartment, Dom would have used a threat she couldn't ignore.

Jane MacGuire.

Shit.

He hung up and flipped his Rolodex for Barbara Eisley's pager. It was the only way he could get the address of the halfway house at this hour.

Eisley called back in less than a minute. But it took

ten minutes for Joe to persuade her to give him the address.

Rage and fear were building inside him with every second. He wanted to *strangle* Eve. She had closed him out again. All the years of being together, and she had turned her back on him. He wished he'd never met the bitch. Who needed to have that kind of torment in their lives? Half the time he wanted to shake her and the other half he wanted to cradle her and take away her pain. She thought she was strong enough to take on anything, but she was no match for Dom.

Don't do it, Eve.

Don't run toward him.

Wait for me.

SHE WAS RUNNING.

The alley smelled of grease and garbage.

Darkness.

A sound to the left.

Her heart leaped to her throat.

Dom?

No, only a cat.

Where was Jane?

"Jane? Do you see her, Mark?"

"Here," Jane called out.

The big cardboard refrigerator box against the brick wall.

"Mike's okay." Jane crawled out of the box, dragging a small boy with her. "He's just scared. He said he kept hearing scratching tonight. Probably rats. He's hungry. You got anything in your purse?"

"I'm afraid not."

"Who are they?" Mike was staring at Eve and Mark warily. "Welfare?"

"I wouldn't do that to you," Jane said. "But you can't stay here any longer. There's some bad people hanging around."

"I'm okay."

"You'll be better where Eve will take you. Get your stuff."

Mike hesitated.

"There will be plenty of food."

"Okay." Mike ducked back into the box.

"Where are you going to take him?" Jane asked. "He's going to want to know."

So did Eve. "I've got to think about it."

"Not welfare."

"No."

"Not back to his father."

"Okay, Jane, I get the point."

"You promised."

She inhaled sharply. Something was gleaming wetly on the cardboard box. "I'll keep my promise."

Mike came out of the box carrying a duffel bag. "What kind of food? I like french fries."

"I'll see what I can do." She turned to Mark. "Take them back to the car, will you?"

Jane looked at her.

Mark raised his brows. "You're not coming?"

"In a minute."

He nodded and began to shepherd the children up the alley.

She reached out and gingerly touched the dark stain on the box. Not as wet as she'd thought, only a little came off on her fingertips. Her hand was trembling as she reached into her handbag and drew out a small flashlight.

The stain on her fingers was dark red, almost rusty. Blood.

*He kept hearing scratching tonight.*

She shone the light on the box.

*You've done well, Eve. A small reward . . .*

She felt sick as she realized how close Dom had been to the little boy.

Reward?

Mike's life was her reward?

No.

The dots at the end of the sentence were leading downward.

Something white lay on the ground.

She slowly knelt down and shone the light on the small object.

A bone. Tiny, delicate. A child's finger bone.

Bonnie?

She felt faint and held on to the cardboard box to keep from falling to the ground.

Hold on. He wants you to hurt.

Oh, God, Bonnie . . .

Don't touch it. Don't touch anything. Maybe he's made a mistake this time.

See, she was getting better. She hadn't been able to leave the rib he'd left for her on the porch.

She could do it now. She could leave that fragile bone lying in the alley if it meant a chance at catching the bastard.

She struggled to her feet and turned off the flashlight.

Fight the pain. Walk.

Don't think of the bone. Don't think of Bonnie.

She couldn't save her daughter, but she might be able to save Jane and Mike.

Are you there, Dom? Go ahead, show me blood. Show me my daughter's bones. Everything you do is making me stronger.

I won't let you win this time.

# CHAPTER NINE

The man's throat had been slashed.

"Son of a bitch."

Joe looked up to see Barbara Eisley standing a few feet away. She took a step closer and looked down at the body that had been rolled into the bushes bordering the house. "The security guard?"

"What are you doing here?"

"Why shouldn't I be here? You wake me up in the middle of the night and tell me that you're coming out here to disturb my people and you expect me to just go back to sleep?" She glanced back at the halfway house in which every light was blazing. "This is my responsibility. Where's Jane MacGuire?"

"I don't know."

"The house mother says she's not in her room. The guard's dead. Could she be dead too?"

"She could be." When Eisley flinched, he added, "But I don't believe so. There was a knotted sheet hanging from her window."

"So she climbed down—and dropped right into a murderer's hands."

"Maybe not."

Eisley's gaze raked his face. "Eve Duncan." She swore

beneath her breath. "I told her to stay away from the kid."

"And she told you Jane was in danger. You wouldn't listen. You'd better pray Eve got to her before the man who killed your security guard did." He rose to his feet. "Don't let anyone touch anything or track around this area before the forensic team gets here."

"Where are you going?"

"To find Jane MacGuire."

"If Eve Duncan took her, it's kidnapping." She paused. "But since there are mitigating circumstances, if she returns the child within twenty-four hours, I might persuade the department not to press charges."

"I'll convey your generous offer to her. Providing she ever makes contact with me."

"You have to know where she is. That child has to be found." There was a hint of panic in her voice. "You're friends, aren't you?"

"I thought we were."

He could feel her gaze on him as he walked toward his car at the curb.

*You're friends, aren't you?*

Friends. Through all the years he'd forced himself to accept the relationship, and now she was even edging away from that.

At the worst possible time.

Screw friendship. Screw hope. I don't give a damn.

Just call and let me know that bastard hasn't gotten to you.


MARK PARKED THE car in front of the Peachtree apartment building. "Who lives here?"

"My mother and her fiancé," Eve answered. "She's the only one I could think of who'd be willing to take care of Mike."

Jane looked up at the thirteen-story high-rise. "Your mother?" she said doubtfully.

"She managed to raise me. I believe she can be trusted with Mike."

"Maybe."

Eve sighed with exasperation. Not only would she have to persuade Sandra to help, but her mother also had to win Jane's seal of approval. "He'll be safe here, Jane. The building has security, and my friend, Joe, arranged additional protection for my mother. He'll be fed and protected. What else can you ask for?"

Jane didn't answer as she headed for the front entrance with Mike trailing at her heels.

Eve looked at Mark. "Coming?"

"I don't think so. It's after one in the morning. I'd much rather face our serial killer than wake your mother and her boyfriend from a sound sleep and try to convince them to be instant parents. I'll wait here."

"Coward."

He smiled. "Yep."

She started after the children. She wasn't eager to face the task at hand either. She scarcely knew Ron Fitzgerald. She'd met him only once before she'd left for Tahiti. He'd seemed pleasant, smart, and genuinely devoted to her mother. But he owed Eve nothing.

Then she would tackle him first. Even though she hated imposing on Sandra, she didn't doubt her mother would help. She just didn't want to do anything that would mess up a relationship her mother obviously treasured. She'd ask her to take the kids into the kitchen and fix them something to eat, then explain the situation to Ron and appeal for his help.

"NO," RON SAID flatly. "I won't have Sandra involved in any illegal activities. Take the kids to the police."

"I can't do that. I told you—" Eve stopped and drew a deep breath. "I'm not asking you to accept Jane. That might put you both in danger. But Dom has no interest in Mike, or he would have killed him when he had the chance. I just need someone to take care of him until I can work my way through this mess."

"He's a runaway. There are serious repercussions for not returning him to his parents."

"For God's sake, according to Jane he's been on the street for days and no one's reported him missing. Do you think his parents care?"

"It's against the law."

And who should know better than a lawyer? "I need help, Ron."

"I can see you do, but Sandra is my concern. I'd like to help, but I can't afford to let her—"

"We'll do it." Her mother stood in the doorway. "Stop being a protective ass, Ron."

He turned to face her. "How long have you been standing there?"

"Long enough." She came toward them. "Do you think Eve would have come here if she'd had any other choice?"

"Let me take care of this, Sandra."

She shook her head. "That little boy is scared. We're not going to toss him back to his parents, and I'm not going to send Eve away when she needs me. I did that too many times when she was a kid." She paused. "But she's not your daughter. I can take Mike back to my own house."

He scowled. "The hell you will."

"Believe it." Her tone was quiet but firm. "We've been very happy, but there's more to my life than just you, Ron."

"Harboring a runaway is illegal, and I won't have you—"

"Did I ever tell you how many times Eve ran away when I was on crack?" She looked at Eve. "He doesn't mean to be hard. He's just never been there."

"I don't want to mess up anything for you, Mom."

"If taking a kid in from the cold can mess up what

Ron and I have, then it's not worth keeping." She turned back to Ron. "Is it?"

He stared at her for a moment, and then he gave a faint smile. "Damn you, Sandra." He shrugged. "Okay, you win. We tell the neighbors he's my brother's kid visiting from Charlotte."

Relief surged through Eve. "Thank you."

Sandra shook her head. "You're so stubborn about standing alone and not letting anyone help you. It's nice to be able to do something for you."

Eve warily glanced at Ron.

"It's okay. I don't like it, but it's okay." He slipped his arm around Sandra's waist. "But you stay away from her until this bastard is behind bars. Do you hear me? I won't have Sandra in danger."

"I didn't intend anything else. Keep your digital phone on, Mom. I'll call periodically to make sure everything's okay." She stood up. "Now I'll go and find Jane and get out of here."

"I'm ready." Jane stood in the doorway. "Mike's having another pancake, Mrs. Duncan. You'd better stop him or he'll have a bellyache tonight."

"Another? Good heavens, he's already had six." Sandra hurried toward the kitchen.

Jane came forward. "We should leave now. I've explained things to Mike, but he may make a fuss if he starts thinking about me leaving." She looked at Ron. "You take good care of him. He may be scared of you at first. His father is big like you."

"I'll take care of him."

She studied him. "You don't want to do it." She turned to Eve. "Maybe we shouldn't—"

"I said I'll take care of him," Ron said testily. "I don't have to like it. I promised and I'll do it."

Jane was still frowning.

Christ, she had to get her out of there. "Come on,

Jane." Eve pushed her toward the front door. "They'll be better off alone."

"I'm not sure that—"

Eve pulled her out into the hall and closed the door. "He'll be fine. Mom will take care of him."

"She doesn't cook very well. The pancakes were runny."

"Cooking isn't one of her talents. But she's a good person. You'd like her if you got to know her."

"I do like her. She's sort of like . . . Fay."

"And Fay was very protective, wasn't she?"

"Yes." Another silence. "That man."

"He's a nice guy. He won't hurt Mike."

"I don't like him."

Eve had liked him a lot better the first time she'd met him. But no one was perfect, and she should be glad he was protective of Sandra. "He's worried about my mother. Do you think I'd leave Mike if I wasn't certain?"

Jane stared at her with a frown and finally shook her head. "I guess not. Where are we going?"

"Someplace out of town where we can find a motel and get some sleep. I'm tired, aren't you?"

"Yes."

Eve could see Jane was exhausted. Her face was pinched and pale with strain and yet she had doggedly held on until Mike was settled.

Jane was silent until they got into the elevator. "Why?" she whispered. "Why is it happening?"

"I'll tell you, but not now. Trust me."

"Why should I?"

What could she say? After what Jane had gone through in the last twenty-four hours, why should she trust anyone? "I don't know. I'm not sure if I'd trust anyone either. I guess because I'm your best bet."

"That's not saying much."

Frustration made Eve speak sharply. "Well, it's all you'll get from me. It's all I can give you."

"You don't have to get nasty."

"Yes, I do. I feel nasty. I'm mad as hell and I don't need—" She bit her lower lip. "Sorry. Things are piling up on me."

Jane was silent until they reached the front entrance of the apartment building. "It's okay. I'd rather you be nasty and honest. I hate those soppy caseworkers who ooze all over me."

As a child, Eve had hated them too, but as an adult she felt bound to defend them. "They want only to do their—" Oh, what the devil. She was too tired for hypocrisy. "I promise I'll never ooze." She opened the back door of the car. "Jump in. We have to get out of here."

Mark looked over his shoulder at them. "I see we've lost one of our orphans."

"Mom will take care of him."

"So where to now?"

"Away from here. Fast. One of the first things the police will do to find me is talk to Mom. We're lucky we got here before they did. Go somewhere outside the city. A motel."

"Any preference?"

She shook her head. "Somewhere safe."

"Safe from Dom or safe from Joe Quinn?"

Joe.

Mark's narrowed gaze met hers in the rearview mirror. "Joe will find you, Eve."

She knew he would. It was only a matter of time. So she had to take advantage of that time. "I'll deal with Joe later."

He gave a low whistle. "Better you than me."

But no matter how much she dreaded it, she needed to call Joe at least one more time. She had to tell him about the scrawl on the cardboard box and the bone. Perhaps Dom had left some scrap of evidence.

He had made no detectable mistakes so far.

But wasn't he showing signs of recklessness? Mere hours after killing Fay Sugarton, he risked discovery by planting that bone only blocks from the crime scene.

Maybe he wasn't invulnerable. Maybe this time he'd left a clue to his identity.

So call Joe, take the flak, and tell him.

MARK GRUNARD DROVE them to a Motel 6 near Ellijay, Georgia. He arranged for a single room for himself and a double for Eve and Jane.

"As you ordered." He handed Eve a key. "I'll see you in the morning."

"Thanks, Mark."

"For what? I'd like to say I'm doing everything to save the kid, but I'm really interested only in the story."

"Thanks anyway."

She pushed Jane into the room and locked the door. "Bathroom. Wash up." Jesus, it was cold. She turned up the thermostat. "You can sleep in your underclothes tonight. I'll get you something else to wear tomorrow."

Jane yawned. "Okay."

She called Joe's digital number as soon as she was sure Jane was asleep in the twin bed next to her.

"Joe?"

"Where the *hell* are you?"

"I'm fine. And I have Jane MacGuire. She's safe."

"I've been hunting all over the city for you. Sandra wouldn't tell me a damn thing."

"Are the police bothering her?"

"Of course they are. What do you think?"

"Help her, Joe."

"As much as I can. She's not the one they want. Where are you?"

She didn't answer the question. "I just called to tell you there may be usable evidence in the alley off Luther Street. Dom left a message in blood on a cardboard box and a child's finger bone on the ground."

"Does the message say who the child is?"

"No."

*Bonnie.*

Close it out. Don't think about Bonnie.

"And I don't know who the blood belongs to."

"I do. The security guard at the welfare house you busted her out of."

"Christ." She shivered as she realized Dom might have already been preparing to go after Jane. "How long has he been dead?"

"We don't know yet. It was cold tonight. Time of death can be hard to determine when the body's been exposed to low temperatures. The last time anyone saw him was about eight-fifteen."

So his death could have occurred in the early evening, hours before she appeared on the scene. The eerie feeling she'd had as she had stood beneath Jane's window could have been imagination.

"Which makes you both a kidnapper and a suspect in a murder," Joe said.

"Murder?"

"You were at the scene. Though I don't believe anyone's going to seriously believe you're a murderer."

"That's comforting."

"But you'll be considered at least a material witness, and you'll be wanted for questioning. And then there's the kidnapping. There's an APB on you."

"You know why I had to get Jane out of there. Dom told me if I didn't, he'd go in after her."

"I thought as much." His voice was without expression. "It would have been nice if you'd called me and talked it over."

God, he was angry. "I had to do it myself."

"Did you? If I recall, I'm involved up to my neck. Why did you decide to cross me off your list?"

"You know why. I had to get Jane away even if I broke the law. You're a cop, Joe."

"You think that would have stopped me from helping? I'd have done it *for* you, dammit."

"I know." She swallowed to ease the tightness of her throat. "I couldn't allow it."

"You couldn't allow—" He had to stop to temper his tone. "Who the hell gave you the right to make my decisions for me?"

"I took the right."

"And you shut me out."

"I shut you out. Stay out, Joe."

"Oh, no. I've let you sweep me into the background too many times. I can take that but I won't have you walk away from me."

"I wouldn't be a good friend to you if I let you—"

"Screw friendship." His voice was hoarse with barely contained violence. "I'm sick to death of it. Just as I'm sick of standing on the sidelines and having you treat me like some old hound that needs nothing more than an occasional pat on the head."

Shock surged through her. "Joe."

"It's happened too often, Eve."

"The hell it has."

"The hell it hasn't. You're not even aware of it. You block everything out, and what you don't block out, you interpret to suit yourself. You'll hang up the phone tonight and you won't look beyond what you want to see."

"I've never taken you for granted," she said in an uneven voice, "and I've never treated you as anything but my very dear friend."

"Then why didn't you tell me? Why don't you tell me where you are?" He took a deep breath and then his voice lowered persuasively. "Last chance. Let me come to you now. Afterward I'll step back. I'll let you bury your head and not—"

"I can't. You can't help me. Not this time."

He didn't speak for a moment, and she could sense his emotions seething in that silence. "Your choice. You know, I'm almost relieved. But I'll find you. I'm not going to let you close me out, and I'll be damned if I'm going to let that son of a bitch kill you."

"I don't want you to look for me. If you call me, I'll hang up. Do you understand?"

"I'll find you." He hung up.

She was shaking as she punched the off button. Joe was one of the bedrocks of her life, and she felt as if that rock had exploded beneath her feet. She had seen him angry before, but this was different. He had attacked her. He had said terrible, false things. She had never taken him for granted. She didn't know what life would be like without Joe. Why couldn't he understand she was doing only what was best for him?

Smother the hurt. Go to sleep. Try to forget.

She turned off the light on the nightstand.

*I'll find you.*

His words had sounded like a threat. The intimidating Joe she had spoken to tonight was the tough cop, the ex-SEAL. Relentless, unswerving, deadly.

Nonsense. Joe would never threaten her. Joe was closer than a brother, more protective than a father.

*You treat me like some old hound that needs nothing more than an occasional pat on the head.*

She couldn't think about Joe. She didn't need any more turmoil in her life.

*You block everything out.*

Hell, yes, she'd block out Joe for now and she'd be damned if she'd feel guilty.

She closed her eyes, ignoring the stinging behind her lids. Go to sleep. Tomorrow she would find a way to make sure Jane was safe from Dom. That was much more urgent than Joe's hurt feelings and lack of understanding. That could be solved later. It was Jane who was important now.

*I'm sick of standing on the sidelines.*

God, it wasn't that she thought Joe was less import—

Don't think of him. The message beneath those words was as disturbing as a volcano ready to erupt. She'd always known it was there but had chosen not to see it. And she couldn't permit herself to see it now.

She turned over, willing herself to go to sleep.

*I'll find you. . . .*

HER PHONE RANG, rousing her from sleep.

Joe? She wouldn't answer. She couldn't face any more arguments or—

It rang again.

Dammit, she had to answer or risk Jane being woken up.

She kept her voice to a whisper. "Hello."

"Did you go to the alley off Luther Street?"

Dom.

"Yes."

"Then you must have our sweet Jane. I thought she'd insist on going to help her little friend. She appears very fond of him. It's the kind of thing you would have done as a child, isn't it? Did I mention how much alike you are?"

"You killed the security guard."

"Just helping you a little. He would have gotten in your way. How did you get her out? The drainpipe? I had considered it, but—"

"Why are you calling?"

"I like to hear your voice. Do you realize how full of tension and emotion you are? I can hear every nuance of it. It's very exciting."

"I'm hanging up."

"Then I guess I'd better get down to the business of guiding you in the direction I want you to go. It's too dangerous for either of us to remain in Atlanta. They could arrest you for kidnapping, and that would spoil everything. You wouldn't be able to bond with Jane and

I'd have to slit her throat. I'm sure you'd surround her with protection, so it would be a very difficult kill."

Her hand tightened on the phone. "If I were arrested, you would have no reason to kill Jane. Your little scenario would be spoiled."

"But I gave my word," he said gently. "I always keep my word. So you have to be careful not to get caught, don't you? That's why I want you to leave Atlanta."

"Are you afraid I might find you if I stayed?"

"On the contrary, I like raising your hopes. The idea of you searching for me is wonderfully stimulating. It's been a long time since I've felt this much excitement. I was always so concerned about making the kill perfect and undetectable, I never realized I needed a certain amount of interaction."

"You won't get it if I'm hiding away somewhere."

"I don't want you to hide away. I just want you out of Atlanta. I think it's time for you to take a trip to Phoenix."

"What?"

"I've always liked Phoenix."

"I know. You've killed there."

"You know that?"

"The FBI already has a fix on two murders you committed there years ago. So you're not as clever as you thought. We'll get you, Dom."

"Not from those kills. You won't find any evidence. I was very careful, and time will have erased what I didn't. It's only lately that I may have been bored enough to make a mistake. You have a small chance of catching me if you find a fresh kill."

"What are you talking about?"

"I think it fitting that you find the woman who brought us together. She wasn't very interesting, but that kill made me finally realize that there was something very wrong and eventually led me to you. She showed me the light, and then I showed *her* the light."

"In Phoenix?"

"Ah, you're beginning to sound eager."

"What was her name?"

"I don't remember. It didn't matter."

"When?"

"Five or six months perhaps. I can't remember. There was an earlier kill who gave me a hint of my problem, but she was the one who lit the way. It's important that the way be lighted for us, isn't it? Find her, Eve, and you may find me."

"Tell me where she is."

"You know better than that. You have to work for it." He paused. "She had a lovely voice, I understand. A soprano."

"She was a singer?"

"Go to Phoenix. Take Jane with you. Cling to her, nurture her . . . mother her. Did you find the bone?"

"Damn you."

He laughed. "You may have the complete set soon, and I'll have to start again. Doesn't Jane have an interesting bone structure?"

Don't lose your temper. He wanted to flay her with words so he would get a response. "Scatter all the bones you please. They're not Bonnie's."

"You did that very well. I could almost believe you meant it. Go to Phoenix, Eve."

"You bastard, why should I do anything you want me to do?"

"Phoenix. That's my last word on the subject." He hung up.

The last word. How many last words had the son of a bitch heard over the years? How many screams, how many pleas?

Had the woman in Phoenix pleaded with him before he killed her?

"It was him, wasn't it?" Jane asked out of the darkness.

Oh, shit.

"The man who killed Fay? Why did he call you?"

"It's a long story, Jane."

"I heard you say he wanted to kill me. Why? I didn't do anything to him. Neither did Fay."

"I told you he wasn't sane."

"But why does he want to kill me?" Jane's tone was fierce. "You *tell* me, Eve."

Eve hesitated. How much could she explain without terrifying the poor kid?

"Tell me."

Forget trying to be kind and soothing. Jane needed to know the threat and where it was coming from. If she'd made Bonnie more knowledgeable about the beasts out there, maybe she'd still be alive.

"Okay." She turned on the light. "I'll tell you, Jane."

"HE DIDN'T WRITE with his finger," Spiro told Joe, who waited by his car in the entrance to the alley. "That would have been too lucky. We found a stick with blood on one end behind the box. We'll probably find wood particles in the blood on the box. We'll examine the stick for fiber, since he probably wore gloves. What the hell was he doing here anyway?"

"I've no idea." Joe's gaze remained fastened on the four agents who were still swarming about the cardboard box. "Eve didn't confide in me. She just told me about the box and the bone."

"She must have been pretty shook up."

"No doubt." Joe got back in the car. "How fast can you process the tests?"

"Couple of days."

"Odds are the blood's the security guard's." He started the car. "Let me know as soon as you can."

"Where is she, Joe?"

"I don't know."

"Kidnapping's a serious offense."

"I know that." He lifted his gaze to meet Spiro's. "And you know why she took her."

"That's not my business. It's the court's. It's my job to catch her."

"Your job is to catch Dom. For God's sake, get your priorities straight."

Spiro smiled faintly. "My priorities *are* straight. I want Eve because she's my strongest lead to Dom." His gaze narrowed on Joe's face. "Where is she, Joe?"

"I told you, I don't know."

His brows lifted in surprise. "My God, maybe you don't."

"But I'm going to find out." He looked away from Spiro and said stiltedly, "I'd appreciate any information you can give me."

"My, that was hard for you, wasn't it? You must be desperate."

"I have to find her."

"I was wondering why you didn't try to talk your department out of issuing that APB on her. You want her found even if it means she gets tossed in jail."

"You didn't try to stop the APB either. You don't want her running around or hiding someplace where you can't contact her."

Spiro didn't answer.

"Will you tell me if you find out anything?"

"Maybe." Spiro shrugged. "Okay. Not that I have any faith that you'd return the favor."

Joe started the car. "Don't be too sure. Wherever Eve is, Dom is. I might need your help."

Spiro was still standing there as Joe drove off. He looked grimmer and more tired than ever in the harsh headlights. Would he call Joe if he got a lead on Eve? Joe wasn't sure. So don't trust Spiro to tell him.

All right, he had done all he could here.

Now it was time to stop feeling and start thinking.

And then go on the hunt.

• • •

"IT DOESN'T MAKE sense," Jane said. "I don't have anything to do with you. Neither did Fay."

"I know."

"I hate it. I hate you."

Eve flinched. She should have expected Jane's reaction. "I don't blame you. But the fact exists that Dom is a danger to you. You have to let me help protect you."

"I don't have to do anything."

"All right, you don't have to do anything. You can run away and maybe Dom won't find you. You can get yourself picked up by welfare and let the police protect you." She paused. "But you told me you don't trust the police."

Jane glared at her.

"Or you can go with me and work with me to keep yourself safe."

"I don't want to go anywhere with you." She was silent a moment. "You're going to Phoenix, aren't you? You're going to do what he wants."

"I don't think I have any choice, do you? He has to be caught, Jane."

"Yes." She lay as stiff as a stick in the bed. "He killed Fay. She never did anything to him and he killed her. I hate him. I hate the son of a bitch."

"So do I. We, at least, have that in common."

"He really thinks I'm your daughter? He's got to be crazy."

"I believe he just wants me to consider you my daughter."

She was silent a moment. "Was Bonnie much like me?"

Eve shook her head. "No. She was younger, softer, dreamier. You're more like what I was when I was growing up."

"I'm nothing like you."

"Have it your way."

"I will."

"But I believe you'll be safe as long as you stay with me. He wants us together. Will you come with me, Jane?"

Jane turned her back on Eve.

Don't push. Let her think. She's smart.

Eve turned out the light. "Let me know in the morning."

No answer.

What would she do if Jane refused to go with her? The question scared her to death.

She would face that possibility when it confronted her.

*You bury your head.*

And she wouldn't think about Joe or his unfair words. They stung too much.

Joe . . .

"What do you mean? Softer?"

"What?"

"Your daughter."

"I loved her very much. I wanted everything to be sweet and sunny for her. I've been thinking lately that maybe if I'd shown her—Never mind."

"You're saying you were stupid. Like I was about not talking to Fay."

"I guess that's what I'm saying."

Another silence. "I don't think you're stupid very often."

"Once is enough."

"Yeah."

Christ, she was saying all the wrong things. Jane was feeling guilty enough. "Fay's death had nothing to do with you, Jane. If there's someone besides Dom who was responsible, it's me. Let me try to make sure you don't get hurt too."

Minutes passed.

Go to sleep. She's not going to answer.

"I'll go with you," Jane said.

Eve breathed a profound sigh of relief. "Good."

"Not because I like you. I don't feel anything for you. I wouldn't care if he killed you. But I hate *him*. I hate what he did to Fay. I hate what he wants to do to me. I wish someone would slit his throat."

"I understand."

Yes, she understood the hatred and helplessness Jane was feeling as if the emotions were her own.

As if Jane were her own.

She instantly rejected the idea. It was what Dom wanted, the growing closeness and empathy, and she would not let him have it. Keep Jane at a distance. It should be easy. Jane was tough and wanted nothing to do with Eve.

She hadn't been very tough with Mike. When she had smiled at him, she had reminded Eve a little of Bonnie. The same luminous, loving quality . . .

Crazy.

Bonnie and Jane were nothing alike.

Thank God.

So stop thinking of either of them. Think instead of how to keep Jane safe in Phoenix.

And stop letting Dom call all the shots.

It was time to go on the hunt.

Her phone rang again.

What the hell?

"PHOENIX?" MARK'S TONE was thoughtful. "It is a long way from Atlanta. You might have a better chance of hiding the kid there." Standing outside McDonald's, Mark looked at Jane, who was inside, seated at a booth eating breakfast.

"Bull," Eve told him. "There's no place that's a long way from anywhere these days. You guys in the media have made sure of that."

"Technology has a little something to do with it."

Mark took a drink of his coffee. "Going to Phoenix is a big risk, isn't it?"

"It's a bigger risk staying here."

"What about protection for the kid?"

"I have an idea what I can do."

"But you won't tell me?"

She shook her head.

"And that means you don't want me to go with you to Phoenix."

She shook her head again. "No one knows you're involved in my taking Jane. You've helped me enough."

"For a reason. I want the story, Eve. You *owe* it to me."

"I'll call you when I'm getting close."

"And I'm to trust you?"

"I won't turn my back on you."

He studied her. "I don't think you will." He shrugged. "Okay, I'll go back to work. I might run into something that'll help you. You'll let me know where you are?"

"I'll let you know."

"How are you going to get there?"

"I hope you'll let me borrow your car. I'll drive it to Birmingham and leave it at the airport."

"And how will you get on a plane without being recognized? You have to have an ID to go to the bathroom these days."

"I'll manage."

"I could drive you to Phoenix."

"You've done enough."

"Just thought I'd give it a shot." He glanced at Jane again. "She's not going to give you any trouble?"

"I didn't say that. She's wary of everyone, and that includes me. She hasn't said more than two sentences since we got up this morning. But at least I can reason with her." She held out her hand. "Thanks for everything, Mark."

He shook it and then dropped his car keys into her

palm. "Remember, you owe me. I'm letting you off the hook right now, but I want that story."

"You'll get it." She started for the booth where Jane was sitting.

"Eve."

She looked back over her shoulder.

Mark's gaze narrowed on her face. "You're too damn confident this morning."

She made a face. "I wish I were."

"You're in better shape than you were last night."

"Things always look brighter in the morning."

"Not necessarily. I think you have an ace in the hole you're not telling me about."

She waved. "Good-bye, Mark. I'll be in touch."

He was wrong. She wasn't at all confident; she was scared and confused. What Mark had seen as confidence was only the faint glimmer of hope.

But she'd take it.


HE WAS WAITING at the parking lot at the Birmingham airport.

"You're an idiot." Logan drew Eve close and kissed her hard. "And Joe's a criminal idiot to allow you to get into a mess like this."

"Joe had nothing to do with it." She felt a deep sense of comfort as she stepped back and stared at him. He looked dear and strong and familiar. "He doesn't know anything about it."

"You made sure of that to protect the SOB."

"Let's not talk about Joe." She gestured for Jane to get out of the car. "Did you bring the ID?"

He handed her a leather pouch. "Cash, phony birth certificates, two credit cards, and a driver's license."

"Is he a crook?" Jane asked.

Logan glanced at her. "It depends on who you ask."

"On the streets they sell phony IDs to anyone who wants one."

"I don't sell, I buy. And you should be glad I was able to buy these at such short notice."

"This is John Logan, Jane. He's not a crook, he's a well-respected businessman."

"And he's the one you said would help us?"

"We couldn't board a flight without phony IDs."

"I've arranged a place for you to stay—it's on the outskirts of Phoenix. Two of my company's top security people will be there to keep an eye on you." He took Eve's elbow. "Come on, let's go."

"We say good-bye here." She hung back. "I don't want to be seen with you, Logan."

"You're not going to say good-bye to me until we reach Phoenix. I have a private jet waiting. That way you won't have to chance being recognized."

"No." She dug in her heels. "I know I agreed to let you help me when you called last night, but I don't want you to do anything more."

"Too late." He smiled. "I can handle the heat. Just watch me."

"I don't want to watch you. I don't want to be responsible for anyone else getting involved in this mess."

His smile faded. "Listen to me. I'm not backing away when you're in trouble. You should have called me instead of letting me hear secondhand from one of my associates in Atlanta."

"Associates? Are you having me watched, Logan?"

"Just keeping an eye on the situation." His lips tightened. "I couldn't be sure what Joe would do to keep you here."

"Joe's my friend, and he's done—"

"Okay." He held up a hand to stop her. "I'm just glad that you called on me instead of him. Too bad I won't see him. I'd like to rub his nose in it."

"He has more to lose than you. He's a cop and you're—"

"Just another philistine tycoon." Logan pushed her

across the lot toward the exit. "With enough money to cover my tracks. So use me, dammit." He glanced at Jane, who had fallen into step with them. "Am I making sense, kid?"

She studied him. "Yes. Use him, Eve."

He looked a little surprised. "Very cool."

"I don't use people," Eve said. "Not if I can help it."

"Why not?" Jane asked. "He wants you to do it. We might need him."

"Very clear-thinking child." He tilted his head. "How about participating in my executive training program? I have a lot of employees who—"

"Is that supposed to make me feel good?" Jane gave him a disgusted glance. "Use him, Eve."

"The child's obviously of the opinion I'm not worth anything else," he murmured. "Use me, Eve."

"I'll let you take us to Phoenix," Eve said. "After that you get away from me, Logan."

"We'll discuss it in Phoenix."

It was almost dark when Logan drove up to the small red-tiled house near Scottsdale. She could catch just a glimpse of the house through the thick stand of trees and ornate Spanish-style gates.

Logan got out of the car, pressed a code into the panel by the gates, and the gates swung open. He returned to the car. "There are two remotes in a drawer in the hall," he told Eve. "Use them so you won't have to get out of the car. There are two security guards in a cottage to the north of the house. Herb Booker and Juan Lopez. They'll make the rounds regularly, but they won't bother you unless you press an alarm button."

"And where are the alarm buttons?"

"Kitchen, master bath, bedroom, living room beside the phones. You'll never be farther than a few feet from one."

"You seem to know the setup pretty well."

"I use this house when I come here for business. A little security never hurts."

"Are you sure he's not a crook?" Jane asked Eve.

"Charming," Logan said, amused.

"I'm sure." Eve got out of the car. "He's like a politician. They always have to have someone around to protect them."

"Ouch." Logan unlocked the front door. "Knowing the way you feel about them, I'd rather you think I'm like a crook. Why can't I convince you that there are honest, stalwart politicians out there?"

"We've always agreed to disagree." She pushed Jane in ahead of her and turned to face Logan. "Thank you. Go."

"There are two extra guest rooms."

"Go."

"I'm going to find the kitchen and make a sandwich." Jane moved down the hall away from them.

"See, she couldn't bear to see me cast out. I think she likes me. Smart girl."

"Only you could translate indifference into affection." Eve crossed her arms over her chest. "Go."

"She's not indifferent to me. We'd get along once we got used to each other. She reminds me a little of you when we first met."

"She's *nothing* like me."

He gave a low whistle. "Evidently, I said the wrong thing."

"Go, Logan. Please."

He smiled and stroked her cheek with a finger. "I'm going. I'm flattered you care so much about protecting me."

Joe had not been flattered. Joe had been angry and completely unreasonable, damn him.

"Is there anything else I can do for you?"

"I assume there's a computer and plenty of search software."

"Come on, I *manufacture* computers. The office also has an excellent library."

"Then, that's all I need."

"You'll find clothes for both of you in the two main bedrooms. I'm not sure Jane's will fit. She's kind of small for a ten-year-old."

"She's big enough to be a presence."

"I noticed." He leaned forward and kissed her. "Then I'm on my way. If you need me I'll be at the Camelback Inn."

"Dammit, Logan, I meant for you to go back to Monterey."

"I know you did." He started down the steps. "I'll leave you this rental car. I'll go to the cottage and get a lift to the hotel from one of the security guys."

"You listen to me, Logan. I've already taken more than I should from you. I'll feel guilty as hell if I get you in trouble."

"Good. Guilt can be useful in the hands of a clever man, and it shows you care about me."

"There was never any doubt about that, and you know it. After all we've been through together, I'd have to be a robot not to care about you."

He smiled back at her over his shoulder. "That's what I'm banking on."

"Logan."

He shook his head. "No, Eve. You can keep me from living in the same house with you, but you can't keep me from being nearby." He winked. "Besides, I'm anticipating the moment when Joe finds out that I'm the one who's been helping you."

Before she could answer he'd disappeared around the side of the house.

She should probably never have let him help her. Logan didn't know the meaning of a limited involvement.

No, that wasn't really true. He'd been very careful about observing the parameters she'd put on their relationship. He never moved too fast or too far for her. Considering his dominant nature, it must have been very difficult for him, and she valued him all the more for it.

At least, this time she had won a partial victory. With Logan, that was a major accomplishment. She'd worry later about convincing him to leave. For now she had work to do. But first, she needed to call Mom and check on her.

She crossed to the foyer table and dialed her mother's digital number. Sandra answered on the third ring.

"Everything okay?" Eve asked.

"Yes and no. Your killer hasn't shown up, but Ron was ready to strangle Mike himself. I don't think anyone ever made him take a bath before. He was ready to hit the streets again."

"Damn."

"Don't worry. They worked it out. Ron likes a challenge. He bribed him. He told him he'd bring home dinner from McDonald's each day he took a bath." Her mother chuckled. "He jumped at it. I think I'm insulted."

"All kids like McDonald's."

"Don't try to spare my feelings. We both know I'm a lousy cook. How are you?"

"Fine. I'll try to call you every other night. If there's any problem, even a suspicion of one, you call me."

"I will." Sandra paused. "Joe has no idea where you are or what you're doing."

"I thought it best."

"He's wound tight as a wire, Eve. I've never seen him that way before."

"Don't tell him anything."

"He's our friend. I'd feel better if he were with you. Why can't I—"

"No, Mom."

"Okay." She sighed. "But he's going to nag the hell out of me."

"You're tough. You can take it."

"He's tougher. But he likes me, so he won't run over me. Are you going to tell me where you are?"

"Phoenix."

"And I'm not to tell Joe."

"Please."

"It's a mistake."

"I've got to go, Mom. Take care."

"*You* take care."

Eve slowly hung up. Joe was doing what he did best, hunting. What would his next move—

"Want a sandwich?" Jane stood behind her. "It's turkey. I made two."

"Thanks." She wasn't hungry, but the overture was the first Jane had made since she'd agreed to come to Phoenix. "I'd like that." Eve followed her down the hall toward the kitchen. "I guess we're on our own as far as food is concerned. I'm afraid I'm not much of a cook."

"You've got to be better than your mother." She hopped up on a stool at the breakfast bar.

"You might change your mind. I haven't had much experience."

They ate in companionable silence.

"I can help," Jane suddenly offered. "I did most of the cooking in one foster home I was in."

"Was that at the Carbonis? Mrs. Eisley said you had a rough time with them."

"I did okay." Jane finished her sandwich. "You want me to help clean up?"

"There's not much to do. I can handle it." She had an idea. "Logan says there's a good library. I don't know if there's anything that you might want to read, but—"

"Books?" Her face lit up. "There are books here?"

"So Logan says."

Jane quickly covered the flicker of excitement. "I might take a look at them. There's probably nothing else to do." She got down from the stool, took her plate to the sink, and turned on the water. "Logan likes you. Do you sleep with him?"

Eve blinked. For God's sake, the kid was only ten. Ten but no child, Eve reminded herself. She'd probably been through more in her short life than a woman of thirty. "That's none of your business."

Jane shrugged. "He's doing a lot for us. I just wondered if you have to pay him."

Sex for pay. Another aspect of life on the streets.
Day-to-day contact with prostitutes had been a part of
Eve's childhood, and, of course, Jane had been exposed
to the same life. "No, Logan's my friend. Friends don't
ask to be paid. He's a good guy." She added with a
smile, "And he's *not* a crook."

"I didn't really think he was. I just wondered if I
could piss him off."

"Jane."

"He didn't mind. He's pretty tough. Where's the library?"

"I have no idea."

She started for the door. "I'll find it."

"If you don't mind, take your books to another room
after you choose them. I need to work at the computer."

"Why?"

"I need to see if I can access back issues of the local
newspaper."

"Oh, to find that murdered woman?"

She nodded. "I don't have a lot to go on. Dom was
very careful not to give me too much information. Just
that the murder happened five or six months ago, she
was a singer, and that her body hasn't been found. So
I'm looking for a disappearance, not a murder."

"I'll stay out of your way." Jane vanished down the
hall.

At least she didn't have to worry about keeping the
child amused. It was clear Jane was an avid reader and
eager to find the library. As for Eve, she'd grab a
shower, change into jeans and a shirt, and hit the computer.

"YOU WANT ANY coffee?" Jane put the carafe and a cup
down on the desk beside Eve. "It's pretty strong. I don't
know how to make it any other way."

"That's fine." Eve leaned back in the chair and rubbed her eyes. "You didn't have to do this."

"If I'd had to, I wouldn't have." Jane curled up in a leather chair across the room. "You're not finding anything, are you?"

Eve shook her head. "I've gone back seven months. Maybe he was lying to me." She poured coffee. "It's after midnight. You should be in bed."

"Why?"

"Aren't you tired?"

Jane lifted her chin. "Aren't you?"

She was too tired for challenges at the moment. She made a face. "Yes, maybe I'll put you to work on this and go to bed."

"I'll try. But we work on Macs at school. What's that computer?"

"A Logan." Kids these days were so far ahead of where Eve had been at the same age.

"Logan?"

"John Logan makes computers."

"Like Bill Gates?"

"Sort of. But hardware, not software. And they're nothing alike. Did you find something to read?"

She nodded. "A book about some scientists who are trying to locate Troy. It's pretty cool." She paused. "And a book about forensic sculpting. You told me that's what you do for a living. Does it belong to you?"

"No, Logan hired me to work on a case and he believes in doing his research."

"The pictures are icky."

Eve nodded.

"Can you really do that?"

"I really can."

"Why?"

"It's my job. And sometimes I can help make parents feel a little better about losing someone."

"They should just go on and not think about them."

"Is that what you do?"

"Sure. Why not?" Jane stared at her defiantly. "I haven't thought about Fay since he killed her. She's dead. Why should I?"

Eve stared skeptically at her.

"It's true. I've thought about the creep who did it but not her." She got to her feet. "I'm going to bed." She strode out of the room.

So full of pain. What would it take to get such a damaged child to lower the walls she'd built around herself? Eve mustn't try to overcome that barrier. It would be the most dangerous course to follow just then.

The safest thing to do for both of them was to find the missing woman. Provided Dom had really killed that woman. As she'd told Jane, he might have lied to lure her out of Atlanta.

But why Phoenix?

He'd said he liked the city. Maybe there was something about the atmosphere here that triggered—

Stop analyzing and get to work. There had been nothing helpful in the paper during the five- to seven-month period Dom had specified. Maybe she should go back further. Or maybe not. Check the recent editions . . .

JANUARY 30. Not even a month ago.

Debby Jordan was in her early thirties, married, the mother of two boys. She had disappeared on the way to choir practice.

*I'm told she had a lovely voice. A soprano.*

Eve scanned the initial story about the disappearance and then several follow-up stories.

Her husband had found her car in the church parking lot when she hadn't come home.

An investigation had turned up nothing.

The church had offered a two-thousand-dollar reward for any information.

Choir members had been interviewed and spoken of

her kindness and the loveliness of her voice. "A soprano
sweet as an angel's."

Several heartrending pictures of her husband and two
little boys . . .

Debby Jordan.

Eve leaned back in her chair and closed her eyes.
How Dom must have enjoyed throwing out lies and de-
ceptive hints. You made it hard enough, but I've found
her, Dom, you son of a bitch.

She felt too sick to feel any sense of accomplishment.
A woman with everything to live for had died. Eve
couldn't do anything about her death. But she could
find the man who had killed her. The first step was to
locate Debby Jordan's body.

Okay. Since Dom had wanted her to do just that, he
would have given her some other clue. Think. Remember every word he'd spoken regarding Debby Jordan.

*She showed me the light, and then I showed her the
light.*

*She was the one who lit the way.*

*It's important that the way be lighted for us, isn't it?*

She slowly straightened in her chair.

It was possible, if Dom wasn't making an ass of her.

*The Indians called the falls "the place of tumbling
moonlight."*

Talladega Falls.

What had Charlie said about the two Phoenix killings?

*Two skeletons were found three months ago in
San Luz.*

She jumped up and strode to the bookshelves. A dic-
tionary. Pray that Logan had a Spanish-English dictio-
nary. She found one and quickly rifled through it.

*San*—saint.

Her hands were shaking as she thumbed through the
pages once more.

*Luz*—light.

Yes!

*Light.*

She drew a deep breath.

I've got it, you bastard. I've *got* it. Now give me a little more time and I'll find Debby Jordan.

She leaned forward and accessed the Internet search engine. Then she typed in one word.

*Cadaver.*

"WHERE ARE WE going?" Jane asked as she looked out the car window at the cactus-dotted terrain. "We're out in the desert."

"We'll be there soon."

"Where?"

"I told you I need help to find Debby Jordan. There's someone out here who may be able to give me that help."

Jane glanced over her shoulder. "There's someone following us."

"I know. It's one of Logan's security people."

"Oh." Jane looked back out the window. "It's ugly out here. Flat and brown. I like it better at home."

"Me too. But it's getting greener the closer we come to the mountains."

"A little."

Where was the turnoff? The directions in the Internet ad had been precise, but all she'd seen had been— There it was!

A wooden sign with an arrow and a single name painted on it.

PATRICK.

She turned left onto a bumpy dirt road. One more mile should bring her to the ranch.

"Patrick?"

"That's the name of the person who's going to help us. Sarah Patrick. She trains dogs for a living."

Jane's face lit with a smile. "Dogs?"

It was the first time she'd smiled since she'd left her friend Mike.

"These are working dogs, Jane. Not pets."

"What kind of work?"

"Obedience training. But I researched and found a few stories about her in the local newspapers. She belongs to a volunteer search and rescue team based in Tucson, and she's also affiliated with the ATF. She and her dog were at the Oklahoma City bombing a few years ago, in Tegucigalpa after Hurricane Mitch, and in Iran after the earthquake last year."

"What did they do there?"

"They tried to find survivors buried in the rubble." She paused. "And later they searched for the bodies of the dead. Evidently Ms. Patrick's dog has a very good nose."

"He smelled the bodies?"

"That's what search and rescue dogs are trained to do. They're pretty smart. The Atlanta PD uses special cadaver dogs occasionally."

"And that's what you want him to do? Find that woman Dom killed?"

Eve nodded. "Look, there's the ranch."

If it could be called a ranch. A log cabin, several spacious wire-pen enclosures, and a large corral that was equipped with apparatus that could have belonged in a child's playground. An old Jeep with faded, chipped green paint was parked on one side of the cabin.

"No dogs," Jane said, disappointed. "The pens are empty. She must not be a very good trainer if nobody wants to hire her."

Eve parked in front of the cabin. "Don't jump to conclusions. Maybe this is a slow time for her. Every business has its—"

The door swung open and a woman dressed in tan shorts and a plaid shirt came out of the cabin. "You lost?"

"Sarah Patrick?"

The woman nodded. "Don't tell me. You're from Publishers Clearing House. Where are my flowers and the six-foot check?"

Eve blinked.

"I guess you're not." Sarah Patrick sighed. "Too bad. The cash would probably have corrupted me, but I could have used the flowers. I can't grow anything out here. The soil's too sandy." Smiling, she stepped closer and looked in the window at Jane. "But kids are as good as flowers. My name's Sarah, what's yours?"

"Jane."

"It's a hot day. Come inside and have some lemonade, Jane." Her glance shifted to Eve. "You too, I suppose. Unless you're from the IRS. Then I'll sic my dog on you."

Eve smiled. "I'm Eve Duncan. You're safe. I came to offer you a job."

"No one's safe from the IRS. I make barely enough money to support myself and Monty, but I'm self-employed, so my tax returns always get noticed. They never understand when I claim Monty as a dependent."

Eve followed Sarah Patrick into the house. "Monty?"

"That's Monty." The woman nodded toward the fireplace.

A golden retriever lying full-length on the floor lifted his head, yawned, and wagged his tail.

"Lazy beast." Sarah went to the refrigerator. "We just came back from a five-mile run and *I'm* not in a state of collapse."

"You don't have all that hair," Jane said indignantly as she went down to her knees beside the dog. "He got hot."

Monty looked up at her with mournful eyes and then licked her hand.

Jane was melting, Eve saw in surprise. She turned to

Sarah. "He's beautiful, but I can see how you'd have trouble with the IRS."

Sarah smiled. "It amused me to see if I could get away with it. Everything was fine until they audited me." She poured lemonade into two glasses. "I don't think Jane wants to be interrupted yet. Sit down." She went over to the sink and leaned against it. "I'll take pity and stay downwind of you. I haven't had a chance to shower yet."

She did have a gleam of perspiration on her tanned face and legs. Sarah Patrick was possibly in her late twenties, of medium height with short dark brown hair and a wiry, slim body. She wasn't a pretty woman, but her large, sparkling brown eyes and well-shaped mouth were appealing. What made her arresting was the forceful energy she exuded.

"She your kid?" Sarah's gaze was on Jane. "She's very loving. Loving's good."

Jane *was* being loving, Eve noticed. Who would have guessed that Jane would succumb to a retriever? "No, she's not mine."

"I like kids."

"You don't have any of your own?"

She shook her head. "I don't even have a husband." Her eyes twinkled. "Thank God. I have enough trouble."

"You're alone here?" Eve frowned. "You shouldn't advertise where you live."

"I get lonely. I can take care of myself." She looked at the retriever. "And I have a great guard dog. Didn't you notice?"

The guard dog had rolled over on his back in the most submissive position and caught Jane's hand playfully between his front paws. He made a *woo-woo* sound and stretched his neck to nibble at Jane's wrist.

"Yeah, sure," Eve said doubtfully.

Sarah chuckled. "I can see you aren't confident about my training program. Monty isn't a very good example. He has a few psychological problems. He's not sure which one of us is the dog."

"He's adorable."

Sarah's face softened. "You know it." She set the glass down on the sink. "Who recommended me as a trainer?"

"I found you on the Internet."

"I'd forgotten I'd posted an ad. That was years ago, and no one's ever answered it. I guess the directions out here are kind of discouraging." Her gaze narrowed on Eve's face. "Why weren't you discouraged?"

"I need you."

"There must be a dog trainer closer to where you live."

"I need a cadaver dog."

Sarah stiffened. "I should have known. Who are you with? ATF? Did Madden send you?"

"No ATF. No IRS. I don't know any Madden."

"I wish I didn't. That's one plus on your side." She shook her head. "I'm not interested. Are you with a police department? I can give you the names of several handlers who work with the police."

"I want you. According to the newspapers, you're the best in the business."

"I'm not the best. Monty's the best."

"Well, I don't believe he'll make a deal with me."

"Neither will I."

"Please. It should take only a few days."

Sarah shook her head.

"You don't appear too busy. I'll pay you more than your usual fee."

"I said no."

"Why not?"

"I don't like searching for cadavers."

"But you do it."

She glanced away. "Yes, I do it."

"Then do it for me."

"I think it's time you left."

Eve rose to her feet. "Please think about it. I need you."

"Well, I don't need this job." She turned toward Jane and the dog. "Come on, Monty. It's time you stopped making an idiot of yourself." She snapped her fingers.

What happened next was amazing. Monty rolled over, leaped to his feet, and was by Sarah's side in the space of seconds. His entire demeanor had changed. He was alert, charged with energy, and gazed at Sarah with total absorption.

"He's very obedient," Eve said. "I don't think there's any doubt who's the dog and who's the boss."

"I'm not his boss. We're partners. Monty obeys because he knows there are situations where we could both get killed if he didn't trust me." She moved toward the door and Monty was on her heels. "Please leave. You're not going to get what you want."

"I'm sorry you feel that way. Come on, Jane."

Jane frowned at Sarah. "Don't make him run when it's hot. It's bad for him."

"No, it's good for him. We run five miles twice a day, rain or shine. We have to keep in shape and tolerate every kind of temperature. It's important."

"He got tired." Jane reached out a hand to pet the dog. "You shouldn't—" Monty was backing away from her touch. "Why is he doing that? I thought he liked me."

"He does like you. He's just in work mode."

"Let's go, Jane." Eve headed for the car.

Jane reluctantly trailed her, gazing over her shoulder at Monty and Sarah Patrick. "I don't like him this way. He was different before."

They'd both been different before Eve had mentioned the cadaver search. The woman and the dog standing in the doorway were not the duo that had welcomed them into the cabin. No hint of humor or warmth showed in Sarah's face now. She looked tough as nails, and Monty reminded Eve of a witch's familiar, remote and clinging only to Sarah.

"It's very important," Eve called out to Sarah. "Think about it."

Sarah shook her head.

"Do you mind if I phone you and ask if you've changed your mind?"

"I won't change my mind."

Eve started the car.

"Wait." Sarah looked at Jane's disappointed face, and then she glanced down at the dog. "Go say good-bye, Monty." She snapped her fingers.

Metamorphosis. Monty bounded out of the cabin and stood up on the door of the passenger seat, trying to reach Jane through the open window.

Jane opened the door and Monty was on her, practically in her lap, whimpering and nuzzling her. She buried her face in his neck, her arms hugging him tightly.

"Enough," Sarah said.

Monty gave Jane a last slurp and backed away. He sat down, but his tail was pounding a drumroll on the ground.

"Thank you," Eve said.

Sarah shrugged. "What can I say? I'm a sucker for kids and dogs."

"Then listen to what I have to say. You could help—"

Sarah went into the cabin and closed the door.

Eve gritted her teeth in exasperation. Stubborn woman.

"She left Monty outside," Jane said. "What if he runs away and gets lost?"

"He won't get lost." She started to drive and glanced in the rearview mirror at Monty. No witch's familiar now, he was again the adorable dog who had melted Jane's reserve. He turned, padded to the door, and struck it with one paw. It was opened immediately and he entered the cabin. "She takes good care of him."

"She makes him run." Jane scowled. "I don't think I like her."

"I do. Sometimes if you're too soft, it does more harm than good."

"But he's a dog. He wouldn't understand."

Wouldn't he? Eve remembered her odd feeling when Sarah had looked into Monty's eyes and told him to say good-bye. It was as if they'd read each other's minds.

Witch's familiar . . .

Crazy. The golden retriever was not sinister. Even when he'd been in work mode, he'd been remote rather than intimidating.

"You like her even though she won't do what you want?" Jane asked.

"Maybe she'll change her mind."

Jane looked at her skeptically.

Eve felt skeptical herself. "I'll call her later." In the meantime she'd hit the Internet again and search for other options.

She had a hunch changing Sarah Patrick's mind would be almost impossible.

THE PHONE WAS ringing when Eve walked into the house.

"Did you get her?" Logan asked as soon as Eve answered.

"You had me followed."

"You wanted protection for the little girl."

"I take it they phoned back to tell you who I went to see?"

"Sarah Patrick. Cadaver dog. Smart move."

"She turned me down."

"Did you offer her enough money?"

"We didn't get that far. The minute I mentioned using Monty as a cadaver dog, she iced down. She accused me of being with the ATF and being sent by someone named Madden, whom she evidently doesn't like."

"Do you want me to help?"

"No, I want you to butt out. If I can't get Sarah, I'll get someone else to help me."

"But you want Sarah Patrick."

"Of course I do. She's the best in the business and she's a loner. She'd be less likely to turn me in to the police." She added dryly, "And she can't stand the IRS, which should prove she's the right stuff to you."

"Definitely."

"But if I can't have her, I'll find someone almost as good."

"I could try to—"

"No, stay out of it, Logan." She hung up.

"We're not going to see Monty again?" Jane asked.

My God, her voice was almost wistful. "Have you ever had a dog?"

Jane shook her head.

Eve felt sorry for her. She had fallen like a brick for Monty. Who wouldn't? He was utterly adorable. "I'll try again tomorrow."

"If you want to. He's kind of cute, but I don't really care." Jane headed down the hall. "I think I'll go read my book."

Sure she didn't care. She was just raising the walls again. An entirely natural response by a child who'd been betrayed too many times in her short life. Eve couldn't let the opportunity for Jane to have warmth and contact slip away.

She would try to get Sarah Patrick and Monty. If she

couldn't, she'd find another handler with a dog as smart and appealing as Monty.

Fat chance.

Dammit.

She reached for the phone and dialed information for the number of the Camelback Inn.

# ELEVEN

The desert night was chill, the breeze sharp and cool on Sarah's face as she ran. Monty ran beside her, pacing her. She could feel the blood pumping through her veins, the muscles of her calves flexing with every step.

Monty was getting impatient. She could *feel* it. He wouldn't leave without permission, but he wanted to stretch out.

Halfway up the knoll, her pace faltered.

Monty looked back at her.

She chuckled. "Go on. Make me look bad. Beat it."

Monty flew.

She watched the moonlight brush a silver sheen on his golden coat as he ran straight up the incline. Beautiful . . . Scientists believed dogs were descended from wolves, but she never associated Monty with wild animals except in moments like these.

He was waiting for her on the top of the knoll.

She could almost see his satisfaction.

*Weakling.*

"I have two legs, not four." She stopped, trying to get her breath. "And I think you're part billy goat."

*Excuses.*

Monty loped over to lean companionably against her. Silence. Wind. Night.

She closed her eyes, tasting them all. God, this was good.

Monty whimpered.

She opened her eyes and looked down at him. "What's wrong?"

He was staring down at the cabin miles below them. "Monty?"

She moved closer to the edge, and then she could see it too. Lights. A car approaching the cabin.

She stiffened. Eve Duncan again? She had thought she'd made herself more than clear yesterday. But Eve had impressed her as being very determined. Maybe she'd decided to drive out and give it another try.

She was tempted to just stay up here until the woman got bored and went home.

Monty had other ideas.

He was already on the trail going down.

"Did I say we were going down?"

*Child.*

Monty loved kids, and he remembered the little girl Jane.

Okay. Face Eve Duncan, be brief, get rid of her.

Sarah started down the trail at a trot. "Wait for me, blast it."

*Child . . .*

It was not Eve Duncan's car.

Madden?

She stopped abruptly, her heart pounding. "Monty."

Monty stopped, tensing as he heard the note of panic in her voice. He looked back at her. *Fear?*

Damn right she was scared.

*No child.*

"I don't think so."

What should she do? Run? Face Madden?

Even if she and Monty stayed away from the cabin for days, Madden would still be there when she got back. She knew from experience he was totally relentless.

Okay, face him. She could always disappear later.

She strode forward, Monty trotting anxiously beside her.

*Help?*

"No. It's okay."

Monty whimpered.

"I said it's okay, dammit."

"Ms. Patrick?" A man was waiting by the cabin door. "I wonder if I can speak to you? My name is John Logan."

Not Madden.

Monty started to wag his tail as he sensed her relief.

"Always the optimist," she murmured. "He could be a bill collector, you know."

"Ms. Patrick?"

She strode toward him. "It's after nine at night, and Monty and I keep early hours. Call me in the morning."

"I've driven a long way, and I need to talk to you now." He smiled. "I assure you I'm very respectable."

His clothes and shoes were impeccable, but so were a lot of drug dealers'. "I don't like people dropping by late at night."

"Eve said you were difficult."

She should have known. "Eve Duncan? She asked you to come?"

"Not really. It was my idea, but she did ask for a little help." He gazed admiringly at Monty. "Beautiful animal."

He was a beautiful animal himself. Sleek like a cougar. Cougars could be dangerous. "Yes, he is." She opened the door. "And he's tired. Good night, Mr. Logan."

"Wait." His smile faded. "Could I come in? I'm expecting a telephone call."

"On my phone?"

"I took the liberty. It's from someone you know. Senator Todd Madden?"

She froze.

"May I come in?"

She went into the cabin and slammed the door.

He knocked. "It would really be better if I talk to you before he does. He strikes me as a man who could be very unpleasant when he's crossed."

Madden and everything connected to him was never pleasant. Calm down. Face the problem.

She opened the door. "Come in." She sat down in the rocking chair. "Get to the point and then get out."

"I'll be as quick as I can. Eve needs you to find a body buried somewhere in the area."

"Tell her to get someone else."

He shook his head. "She wants you. I can't blame her. I had my people do some research on you. You're quite remarkable."

"Am I?"

"Your work in Oklahoma City was incredible. And that earthquake in Iran last year that killed two thousand—you managed to save twenty-seven people buried in the rubble."

"And found sixty-eight dead."

"You remember the number?"

"I remember some of the numbers. I remember all the faces."

"Eve's not going to make you look at the face of this cadaver."

"I've always hated the word *cadaver*. It dehumanizes."

"All she wants you and Monty to do is locate the body. Then you can fade back into your little home in the desert."

"It's not that easy."

"You've worked with the police before on cadav— body searches. The Salt Lake City Police Department thinks very highly of you."

"Whoop-de-do."

He smiled. "Sergeant Levitz believes you can read

that dog's mind. He said it's uncanny how you understand each other."

"Levitz isn't very bright. All dog owners will tell you their pet can almost talk. When you've been with someone as long as Monty and I, you learn to understand each other."

"Still, you'll admit it's an unusually strong bond." He gazed at Monty, who was lying at her feet. "Even I can see that."

She didn't answer.

"And you've been through a lot together."

"Yes. No body search."

He sighed. "We really need you. I'm afraid I'll have to insist."

"Screw you."

He checked his watch. "Is Madden very prompt? If so, he should be—"

The phone rang.

She picked up the receiver.

"Is he there?" Madden asked.

"He's here."

"He's a very important man, Sarah. He has a lot of political connections. I don't want to antagonize him, especially since pleasing him is such a simple matter."

"Simple for you."

"We've discussed this before. Logan assures me the task shouldn't take more than a day or two."

"That's too long. An hour is too long if it's not a case of life and death."

"I know you don't like cadaver searches, but it's necessary."

"How do you know it's not illegal?"

A pause. "Logan is a respectable businessman."

With political connections. Sarah's hand tightened on the receiver. "I don't want to do this, Madden."

"But you will do it." His voice lowered to a silky mur-

mur. "Because you know the consequences if you don't, Sarah."

Son of a bitch.

"Two days. I'll give them two days."

"That's all I promised Logan. Good-bye, Sarah. Good hunting."

He hung up.

She turned to Logan. "Two days."

"Eve will be very happy."

"I don't give a damn if she's happy. I wish she'd never heard of me. I told her no and then she called you in to do her dirty work."

"Contacting Madden wasn't her idea. I didn't even tell her that Madden was the key. She wouldn't have used it. She just wanted me to find out if there was something she could offer you that would entice you to do the job."

"But you did use it."

"I'm more ruthless than Eve. I dug deeper and discovered a weapon in Madden. She wanted you, I got you." He glanced around the cabin. "You don't have a TV or a radio?"

"I don't need them."

"It keeps you a little uninformed."

"Blessedly uninformed."

"Eve mentioned she didn't see a TV." He held out the manila envelope he'd been carrying. "I believe you should know who you're dealing with. This is a dossier on Eve Duncan and newspaper articles about Talladega and the murder of a security guard. It won't tell you everything, but it gives you a good starting place."

"I'm not interested in Eve Duncan unless it will get me out of this job."

He shook his head. "But it may make you more willing to do it. Eve's trying to save a child's life."

"By forcing me to find a dead body?"

"Unfortunately." He moved toward the door. "By the

way, if I were you, I wouldn't call the police and tell them where to find Eve. That would make me angry and I'd have to call Madden. My impression is that he doesn't give a damn about anything except his career. Am I right?"

"Police?"

"Read the file." He opened the door. "I'll tell Eve you're delighted to be of service."

She cursed.

"Eve will be in touch." His lips tightened. "Get the job done. I don't care if you like it or hate it."

Sarah watched the door close behind him. Her hands clenched into fists on the arms of the rocker. Keep your temper. Losing control won't do any good. It's only two days. Maybe there wasn't even a body.

But if there was, Monty would find it.

He whimpered and got to his feet, looking up at her.

She bent down, put her arms around him, and buried her face in his coat. "I'm sorry, boy," she whispered. She could feel tears sting her eyes. "We have to do it."

EVE RECEIVED A call from Sarah Patrick later that evening.

"Logan told me you'll help. That's very kind of you."

"I want it over as soon as possible," Sarah said. "We'll start the search tomorrow. Do you have a general area?"

"Maybe. I'm not sure. We may have to try a couple—"

"You have two days," Sarah said. "Try to get me a piece of the victim's clothing. Sometimes Monty responds more to the scent clinging to clothes than to a body."

"That may take a little while. I don't know if—"

"It's up to you. I told you what I need. I don't care if we find her or not. I'd rather we didn't. After you've got the clothing, call me and I'll meet you at the search site." She hung up.

Eve sat there a moment and then dialed Logan. "What the hell did you do to Sarah Patrick?"

"I got her to go to work for you."

"How? She was cold as ice."

"It's done. You have her for two days. Make use of her."

She should have known Logan would do whatever he had to do to make it happen. He'd been ruthless as hell in getting Eve to work for him. "I didn't want her hurt."

"She's not hurt. You're not hurt. And Jane isn't hurt. If you'll use Sarah instead of having qualms, you'll all stay alive and well. That's what's important, isn't it?"

He's right, she thought wearily. That's what's important. "She wants an article of Debby Jordan's clothing. Do you suppose you could get it without breaking into her house and scaring her family?"

"I'll manage. And no thanks are needed for my help with Sarah."

She felt ashamed. Why was she blaming Logan? She had made the call that had started him into action. Maybe she'd even subconsciously hoped that he'd go far beyond what she'd asked. "I'm sorry. I guess I'm a little discouraged. I don't know if Sarah will be able to find the body. I'm not sure where it's buried. I'm just taking my best shot."

"I'd like to go with you tomorrow. Any chance?"

"You've already done too much. I won't have you seen with me."

"There's no such thing as doing too much."

"Tell that to Sarah Patrick. She's giving me two days."

"Try to make it within her framework. I'd prefer not to have to squeeze again. As I dodged insults, I actually found myself liking her."

"I don't think she reciprocates. I got the impression she'd just as soon bury both of us as find Debby Jordan."

"Since you won't let me come with you, you'll just

have to deal with her. I'll have your article of clothing by tomorrow morning."

IT WAS A white baseball jersey with the Arizona Diamondback logo on the front.

Sarah Patrick took the shirt without looking at it. "Has it been washed since she wore it?"

"No, Logan said she slept in it the night before she disappeared."

"Then how did he get it?"

"I didn't ask."

"He probably stole it from a bag for the homeless."

"He's not as bad as you think."

"No, he's probably worse."

"I was surprised you wanted the shirt. She's been buried for almost a month. The scent can't be—"

"I could have used a substance that simulates the decay smell, but that would have upset Monty. Not that the shirt may do any good anyway." She shrugged. "But we'll try." She glanced around the open field. "Why are we here?"

"This field is in back of the Desert Light subdivision."

"So?"

"Bodies have been located in two other places associated with light. Dom repeatedly mentioned light in our last conversation. I think he was trying to tell me something."

"Why didn't he just come right out and say where he buried her?"

"That wouldn't be as much fun for him. He wants to make me work."

"You mean he wants to make Monty and me work."

"He doesn't know about you." Eve wasn't sure that was true. Dom had not contacted her since she'd arrived in Phoenix, but that didn't mean he wasn't here, watching her.

"And you want me to search this field just because of the subdivision's name?"

"It's also close to the church where Debby Jordan disappeared."

Sarah gazed at her dubiously.

"Okay, it's not much to go on." Eve's lips tightened. "But it's all I've got."

"Whatever you say. I'll go on any wild-goose chase for two days. That's all you're getting from me." She took a canvas bag from her Jeep, then glanced at Jane, who was kneeling beside Monty. "Why bring her along?"

"Dom likes her with me and I can't chance leaving her alone. She won't get in the way."

"I didn't say she would. She seems a smart kid. But Monty's not going to be able to keep her company." She strode over to Jane and smiled down at her. "Sorry. It's time for Monty to work."

Jane got to her feet slowly. "May I go with you?"

Sarah looked at Eve.

Jane was already there. Was it any worse for her to search actively than sit in a car and wait? At least she'd be busy. She slowly nodded.

Sarah turned back to Jane. "We cover ground pretty fast and I usually take him over the terrain twice just to make sure we don't miss something."

"I'll keep up."

"Suit yourself." Sarah knelt down and opened the canvas bag. She pulled out a leash and fastened it to Monty's collar.

He went still.

"He knows something's happening?" Jane asked.

She nodded. "But he doesn't know what yet. I'm leashing him for my benefit, so I can better control our steps. I don't usually put a leash on him at all, only when we're in an unfamiliar environment or a leash makes people feel safer around him."

"Safer?"

"He's a big dog. Some people don't like big dogs."

"Then they're crazy," Jane said.

Sarah smiled. "I'm with you, kid." She reached into the canvas bag again and pulled out a denim belt that contained a multitude of pockets.

Monty stiffened.

"Now he knows we're on the job." Sarah fastened the pack around her waist. "It's his signal."

Monty lifted his head, his eyes bright and eager.

Sarah reached down and let him sniff the jersey. "Find her, Monty."

Eve leaned against the fender of her car and watched Sarah, Jane, and Monty walk the field. They moved fast, as Sarah had said they would, but the field was large and it took time to traverse every foot of it.

Monty held his head down, every muscle tensed as he moved over the terrain. Twice he stopped, hesitated, and then continued on. It was early afternoon before Sarah brought Monty back to the car. "Nothing."

"You're sure?" Eve asked, disappointed.

"Monty's sure. That's enough for me."

"How good is he?"

"He's damn incredible."

"Why did he stop those two times?"

"He sniffed something dead."

Eve stiffened. "What?"

"Nothing human. Monty knows the difference." She took off the dog's leash, then her own belt, and turned to Jane. "He's off duty now. Why don't you go play with him? He'd like that."

"Okay." Jane didn't have to be asked twice.

Sarah watched her run out into the field with Monty at her heels. "Monty likes her."

"She absolutely loves him."

"She's got good taste."

"Thanks for letting her trail along with you. She's had it pretty rough. Being with Monty is good for her."

"It's not her fault I've been railroaded into doing this." She looked pointedly at Eve. "It's yours."

Eve flinched. "You're right. So I might as well drive you as hard as I can while I've got you. You're not going to think any less of me."

"You have other sites in mind?"

"About eleven. They all have 'light' in their names."

"Eleven?"

Eve got out her city map and pointed to areas she'd circled. "Maybe twelve."

"You'll never make it in two days."

"We'll do the ones closest to Debby Jordan's church first. Is there any limit to how long Monty will be effective?"

"No, we worked for seventy-two hours straight in Tegucigalpa with only short rests. But you saw how long it took to rule out just this field."

"Then we'd better get moving." Eve folded the map. "Moonlight Creek is just fifteen minutes from here. We need to search both sides of the bank."

"That will take even longer than this field."

Eve got into her car. "Call Monty and Jane."

Sarah stared at her for a moment and then smiled grudgingly. "You don't know when you're beaten, do you?"

"Do you?"

Sarah turned and called, "Jane, bring my dog back. We've got work to do."

THEY SEARCHED UNTIL almost midnight but managed to rule out only four other sites. Seven left.

"That's it." Sarah took the leash off Monty. "We're calling it a day. I'm so tired, I can't see anymore."

"You don't have to see. Monty just has to smell."

Sarah shook her head. "God, you're one hard bitch."

"I have to be." Eve looked at Jane, who was asleep in the backseat.

Sarah's gaze followed hers. "He really kills kids?"

"He really does."

"Bastard."

"One more hour."

Sarah shook her head. "We can't see. I could get Monty hurt. I don't have that right."

"You said you worked longer in Honduras."

"We were trying to save lives, not find bodies." She gestured to Monty, and he jumped into the Jeep. "We're quitting for tonight."

"We didn't cover as many sites as I hoped."

"I told you we wouldn't."

"I know. I just wanted . . . you're not giving me enough time."

"Too bad."

"Yes, it is."

Sarah got into the Jeep. "We'll start at dawn tomorrow," she told Eve.

"Dawn?"

"Don't you want a full day?"

"Of course I do. But I thought that you—"

"Monty and I don't work banker's hours. I promised you two days. You'll get them."

Before Eve could reply, Sarah's Jeep was roaring down the road.

She got into her car and headed home.

Sarah was tough but not as tough as Eve had first thought. She had worked tirelessly, to the point of exhaustion, and would get only a few hours' sleep tonight before starting out again in the morning. Obviously, she had a soft spot for kids. Maybe Eve could persuade her to search more days and—

Her digital phone rang.

"You're keeping late hours," Dom said. "Are you becoming a little frantic, Eve?"

Oh, God.

"You woke me up."

"Not unless you're asleep at the wheel."

Don't panic. It could have been a guess. "You haven't called in a while. I was hoping I was rid of you."

"It's been only a few days. I've enjoyed watching you scramble to find the lovely soprano."

"You're bluffing. You don't know where I am."

"I didn't for a little while. You slipped out of Atlanta very quietly. But I knew it was only a matter of time before you figured out the identity of my soprano. I only had to stake out Debby Jordan's home."

"I never went to her home."

"But one of John Logan's men did. It was easy to track him to Logan and Logan to you. Is he the one who helped you get out of Atlanta?"

"I don't know what you're talking about."

He chuckled. "You're trying to protect him. I'm not annoyed with Logan. He's just made the situation more interesting. Though I admit I was puzzled when you didn't show up on the grieving widower's doorstep and question him yourself. But I should have known you wouldn't do the obvious thing. Using Sarah Patrick is a stroke of genius. Too bad you went to the wrong places."

"I'll find her."

"I hope not too soon. I'm enjoying the hunt."

"Dammit, tell me where she is. You know you want me to find her."

"Not yet. Every day is making you more tired, more tense, more angry. I want it to go on."

"I'll find her tomorrow."

"That would disappoint me. I'd like the search to last at least a week."

"Then why don't you go dig her up and bury her somewhere else?"

"You know moving a body is a killer's worst mistake. I could be discovered, leave evidence. Anything. No, I think I'd do better to slow you down. Did I mention how much I liked the idea of you taking Jane wherever you go? She's with you now, isn't she?"

Eve didn't answer.

"You're growing closer, aren't you? Older children are smarter. You're able to talk to them. Bonnie was a little too young for you to—"

"Shut up."

"You see how tense you are? This hunt is terribly exciting. I'm beginning to wonder if little Jane is redundant. Killing her would slow you down, wouldn't it?"

"It would stop me in my tracks."

"No, I think you'd be angry enough with me to continue. Anger and sorrow are almost as good as fear."

Damn vampire. "I'm hanging up."

"Maybe I'll take the little girl tonight."

Her hand tightened on the receiver.

"Yes, that would slow you. Look in your rearview mirror."

Headlights.

"Do you see me?"

"It's not you. One of Logan's security men has been following us all day."

"He lost you at the last search site. But I felt bound to keep you company."

"You're lying."

"How long until you get home?"

She didn't answer.

"You'd better hurry."

She pressed on the accelerator.

"Yes, I think it's time I took Jane."

He was only bluffing.

Oh, God, the car behind her was going faster.

Her heart was pounding so hard it hurt.

Faster.

Ten blocks more to the house.

Were the lights closer?

Yes.

She went around the corner on two wheels.

Jane murmured something in the backseat as the car jerked.

"Did I ever tell you how I kill children? I do it slowly, since every emotion they emit is pure and singing. They're the only ones who deserve white. Fear and pain aren't clouded as they are in adults. Do you think Jane will be as brave as Bonnie?"

She wanted to kill him.

Four blocks.

"I hear you breathing. How frightened you are."

Headlights blinding her in the rearview mirror.

She dropped the phone on the seat.

And stomped on the gas.

Gates up ahead.

The remote. Open the gates.

They were moving too slowly. The car was right on top of her.

She almost tore through the gates.

Up the driveway.

The lights were still behind her. Coming through the gates.

She screeched to a halt in front of the house and leaned on the horn.

Come. Somebody come before he—

Knocking on the window. A face pressed against the glass.

"Ms. Duncan. Are you okay?"

Herb Booker.

She rolled down the window.

Headlights were still glaring in her rearview mirror from the car parked behind her. The driver's door was open.

"Eve?" Jane was sitting up sleepily.

"It's okay." Her hand tightened on the steering wheel. "Is that your car, Herb?"

"Sure. I've been behind you all day. Is something wrong? I got worried when you started speeding."

She slowly lifted the phone to her ear. "Damn you."

"Just kidding." He hung up.

"YOU LOOK BEAT." Sarah's gaze narrowed on Eve's face. "You okay?"

"I didn't sleep well. How are you?"

"Fine. Monty and I are used to getting by with a few hours' sleep."

Eve got out her map. "We hit the areas south of the church yesterday. I thought we'd go west today." She tapped a spot on the map. "This one first. Woodlight Reservoir."

"Are you sure? That will be a lot of ground to cover. You've got to pick your best shot," Sarah said. "I'll give you until midnight tonight."

"You won't change your mind?"

"No." Sarah turned and tossed Monty's leash to Jane. "Come on, kid, we've got to get this show on the road."

Eve looked at her in despair. After last night, the search seemed futile. Why were they doing it? Just to entertain that bastard?

No, they were doing it for the same reason Eve had in the beginning. The possibility that Dom might have made a mistake.

God, let him have made a mistake.

"WE HAVE TO stop now," Sarah said quietly. "Sorry."

Eve's hands clenched into fists. "It can't be midnight."

"It's one-thirty." She gestured, and Monty jumped into the Jeep.

"I suppose I should thank you for the extra time," Eve said dully.

"You'd rather spit in my eye."

"That's not true." Eve was frustrated, but she couldn't

fault Sarah's work. The woman had worked from dawn until then with only short breaks for Monty to drink and rest. "I only wish you'd give in and let me have one more day."

"I can't do that." Sarah didn't look at her. "I know you have good reason to search, but it's not my reason. My job is to protect Monty. I didn't want to do this job, and I've given you two days."

"It's not enough."

"I've given you all I can. And every hour of the past two days I've hoped we wouldn't find that woman." She shook her head. "So maybe it's just as well I'm out. Maybe I'm not working as hard as you want me to work."

"Bullshit. You'd never cheat."

"Find someone else."

"You know I can't afford a delay."

"I can't help you." She started the Jeep. "Sorry."

"If you were sorry, you'd help me. Finding bodies isn't pleasant, but I'd think you'd—"

"Pleasant?" Her voice was strained. "My God, you don't know what you're talking about."

"I know catching Dom and protecting Jane are more important than any objections you have to working another day or two."

"Your opinion. You have a right to it. I know only that I have to protect my world the way you're protecting yours." She paused. "Sorry."

Eve's eyes were stinging as she watched the taillights disappear. She would feel all right soon. She was just tired and discouraged. She'd go back to the house and hit the Internet and see if she could find another Sarah Patrick.

Monty whined.

"Shut up." Sarah pressed the accelerator. "You don't know when you're better off."

*Sad.*

"I can't help it if she's sad. I have to take care of us."

*Alone.*

"We're all alone."

*Not us.*

She reached out and scratched his ears. "No, not us," she whispered.

He whined again.

"I said no."

*Child.*

That thought was tearing at Sarah too.

"It's not our business. Eve will take care of her."

*Sad.*

"Go to sleep. I'm tired of you nagging me. We're through. We got lucky and I'm not risking another day."

Monty settled down in the seat and laid his head down on his paws. *Child* . . .

"WHERE IS SHE, Mark?" Joe asked.

There was silence on the other end of the line. "How did you track me down?"

"It wasn't easy. The station was very cagey about giving me your new digital phone number. You changed it two days ago. Why, Mark?"

"I get a lot of nuisance calls. All media people do."

"And you took a two-week leave from the station."

"I was tired. I decided to come down here to Florida to bask in the sun."

"Or you knew I'd be searching for you."

"Really, Joe, I'd hardly go to all that trouble to avoid you."

"I think you would. Where is Eve, Mark?"

"How would I know?"

"She didn't have the address of the welfare house. It took me fifteen minutes to bully the information out of Eisley. Yet Eve was able to go there and take the kid away. I put two and two together and came up with you, Mark."

"Do you think Eisley would tell me where it's located?"

"I think you know where every body in the city is buried."

"That's an unfortunate turn of phrase."

"Where is she, Mark?"

"I've invested a lot of time and effort in this story. Eve doesn't want you to know where she is."

"I'm going to find her."

"Then you'll do it without my help."

"I don't think so. I'll find her or I'll find you. Believe me, you'll prefer that I find Eve."

"Is that a threat, Joe?"

"You'd better believe it. Where is she?"

"Let's just say that she's following Dom's lead."

"What lead?"

"That's for me to know and you to find out," Mark said silkily. "I don't like being threatened, Joe." He hung up.

Joe leaned back in his chair, chilled to the bone.

Christ.

Don't let fear get to you. Just find her. Keep at Mark until you've wrung every drop of information out of him.

He dialed Mark's number again.

Just find her.

MONTY WAS HOWLING.

Sarah sat upright in bed.

Monty almost never howled.

She turned on the bedside lamp and swung her feet to the floor.

He howled again and then broke off.

Oh, God.

She was through the front door in a heartbeat. "Monty?"

No answer.

She turned on the living-room light, then walked back outside, keeping the door open.

"Monty?"

No sound. Her hands clenched at her sides.

"Monty, where are—"

Something beside his water dish.

A large steak with bites taken out of it.

She never gave Monty red meat.

"No."

She ran out into the darkness. "Monty!"

She tripped over something furry. Something limp that—

Please. Please. No.

"*Monty!*"

SOMEONE WAS HONKING, lying on the horn until it ripped through the night.

What the hell?

Eve pushed away from the computer and stood up.

The phone on the desk rang.

"We have an intruder at the gates," Herb Booker said. "Please stay inside the house until we check it out."

"For God's sake, it has to be a drunk. I can't imagine anyone very menacing waking the entire neighborhood."

"Please stay inside."

"He'll wake Jane up, dammit." She headed for the front door.

The horn was still blaring as she walked down the driveway toward the gates. Juan Lopez was there before her.

Sarah Patrick's Jeep was stopped outside the gates. "Let me in, dammit."

"Open up," Eve told Lopez.

He pressed a remote and the gates swung open.

Sarah drove past Eve and up to the front door.

"It's okay," Eve told the security men.

Sarah was climbing out of the Jeep when Eve caught up with her. Eve took one look at her face and asked, "What's wrong?"

"What's not wrong?" Sarah said. "Son of a bitch. Dirty son of a bitch. I want to kill him."

"Dom?"

"Who else? No one else—"

Fear suddenly surged through Eve. "Sarah, where's Monty?"

"Dirty son of a bitch."

"Sarah."

"He tried to kill him." Tears were running down her face. "He tried to kill Monty."

"Tried?"

"He scared me to death. I thought he—"

"Sarah, what happened?"

"He threw a slab of beef next to Monty's water bowl. It was poisoned."

"You're sure?"

"A coyote got hold of it. He was dead when I found him."

"Thank God Monty didn't eat it."

"I didn't think he would. I've taught him not to eat anything I don't give him. But I didn't know—and then he wouldn't answer me." She wiped her damp cheeks with the backs of her hands. "Shit."

Eve nodded. "I know." She opened the door. "Come in."

"Just a minute. I've got to get Monty out of the back." She couldn't see the dog. "Where is he?"

"On the floor."

"Why? Did he eat any poison at all?"

"No." She knelt beside the Jeep and her tone became soft and loving. "Come on, baby. Time to go."

Monty whined.

"I know. But we have to get out of the Jeep and go inside." She put the leash on him. "Come on, Monty."

He finally got to his feet and jumped down from the Jeep. His tail tucked between his legs, he moved slowly toward the front door.

"Are you sure he didn't get any poison?"

"I'm sure."

"Then what's wrong with him?"

"What do you think's wrong? He's sad. I had a devil of a time getting him away from that dead coyote. It must have been alive when Monty found it. Monty has trouble dealing with death." She shrugged. "Don't we all?"

"You're saying he has psychological problems?"

Sarah glared at her. "What's odd about that?"

Eve held up a hand. "Not a thing." Looking at Monty, she could tell something was drastically wrong. His ears were pressed to the sides of his head, and his expression was terribly woebegone. "What can we do?"

"He'll be okay. He just needs a little time." She led Monty to the hall. "Is it okay if I take him to Jane's room?"

"She's asleep."

"He won't wake her."

"But what good would that do?"

"There's no one more alive than a child. It will help Monty to be near her."

"Therapy?"

Sarah stuck out her chin. "Jane won't mind. She's crazy about Monty."

Who wouldn't be crazy about Monty? Eve thought. Those big, soft eyes were so sad, it almost broke her heart. "Up the stairs. First door."

"Thanks."

Eve watched her lead Monty up the stairs, then went to the kitchen and started brewing a pot of coffee.

The coffee was almost done when Sarah appeared in the doorway.

"Get him settled?"

She nodded. "Sorry. Jane woke up."

"She'll go back to sleep."

Sarah said hesitantly, "He's in bed with her. But he's clean. I washed him off after I brought him home tonight."

"Do you take cream or sugar?"

Sarah shook her head.

Eve handed her a cup of coffee. "Stop looking so guilty. It's okay."

"No, it's not. Monty and I don't like to depend on other people."

"I don't think Monty minds as much as you do."

"You're right." She made a face. "He's probably better adjusted than I am."

"Why did you come here, Sarah? I don't think it's because Monty needed therapy."

"I was mad." Her lips tightened. "I wanted to kill the bastard. I still do."

"You're sure it was Dom?"

"Aren't you? I've no near neighbors who could be annoyed by Monty. He always stays close to me. No one ever tried to hurt him before he started to look for Debby Jordan. Someone wants to stop you from finding her."

Eve shook her head. "Just slow me down. Dom's having too much fun to stop me cold. He didn't realize that you'd refused to help me any longer."

"So he tried to kill Monty."

Eve nodded.

Sarah's grip on her cup tightened. "I won't stand for it. I'm going to get the bastard and hang him out to dry."

"I thought you were through."

"Don't be stupid. He tried to kill my dog. He might try again. The only way to protect Monty is to catch that son of a bitch." She took one more sip of coffee and set the cup down. "Time to get to bed. We have only a few hours to sleep. We'll set out at dawn."

"We will?"

"I'm staying here. It's safer for Monty. I'll need a room. Or if that's not possible, I can go get my sleeping bag. I'm used to roughing it."

"I can give you the bedroom across the hall from me."

"Thanks. I'll get my bag and Monty's things out of the Jeep." Sarah left the kitchen. "You go on to bed. I'll lock up."

Eve stared after her. An angry, protective Sarah Patrick was clearly a power to be reckoned with.

She turned out the light and started up the stairs. Well, this was what she'd wanted. She'd asked Sarah to continue to help. But she hadn't imagined the woman would barge in and take over.

Eve stopped at Jane's door and opened it. Jane was asleep again. Monty was in bed with her and she had an arm flung over the big dog.

What the hell. She could hold her own with Sarah Patrick. The dog was good for Jane, and the attack on him pointed out how close Dom was. He was getting tired of staying in the background and watching and waiting.

She shivered as she closed the door of Jane's room. It might not be bad having Sarah and Monty in the same house. She was feeling very much alone right now.

"Get to bed." It was Sarah passing her in the hall.

"Go to hell."

Sarah stopped at her bedroom door. "Sorry. I'm used to running things and I've been feeling pretty helpless lately. I'll try to watch it."

Eve smiled faintly. "Do that."

It was going to be all right. She and Sarah would adjust to each other. After all, they had a common goal now.

You made a mistake, Dom. You're not perfect. If you'd left it alone, Sarah would have stopped helping me. Now I have an ally.

Did you make another mistake with Debby Jordan?

"NOTHING?" EVE ASKED, disappointed.

Sarah shook her head. "Not a sign." She gestured to Monty, and he jumped into the car. "He thought there was something beneath that fallen tree, but then he changed his mind."

"Should we go back? Monty must be as tired as we are. Maybe he made a mistake."

"He doesn't make mistakes. He'll know it when he runs across it."

"It's been three days."

"She's not *there*." Sarah paused and then tempered her tone. "Sorry. It's been a long day."

They had all been long days. From dawn to midnight and sometimes later. Sarah had a right to be annoyed. While she had sat in the car or stood watching, Sarah and Monty had hunted. It was a wonder they kept pushing.

Sarah was silent until they were almost back at the house. "How many sites are left?"

"Four."

"That's not many. Could he have lied to you?"

"He's capable of anything. But if we aren't on the right track, why did he try to kill Monty?"

"To make the scenario more believable?"

"It's possible," she said. "Maybe he likes seeing me run in circles."

"But you don't believe it."

"No, I think there has to be a payoff. He likes the excitement, the ups and downs. Hope and then disappointment. Tension and then release. If we found Debby Jordan, it would be a tremendous release for him."

"You sound like you know the bastard."

Sometimes Eve felt as if she did know him. He was always on her mind. And there were moments when she felt that if she turned around quickly, she would catch sight of him.

Imagination. Since that night he'd phoned her in the car, Juan Lopez and Herb Booker had been very much on guard and had assured her no one had been following her.

Maybe.

She turned the corner and saw the familiar gates of home. "We'll find her tomorrow," she told Sarah. "He didn't lie to me. I know that—"

"Watch out!"

Eve stomped on the brakes when she saw the man in the street. "Christ."

Lopez had stopped his car behind her and was running toward the man, gun drawn.

"No!"

Then Lopez was down, lying in the middle of the street.

My God, he was going to kill Lopez.

She jumped out of the car.

"Eve, are you crazy?" Sarah shouted.

"Stop it. Do you hear me? Dammit, stop it. You'll hurt him."

"I feel like hurting someone." Joe released his hold on Lopez's neck and stood up. "He was stupid to run at me."

"He was trying to protect me."

"He didn't do a good job. Logan's wasting his money."

"He does a very good job."

The gates were swinging open and Herb Booker was running out into the street.

Joe whirled, immediately on the offensive.

Eve stepped in front of him. "No, it's okay. I know him, Herb."

Herb looked at his partner, who was on the ground, slowly sitting up, and then at Joe. "It's not okay to me."

"He's a police detective."

"Since when do cops use Rambo tactics?"

"Joe's a little different." She turned to Joe. "Go on up to the house."

He smiled sardonically. "You're actually letting me in?"

"Shut up. I'm mad as hell at you. There was no call for hurting Juan."

"He had a gun."

"And you nearly killed him."

He shrugged. "Like I said, I was annoyed."

"Well, so am I." She got back in the car. "No one invited you here."

"Oh, I'm well aware of that." He turned and strode through the gates.

"*Who* is that?" Sarah asked Eve. "Herb was right. He reminded me of Rambo too."

"Joe Quinn." She drove up the driveway. "An old friend."

"Are you sure? The vibes he's giving off are more explosive than friendly."

"He's upset with me." Her lips tightened. "But no more upset than I am with him."

"He was at Fay's," Jane said from the backseat. "He jumped on me."

"You jumped on him first. With a baseball bat."

"You're defending him," Sarah noticed.

"It's habit." She parked and got out of the car. "You all go on to bed. I'll deal with him."

"He'll take some dealing," Sarah murmured. "But Monty and I are too tired to volunteer, and Jane doesn't have her baseball bat."

Jane chuckled. "Can Monty sleep with me tonight, Sarah?"

"Not tonight. You know that's only on special occasions." Sarah nodded at Joe, who was waiting by the door. "Be nice to Eve, or I'll sic my dog on you."

She didn't wait for an answer as she ushered Jane and Monty inside.

"Who is she?" Joe asked Eve.

"Sarah Patrick. Monty is her dog. If you knew where I was staying, I'm surprised you didn't know about Sarah. Didn't Logan tell you what was going on?"

"You've got to be kidding." He followed her into the house. "Logan told me no more than he had to, just that you were safe, he had two men guarding you, and that I should go jump in the lake."

"Then how did you find me?"

"Mark told me you were heading for Phoenix and that he thought you had an ace in the hole. I immediately thought of Logan. I started looking for him and learned that he'd left Monterey and was staying at the Camelback Inn. I'd also discovered that he owned this house, and I thought it logical that he'd provide you and Jane with a place to stay."

"How astute of you."

"I wouldn't be sarcastic if I were you." His tone was thick. "I've gone through hell trying to find you and not knowing if I'd get here before Dom did. I don't know how much control I have left."

"Not very much judging by that display you put on outside."

"Did it upset you? Too bad. But then, I've always known that violence upset you. You've had too much of it in your life. So I kept that part of me turned low. I'm tired of it, Eve. Accept me as I am." He looked around the foyer. "Very nice. Very cozy. Logan did you proud."

"He's been a great help."

His eyes narrowed. "Oh? How great a help? Lots of sympathy and intimate little chats?"

"Of course I talk to him. I call him whenever I get a chance, to tell him how things are going. Was I supposed to just drop him after he helped me get Sarah and all the other— Why am I defending myself? It's none of your—"

"There's only one thing I want to know. Has Dom contacted you since you've been here?"

"Yes."

He muttered a curse. "How does the bastard do it? He must be sticking as close as molasses to you."

"Why are you surprised? He's had decades of experience in stalking, and he must know every trick in the book. It wouldn't be any fun for him if he couldn't check my pulse." She walked into the living room and turned to face him. "I'm tired, Joe. Say what you've got to say to me and let me go to bed. We've got to get up at dawn and start searching again."

"Just like that?"

"Just like that." She lost patience with him. "Dammit, Joe, do you expect me to apologize to you for trying to save your job? I'd do it again. This is my concern, not yours."

"Your concerns have been mine since the day I first

met you. They'll be mine until the day I—" He shook his head. "You're backing off, closing me out. I can feel it, dammit. How long do you think I can—" He took two steps forward and grasped her shoulders. "Look at me. For God's sake, look at me and see me as I am, not what you want me to be."

His eyes . . .

Her chest was so tight, she couldn't breathe.

"*Yes.*" His voice vibrated with intensity.

"Let me go." Her voice sounded faint even to her ears.

His grasp tightened and then he slowly released her. "I'm not stupid. After all these years, I'm not going to rush it. But you've kept me chained too long by pity. I can't take it anymore."

"Pity? I've never wanted your pity."

"How could I not feel pity? I ached with it. I ate and slept with it. It was dry as dust, but it was all I had. And every time I thought I couldn't take one more minute of it, you made me bleed again and I was caught." He held her gaze. "No more pity, Eve."

"I'm going to bed." She backed away from him. "We'll talk in the morning."

He shook his head. "No, we don't have to. I can wait now." He glanced at the couch. "I'll bunk down here."

"There's another spare bedroom."

"You can show me tomorrow. Go escape now."

She needed to escape. She was confused and panicky and there was a funny feeling in the pit of her stomach. And Joe, damn him, knew her so well, he was probably aware of exactly what she was feeling. "I'll see you tomorrow."

"It will be okay, Eve." he said quietly. For the first time, a faint smile lit his face. "Don't think about it. Ride with it, live with it for a while. I'm the same man you've known for the past ten years."

But he'd been almost a stranger during those moments when he was looking down at her.

When he was touching her . . .

How many times had he held her in the last ten years? In friendship, in sympathy, quieting the pain, helping her through nights of torment and loneliness.

Never like this.

"Good night," she murmured, then fled the room.

It was crazy, she thought as she took off her clothes and slipped into bed. It shouldn't be happening. Damn you, Joe. You shouldn't be feeling like this.

*She* shouldn't be feeling like this.

Her breasts were taut, aching against the coolness of the sheet, and there was an unmistakable tingling between her thighs.

Oh, shit.

Not for Joe. She didn't want to feel this animalistic lust for Joe. It didn't have any place in the compartment she'd given him in her life.

*Compartment.* Where had that thought come from? Because she couldn't bear to let him go, had she kept Joe in the one area of her mind and heart where she could accept closeness? How incredibly selfish.

It couldn't be true. She wouldn't let it be true. Yet that night at the motel in Ellijay, hadn't she known there was something else between them, something she wouldn't permit to come to the surface?

Perhaps tonight was only a temporary aberration on Joe's part. Maybe tomorrow he'd be back to normal.

But what about her? Could she ever look at Joe again in the same way? When he'd touched her and stared down at her with such intensity, he seemed to have changed before her eyes. She'd suddenly become *aware* of him. The physical, sexual Joe Quinn. The broadness of his shoulders, the slimness of his hips, his mouth . . .

She'd wanted to reach out and touch that mouth.

Heat. Tingling. Hunger.

Stop thinking of him that way. She had to regain her balance so she could convince Joe how destructive going in a new direction could be. Be logical, be cool. . . .

She was so upset, there wasn't any way she could be logical or cool.

Damn you, Joe.


JOE, DRESSED IN jeans and sweatshirt, his hair wet from the shower, met her in the hall when she came downstairs the following morning. "Coffee's made. Sarah, Jane, and Monty are in the kitchen. You're late." He smiled. "Didn't sleep well?"

She stiffened. "I slept fine."

"Liar." He started toward the kitchen. "Sarah filled me in on your progress, or lack of it."

His manner was casual, she noticed with relief. This was the Joe she knew. It was almost as if last night had never happened. "We still have a chance."

"If Dom didn't lie to you. Don't bank too much on there being evidence even if we find Debby Jordan. Spiro says nothing of value has been uncovered at the graves at Talladega."

"What about the cardboard box in the alley?"

"The same. The blood belonged to the security guard at the welfare house."

"And the two graves in Phoenix?"

"Spiro sent Charlie here to help look into that. Nothing yet."

"That doesn't mean we won't find something."

"He wouldn't have told you about Debby Jordan if it had a chance of incriminating him."

"Yes, he would. He's tired of being safe. He needs—I don't know what he needs, but I'm part of it. And he's made at least one mistake since I came here."

"Sarah's dog."

She nodded. "If he made one mistake, he may have made another."

"And if he didn't?"

"Then we'll find a way to get him. I can't let this go on indefinitely. I won't be made to hide and I won't be taunted by that bastard." She grimaced. "I can't *stand* it. He's feeding on me, Joe."

"Maybe you're right. Maybe Debby Jordan will be the key." He paused. "So let's get breakfast and hit the road."

"You're going with us?"

"You let the kid go. Why not me?"

"Jane has to stay with me."

He started to open the kitchen door, but she stopped him. "I don't want you to go with us, Joe."

"I'm going. You're not going to get rid of me again."

"Look, I've been careful. I've stayed out of sight. I've let Sarah handle the people who've come up and questioned us while we were searching, but there's always the possibility the police might find me. I don't want you to be with me if that happens."

He grinned. "Then I'd make a quick arrest myself. Did I forget to tell you that I persuaded my department chief that it was his idea to send me here as the Atlanta liaison on the interstate task force? So my job you're so worried about is safe."

"The hell it is. You're walking a tight line, and I don't want you to go with—"

"You're repeating yourself."

"And you're not listening. I don't need your help."

He looked at her pointedly. "You let Logan help you."

"I didn't want his help."

"But you still let him help you."

"That was different."

"Yes, it was different. I wanted to strangle you when you left me and went to him for help." He smiled. "But now I believe it's an encouraging sign. Think about it."

She didn't want to think about it. Suddenly she was feeling the same tightness in her chest, the same awareness she'd experienced the night before. Dammit, she didn't want to feel this way around Joe. He was her best friend, almost her brother. "It's all wrong. You're spoiling everything."

He went past her into the kitchen. "Adjust."

"EASY, BOY. YOU'RE going too fast." Sarah tightened her grip on the leash. Monty had been tense and moving at top speed since he'd reached this field at the rear of Dawn's Light Elementary School.

Instinct or impatience? He'd gone through days of search with nothing to show. God knows Sarah was tired and impatient.

It had to be nearly six. It was getting dark and the scraggly trees were casting longer shadows on the sparsely covered ground.

"How much longer?" Joe called from the car, which was parked at the edge of the field.

"Another fifteen minutes." She paused a moment, giving both herself and Monty a chance to catch their breath, her gaze fixed on Joe and Eve. It was odd watching them together. It was clear they were old friends; they had the comfortable habit of almost finishing each other's sentences. Yet there was something disquieting about the tension between them. People were too complicated. Dogs were much easier . . . most of the time.

"Are we almost done?" Jane asked.

"Soon." She started moving again. "Why don't you go to the car and get a sandwich? You must be hungry."

Jane shook her head. "I'll wait until you go back." She smiled eagerly. "Monty's going faster, isn't he? Why do you suppose he's doing that?"

"How should I know? I'm just along for the ride."

Jane frowned. "What's wrong with you?"

"Nothing." Her stride lengthened. "Go back to the car. You can't keep up."

"I always keep up."

"I told you to go back," she said sharply. "We don't need you."

Jane stopped, stared at her for a moment, and then turned on her heel and walked away.

She'd hurt the kid's feelings. But it couldn't be helped. She couldn't afford to concentrate on anything but Monty just then.

Faster.

To the left.

Faster.

Monty was straining at the leash.

*Close.*

*Eagerness.*

*Hope.*

*Found!*

Monty started to dig.

"No, Monty."

*Found.*

She didn't try to stop him again. He'd find out soon enough.

He froze into stillness.

*Gone?*

"Yes."

He backed away. *Gone.*

He was whimpering.

Christ, he was hurting.

She fell to her knees and put her arms around his neck.

*Child?*

"I don't think so."

*But gone.*

She felt tears sting her eyes as she rocked him gently. "Shh."

"What's wrong? Is he hurt?" Eve was standing beside her.

"Yes." And it was her fault. She had tried not to think about this moment, but she had known it would come. "He's hurt."

"Should we take him to a vet?"

Sarah shook her head. "It wouldn't do any good." Please stop whimpering. You're breaking my heart.

*Gone*.

"What happened?" Joe knelt beside the dog. "Does he need first aid? I've had training in—"

"He found her."

"Here? Debby Jordan?"

"I guess it's her," she said dully. "It's a human being and it's dead." She rose to her feet. "I'm taking Monty back to the car. He's done his job." She gently tugged on the leash. "Come on, baby."

Monty wouldn't move.

"You can't help, Monty. It's time to go."

He lay there, whimpering.

"Can I help?" Joe asked quietly.

"He won't leave her. He knows she's dead, but he won't accept it." She tried to steady her voice. "The damn idiot never accepts it."

"Then we'd better get him away from here." Joe picked up the retriever. "Easy, boy. I won't hurt you. Sarah wants you to go back to the car."

"Should I come with you?" Eve asked.

"Stay here." Sarah followed Joe. "There's no way I'm bringing Monty back if we lose the exact location."

Jane ran toward them when she saw Joe with Monty in his arms. "What's wrong? What happened to Monty?"

"He's okay." Joe set Monty carefully on the backseat. "He didn't want to come back to the car."

"Why not?"

Joe turned to Sarah. "I've got to get back to Eve and mark the site. Will you be okay?"

Sarah nodded, then she climbed into the backseat and lifted Monty's head onto her lap.

Jane stood watching her. "He looks sick."

"He's not sick, he's just sad."

"Why?" Her gaze flew to where Eve was standing. "He found her?"

"He found someone."

Jane shivered. "You know, I didn't really think it would happen. I knew it was right to search for her, but I—"

"I know." Sarah tried to smile. "I had mixed feelings about finding her too."

"Because you were afraid it would upset Monty?"

"I knew it would hurt him."

"He's been like this before?"

"Every time. When I brought him back from Tegucigalpa, he wouldn't leave the cabin for a month. He lost seven pounds. I had to coax him to eat."

"Will it be like that this time?"

"I hope not." She stroked Monty's head.

"You shouldn't have taken him there."

"He saved many, many lives. Was I to stop him from doing that?"

Jane frowned. "I guess not. But I don't like it."

"Neither do I."

"Are all dogs like him?"

"Golden retrievers are wonderful family and handicap dogs because of their gentleness. They're full of love, and Monty seems to have gotten a double dose."

Jane's hands knotted into fists at her sides. "I hate that he's hurting like this. Tell me what to do to help him."

Sarah knew from past experience that there was no quick fix. But the child was hurting almost as much as the dog, so she had to do something. "Climb in and sit with us. Pet him. Let him know you're here."

"He'd like that?"

"He likes children, and he particularly likes you, Jane. It could help."

Jane scrambled into the backseat and started stroking Monty. "He's still whimpering. You're sure this is helping?"

Sarah wasn't sure of anything but that love and a child's life force were miracles in themselves. She could use a little of that life force herself. "It couldn't hurt. Just stick with it."

There was silence in the car for several minutes. "Why do you do this?" Jane whispered. "You love Monty. You have to hate it."

"Not many other people are able to do what we do." She cleared her throat. "But I have to be careful how I use Monty. I'm responsible. I have to be the one who protects us."

"Why?"

"Because Monty is what he is and he loves me." Her hand moved caressingly on the dog's head. Come on, boy. Please don't hurt anymore. It's killing me. We have to get you over this. She whispered, "And he'll never, never tell me no."

DEBBY JORDAN WAS lying beneath this ground. Eve stared down at the area Sarah had indicated. It didn't look like a grave.

"Here?" Joe was standing beside her, carrying a red emergency flag he must have taken from the trunk of the car.

She gestured to the spot. "I can't believe Monty found her. I'd almost given up hope."

"Not you." He anchored the flag and stood up. "That should do it. Have you thought about what we should do now?"

"We can't excavate ourselves. We'd disturb any evidence. The local police?"

"We could go that route." He paused. "Or we could call Spiro."

"I'm wanted for kidnapping. I won't let him take Jane away from me."

"Then we'll have to work a deal, won't we?" His lips tightened. "One that won't make you the bait."

"We don't even know for sure it's Debby Jordan who's buried here."

"But you have a hunch it is, don't you?"

"Yes, I think it's her. He wanted me to find her, and we found her. But he wanted to stretch it out. This was probably too soon for him. We'll have to see what he does next."

# C H A P T E R
# THIRTEEN

"How's Monty?" Joe asked as Eve came down the stairs later that evening.

"Sarah's worried. He wouldn't eat his supper. Jane's hanging over him." She shook her head. "I thought he was going to be good for her, but I didn't foresee this."

"He probably *is* good for her. Caring never hurt anyone. There's not enough of it in this world."

Joe had cared. She remembered how tenderly he'd lifted the retriever and carried him back to the car. Strange how moving the gentleness of a tough man could be. "Did you reach Spiro?"

"Yes, he's on his way. He said he would have come anyway. Charlie's come across something pretty interesting about the other two cases."

"What?"

"He wouldn't talk about it."

"So much for sharing information."

"We'll get it out of him. Right now he thinks he's doing us a favor. We just have to convince him that we stand on equal ground."

The phone rang.

She tensed.

Joe looked at her. "Shall I get it?"

It wouldn't be Dom. Dom always called on her digital phone. "No, I'll answer it." She picked up the receiver.

"Good to hear your voice, Eve," Mark Grunard said. "Though I wish I'd heard it earlier. You promised you'd contact me."

"There wasn't any reason. I didn't know anything. How did you find out where I was?"

"Joe and I made a deal, and *he* keeps his word. Is he there?"

"Yes." She handed the phone to Joe. "Mark Grunard."

She sat and watched his face as he talked to Mark. No expression. The wariness and stillness were firmly back in place.

"He's coming." Joe hung up. "He wants to be on the spot in case anything interesting happens."

"He said you made a deal."

"It was the only way I could get him to tell me where you'd gone. I called him after I found out about this house."

"Without asking me?"

"Did you ask me before you flew the coop?" He added softly, "I'd have made a deal with the devil himself to find you, Eve. Shall I tell you what I'd do to keep you?"

The words came out of left field, surprising her, shaking her. "I don't want to—"

"I didn't think you'd want to know." He turned and moved toward the front door. "I'll drop it for now."

"Where are you going?"

"Back to the burial site. I don't like the idea of leaving it unattended."

Her eyes widened. "You think he'll come back to it?"

"If he's watching you, then he knows we found the grave."

"He won't try to move the body. He told me once that it would be stupid."

"Then I'll be guarding it for nothing. But it won't hurt."

"How long will you be there?"

"Until Spiro meets me there tomorrow morning. Don't expect me back until—"

"I'll go with you."

"Go to bed, you're not invited." He opened the door. "My job, Eve. You and Sarah have done yours."

"It's idiotic of you to go there tonight if you think he—"

She was talking to air. He was gone.

How dare he upset her and then terrify her by going back to Debby Jordan's grave? And how could he think that she'd be able to sleep? She'd be up all night, imagining him by himself in that field.

She *would* sleep. She wouldn't think of him. Let him risk Dom coming back and finding him. It would serve him right. He'd probably enjoy facing that son of a bitch. Joe'd karate-chop him as he had Lopez and walk away.

Her heart was pounding hard. Stop it. Don't think of him.

Go to bed and go to sleep.

JOE WAS SITTING several yards away from the grave site, and she could feel his gaze on her as she approached, but she couldn't see his expression in the darkness. There probably wasn't any expression. She usually had to watch for the faintest flicker of an eyelash or the movement of his mouth to know what he was feeling.

Though he'd made his feelings more than clear lately.

"I was expecting you." Joe patted the ground beside him. "Sit down."

"Well, I didn't expect to be here." She sat down and linked her arms around her knees. "I told you he wasn't coming."

"But you couldn't let me run the risk alone."

"You're my friend . . . sometimes."

"All the time. You shouldn't have come here by yourself."

"I'm never by myself. One of the security men followed me."

"Which is the only reason I feel the slightest gratitude to Logan."

"He's a good man."

"No comment."

She was silent as she gazed across the field at the red flag marking the grave. Are you there, Debby Jordan? I hope you are. God, I hope we can bring you home.

"She had two children?"

"Two little boys. According to the newspapers, she had everything. A happy marriage, a family, friends. She was a good person trying to live a good life. Then one day she left home and never came back. No warning. No reason. Dom saw her and wanted her dead." She shook her head. "That's what's most frightening. You can live your life in the best way, the most moral way possible, and it doesn't make any difference. A madman chooses you at random and takes away everything. It's not fair."

"That's why we all have to live every moment as if it were our last and not close ourselves off."

He was no longer talking about Debby Jordan. "I don't close myself off. I just choose what I want in my life."

"Then you should widen your selection. It's pretty damn miserly."

"I'm content with the way things are."

"Bullshit."

"Dammit, why do you want to change everything?"

"Because I'm too selfish. I want more."

"I can't— I don't want—"

"Sex?"

Eve stiffened. It was the one subject she hadn't wanted to bring out in the open. God knows, she'd tried to push it away a hundred times while lying in bed last night.

"I think you do want it." He wasn't looking at her. "You've had a few sexual relationships since Bonnie died. Nothing serious. You wouldn't let them be serious. That would have interfered with your work."

Joe had never spoken to her before about those fleeting relationships. She hadn't known he'd even been aware of them. "It still would interfere."

"Then you'll have to learn to deal with it." His tone was almost offhand. "Because I'm here and I'm serious as hell. I've watched and I've waited. I learned to control jealousy and anger and desperation. I never tried to stop you from going to other men because I knew that every step would help you heal. But you needed something else from me. Well, you got it."

"Joe . . ."

"Everything I've done since I met you has been centered on you. You *became* my center. I don't know why. I never wanted it." He finally turned to look at her. "But if you can see beyond Bonnie and all those other lost kids, you'll find I'm pretty damn close to your center too."

"You're my friend, Joe."

"Forever. But I can be more. I can please your body." He paused. "And I can give you a child."

"*No.*"

"That scared you. You're afraid to even think of it, but it would be the one act that might heal you. For God's sake, it wouldn't be a betrayal of Bonnie."

"No."

He shrugged. "I'm not pushing it. We have a long way to go before we get that far."

She stared at him in pain and bewilderment. "Joe, it wouldn't work."

"It *will* work. I'll make it work." He smiled. "My first

goal is to get you to think of me as a sex object instead of as a brother. Shall I tell you how good I am in bed?"

He was joking. Or was he? She was so confused, she wasn't sure of anything about him anymore.

"No, I'd rather show you." His smile faded. "And I know this isn't the time or place. Though it seems as though we've spent most of our years together balanced on the edge of a grave." He reached over and touched her cheek. "You should think about the fact that a good portion of the time I'm looking at you I'm not seeing my friend. I'm seeing you in bed or on top of me or putting your hands on—" He threw back his head and laughed. "Your eyes are as wide as saucers."

"Damn you, Joe." She felt as if her face were on fire. "I won't think about it." But she would. She wouldn't be able to stop herself from remembering his words.

And he knew it.

"It's okay." He was still smiling as he pulled her into the crook of his arm. "Relax. I don't mind occasionally being just a shoulder to lean on. I'm only opening our relationship to more interesting possibilities."

She shouldn't take comfort from him. It wasn't fair. Besides, it confused the issues. And what the hell were the issues? Sex? Love? Friendship? Whatever they were, she should probably stay remote until she could think clearly.

Yet they had sat like this a hundred times, touched and shared thoughts and silences. How could she push him away? It would hurt too much. It would be like tearing out a part of herself.

"Stop fretting," Joe murmured. "This part will always stay the same. I'm not trying to take anything away from you. I'm just trying to give us both more."

"You must think I'm a selfish bitch," she said unevenly. "You've already given me so much. You saved my life and you saved my sanity. I'd give you anything you wanted if I wasn't afraid I'd end up hurting you. Sex is nothing. You'd ask for more and I don't know anything about a man-woman relationship. The boy who got me pregnant with Bonnie left as soon as I told him I wouldn't get an abortion. That wasn't exactly great training. I don't know if I could handle such a big commitment."

"You can handle it. You can handle anything."

"Yeah? I haven't handled any sexual relationship since with great skill."

"That's because it wasn't with me."

She suddenly chuckled. "You arrogant bastard."

He smiled. "Nothing but the truth." He pressed her head into the curve of his shoulder. "Go to sleep. You might get lucky and dream of me."

"I wouldn't give you the satisfaction. Your ego is too big as it is." She gradually relaxed. Weird, she thought drowsily, she shouldn't be able to fall back into the comfortable groove of years. But Joe seemed able to switch back and forth effortlessly and bring her along with him. "I shouldn't go to sleep. I came here in case Dom—"

"I know. The minute you showed up I knew I was safe."

"Shut up."

"Whatever you say."

"Yeah, sure. Catch me hurrying out to try to save your neck again."

"You'd do it."

Yes, she would. Without question and without thought. Because the concept of Joe hurt or killed was too frightening to contemplate.

To live without Joe . . .

SPIRO ARRIVED AT the field at ten-fifteen the following morning.

"Hello, Eve. You've been a very busy woman since I last saw you." His gaze went to the red flag. "That's it?"

Joe nodded. "That's it."

"We'd better hope that cadaver dog has a damn good nose. I'm going to look like an idiot if he's found a dead gopher."

"He has a good nose," Eve said. "Sarah says he can tell the difference."

"Sarah?"

"Sarah Patrick, his trainer."

"That's right, Joe told me about her." Spiro turned back to Joe. "And what if it's not Debby Jordan?"

"Then we start searching again."

"And I'm supposed to ignore the fact that I know Eve and the kid are here? You're asking a lot of me. I could lose my job. Besides possibly facing criminal charges for harboring a felon."

"Stop dancing around, Spiro. If you hadn't intended to deal, you wouldn't be here. You'd have sent a squad car of Phoenix's finest to pick us up."

"And tell me why I shouldn't do that?"

"We've given you one major lead. We may be able to get you more."

He was silent a moment. "The kid. Give her back to welfare and maybe we can—"

"No," Eve said flatly. "That's not negotiable."

Spiro turned to her. "Everything's negotiable."

"I'm not returning Jane." She paused. "But I'll make it easy for you. I'll give you what you want."

"No," Joe snapped.

"Be quiet, Joe. I knew it was going to come down to this." She stared directly into Spiro's eyes. "I'll give you my word to let you use me any way you want. But only if there's no other solution."

"And who's to decide if there's no other solution?"

"I will."

"That puts you in control. I don't like that."

"But you'll take it." She smiled wryly. "Because you're

an obsessed man, Spiro. You want Dom almost as much as I do."

"More. Because I know what he is and what he can do. You're seeing him only from a personal point of view."

"You're right, my interest couldn't be more intensely personal. Deal?"

Spiro hesitated. "Deal."

"May I speak now?" Joe asked grimly. "I seem to have been left out in the cold again."

"We need him, Joe. It was the only way to get him."

"You could have let me give something else a shot first." He turned to Spiro. "You'd better try damn hard to catch that bastard, or I may declare your little deal null and void. In the most violent way possible."

Spiro acted as if he hadn't heard him. His gaze had shifted back to the grave site. "I'm calling the Phoenix PD to help excavate the site. That means I don't want either of you anywhere near this place. I'll tell them I received a tip about the grave from one of my informants." He looked at Eve. "I'm sending a man to your house with equipment for tracing and taping Dom's calls. I don't have much hope, but we've got to give it a try." He headed for the car. "I'm calling the Phoenix PD now. Get out of here."

"When will we know what you find?" Eve asked.

"I'll phone you tonight with a preliminary report." He smiled sardonically over his shoulder. "Just so you can be sure I'm working my ass off. Okay?"

"Okay." She looked at Joe. "I'll see you back at the house, Joe."

"I'll be a while," he said. "I believe I'll go down to the precinct, look at the files, and talk to Charlie Cather. I'm feeling uptight as hell. I need to *do* something."

THE CALL FROM Spiro came at eight forty-five that evening. "It's Debby Jordan."

"Positive?" Eve asked.

"Too early for DNA, but we got a match on the teeth."

"He didn't pull her teeth?"

"I was surprised too. Or maybe not. From what we could tell, he nearly carved her to pieces. He must have been in a frenzy."

"Enough to forget something as important as her teeth?"

"I'm just telling you what we found."

"Anything else?"

"Yes, there was a candle in her right hand. A taper. Pale pink."

*She showed me the light and then I showed her the light.*

"Can you trace the candle?"

"We'll give it a try. The problem is that candles have become so popular, everyone's manufacturing them these days."

That was true. Even Mom liked to light candles in the bathroom when she soaked in the tub. "When will you get the autopsy report?"

"Tomorrow at the earliest."

"Good-bye. Call me if you learn anything else, Spiro."

"Oh, you've decided you've wrung me dry and are throwing me away? I'll call you tomorrow." He hung up.

Candles.

Light.

*I showed her the light.*

What did it mean to him?

Frenzy. It was difficult to imagine Dom in a frenzy. He was too cool and deliberate. Yet he had said that Debby Jordan was a turning point for him.

"Eve."

She saw Jane standing in the doorway. "Hi. How's Monty doing?"

"I don't know." She shrugged. "Okay. I guess. I'm hungry. You want me to make you a sandwich too?"

Something was wrong. She was too indifferent. Why had she left Monty's side? "Sure. I'd like that."

"You don't have to come with me. I'll bring it here to the office for you." She disappeared down the hall.

Was she worried about Monty? Was she scared? It was always difficult to know what Jane was feeling. But she was reaching out, and it was important that Eve be there for her.

She dropped down on the couch and rubbed her eyes. Too many things to think about. Too many needs to be met. Stop whining. At least things were moving forward.

"You asleep?"

She opened her eyes. Jane stood before her with a tray. "No, just resting my eyes. I didn't get much sleep last night."

Jane set the tray down on the coffee table. "I brought my sandwich too, but I guess you don't feel like company."

It was Jane who never admitted the need for companionship. "I was just thinking I was a little lonely. Sit down."

Jane curled up on the far end of the couch.

"Aren't you going to eat?" Eve asked.

"Yeah, sure." She picked up her sandwich and nibbled at it. "You're lonely a lot, aren't you?"

"It happens."

"But you've got your mother and Joe and Mr. Logan."

"That's true." She took a bite of her sandwich. "Are you lonely sometimes, Jane?"

She lifted her chin. "No, of course not."

"I just wondered. You haven't asked about Mike lately."

"You said that your mother was trying to get him taken away from his father. He'll be okay if they do that." She suddenly looked at Eve. "Why? Is something wrong? Did that lawyer toss him out and—"

"No, Mom says they're becoming buddies. Nothing's wrong." Not with Mike, but she was beginning to think something was wrong with Jane. "It's hard being far away from friends, and I know you like Mike. I've always found loneliness sometimes sort of ambushes you."

"Not me."

Try another road. "I'm surprised you're not with Monty. I'm sure he needs you."

A silence. "He doesn't need me. Sarah said I was helping, but he needs only her. He barely knows I'm there."

Ah, there was the pain. "I'm sure he does."

Jane shook her head. "He's her dog. He belongs to her." She didn't look at Eve. "I wanted him to belong to me. I thought if I loved him enough, he'd love me more than Sarah." She added defiantly, "I wanted to take him away from Sarah."

"I see."

"Aren't you going to tell me how bad that is?"

"No."

"It was bad. I . . . like Sarah. But I love Monty. I wanted him to belong to me." Her hands balled into fists. "I wanted *something* to belong to me."

"He does belong to you. He just belongs to Sarah more. It's natural. She was first in his life."

"Like Bonnie was first in yours?"

Shock rippled through her. "I thought we were talking about Monty. How did we get to Bonnie?"

"She belonged to you. That's why you're helping me, isn't it? It's for Bonnie, not me."

"Bonnie's dead, Jane."

"But she still belongs to you. She's still first." She took a bite of her sandwich. "Not that I care. Why should I care? It's nothing to me. I just thought it was funny."

My God, her eyes were glistening with tears. "Jane."

"I don't care. I really don't care."

"Well, I do." She slid across the couch and pulled Jane into her arms. "I'm helping you because you're a very special person and that's the only reason."

Jane's body was ramrod stiff in her arms. "And you like me?"

"Yes." Christ, she'd almost forgotten how small and dear a child's body felt. "I like you very much."

"I . . . like you too." Jane slowly relaxed against her. "It's okay. I know I can't be first, but maybe we can be friends. You don't belong to anyone like Monty does. I'd like to—" She stopped.

"Maybe we can," Eve said. Jane was breaking her heart. So defensive, so resistant, and yet so in need. "I don't see why not, do you?"

"No." Jane lay still against her for a moment, and then she pushed her away. "Okay. That's settled." She stood up and hurried to the door. "I'm going to get Monty some food and then I'm going to bed." The moment of softness was clearly over. Now Jane was eager to escape a situation that must have made her uneasy.

Well, wasn't Eve equally uneasy? The past few minutes had been as awkward for her as for Jane. They were quite a pair, she thought ruefully. "I thought you said Monty didn't need you."

"Well, he needs to eat. Sarah would have to leave him to get food, and that would make him sad." She added just before leaving the room, "He can't help it if he doesn't love me best."

Adjustments and compromises and acceptance. Jane's life had never been anything else, and she was afraid to ask for anything more, Eve thought as she rose to her feet. But there had been a breakthrough tonight.

She was beginning to admit that she did need someone, and Eve had been chosen to fill the void.

Eve smiled in amusement as she started up the steps. Jane wasn't the only one who had to make compromises. Eve was playing second fiddle to a golden retriever.

It wasn't until she was in bed and had turned out the light that the significance of what had happened hit home.

*Dom had gotten what he wanted.*

Jane had crept beneath Eve's defenses and was becoming important to her.

Calm down. It's fine. Jane had not become Bonnie to Eve. What Eve felt for Jane was entirely different; Jane was more like a friend than a daughter.

But that might be close enough for Dom to make his move.

The thought sent a bolt of panic through her. It wasn't too late. She could push Jane away. She could pretend they'd never shared those moments in the office.

The hell she could. She could never hurt Jane that way.

Dom didn't know anything had changed. She could keep it from him. She'd just be careful to be distant with Jane whenever they were out of the house.

She could keep the truth from Dom.

"HI." JOE CAME into the kitchen and dropped down into a chair. "I could use some coffee."

"It's made. On the counter." Eve lifted her own cup to her lips. "You didn't come home last night."

"How do you know?" He got up and poured himself a cup. "Are you checking up on me? Good."

"I just knocked on your bedroom door and looked in when you didn't answer. You could have called."

"I hoped you were asleep." He grinned. "We sound like an old married couple."

"Why didn't you come back last night?"

"I went with Charlie to his hotel and had a few drinks." He made a face. "Well, more than a few."

"You tried to get him drunk?"

"Just mellow. Charlie's being very cagey. Spiro has him on a short leash since he went over Spiro's head about the VICAP report."

"I don't want to get him in trouble. You should have tried the Phoenix PD first."

"I did, but I ran into a stone wall. The local police are royally pissed at Spiro for not giving them the name of the informant who supposedly told him where Debby Jordan was buried."

"What's that got to do with you?"

"They think I'm a little too friendly with Charlie and Spiro. So I'm out in the cold unless I can find out information from either one of them."

"And did you?"

"It took me a long time before I could persuade him to tell me what he'd found out from the Phoenix police about the murders."

"Candles?"

"There were wax traces that turned out to be candles, but that's not it. The bodies had been buried much longer than the ones at Talladega."

"How long?"

"Between twenty-five and thirty years."

"My God." The time span staggered her. How many deaths, how many graves, Dom? "And no one's ever caught him. It seems impossible."

"As Spiro said, he was probably lucky in the beginning and then got smart." He paused. "But we may have gotten lucky ourselves. These two killings may have been a couple of the first he committed."

"What difference does that make? There can't be any evidence left after all this time."

"The bodies have been identified."

"How? The teeth had been pulled."

"DNA. Remember, the bodies were found almost three months ago. The lab reports came back two weeks ago." He lifted his cup to take a sip. "The police went through old records and came up with four possible missing persons cases. They visited surviving relatives and finally narrowed it down to Jason and Eliza Harding. Age fifteen and sixteen, brother and sister. Disappeared on September 4, 1970. Nice kids. Maybe a little wild. Jason played the guitar and was always talking about going to San Francisco someday. When they disappeared, their father told the police to check in Haight-Ashbury or L.A. There had been a young kid hanging around with Jason and Eliza, a likable kid, but Mr. Harding had begun to think maybe he was a bad influence. He and his two brothers had drifted into town a few weeks before. His brothers were quiet, almost moody, but Kevin was chatty, a ball of fire. He went on and on about different singing groups and musicians who were making a fortune in the coffeehouses on the West Coast. A regular pied piper."

"Dom?"

"His name was Kevin Baldridge. He and his brothers disappeared at the same time as Jason and Eliza."

"Could they trace him?"

Joe shook his head. "But there may be a picture of him."

"Oh, my God."

"Don't get excited. Mrs. Harding offered it to the police, but it wasn't in the file." He smiled. "Charlie's located the Hardings in Azora, a small town north of here. I don't think it's a photo that a mother would throw out, do you?"

"No." Joe was right. She shouldn't get excited, but,

dear heaven, what a break. "Do they know their children's bodies have been found?"

"Not yet. Charlie's just located them. He's going to visit them tomorrow."

"I want to go with him."

"I thought you would. Sorry. It's not a good idea for him to be seen with a kidnapper. But I got him to promise to let you look at the photo as soon as it's logged in as evidence."

"A photograph."

"It might not be Dom."

"And it might be."

Tomorrow she might be able to see his face.

Joe set his cup down on the table. "I'm going to take a shower and get a little sleep." He stood up. "And then I'm taking you out to lunch."

"What?"

"It's going to drive you crazy marking time with nothing to do until we hear more from Spiro or Charlie. Unless you have another body you want to dig up." He headed for the door. "Be ready at noon."

Bossy bastard. "Maybe I don't want to go out to lunch. And maybe you shouldn't be seen with a kidnapper either."

"Then stand me up. I'll take Monty. He'd probably appreciate me more anyway. Though Sarah won't be pleased with me for giving him spicy Mexican." He left the room.

It was the second time in twelve hours she'd come second to that dog, she thought in amusement. It was enough to give a woman a complex.

But, at least, Joe's attitude had been light. She didn't need to deal with weightier personal matters just then. Not that she'd have a choice if Joe decided to— She wasn't going to worry about it. Joe was right. She'd go crazy if she didn't keep busy.

"Could I have some coffee?" Sarah stood in the doorway with Monty beside her. The woman looked as tired and shaky as the dog.

"Sure." Eve jumped to her feet. "Sit down. Would you like something to eat? You haven't had a bite since Monty found Debby Jordan."

"Is it her?" Sarah sat down at the table and Monty lay down at her feet. "Positive identification?"

Eve nodded.

"Thank God." She reached down and patted Monty on the head. "It's over, boy. No more."

"Eggs?"

"Just cereal. Please."

Eve put the cereal, a bowl, and milk before her. "Has Monty eaten?"

"A little last night. He's getting better." Sarah poured milk on the cereal. "Is it going to help? Are they going to find him?"

"There's one lead that looks promising." She told her about the photograph. "It's a lot more than we knew before."

"Yes." Sarah was silent. "I've been thinking about going back to my cabin tomorrow. The search is over. There's no reason for Dom to target Monty now."

*He must have been in a frenzy.*

"Dom doesn't have to have a reason. You found her body quicker than he wanted. Stay here."

"We can take care of ourselves. We were just caught without warning." Sarah rubbed Monty's ears. "And we like our own space."

"Please. Stay here. Just for a few more days. There's a chance that we may get a break soon." She paused. "And Jane will be worried about Monty. You know that."

"I know." Sarah shrugged. "Okay, a couple of days. But Monty will get well sooner at home."

And Monty's well-being was obviously the key to Sarah's existence. "Thanks."

Sarah finished the cereal and stood up. "I'm taking

Monty for a run around the grounds. He needs the exercise." She made a face. "And so do I. Neither of us can stand being cooped up."

That seemed to be the consensus of opinion. Keep moving. Stop thinking of Dom. Mark time. "I'm going out to lunch with Joe. Will you and Monty keep an eye on Jane for me?"

"Sure. But she's more likely to be the one keeping an eye on Monty and me." Sarah grinned. "She's a nice kid. I'm going to miss her." Her smile faded. "It seems impossible that monster wants to kill her."

"But he does."

"Yeah, I know." She moved toward the door with Monty at her heels. "I learned a lot about monsters when I was at Oklahoma City."

"I don't know how you handled it."

"Yes, you do. You handle it one day at a time. One minute at a time. And try to find something in between to balance the craziness."

"You go take your dog for a run."

Sarah smiled faintly. "Or you go out to lunch with Joe. Whatever works."

Eve nodded. "Whatever works."

Logan called Eve on her digital phone when she and Joe were on their way to lunch. "You found Debby Jordan."

"Yes."

"You could have called and told me and not let me read about it in the newspapers."

"I told you, I wanted you out of it." She'd wanted all of them out of it, but that didn't seem to be happening, she thought ruefully.

"Is Quinn still staying at the house?"

"Yes."

"Herb told me he was there. I didn't call you because I hoped you'd send him on his way, but I seem to be the one left out of the circle."

"I'm getting rid of Joe as soon as possible." She glanced at Joe. "But he's making that very difficult."

"Tell me about it. I should have known he'd find out about the house. Is he with you now?"

"Yes."

"Dammit, let me come and help you."

"No, Logan."

There was a silence. "You're closing me away from you. I can feel it."

"I have to do it."

Another silence. "That could mean a lot of things, couldn't it?"

"It means exactly what I said."

He muttered a curse and hung up.

She pressed the off button.

"He's pissed?" Joe asked.

"Yes."

"Good."

"Shut up." Tears stung her eyes. Maybe it would be better if Logan was angry with her. Perhaps she hadn't called him because she wanted him to be the one who walked away. Logan had pride and she had not wanted to hurt that pride.

*You're closing me away from you.*

It had struck a truthful note. My God, had she been pulling away from Logan, distancing herself? When had it started? Joe had come back into her life and turned everything upside down.

"Logan's done everything he could to make things easier for me, and yet he didn't interfere. Not like some people I know."

"That's his mistake. He always took the slow, civilized approach where you were concerned."

"The intelligent approach."

Joe just smiled.

She wanted to slap him.

"Sorry. Actually, I'm feeling fairly mellow toward Logan, and I shouldn't fault him. For years I made the same mistake. There's only one difference between us." His tone was suddenly no longer light. "He doesn't want you enough. You're not his center. He wouldn't do anything to get you. That's why he'll lose." Joe swung the wheel and the car coasted through the entrance gates of a pleasant little park. "And that's why I'll win." He parked at the side of the road. "Now, stop thinking and relax. We're here."

She looked at him in bewilderment. "Where?"

"Lunch." He nodded at a food cart parked by the playground a few yards ahead. "Galindo's. Herb says they make the best fajitas in Phoenix." He pulled a pair of sunglasses from the glove compartment and reached for a black straw hat from the backseat. "Put these on. You'll look like Madonna incognito."

"You've got to be crazy."

"Just hungry. I thought it would be nice to sit on one of those park benches, eat, and people-watch." He got out of the car. "It's too nice a day to be cooped up inside."

It *was* a nice day, and she didn't want to quarrel with him. She wanted to relax and try not to think of Logan or Dom. Tomorrow would be soon enough. Tomorrow they might have the photograph.

EVE AND JOE were sitting on a park bench, eating Mexican food, as if they hadn't a care in the world. She was smiling as she leaned toward Quinn and wiped a corner of his mouth.

Her entire attitude was subtly different today, Dom thought.

Hope?

Perhaps. She had found Debby Jordan.

Dom had no objection to hope. He had wanted to drag the search out a little longer, let the tension build and the relationship with Jane MacGuire grow, but he could deal with optimism. The fall was always greater when you'd climbed to the top. Perhaps it was even better that she'd found the woman so soon. Things were going to move fast from now on, and he'd be walking a tightrope. Excitement seared through him at the thought.

But pitting himself against Eve Duncan was more exhilarating still. She was evolving, toughening, changing just as he had changed. It was interesting to observe and know that he was responsible.

So hope was fine.

But there was something else going on with her. . . .

Watch her. Body language almost always told the story. If he studied her, it would come to him. He had begun to know her very well.

It would come to him.

SARAH AND JANE met Eve and Joe in the driveway.

Monty ran toward Eve, wagging his tail, when she opened the car door.

She gently patted his head. "He looks better."

"He is. Thank God." Sarah gestured and Monty ran back to her. "Nice lunch?"

"Very nice. Fajitas and chili," Joe answered. "I think Eve enjoyed it much more than your Monty would have. I was tempted to bring him a doggie bag, but Eve convinced me it wouldn't be wise."

"I would have murdered you. Monty gets gas."

"Have you been running all this time?"

"No, Jane and I had a picnic." She smiled at the little girl. "Jane said she couldn't remember the last time she had a picnic lunch."

Jane shrugged. "No big deal. Just a lot of ants and dirt in the sandwiches."

Sarah shook her head. "You're tough."

"Well, I guess Monty liked the picnic."

"Because you fed your roast beef to him."

"You told him to take it, and he needed it. He hasn't eaten much lately." Jane headed for the front door. "Come on, Monty. I'll give you some water."

Monty didn't move.

Sarah made another hand gesture and Monty bounded after Jane into the house.

"Thanks for keeping her company," Eve said.

"I enjoy her." Sarah was frowning slightly. "I wish I could— It's not easy for her."

"What?"

"I can't share Monty. She wants him to belong to her, and that can't happen. It's not safe for him to have a divided allegiance." She made a face. "Besides, we've been close too long. It kind of shuts everyone else out."

"She understands about compromises. She's made the adjustment."

"Compromises *suck*."

"I'll second that," Joe murmured. He headed for the front door. "I'm going to call Charlie Cather and then go down to the precinct. I'll see you tonight."

"Why are you calling Charlie? I thought you said he wouldn't let us go with him."

"Another try won't hurt."

Sarah's gaze followed Joe. "You were gone a long time. I was wondering whether Monty and I should come after you."

Eve smiled. "I don't need protection from Joe."

"No?"

"Time got away from us." She tilted her head. "You don't like Joe?"

"I didn't say that. I do like him. He was nice to Monty. I like most people who are nice to Monty. I just think he's a powerhouse and you have to be careful not to be run over by people like him. I've had a few experiences with powerhouses myself."

"For God's sake, we only had lunch. I won't be run over."

Sarah gave her a shrewd look. "Unless you want it to happen." She held up a hand as she strode toward the door. "It's none of my business. I think I'll go and see how Jane and Monty are doing."

Eve slowly followed her into the house. She could hear the sound of Jane's and Sarah's laughter in the kitchen. Joe must be in the office making his call.

Joe . . .

*Unless you want it to happen.*

Of course she didn't want it to happen. She wanted

everything to go back to the way it was. It was too dangerous to let herself be swayed by the—

The house phone rang.

"There's a Mr. Grunard at the front gate," Herb Booker said when she picked up the receiver. "He said you're expecting him."

"Let him in, Herb." She felt a ripple of relief as she replaced the phone. The arrival of Mark Grunard brought her mind back to what was important.

She opened the front door before he could ring the bell.

"Well, this is more welcome than I've come to expect from you." Mark got out of the car. "I anticipated having to storm the gates."

She smiled. "I've never meant to close you out. I just didn't have anything important to share with you."

"I'm a journalist. I can make a story out of a trip to the grocery store."

"That's what I'm afraid of," she said dryly. "Come in and I'll fill you in on what's been happening. Off the record."

"Of course." He followed her into the living room. "Where's Quinn?"

"In the office, I think. He's going to the precinct later."

"Yeah, I heard how he finagled that job as liaison. Smart. And very convenient for me."

She turned to face him. "I want to cooperate with you, Mark. But I won't let you put Joe on the spot."

"Quinn can take care of himself."

Mark wasn't going to listen. Now that he was in the center of things, he was going to push until he got what he wanted. "I've been feeling a little guilty about you, Mark. I don't like the idea of breaking my word to anyone. But the minute you start making Joe's job awkward for him is the minute you'll be out of the loop."

Grunard smiled. "Now, why would I make Quinn's

job difficult? We're all after the same thing. I'll go down to the precinct after I check into a hotel, but I won't get in Quinn's way." He was glancing around the room. "Nice place. Quinn told me Logan had set you up."

She gave him a blank stare. "I don't know what you mean."

He chuckled. "He also said you'd deny it."

"Logan has nothing to do with this. Leave him out—"

"I brought you a glass of milk, Eve." Jane was standing in the doorway. "Mrs. Carboni used to say that milk settled her stomach after she ate spicy food."

"I don't like being compared to Mrs. Carboni." She smiled as she took the milk. "But thanks anyway."

"No offense." Jane smiled back at her. "I used to sneak jalapeño juice into everything she ate. It's pretty hard to tell in spaghetti sauce. Sometimes the milk didn't help and she'd be up all night throwing up."

Eve laughed. "Good."

"This milk's safe. I wouldn't do that to you."

"My, my," Mark murmured. "I believe our little chickadee has mellowed."

Jane gave him a cool glance.

"Or maybe not." Mark smiled. "How are you, Jane?"

"I'm no chickadee." She left the room.

"Ouch." Mark wrinkled his nose. "It seems you're the only one she's tolerating these days."

"I'd have snubbed you too if you'd been that patronizing toward me. She's been holding up better than anyone could expect. She's been wonderful."

"Okay, okay." He held up his hands in surrender. "I see the two of you are presenting a united front. I think I'd better go find Quinn and get him to fill me in on what's been going on. It's safer. Where's the office?"

"Second door on your left," she said curtly.

He glanced back at her from the door. "Dom's done it, hasn't he? The kid's gotten to you."

"Don't be stupid. We're just used to each other, that's all. We live together."

He shook his head. "Then Dom had better never see you with her. He might make the same mistake I did."

Chill iced through her. Had the growing bond been that obvious? "He won't see her with me."

"Then that's okay." Mark left the room.

It wasn't okay. If Mark had made the connection so easily, maybe anyone would be able to see it also. She wouldn't let it happen. She would never take Jane from the house. Still she felt shaken and scared and a little sick. She needed warmth and life and—

Joe.

No, she couldn't go running to Joe.

Jane and Sarah were in the kitchen. She'd go there and sit down at the table and listen to them talk and laugh. She'd pet Monty and then maybe she'd call her mother. She'd keep busy and try not to think of the photograph or Dom or anything but the precious things in life.

And soon the chill would go away.

THE RED-HAIRED DOLL stared up at Eve with glassy brown eyes. Its porcelain throat was cut from ear to ear.

"It was in the driveway. Someone must have tossed it through the gate," Herb Booker said quietly. "The video camera at the gate went out and Juan found the doll when he went to check it. The camera lens had been shattered. Probably a shot from a long-range weapon, since the camera didn't pick up anything. I was going to call Mr. Logan, but I thought you should see this first."

"Yes," she said numbly.

"It wasn't there when Mr. Quinn or Mr. Grunard left earlier. I checked the gate myself." He hesitated. "It's a little girl doll."

"I can see that."

*Bonnie.*

*Jane.*

"It's nasty. I think we should call someone."

"I'll take care of it."

"No offense, ma'am, but it could mean the little girl is—"

"I'll take care of it, Herb." Her hand tightened on the doll. "Thank you for your concern."

"I think you should reconsider—"

"*Go away.*" She stopped and tempered the sharpness of her tone. "I'm sorry. I'm upset. I need to be alone to think about this. I don't want you to call anyone, not even Mr. Logan. Do you understand?"

"I understand."

But he didn't say he wouldn't do it. Why should he? Logan paid his salary.

"Not even Mr. Logan," she repeated, and then gave him an out. "At least, not until tomorrow. Okay?"

He shrugged. "I guess so. Juan and I will both patrol the grounds tonight. You don't have to worry."

"Thank you."

Not worry? Dom had been close enough to toss this savaged doll practically on her front doorstep.

Booker still didn't move.

"Good-bye, Herb." She went into the living room and a moment later heard the front door close behind him.

She sat down on the couch, took out her digital phone, and laid it on the coffee table in front of her.

And waited for him to call her.

It was almost midnight when the phone rang.

"Just a reminder," Dom said.

"What's wrong? Did you get tired of sending me bones?"

There was a surprised silence. "You're angry."

"You bet I am."

"What an interesting development."

"Did you expect me to sit shivering in the dark, you son of a bitch?"

"I didn't really think about it. As I said, I only meant it to remind you of what was important in your life. I believe you may be forgetting."

"Important? You?"

"Yes. Right now there's no one more important to you than I am."

"Screw you." She hung up.

The phone rang again five minutes later.

She ignored it.

It rang four times more in the next hour.

She didn't answer.

IT WAS AFTER two in the morning when Joe came home.

She was still sitting on the couch, holding the doll, when he walked into the living room.

He took one look at the doll and then at her expression. "Shit. What the hell happened?"

"Dom tossed it onto the driveway. Herb didn't tell you?"

He shook his head. "I was wondering why they were both at the gate when I drove in. Did he call?"

"Yes."

He fell to his knees before her. "Bad?"

"The bastard's always bad. It's what he does." Her voice was shaking. "He thought I wasn't paying enough attention to him. He wanted to remind me that he was still around."

Joe gently stroked her hair back from her face. "You could hardly forget."

"That isn't enough for him. He wants to dominate my life. He wants to *be* my life." She looked down at the doll. "He tossed this ugliness at me so I'd remember Bonnie and Jane and all those other—"

"Shh."

"Don't shush me. I won't have it." She jumped to her

feet. "You're treating me like the victim he wants me to be. I won't be a victim. I won't let him run my life."

"Easy." He rose to his feet. "I'm not the enemy here, Eve."

"I know." She took a step closer and buried her head in his shoulder. "Hold me."

He carefully slid his arms around her.

"No, dammit." She pressed against him. "*Hold* me."

He went still. "Are we talking about what I think we are?"

"I won't think of him. I won't think of death. That's what he wants me to do. I want to *live*."

"And you're equating sex with life?"

"Aren't they the same thing? If not, I don't know what the hell all the shouting is about."

"Sex can be a big part of life."

"I won't let him do this to me. I'm not going to sit around and wait for him to come knocking on the door or dictate to me. I'll do what I damn well please."

"Your declaration of tenderness is amazing."

"Do you think I don't know it's not fair to you? But you want it. You told me you wanted it. Have you changed your mind?"

"Hell, no." His lips firmed. "But this isn't what I had in mind."

"It's not what I had in mind either. But I won't have him—" Christ, what was she doing? This was *Joe*. Where were all her good intentions? Tears were suddenly running down her cheeks. "I'm sorry. Forget it. I don't know what I was thinking. Hell, I wasn't thinking. I was only feeling. Try to forgive me. I must have gone a little crazy. He made me so damn—"

The digital phone rang.

"Don't answer it. It's him. I hung up on him and he keeps calling back."

"Turn off the phone."

"Then he'd know he's won."

"Are you sure it's him?"

"It's Dom. I upset him. He wasn't getting what he wanted from me." She picked up the ringing phone and stuffed it in her purse. "He expected more of a payoff from that doll. You might as well give it to Spiro," she said, handing it to him. "See if he can get anything from it or trace it."

"I'll do that." His gaze narrowed on her face. "Are you okay?"

"Other than going temporarily insane, I'm in great shape," she said jerkily. She turned on her heel. "I'm going to bed. I'll see you in the morning."

"Yes."

The phone had stopped ringing by the time she had showered and gotten into bed. Maybe he'd given up. Thank God he didn't know the damage he'd almost done. No, that *she'd* almost done. She had to accept responsibility for her own actions. Anger and frustration were only excuses.

She reached over and turned out the light.

"You shouldn't have done that. I wanted to see you."

Joe was standing in the doorway, a dark figure silhouetted by the light in the hall.

An unmistakably naked figure.

"No," she whispered.

"Too late." He came toward her. "I've been invited."

"I told you I'd made a mistake. I said I was sorry."

"I'm not. You caught me off guard down there and hurt my ego. But once I had time to sort things out, I realized that opportunity was knocking."

"I didn't want to hurt your ego," she said unevenly. "I don't want to hurt you at all, Joe. That's why this can't happen."

"You want it to happen."

"No."

"Dom may have triggered it, but it must have been on your mind or it wouldn't have occurred to you."

"Of course I've been thinking about it. You made sure of that. I'm human, dammit."

"And I mean to make the most of it. It's been a night of revelations. You actually said you wanted to live. That's the first time I've ever heard you say that." He lifted the blanket. "Scoot over. I'm coming in."

His naked thigh touched hers.

She moved over. "It's a mistake, Joe."

His hand covered her breast. "Never."

She couldn't breathe. "Please."

His hand was between her thighs. "Do you know I've never really kissed you?"

She arched upward as his thumb found her. "You're not kissing me now."

"I'll get around to it. I'll get around to everyth— My God, you're ready for me. I thought I'd have to—"

Her digital phone rang.

Joe muttered a curse.

She whispered, "Turn it off."

He started to get off the bed and then stopped. "No." He moved back over her. "I promise you won't hear it soon."

She cried out as he plunged deep within her.

The phone was ringing.

He moved fast, hard.

The phone . . .

He lifted her, crushing her to him as he moved deeper, faster.

Was the phone still ringing?

She no longer heard anything but the beat of his heart against her ear.

"WHY DIDN'T YOU turn off the phone?" she asked drowsily.

"Why do you think?" He kissed her breast. "I was busy. Maybe I didn't want to take the time."

"Tell me."

"Ego. I wanted to be more important to you than Dom. I wanted to beat him." He kissed her nose. "You hurt my feelings a little."

"Not enough to stop you."

"It would have taken a major catastrophe to stop me. Dom doesn't qualify."

"He qualifies."

"He didn't win, did he? Therefore, he's out of the running."

For the time being.

"Stop thinking about him." He reached over, turned on the light, and switched off her phone. "I want to look at you."

She was blushing. "For heaven's sake, give me a blanket, Joe."

He shook his head. "I've wanted to see you like this for too long. Let me have my kicks."

Not when she felt as if she were melting wherever he looked at her. "Turn off the light. Please."

"Not until—" He saw her expression and turned off the light. "Maybe later?"

"Maybe."

"I forgot you're not all that experienced in this sport." He pulled her closer. "But you liked it? You like me?"

She didn't speak.

He was silent a moment. "After ten years I think I deserve the words."

Ten years. She felt tears sting her eyes. "If I weren't afraid you'd be completely impossible, I'd tell you that you were pretty good."

"*Pretty* good?"

"Very good."

"More."

"A stud, a stallion. Brad Pitt, Keanu Reeves, and Casanova rolled into one. I don't know why Diane ever let you go."

"She was a smart lady. She knew she deserved more

than I could give her. It was a mistake from the beginning."

She raised herself on one elbow to look down at him. "Why did you marry her, Joe?"

"It will scare you if I tell you."

"The hell it will."

Silence.

"Why, Joe?"

"For you. I married her for you."

"What?"

"You were too isolated. I thought you needed a friend of your own sex."

"You're kidding."

"I told you it would scare you."

"Men don't get married to provide—"

"I did," he said simply.

She stared at him.

"You were my center. Everything revolved around you. It was a time in my life when I'd almost given up hope of being anything else to you. I thought I'd chosen someone who could give you the companionship you needed. Diane liked the nice things I could give her, and I honestly tried to make a go of our marriage." He shrugged. "It didn't turn out the way I hoped."

"That *is* scary."

"Obsessions always are." He put his finger on her lower lip. "As you should know, my love."

She stiffened.

"Love," he deliberately repeated. "Get used to it."

"I don't have to get used to anything."

"No, but you might as well. It will be more comfortable for both of us." He paused. "Don't be afraid to love me, Eve. I'm not a helpless child who can be taken from you. I'm tough and mean enough to survive for another fifty years or so."

"I'm not afraid."

"The hell you're not." He lowered his head, his lips

barely touching her own. "But that's okay. You don't have to say you love me. I can wait."

"I don't love you. Not the way you want me to love you."

"I think you do." His lips moved back and forth in a gossamer caress. "But if you don't, that's okay too."

"It's not okay. It's all wrong. I'm damaged. No one should know that better than you. You should have someone who—"

"*You're* damaged? I'm the one who's been obsessed for the last ten years."

"It's not the same. I can't—"

"Shh." He moved over her again. "Don't think. Don't analyze. Let everything fall into place. Enjoy . . ."


HE WAS GONE when she woke.

Emptiness.

Loneliness.

It was stupid. She was acting as if she'd never slept with a man before. Sex, pleasure, departure—it was the way she liked her relationships. No lingering that might interfere with her work.

"Time to get up." Joe opened the door and came toward the bed.

"It's almost noon. I called Charlie and he's on his way back from Azora. He has the photograph."

She sat upright. "Are you sure I'll be able to see it?"

"You can ask Spiro yourself. He's on his way here."

"Why?"

"To pick up the doll."

Of course. "You called him this morning?"

"As soon as I got up. I told the security guys to let him in." He went to the closet. "Hit the shower. I'll get your clothes. What do you want to wear?"

"Anything. Jeans . . . a shirt." She ran into the bathroom and got in the shower. Joe could not have been more cool or businesslike. It was as if last night had never happened. Not that she objected. She would have felt awkward if he'd been any other way. Last night had been too—She shook her head. She didn't want to remember how erotic those hours with Joe had been.

"Come on. You need to eat before Spiro gets here." It was Joe standing outside the glass shower door. "Hurry."

"I *am* hurrying."

She opened the door, and he enveloped her in a huge bath towel and started patting her dry.

She reached for the towel. "For God's sake, I can do that."

His gaze dropped to her breasts. "I'm enjoying it."

*Enjoy.*

She felt heat move through her.

"I brought that blue plaid shirt. I like you in blue. Is that okay?"

"I guess so." She should stop him. The lazy movement of his hands beneath the soft towel was incredibly arousing. For some crazy reason the act seemed as intimate as sex. She moistened her lips. "You never told me you liked blue."

"I never told you a lot of things." He bent his head and kissed the hollow of her shoulder. "But I mean to make up for lost time. Want to go back to bed and hear the story of my life?"

Yes, she wanted to go back to bed. "If you promise to tell it. I've never had much luck in getting you to confide in me."

He chuckled. "You wouldn't this time either. We don't have any time." He stepped back and handed her the towel. "Get dressed. I'll wait outside for you."

"Now you tell me to get dressed. Why the hell did you come busting in here and make me—"

"I wanted to make sure you knew I wasn't going to let you make me a one-night stand." He smiled. "You're not going to be able to focus on me for a little while, but I'm going to be around every minute of your day. Don't forget it."

She stared at the door as it closed behind him. How was she supposed to focus on anything else *but* him? He had brought sensuality back into her life.

She was acting like some nympho. She would not be controlled by either her body or Joe Quinn. She could forget everything but what was important. It would just take will and determination.

She tossed aside the towel and began to dress.

JOE WAS SITTING in the chair beside the bed when she came out of the bathroom. His gaze searched her face and he slowly nodded. "I was expecting that reaction. No problem." He got to his feet. "Let's go down and get you some breakfast."

She had been girded for battle, and it was frustrating to have him sidestep before she could even say a word. "I'm not hungry."

"Okay, then you can watch me eat." He held out his hand and she realized he was holding her digital phone. "But first turn your phone back on. Dom may call and you'll need to talk to him."

Her gaze flew to his face.

"It's time to face him again," he said quietly. "Yes, I want to protect you, but I can't protect you from someone I can't see. We have to bring him out into the open."

"That's what I've been telling you all along."

"I was too scared for you to listen. Now I'm too scared not to listen. You're not going to stop, so I can't stop. We have to finish it. Turn on the phone."

She took the phone and pressed the on button.

It was silent.

Joe smiled. "Now, how's that for anticlimax? I think we both expected an ominous clash of cymbals." He gently pushed her toward the door. "Come on, let's get this show on the road."

Spiro was waiting in the living room when they came downstairs. "Where's the doll?"

"I put it in a box and slid it behind some books on a shelf." Joe crossed the room to the built-in bookcases. "I didn't want Jane to run across it."

"I can't see her flinching," Spiro said dryly. "Your Jane let me in when I rang the doorbell and she gave me the third degree. She even called security to make sure I hadn't leaped over the electric fence."

"Where is she?"

"After grudgingly allowing me to sit down, she said she was going to the kitchen to fix you something to eat." He took the box and glanced at the doll. "Ugly. It must have scared you."

"No. It made me mad."

"Did he make a follow-up call?"

"Yes, I hung up on him."

Spiro looked up. "That might not have been smart."

"I'm tired of being smart and cautious. What about the photograph? Can I see it?"

"Not before it's logged in."

"Can I get a duplicate?"

"Not before it's logged in."

Eve had very little patience left. "What about this Kevin Baldridge?"

Spiro smiled. "According to Charlie, Mrs. Harding remembers Kevin Baldridge and his brothers very well. Kevin was closemouthed about where they were from, but one of his brothers mentioned Dillard."

"Where is that?"

"A small town in northern Arizona."

"Small enough to trace Kevin Baldridge?"

"Maybe. We have to hope the townsfolk have long memories."

"What about his brothers? Even if Kevin Baldridge

has moved on, perhaps they might have gone back home."

"It's possible." Spiro stood up. "We'll soon find out. Charlie will call and check on birth and school records after he gets back with the photograph. And I'm heading up to Dillard today."

"Could we come along?"

He shrugged. "I suppose it wouldn't hurt. And if Dom is Kevin Baldridge, seeing you invade his turf might trigger him to act." He glanced at Joe. "I'm surprised that didn't arouse a reaction from you. No objections? No accusations that I'm using her?"

Joe ignored the mockery in Spiro's voice. "How soon can we leave?"

"Later this afternoon. I have to go back to the precinct, wait for Charlie, and make sure the photograph is logged in." He paused. "Mark Grunard came to see me at my hotel this morning. He said you were still cooperating with him." His lips tightened. "I told him that doesn't mean *I'm* cooperating. I've never approved of your involving him."

"He helped me," Eve said. "I owe him."

"I don't owe him and I don't like how he's been hanging around Charlie."

"He could have turned Jane and me in to the police a dozen times and he didn't do it."

"Why not?"

"Because I promised him an exclusive when we get Dom."

"Indeed?" He moved toward the door. "Whatever your deal with him, we're not bringing him along to Dillard."

"I fixed you an egg and bacon sandwich, Eve." Jane stood in the doorway. "Come on."

"I'll be right there."

Jane gave Spiro a cool glance. "He can talk to you while you're eating. Your food will get cold."

"Heaven forbid I interfere with your nourishment." Spiro mockingly bowed to Jane. "You'll be relieved to know I was just on my way out, young lady."

"Wait."

Spiro glanced back at Eve.

"How long will we be gone?"

"A few hours, a day. It depends on how much advance work Charlie is able to do."

"We're taking Jane with us."

Spiro shook his head. "For God's sake, I'm already sticking my neck out enough without being seen with a kidnap victim."

"She has to go with us."

"She's very well protected here."

"I wouldn't mind going without her if it's only for an hour or so. But you're not sure when we'll be back."

"Is taking her with us wise?"

"Dom wants her with me."

Spiro glanced from her to Jane. "But do you want him to see you with her? You're obviously on close terms."

"If Eve wants me, I'm going with her." Jane took a step closer. "And I wasn't kidnapped. How stupid can you get?"

"Evidently very stupid," Spiro said. "I don't recommend it, Eve."

"I'll take care of Eve and Jane," Joe said. "You handle tracking down Kevin Baldridge."

Spiro shook his head. "It's a mistake." He opened the door. "I'll pick you up at four this afternoon."

Was it a mistake? Eve wondered. She didn't want Dom to see her and Jane together, but what could she do? Jane was her responsibility. She couldn't leave her for hours or maybe days; she would never forgive herself if anything happened to Jane. She'd been down that road before.

She turned to Joe. "I have to take her."

"I know." Joe smiled.

"Of course I'm going," Jane said. "We're not going to let him tell us what to do. Now, come on and eat your breakfast." She started down the hall. "And then you can tell me *where* I'm going."

The small plane landed at a tiny airport north of Dillard, Arizona, at eight-thirty that night. There had been a recent snow in the mountain town, and the weather was icy. The airport had only two runways and the tarmac was bumpy. One taxi was parked outside the terminal.

Spiro got a call from Charlie in the taxi on the way to town. He didn't look pleased by the time he hung up.

"The courthouse burned down six years ago," Spiro said. "And there were no records of any Baldridge children attending the local school."

"Maybe they went to school in a nearby town."

"We're checking Jamison. It's thirty miles from here." He looked out the window. "But the schools will be closed until tomorrow morning. We'll have to stay overnight at a hotel . . . except Charlie said there isn't one. I think Dillard's population is only a little over four thousand."

"Six thousand five hundred," the cabdriver said.

Spiro reached into his pocket and drew out his notebook. "Charlie mentioned a bed and breakfast. Mrs. Tolvey's on Pine Street."

"Good choice," the cabdriver said. "Mrs. Tolvey puts on a great breakfast spread."

"Then that will be fine"—Eve looked at the driver's ID on the panel—"Mr. Brendle." She put her arm around Jane, who was leaning against her. "Anyplace with a bed."

"Bob. Good beds too. Mrs. Tolvey's been running the place for over twenty years, and she changes all the mattresses every five years."

"Incredible," Spiro said.

"Well, they don't get used that often."

"Twenty years," Joe repeated, looking at Spiro. "My, what a coincidence."

"Charlie's a good man. It's a long shot, but still we may find out something from Mrs. Tolvey."

"Will she have enough rooms for us?" Joe asked the cabdriver.

"Six rooms. All clean as a whistle." He nodded. "It's right up ahead. Two blocks."

The bed and breakfast was a large gray house with a wooden swing on the wide front porch. A light gleamed beside the storm door.

"You go on and knock." Bob got out of the car. "I'll get your bags."

"Wait," Spiro said. "Do you have a bar in this town?"

"You've got to be kidding. Four." Bob pulled the overnight cases out of the trunk. "You want to go get a drink first?"

"Is there one where all the regulars go?"

"Cal Simm's place on Third Street."

"Take me there." He turned to Eve. "I want to see if I can find out anything before tomorrow. Check me in and tell Mrs. Tolvey I'll be along in a few hours."

Eve nodded. To Joe, Spiro said, "You'll talk to Mrs. Tolvey?"

"You'd better believe it."

The taxi was pulling away when Mrs. Tolvey opened the front door. Dressed in a pale green chenille robe, she was in her late fifties with short, curly brown hair and a wide smile.

"I saw Bob drop you off. I'm Nancy Tolvey. Need a room?"

"Three." Joe picked up the bags and entered the foyer. "A twin for Ms. Duncan and the little girl, a single next door for me. We have a friend who will be back a little later. We'll check him in too."

"Fine. But we don't have any twins. A queen okay?"

Eve nodded.

"Suppose you show Eve and Jane upstairs and I'll stay down here to sign us in," Joe said.

Eve picked up her and Jane's bags, and Nancy Tolvey led the way.

The room she showed Eve was clean and bright with pale green ivy twining on cream-colored wallpaper. "No private bathroom. It's down the hall."

"You heard her, Jane," Eve said. "You shower first. I'll bring your pajamas to you as soon as I unpack them."

"Okay." Jane yawned. "I don't know why I'm so sleepy."

"The altitude," Nancy Tolvey said. "You must not be from around here."

"We came from Phoenix."

She nodded. "I visited there once. Too hot. I couldn't ever get used to that kind of climate after living here all my life."

All her life . . .

Joe had told Spiro he'd talk to Nancy Tolvey, but Eve might as well do it herself. "We're trying to locate a family who may have lived here a long time ago. The Baldridges?"

"Baldridges?" Nancy Tolvey was silent a moment and then shook her head. "I don't think so. I don't recall anyone by that name living here." She headed for the stairs. "I'll bring you up some more bath towels."

It had been worth a try, Eve thought. Maybe they'd find out something tomorrow.

NANCY TOLVEY WAS frowning as she came down the stairs.

"Something wrong?" Joe asked.

She sat down at the old-fashioned writing desk in the foyer. "It's nothing." She opened the guest book. "Sign here, please. Name, address, driver's license." She was still frowning as she watched him register. "You'll share the bath with your friends. We don't have—" She closed her eyes. "The candles . . ."

"I hoped you had electricity," Joe said dryly.

Her lids flicked open. "No, that's not what I meant. Miss Duncan asked me about the Baldridge family, and I told her I couldn't remember anyone around here by that name."

Joe stiffened. "But you do?"

"I didn't want to talk about it, but, yes, I remember." She smiled bitterly. "There's no way I could forget. And not talking about it isn't going to make it go away, is it? I've done that for years."

"The Baldridges lived here in town?"

She shook her head. "It was up north of Dillard."

"Near Jamison?"

"No, the tent was up farther in the mountains."

"Tent?"

"Old man Baldridge was an evangelist. A real fire-and-brimstone preacher. He had a big tent on this plateau in the middle of the mountains, where he gave his sermons." She made a face. "When I was in my teens, I slept around a little. Well, maybe a lot. My daddy thought I needed my soul saved. When he heard about Reverend Baldridge's tent show, he drove me up there one night. And believe me, it was quite a show. The reverend scared the daylights out of me."

"Why?"

"He looked like death warmed over. White face, dirty gray hair, and his eyes . . ."

"How old was he?"

"Sixty, maybe. He looked real old to me. I was only fifteen."

Then the evangelist couldn't have been Dom, Joe thought.

"He shouted at me," Nancy Tolvey continued. "He stood up there, waving that red candle, telling me what a whore I was."

"Red candle?"

"The whole tent was full of candles. No electricity. Just big iron candelabras filled with candles. We all got a candle when we came in. Children got white ones. The rest of us got red or pink." She shook her head. "I never forgave my daddy for taking me there and letting Baldridge drag me up to the altar and tell everyone what a sinner I was."

"I can see why it's impossible to forget."

"I remember crying and jerking away from him. I ran out of the tent and down the hill to our car. My father came after me and tried to make me go back, but I wouldn't go. He finally took me home. I got married and moved out six weeks later."

"Who else was in the tent that night?"

"There were so many people there. Why are you looking for him? Is he any relation?"

"No. Actually, we're looking for his family."

She shook her head. "I don't know about that. You'll have to ask someone else."

"Can you point me to anyone who might remember anything about the reverend?"

"Daddy heard about him through the Bloom Street Baptist Church. A lot of the members were driving up to the revival on weekends. Someone there might know something." She smiled crookedly. "That was the church where I was baptized, but I never went back. I was too afraid someone had been there when that old devil screamed out what a sinner I was."

"You never heard about the reverend again?"

"You think I'd want to hear or think about him again? I wasn't a bad kid. What's sex anyway? He shouldn't have done that to me." She drew a deep breath. "I'm getting all upset over nothing. It was so long ago. I've lived a happy life since then. Funny how the things that happen to you as a kid leave the deepest scars, isn't it?"

"Maybe not so funny."

She stood up. "I was going to bring up more towels. You're in the room at the top of the stairs, next to Miss Duncan and the kid."

Joe watched her walk down the hall. He had struck pay dirt.


"AN EVANGELIST," EVE repeated. "Dom's father?"

Joe shrugged. "Or grandfather. She said he was nearly sixty."

"Everyone over thirty looks decrepit to a fifteen-year-old."

"True."

"Candles had some sort of significance for the preacher. His flock's state of grace?"

"More likely degree of sin."

"And Dom carries on the judgment?" She shook her head. "He's very smart. He knows why he's killing. He likes it."

"But, as Nancy Tolvey says, things that happen in your childhood scar and stay with you."

"So what happened to him that could have turned him into a mass murderer?"

Joe shrugged. "Who knows? We'll go to the Baptist church tomorrow and see if we can find out anything else."

"Could Dom's father still be alive?"

"Possibly. He'd be pretty old." He bent his head and

brushed a kiss on her nose. "Go to sleep. I'll wait up for Spiro and tell him what we've learned."

"It's more than I expected." Excitement tingled through her. They were getting close. Dom was no longer a complete enigma. "And tomorrow we'll know more."

"Don't get your hopes up."

"Don't be silly. Of course I'll get my hopes up."

Joe smiled. "I shouldn't complain. Hope's very healthy for you."

"Stop sounding as if I'm a nutcase and you're my psychoanalyst."

"Sorry. I've become accustomed to analyzing every move you make. It comes of standing wistfully on the sidelines."

"*Wistful* isn't in your vocabulary." She hurriedly looked away from him. "Jane's in bed. Will you keep an eye on her while I shower?"

"I won't take a step away from your door."

She could feel his gaze on her as she walked down the hall, feeling weak-kneed. Since the trip had begun, Joe had fallen back into the role of old friend. He hadn't said anything too personal until just then, and his words brought the memory of the previous night rushing back to her.

It was very unsettling to realize her feelings for Joe could almost overwhelm her eagerness at what they'd learned about Dom.

JOE WAS WAITING when Eve and Jane came down the stairs the next morning. "I'm afraid we'll have to skip Mrs. Tolvey's breakfast. I have a taxi outside. Spiro's waiting for us."

"He's not here?"

"No, he called me about three in the morning. At the bar he got a lead on Reverend Baldridge, and he's been up all night."

"Did you tell him we should go to the Baptist church?"

Joe nodded. "He said it's not necessary. After he found out about the tent revival, he tracked down Reverend Piper, who's the pastor of the Bloom Street church, and woke him up." Joe shrugged as she stared at him in surprise. "Nobody said Spiro isn't ruthless when he's on the trail."

"He found out something?"

"He found the place where the reverend gave his sermons. It's a fairly long drive. We're going to meet Spiro there."

SPIRO WAS STANDING alone on top of a hill. Patches of snow dotted the ground and gray clouds hovered over the mountains in the distance.

The driver parked at the bottom of the hill.

"Pay off the taxi, Joe," Spiro called out. "I'll drive you back. I commandeered Reverend Piper's car." Spiro smiled sardonically as he nodded at the brown Ford parked some distance away. "There are times when being FBI comes in handy."

Jane ran up the hill and looked around. The ground was utterly barren; tatters of seared cloth clung to the numerous blackened stakes driven into the earth. "A fire?"

"Yes," Spiro answered.

Eve felt suddenly cold. "What happened here?"

"Do you want to send the child to the car?" Spiro asked.

Jane was wandering slowly some distance away.

"No, I won't shut her out. She deserves to know everything we know."

"And what do we know?" Joe had joined them. "When did this happen?"

"Twenty-nine years ago."

"An accident?"

"It was presumed to be an accident. Everyone knew about all the candles. The tent was a fire waiting to happen."

"Any fatalities?"

"No bodies were found. Services were held here every Friday, Saturday, and Sunday. The fire must have happened earlier in the week, because the site was found exactly like this when the first carload of people came that weekend."

"Was there an investigation?"

"Of course. But no one could find Reverend Baldridge. It was decided that he had moved on. Evangelists are usually traveling men, and he wasn't very popular with the authorities anyway. He'd been warned about the candles being a fire hazard."

"*Did* he move on?"

"We'll have to find out, won't we?" Spiro glanced around. "Christ, this place is weird."

Eve felt the same way. "If the fire happened that long ago, why hasn't the grass grown back?"

"What else did you find out?" Joe asked. "What about his family? What did Reverend Piper tell you about Kevin Baldridge?"

"He doesn't remember a Kevin. His father was the pastor of the Bloom Street Baptist Church when Reverend Baldridge was preaching here. He was only a boy when his father brought him up here for services. He met Mrs. Baldridge once, but the only sons he recalls are Ezekiel and Jacob. He never met Kevin."

"But we know there's a Kevin. Mrs. Harding met him."

"If he was here, he was kept out of sight." Spiro shook his head. "Though why is a mystery. It seems old Baldridge kept everyone in the family busy at the services, handing out candles, passing the collection plates . . ."

"I don't like it here." Jane was standing beside Eve. "When can we go?"

Even Jane was feeling bad vibes, Eve realized. "Soon. Want to go wait in the car?"

Jane shook her head and moved closer. "I'll wait for you."

"We might as well all go," Spiro said. "There's nothing we can do right now. We'll hop back to Phoenix and I'll get a team to come here and go over the site."

"After two decades and a fire?"

"No one searched for graves in the area."

"You don't think Reverend Baldridge just moved on, do you?"

"I have to investigate every possibility. The old man seems to have been pretty unpleasant."

"Yes." Joe's gaze wandered around the campground. "Fanatics usually cause a lot of misery."

"Well, if Kevin Baldridge is Dom, he's created more than his share of misery." Spiro started down the hill. "Like father, like son."

"Maybe it isn't Kevin. Maybe it's one of the other brothers." Eve followed Spiro.

"But where was Kevin when the services were going on?" Spiro said. "It smacks of rebellion against the old man." He glanced over his shoulder. "What are you doing, Quinn?"

Joe was kneeling, digging into the soft soil with a hand. "Just checking something." He lifted a palmful of dirt to his mouth and touched his tongue to it. "Salt."

Eve stopped in her tracks. "What?"

"Like you, I was wondering why nothing had grown back." Joe brushed his palm clean as he stood up. "Someone plowed the area with salt either before or after the fire. He didn't want anything to live in this place again."

·   ·   ·   ·   ·

IT WAS EARLY evening when they arrived back in Phoenix. Spiro left them at the airport and Joe, Eve, and Jane arrived at Logan's house after nine o'clock.

To Eve's surprise, Logan himself was sitting on the couch, playing cards with Sarah, when they walked into the living room.

"It's about time." He threw down his cards and stood up. "Why the hell didn't you tell me you were leaving town?"

"I'm glad you're back," Sarah said. "He's been here for hours driving Monty and me bats. He wouldn't leave and then he wanted me to amuse him."

Logan scowled at her. "You cheated."

"I'm just a better poker player than you are. What do you think rescue teams do between searches?" She rose to her feet. "You deal with him, Eve. Monty and I are tired of watching him brood."

"I don't brood."

Sarah didn't argue. "Come on, Jane. You look as tired as I feel. Rough trip?"

"It was creepy there." Jane stooped to pat Monty. "Come on, boy. Let's go to bed."

The retriever stretched and then followed Sarah and Jane from the room.

Logan's gaze followed Sarah. "She's still holding a grudge."

"She played cards with you," Joe said.

"Because she wanted to beat my ass." He turned to Eve and went on the attack. "Didn't it occur to you that I'd be worried when Booker told me you'd left the house?"

"I was in a hurry. Spiro had a lead. I honestly didn't think of it." She supposed she should have called Logan, she thought wearily. "I'm sorry, Logan."

"Leave her alone." Joe was behind her, his hands resting lightly on her shoulders. "She has enough problems without trying to pacify you."

"Be quiet, Joe. He's been trying to help me. I shouldn't have made him worry."

"I don't mind worrying if I can get my teeth into a problem. I can't stand being shut out of—" Logan stopped, staring at Eve and then at Joe standing behind her. "It's over, isn't it? He's done it."

"What?"

"He's won. He's finally got what he wants. God, it couldn't be more clear." He smiled without mirth. "I should have known that I was fighting a lost cause. I could fight Quinn, but I can't fight you, Eve. From the time he came to the island, you wanted to follow him home."

"Because of Bonnie."

"Maybe." Logan looked at them for a long while. "You take care of her, Quinn."

"You don't have to tell me that."

"Yes, I do. Because I'm warning, not stating. If I can help, call me, Eve."

"She won't need your help," Joe said.

"You can never tell."

She couldn't stand it. She wouldn't let him leave like this. "Joe, I want to talk to Logan alone."

Joe didn't move.

"Joe."

"Okay." He left the room.

"Why do I feel that he's lurking in the hall?" Logan asked.

"Because he probably is." She tried to smile. "You should take it as a compliment."

"Should I?"

"He realizes how much you mean to me. How much you'll always mean to me."

"But evidently not enough."

"What's enough? It hurts me when you hurt. It makes me happy when you're happy. If you ever need me, I'll be there for you. Isn't that enough?"

"It's a lot. Not as satisfying as what I wanted, but I'll take it." He paused. "Just for my own curiosity, how did Quinn do it?"

"I don't know," she said frankly. "I didn't want it. It makes me uneasy. It's like being caught in some kind of whirlpool. It just happened."

"Nothing 'just happens' with Quinn. He's a major force. I've always known he was waiting in the wings for you."

"I didn't."

"I know. I hoped I'd have you wrapped up before he decided to make a move. I didn't manage to pull it off." He looked at her for several moments and then gave her a quick kiss. "But it was a good year, wasn't it?"

Tears stung her eyes. "The best."

"Not the best, or we wouldn't have reached this point, but pretty damn good." He took her arm and walked with her into the foyer, where Joe was waiting by the stairs. "Hello, Quinn. What a surprise."

"Not." Joe moved closer to Eve.

"You don't have to act as if I'm going to kidnap her. That's not my style." His lips tightened. "Though I'd like to break your neck."

Joe shook his head. "But you won't do it. That's the difference between us. You're tough, but you never reached the point of no return with Eve. I wonder if you ever have with anyone."

Logan took a step forward and said softly, "I'm tempted to prove you wrong."

"Logan," Eve said.

She didn't think he'd listen to her. Then he turned away from Joe and opened the door. "Good-bye, Eve. I'll be around. Don't close me out entirely. Okay?"

"That couldn't happen." They had become too close. She kissed his cheek. "Not ever."

"Remember you said that." The door shut behind him.

Joe gave a low whistle. "I don't like the sound of that. Am I going to have to be friends with him?"

"You don't have to do anything. But he's my friend, dammit. He always will be."

"I was afraid that was what you meant. I'll have to consider the way to—" He stopped. "You're upset. I'll shut up and leave you alone."

"That would be a first."

"You *are* upset." He scowled. "And I'm jealous as hell."

She used the word he'd once used with her. "Adjust."

He smiled. "I will."

"I've made you no promises, Joe. I still don't think we—"

"Time for me to leave," he interrupted. "You're starting to be introspective, and that could be dangerous. I'm going to the precinct and see about the picture." He paused. "I may not be back tonight. I think you could use some time alone."

She felt a mixture of relief and disappointment. "You don't have to stay away. If I don't want you in my bed, I can always say no."

"I'm trying to display my sensitive side." He leaned forward and kissed her hard and quick. "Sleep well. I'll see you in the morning."

She doubted she'd sleep well, she thought as she climbed the stairs. All the way back from Dillard she hadn't been able to forget the sight of that scorched, ruined hilltop. What had made Dom so bitter that he had ravaged the site? He had ripped and killed the earth as he had the bodies of his victims.

And then she'd faced Logan and hurt him. For the second time.

But she had never thought her feelings for Joe would shift and change. If she was smart, she'd close herself away from him, focus solely on her work. She'd never been this unsure and emotional when she was focused on her job. She had purpose and satisfaction knowing she was helping the lost ones.

Yes, that was the smart thing. Think only of work. Close Joe out . . .

*"IT WON'T WORK, Mama."* Bonnie was sitting in the chair beside her bed. *"Joe won't let you do that. Besides, it's too late."*

*"I can do whatever I wish."* Eve propped her head higher on the pillow. *"He's interfering with my life."*

*"So am I, but you don't shut me out."*

*"You can't shut off your dreams."*

Bonnie chuckled. *"You always have an answer. The reason you don't shut me out is because you love me."*

*"Oh, yes,"* she whispered.

*"And that's why you can't shut Joe out."*

*"That's different."*

*"You're darn right. Joe's alive."*

*"I'd hurt him."*

*"You're just depressed because of Logan. You shouldn't be. It was bound to happen. Remember I once told you that sometimes love started out one way and then became something else? You don't have to lose Logan and you won't lose Joe."*

*"Bull. Loss can happen anytime. I lost you."*

*"Silly. Then why am I here talking to you?"*

*"Because I'm nutty as a fruitcake. Another reason I should walk away from Joe."*

*"I'm not going to argue with you. You're smart, you'll do the right thing."* Bonnie leaned back in the chair. *"I just want to sit here and enjoy being with you. It's been a long time."*

*"Then why didn't you come sooner?"*

*"I couldn't get close to you. It was hard this time. So much darkness . . . Nothing but darkness around him, Mama."*

"He's a terrible man." She moistened her lips. "Was he the one, Bonnie?"

"I can't see through the darkness. Maybe I don't want to see."

"I want to see. I have to see."

Bonnie nodded. "To protect Jane. I like Jane."

"So do I. But also because of you, baby."

"I know. But you're leaning more toward the living now. That's the way it should be."

Eve was silent a moment. "He tried to tell me Jane was you reincarnated. Wasn't that stupid?"

"I think it is. How could I be reincarnated when I'm here talking to you?" She smiled. "And you know she's nothing like me."

"Yes, I know."

"You wouldn't want her to be like me, Mama. We all have our very own souls. That's what makes every one of us so special and wonderful."

"Dom isn't wonderful."

"No. He's twisted and ugly." Bonnie frowned. "I'm frightened for you. He keeps coming nearer and nearer . . ."

"Let him come. I'm waiting for him."

"Shh, don't get upset. We won't think any more about Dom tonight. Will you tell me about Monty? I love dogs."

"I know. I was going to get you a puppy for Christmas the year that you—"

"And you've been regretting ever since that you didn't get me one sooner. Stop it. I was happy. But you should learn something from that. Live every moment. Don't put off anything until tomorrow."

"Stop preaching at me, dammit."

Bonnie giggled. "Sorry. Then tell me about Monty."

"I don't really know much about him. He belongs to Sarah and he's a rescue and cadaver dog. Jane loves him and trails after him every chance she . . ."

•   •   •   •

MARK GRUNARD WAS waiting in the lobby of Charlie Cather's hotel when Joe walked in. "Ah, back from the mountains?"

"What are you doing here?"

"Cather's promised to have a drink with me. He should be down soon. Any luck in Dillard?"

"No school records there, so we're checking a nearby town. It turns out the father was a traveling evangelist."

"Damn, I was hoping there would be school photos to compare with Mrs. Harding's snapshot."

"So were we." Joe sat down. "Spiro's not pleased you're sticking so close to Cather."

"Tough. I didn't get anything from him, so I had to zero in on Cather. He's a hell of an easier mark."

"He's tougher than you'd think."

"But he doesn't have Spiro's experience and just may let something slip." He added shrewdly, "Has he told you anything about the photograph? Is that why you're here?"

Why was he there? He'd gone to the precinct earlier about the picture and was told the duplicates weren't ready. That stone wall again. The Phoenix police were mad as hell at Spiro for not telling them who tipped him off about Debby Jordan's grave. So they were paying him back. A little tit for tat.

Even if Joe could persuade Charlie to describe the photo, he doubted it would help. Face it, he was really there because he'd needed to distance himself from Eve. His impulse had been to move quickly, push hard instead of waiting patiently. It would have been a stupid move. She had been close to Logan, and Joe should be grateful she hadn't been more upset. But he wasn't grateful, and he was tired as hell of waiting patiently. He'd come too close to her to take a step back.

"No one's told me anything," Joe answered Mark. "Have you seen Charlie since he picked up the photo?"

"Yesterday evening at the precinct." He paused.

"Something's bothering him. He's trying to hide it, but he's not good enough."

"Maybe Spiro raked him over the coals for talking to you."

"Maybe." He shrugged. "But I didn't notice it until he came back from the Hardings' with that picture. I'm glad you're here. We'll gang up on the kid and try to find out what's making him so uneasy." He got to his feet. "Here he comes."

Cather was smiling as he walked toward them from the elevators. "I wasn't expecting you, Joe. Spiro said you just got back from Dillard. What is this? A conspiracy?"

Screw ganging up on Cather. If Charlie dropped something, he'd pick it up. But he wouldn't pressure him. Joe rose to his feet. "Yep, and you're the target."

Cather's smile faded. "I can't talk about the photo until I get clearance from Spiro. No way am I stepping on his toes again."

Grunard was right, something was bothering Charlie. But maybe he was just feeling the pressure. "If you can't, you can't. Then I guess if we can't bribe you, you'll just have to buy the drinks." He headed for the bar. "How's your wife?"

EVE WAS SLEEPING when Dom called her very early in the morning. The sound of his voice was hideously jarring, piercing the serenity she usually felt after dreams of Bonnie.

"You've been busy. How did you like the scenes of my childhood?"

"How do you know I was there?"

"I listen. I watch. Don't you feel me watching you, Eve?"

"No, I ignore you . . . Kevin."

He chuckled. "I prefer Dom. Kevin doesn't exist anymore. I've gone through so many transformations since then. And I've noticed you've been trying to close me out. It made me angry at the time. But I got over it. It only whetted my appetite."

"Kevin must have been a nasty little bastard. What happened to your parents?"

"What you think happened."

"You killed them."

"It was inevitable. My father saw Satan in me from the time I was a small child. He'd make me stand and hold a black candle in each hand and then he'd beat me until I fell to my knees. When the beating was over, he'd rub salt into the wounds. Maybe he was right about seeing evil in me. Do you think we're born with the seeds of evil?"

"I think you were."

"But you also think I'm insane. My father was insane and they called him a saint. The line is so thin, isn't it?"

"Did Ezekiel and Jacob think he was insane?"

"No, they were as frightened and fooled by him as all the rest. But I tried to make them see. I took them with me when I ran away. I was lonely then and needed people."

"And you brought them here to Phoenix."

"We were going to California. I'd talked the Harding kids into going with us. But then Ezekiel and Jacob got scared. They packed up one night and ran back to my father. I went into a rage."

"And killed the Hardings."

"It was beyond anything. The ultimate experience of my life. And at last I knew what I was and what I was meant to do. I went back to that tent on the hill and I butchered all of them."

"Your mother too?"

"She stood by and watched him punish me. Is cruelty less painful because it's passive?"

"And your brothers?"

"They made their choice when they went back to him. I had to start over."

"Where are the bodies?"

"You won't find them. I scattered their parts over half of Arizona and New Mexico and enjoyed every moment of it."

"And sowed that campground with salt."

"A melodramatic piece of symbolism, but I was only a boy at the time."

"Like leaving a candle with your victims? You're not a boy now."

"It's difficult to erase the teachings of childhood. Or perhaps part of my satisfaction is showing my father that I use his precious candles in my own way."

"Your father is dead."

"He was sure he was going to heaven, so he must be looking down on me. Or do you think his soul was chopped up with his body? I've often wondered." He paused. "Do you believe Bonnie's soul was destroyed?"

She bit hard on her lower lip. "No."

"Well, you'll know soon. I haven't decided what candle I'll use for you. It's a terrible decision. White for Jane, of course, but your color must reflect—"

She hung up. He was in a mood for confidences, and perhaps she should have held on, but she couldn't take any more. He was dragging her down into the darkness that surrounded him. It was worse because it followed the wonderful dream of Bonnie. At this moment the evil seemed to be overpowering and she was helpless to fight it. It kept coming and coming . . .

*You should learn something from that. Live every moment. Don't put off anything until tomorrow.*

Bonnie's words.

Live every moment . . .

• • •

EVE HEARD JOE come into the house two hours later. She left her bedroom and waited for him at the top of the stairs.

He paused when he saw her. "Okay?"

"No, Dom called. Nothing is ever okay when he talks to me."

"What did he say?"

"Poison. Ugliness. I'll tell you later." She held out a hand. "Come to bed."

He slowly climbed the steps until he stood before her. "I'm being forgiven for not being sorry Logan bowed out?"

"It was never a question of forgiveness."

He took her hand. "You've discovered you can't live without me in your bed?"

"Will you stop joking?"

"Who's joking?" He reached out and touched her cheek. "I'm probing. I have an idea something very important is happening here. Why, Eve?"

She swallowed to ease the tightness of her throat. "I never gave Bonnie a puppy. She wanted it and I put it off. And then it was too late."

His brows lifted. "And what's the connection? Is taking me into your bed the equivalent of giving me a puppy?"

She shook her head. "The puppy's not for you, Joe. It's for me. I'm being entirely selfish. I want to be near you. I want you to talk to me. I want you to make love to me." She smiled shakily. "And I won't put it off. I won't wait until it's too late. Will you come to bed and be with me, Joe Quinn?"

"Oh, yes." He slid his arm around her waist. His voice was as uneven as hers had been. "You're damn right I will."

When Spiro called Eve that afternoon, she told him what Dom had told her of his childhood. "Did the technician monitoring the phone trace the call?"

"No, that's been a washout, dammit. But what Dom told you computes with the little we've learned," Spiro said. "We've contacted the schools in Jamison. No school records for the Baldridge boys. But I managed to track down a couple of reports about an official going out to see Reverend Baldridge and inquiring why the boys weren't in school. The reverend claimed his sons were being home-schooled. He didn't think the boys would get a godly education in public schools."

"Anything else?"

"One more thing. The reports were on Ezekiel and Jacob. No mention of Kevin."

"If he never attended the services, maybe they didn't know he existed."

"Judging by the destruction of that hilltop, I'd say he wanted to make his presence known."

"Not necessarily. He went for years and never seemed to need public recognition of his acts. It's only recently that he's changed."

"He was just starting out then. He hadn't learned. He hadn't evolved." Spiro paused. "But even though he's different now, he would still have traits that fit the usual pattern of the organized offender."

"Above average intelligence, for one," Eve said. "But all this talk isn't getting us anywhere. We need to know what he looks like. Where is that photograph?"

"Don't get your hopes up. The photo may not be the answer."

"What do you mean?"

"Just what I said."

"We're supposed to be working together. Stop being evasive. Tell me."

Spiro was silent.

Dammit, he was stubborn and FBI through and through. She was getting tired of prying information out of him. He had made a deal, but it was clear he wasn't going to budge on this point. Okay, pin him down at least on the time. "When?"

"Soon."

"When?"

"God, you're persistent. Tomorrow, maybe." He hung up.

THEY DIDN'T GET a duplicate of the photograph until two days later. Spiro came to the house and handed Eve a five-by-seven envelope. "Here it is. You're going to be disappointed."

"Why?"

"Look at it."

Joe moved to stand beside her as she opened the envelope and took out the photograph.

It had obviously been taken in a huge backyard. Two teenage boys sat in the foreground at a picnic table; a third was far in the background, coming down porch steps.

"According to Mrs. Harding, the kid on the steps is Kevin Baldridge," Spiro said. "The two at the picnic table are Ezekiel and Jacob."

Dammit, Kevin Baldridge was not only far away but the photo had been slightly overexposed, and because he was in motion, his figure was blurred and completely unrecognizable.

"No wonder the police didn't take this from the Hardings at the time," Eve said. "He's just a blur. He could be anyone. Joe told me that Charlie was troubled about this photograph. I can see why." She looked at Spiro. "Photo technology has improved enormously in the last twenty-five years. They might not have been able to clarify this photograph then, but you can do it now, can't you?"

"Probably. I've sent another duplicate to Quantico." He paused. "But I wondered if you'd like to take a shot at it yourself. You work with photographs too."

"My specialty is age progression, and that's completely different from what you need here."

"Oh." Spiro was disappointed. "Too bad."

Yes, it was, she thought with frustration.

"Nothing you can do?" Spiro asked.

She thought about it. "Maybe." She stood up and got a phone book. "If there's a film developer in town who does global corrections."

"Global corrections?"

"Air brushing and other kinds of—Here it is." She had found an advertisement in the yellow pages. "Pixmore. Now we'll have to see if they have the equipment and the experts to do the job."

"Glamour shots?" Joe was looking over her shoulder at the ad, which showed a close-up of a beautiful woman. "Not exactly scientific."

"How do you think companies like this make their money? They remove everything from zits and facial wrinkles to dark hair roots on photographs." She looked at the photograph again. "They *might* be able to do it. Correctors prefer to work with slides, but I'll take this to them, see if they have someone qualified." She put the picture back in the envelope. "These places are usually backed up for weeks. Can you put a little FBI muscle behind me?"

"I'll have Charlie meet you at Pixmore," Spiro said. "How long should it take?"

She shrugged. "I don't know. Maybe twenty-four hours. It depends on how good the technician is and what kind of overtime he's willing to put in."

"I'll ask Charlie to stay with him until it's finished."

"Good." She moved toward the door. "That will probably help."

"I'll drive you," Joe said.

"That's not necessary."

He made a face. "At the moment I don't seem able to make any other contribution. I'm feeling the need to be needed."

PIXMORE WAS THIRTY minutes from north Phoenix and perched on the summit of a curving mountain road. The one-story building was all glass and stone and gleamed in the sunlight. Charlie Cather pulled into the parking lot right after Joe and Eve.

"I'm glad you think we can get something done with that photo." He shook his head. "I was disappointed. I thought I'd really zeroed in on something."

"You did," Eve said. "It still may be salvageable."

"That's what Spiro said." He nodded at the Toyota driving into the parking lot. "There's Grunard."

"What's he doing here?" Eve asked.

"He was with me at the hotel when Spiro called. He's been bugging the hell out of me." Joe made a face. "But he's not a bad guy."

"Spiro won't like it."

"I cleared it with him. He said give him an appetizer but not the main course. He leaves before they start working on the photo."

Mark was coming toward them, smiling.

"Don't look now, but he appears ready for dessert," Joe said dryly.

"CAN'T YOU GET me a negative?" The technician's name was Billy Sung. He was under twenty-five and definitely not optimistic. "I'm not a miracle worker, you know."

"No negative," Eve said. "Your boss says you're the best technician he has. I'm sure you won't have a problem."

"Don't give me a snow job. I'll have a hell of a problem. This print has multiple errors. One would be easy to correct, but not all of them. You need one of those digital imaging companies in L.A. or a university think tank to enhance those pixels. Pixmore doesn't have the equipment."

"No chance?"

He shrugged. "Maybe. I have a college professor who has a government research grant, and his equipment is way beyond state of the art. He usually lets me use it."

"You're a student?"

"Yeah, I need a degree to get a job with one of those companies on the West Coast. I have to compete with all those whiz kids from UCLA and USC. Those companies are cutting edge. It's incredible what they do with digital computer and software equipment." He looked back at the photograph. "But I do damn well considering what I work with."

"I'm sure you do," Eve said. "Who is this professor and where's his lab?"

"Professor Dunkeil. Ralph Dunkeil. His lab's about five minutes from here on Blue Mountain Drive."

"Could I have it by tomorrow?"

He shook his head.

"Please, it's very important to me."

He looked at her face for a couple of seconds and then slowly nodded. "If you can clear it with Grisby. He's not going to like me putting everything on hold."

"Your boss has already okayed it," Charlie said. "He said that you're ours for the next thirty-six hours."

"That sounds like slave labor." He grimaced. "Though Grisby's pretty much of a slave driver himself. I had to threaten to quit last quarter to make him give me time off to take my finals."

"I'd be grateful if you'll try to hurry it," Eve said. "You'll call me?"

"I'll call you, Eve," Charlie said. "I'll go with Mr. Sung and help."

"I don't need your help." Sung gave Charlie a cool glance. "The government is too much into our business as it is. FBI, CIA, IRS. Now you come in here and try to pressure me."

"Hey, man, I'm only doing my job."

"Yeah, sure," Sung said as he sat down at the bench. "I've heard that before. It's always followed by the crack of the whip."

"Perhaps I could go with you instead." Mark Grunard smiled at Sung. "Do you have any objections to a little publicity? It might help you get that job in California."

Sung looked interested.

"No way," Charlie said firmly. "I told you that you couldn't stay, Grunard."

"But our friend doesn't like you as much as he does me."

Charlie jerked his thumb. "Out."

Grunard sighed. "Maybe I could come back after you've finished your work, Mr. Sung." He handed him a card. "Call me." He left the lab.

"The results are confidential, Mr. Sung," Charlie said.

"Yeah." Sung looked thoughtfully at the card before stuffing it in his pocket. "So were the atomic tests in Nevada that gave everybody cancer."

"Please call me as soon as possible, Mr. Sung," Eve said. "It means a great deal to me."

"I'll let you know."

"WHAT DO YOU think? Can he do it?" Joe asked as he and Eve got into the car.

"Maybe. He seems sharp." She leaned back in the seat. "And I think he likes a challenge. Though Charlie may have a tough time. Sung evidently hates government bureaucrats."

"Maybe you should introduce him to Sarah. So what do we do now?"

"Go home. Wait."

"That won't be easy."

"No." It seemed as if they'd done nothing but sit around and wait lately. "But at least Spiro gave us a chance to hurry the process along."

"He's taking a big risk dealing with us. He's impatient to have it over."

"So am I, Joe." She closed her eyes and tried to relax. "So am I."

IT WAS NEARLY three o'clock in the morning and the lights were still burning in the professor's lab on Blue Mountain Drive.

Eve must be happy she'd found someone passionate enough to work so hard on the photo, Dom thought. Passion could be dangerous.

But it could also be exciting. Every move Eve made was raising the stakes.

He probably should have gotten rid of that photo years ago, but he had moved on and he had not thought it important enough. But what was happening in that lab was important.

Time changed everything. Technology, morals, good, evil. Who would have known how much his needs would change? His priorities were so different now or he would not be sitting outside the lab.

What was happening in there? Were they getting close?

He felt excitement tighten his muscles. Go ahead, Eve. Come closer. Try to find me. . . .

"MORE COFFEE?" CHARLIE asked.

Billy Sung adjusted the computer. "Not right now."

"You didn't eat dinner. I could go out and pick up some fast food."

"No." He was coming close. Screw those L.A. bozos with all their fancy equipment. He was as good as them any day of the week. Just a few more adjustments and he might—

"Are you getting it?"

"You bet I am." He rubbed his eyes and bent forward again over the picture. "I wasn't sure I had a chance, but I'll be able to—" He stiffened. "My God."

"You've got it?"

"Shut up. I have to check the shift." He brought the picture in closer.

The shift was coming in clearer and then clearer still. There could be no mistake.

THE PHONE RANG on Eve's nightstand.

"We're on our way to see you," Charlie said.

"What?"

"Sung wants to see you. He's all excited."

She sat up in bed. "He did it?"

"Not yet. He says he'll be done any minute. He was muttering about shifts and spectrums and he's bringing you the photo. He won't let me see it while he's working on it, but I'll take possession the minute it's completely finished."

"Why the secrecy?"

"Search me," Charlie said sourly. "He evidently

thinks I'm the right arm of Big Brother. He made a phone call and then he said he had to see you right away. He seems to think this is only between you and him, but this is FBI business and he can't fool around with—Where the hell are you going?" He came back on the phone. "I've got to go. Sung must have finished. He just bolted for the front door. We should be there in thirty minutes." He hung up.

"Sung was able to do it?" Joe asked.

"That's what Charlie said, but Sung wants to talk to me." She put down the receiver and swung her feet to the floor. "He'll be here in thirty minutes with the photo. I'm going to get dressed."

Joe sat up in bed. "Why should he want to talk to you?"

"I told you, he doesn't like the government."

"Bad enough to wake you in the middle of the night?"

She headed for the bathroom. "I don't care if Sung comes up here and crawls in bed with us as long as he brings me that photo."

"I'd have a few objections," Joe said. "By all means, let's wait for him downstairs."

"WHERE IS HE?" Eve glanced at her watch again. "It's been forty minutes."

"Maybe they had to go back to the lab for something."

"Wouldn't Charlie have called us?"

"Car trouble?"

"Stop being comforting. Do you have Charlie's digital number?"

Joe nodded and reached for his phone. "No answer." He hung up. "It's time to go looking."

"I'll go with you."

"Stay here. What if all that comforting bullshit is really true and they drive up right after I've left? If they come, give me a call and I'll hotfoot it back."

He was right. She had to stay. But, blast it, it was going to kill her to sit there and wait.

EVE'S PHONE RANG forty-five minutes later.

"There's been a crash," Joe said. "A car went off the road and down into the ravine."

Her hand tightened on the phone. "Is it them?"

"I don't know." He paused. "The car's pretty messed up. It was over a hundred-foot drop."

She closed her eyes. "Christ."

"The medics and rescue team are going down to see if anyone survived. It's not going to be easy. The incline's very steep."

"How could anyone survive a drop like that?"

"It's possible. The car hasn't exploded yet. I have to go now. I'll call you later. I'm going down with the rescue team."

*The car hasn't exploded yet.*

Fear tore through her. "Let them do their job, Joe. Stay out of it."

"I like Charlie Cather, Eve." He hung up.

She liked Charlie too, but the thought of Joe going near that car terrified her.

She dialed Joe back.

No answer. He was already on his way down to the car.

She headed for the front door.

THE FLASHING RED lights of ambulances, fire trucks, and a half dozen police cars dotted the highway. A quartz spotlight was aimed down into the ravine. Yellow tape cordoned off the right lane.

*Joe.*

She parked on the side of the highway and jumped out of the car. She fought her way through the crowd, but dammit, she couldn't see *anything*.

"Eve." Spiro was coming toward her. He nodded to a policeman. "She's all right. Let her through."

She ducked under the tape and ran to the edge of the cliff.

Spiro followed her. "You shouldn't be here, Eve. What are you thinking? This place is crawling with highway patrol and—"

"I don't care. Where's the rescue team?"

Spiro pointed at the line of moving lights at the bottom of the ravine. "They're almost at the car."

What car? It appeared to be only a mass of twisted metal. "Joe's down there."

"I know, he called me. But he was already on his way down when I got here."

"Does anyone know what happened?"

Spiro shook his head. "No witnesses. We don't know yet if they were driven off the road or there was brake tampering. We're not even sure if it's Charlie's rental car. The rescue team is going to try to radio back the license number."

"But you think it is?"

"Don't you?"

"Yes." The lights were almost at the car now. "Do they know how long it's going to take?"

"It depends on what they find down there." He paused. "But I have to warn you. The rescue team is already smelling gasoline. Even worse, gas vapor will be hovering over the vehicle. All it would take is a spark."

She went rigid. "Then tell them to get out of there."

"They have to try to rescue whoever's in the car."

"They don't have to get blown up. I've seen burn victims and—"

"I know," Spiro said quietly. "No one wants that to happen. The squad leader will call off the attempt if it gets too dangerous."

"Joe won't listen. He won't take orders from anybody. He'll do what he has to do to get them out of that car."

God, she wished she were down there so she could *do* something.

"Take it easy, Eve. The rescue team isn't going to make any mistakes that will get anyone hurt. They'll disconnect the battery and then steady the vehicle. And they'll use Hurst tools to force their way into the car to avoid sparks."

The lights were moving, weaving in and around the wreckage.

Ten minutes passed.

Fifteen minutes.

"Why aren't they coming back? Can't you find out what's happening?" she asked Spiro.

"I'll try." Spiro strode over to the command unit and came back a few minutes later. "They've got one man out. They weren't able to make a positive confirmation, but they think the other man is dead. The squad leader's made the decision to pull his team out."

"Why?"

He hesitated. "The car hood is crushed. They weren't able to get to the battery to disconnect it. They managed to turn off the ignition, but anything could blow the car. The catalytic converter, the wiring . . ."

"And everyone's coming up?"

"Look for yourself."

The lights below were moving faster, away from the wreckage, back toward the incline.

Please let Joe be one of those men running to safety.

Her gaze moved back to the wreckage.

One light still burned in the midst of the twisted tangle of metal.

"Joe."

She had known it. Damn him. Damn him.

"My God, he's crazy," Spiro said.

Joe, get out of there. Please.

One minute passed. Two minutes.

Don't stay. Don't stay. Don't stay.

*The wreckage exploded into a fireball.*

She screamed.

*Joe.*

She ran toward the cliff edge.

Spiro caught her.

She struck out at him. "Let me go."

"You can't help him. There's a chance he could be all right."

All right? She had seen that light inside the car when it exploded. "I'm going down there."

"No way." His grasp tightened. "Too many people have been hurt tonight. I'm not going to watch you tumble down that mountain."

She kneed him in the groin and his grasp loosened. She ran, but two highway patrolmen grabbed her and forced her to the ground.

She fought desperately, kicking, frantically striking out.

*Joe!*

Darkness.

"YOU SON OF a bitch. Did you have to hit her?"

"I didn't hit her," Spiro said. "It was one of Phoenix's finest. They were trying to keep her from sliding down that mountain and killing herself. She's not hurt badly. Only stunned."

"You could have stopped them."

Joe. That was Joe's voice. Her eyes flew open. Joe kneeling beside her. Joe's face, oil-streaked, a cut on his cheekbone—but he was alive. Oh, God, alive.

"How do you feel?" Joe was frowning. "Did they hurt you?"

Alive.

She shook her head.

"You're lying. Why are you crying if you're not hurt?"

She hadn't known she was crying. "I don't know." She sat up and wiped her cheeks. "I'm okay."

"You're not okay. Lie back down."

"Shut up, Joe." Her voice was uneven. "I said I was okay. No credit to you. God, you're stupid. I thought you were dead, you idiot. I saw the light in the car right before it blew up."

"I had to drop the flashlight when I wriggled out of the car."

Stop shaking. He was alive. "You shouldn't have been there."

"I know," he said wearily. "The squad leader is mad as hell at me, but I had to make sure." He glanced at Spiro. "I'm sorry, it was Charlie in the car. I thought he was dead, but I had to be sure."

"And he was dead?"

Joe nodded.

Spiro flinched.

"And Billy Sung was alive when we got him out of the car, but he died before we reached the top."

Dead. Both dead. Nice Charlie Cather and Billy Sung, with his plans for taking the world by storm. Joe could have died too. Joe . . .

"Eve?" Joe was gazing at her in concern.

"I heard you. They're dead. They're both dead." She wrapped her arms around her body, but she couldn't stop the shaking. "I heard you."

"You're cold." He reached out to her.

"Don't you *touch* me. I feel fine." Her voice was rising, and she had to stop to control it. "I wasn't down there. I didn't do that stupid—"

"Come on." Joe took her hand to help her to her feet. "I'm taking you home."

She jerked away from him and stood on her own.

"Yeah, get her home," Spiro told Joe. "Those officers may be focused on the wreck, but there's still an APB out on her." He grimaced. "I have to make a telephone call. I'm going to hate this."

Charlie's wife, Eve thought dully. Charlie hadn't

survived, and Joe had been so close to not surviving. Oh, God, she was going to throw up. "She's pregnant. Can you get someone to tell her in person?"

"I'll have someone from the field office go out to see her, but I'm the one who has to do the dirty work."

"Come to the house after you've finished," Joe said. "We have something to talk about." He opened his jacket.

Half of a five-by-seven envelope was stuffed into the top of his jeans.

"The photograph?" Spiro asked.

"I haven't had a chance to look at it yet, but it was on the floor of the car beside Charlie. It was caught under the drive shift, and it ripped when I jerked it out and ran for it."

Spiro held out his hand. "Give it to me."

Joe shook his head. "You'll get it after we take a look at it, and I'm not going to stop and do that now. I need to get Eve home. She's not doing well."

"The hell I'm not. I'd have to be dead before I'd wait to see that murderer's face." She tried to steady her hands as she took the envelope. Disappointment surged through her as she drew out the photo. "No."

A third of the photograph was gone. The third with Kevin Baldridge sitting on the porch steps.

Two lives lost. All for nothing.

Spiro was cursing. "Why couldn't it have been the other half that was torn?"

"Murphy's Law," Joe said. "This is just a print, Eve. Can you do anything?"

She tried to think. "Maybe. Sung might have made copies. Or his work might have been saved on his computer."

Joe looked at Spiro. "Get us permission to go into that lab on Blue Mountain Drive."

Spiro nodded. "Meet me there in two hours."

"We'll be there," Eve said.

"Come on." Joe tried to wrap an arm around Eve's waist. "Let's go home."

"I don't need your help." She pushed his hand away and started toward the car. Put one foot in front of the other. Don't look at him. Keep control or you'll disintegrate into a million pieces. "I'll see you back at the house."

"I'm going with you. For God's sake, you just took a knock on the head."

"That doesn't mean I'm not capable of—"

"I'm not letting you drive."

"And what are you supposed to do with your car? Just leave it here?"

"Screw the car." He opened the car door for her.

"No, I don't—"

"Need my help," he finished for her. "But you're still not driving. Now get in."

HE WHIRLED TO face her as soon as they walked into the living room. "What the hell is wrong with you?"

"Nothing's wrong with me." Except she felt as if she were going to explode any minute. She wanted to scream and pound on him. Damn him. Damn him. Damn him.

"The hell there's not. You're shaking like a malaria victim."

"I'm fine." She couldn't hold on much longer. "Go wash your face," she snapped. "You have oil all over it. All over your hands and that—"

"I'm sorry it offends you."

"It does offend me." A single light in the wreckage and then the world exploding. "I hate it."

"You don't have to bite my head off."

"Yes, I do." She turned away, her back rigid. "Go away."

"Turn around. I want to see your face."

She didn't move. "Go wash up. We have to go to that lab and see if we can get another print."

"You shouldn't go anywhere in your condition."

"There's nothing wrong with me."

"Then look at me."

"I don't want to look at you. I want to go and look at that photograph. It's important, dammit."

"Do you think I don't know that? But there's something else happening here, and it may be more important to me than any picture."

The room seemed to be tilting, exploding beneath her feet.

Like the car had exploded.

Hold on. Don't break down. What had they been talking about? The photograph. "It couldn't be more important. Two men died because of that photograph."

"And I'm sorry as hell, but I'm not to blame." He spun her around to face him. "I did everything I could to help—"

"I know you did. Crawling into that— Stupid, idiotic—" The floodgates broke and tears were again running down her cheeks. "Charlie was already dead, dammit."

"I didn't know that."

"You could have died."

"I didn't die."

"Not for lack of trying."

"Will you please stop crying?"

"No."

"Then may I point out that you're being unreasonable."

"Go to hell." She walked over to the window and stared out into the darkness.

"Eve."

She could feel his gaze on her back. "Go away."

"Are you going to tell me why you're so angry with me?"

She didn't answer.

"Tell me."

She whirled on him, her eyes blazing. "Oh, yes, you're too mean to get killed. You're going to be around for the next fifty years or so. I don't have to be afraid, do I?"

He went still. "Oh, shit."

"You could have died tonight." The words tumbled over one another. "You had no *right*. You upset my life, you barged around and made me feel things I never wanted to feel. You said you'd be around for the next fifty years and then you try to get yourself— Don't you touch me." She backed away from him. "Charlie Cather and Billy Sung died tonight, and I hardly thought about them. I didn't care about the photograph. I didn't care about Dom. Do you know how that makes me feel?"

"I know how it makes *me* feel."

"Are you proud of yourself? You lied to me. You lied about—"

He was holding her, pressing her face to his shoulder. "Stop shaking. It's over."

"It's not over. It's going to go on. Because you'll never change. You'll keep on doing stupid, insane things because you have an ego that tells you that you'll live forever even if you—" Her whole body was trembling. "I can't *stand* it."

"Neither can I. You're turning *me* inside out."

"You shouldn't have done it. You shouldn't have done it."

He was lifting her and carrying her to the couch. "Shh, I'll do anything you say if you'll just stop shaking." He cradled her on his lap. "I thought I was prepared for anything, but I was wrong. I wasn't ready for this. It was always Bonnie who came first with you. I never thought—"

"Because you can't see farther than the tip of your nose."

He was silent a moment. "Are you telling me that you love me?"

"I'm not telling you anything, you bastard."

"It's hard to judge because of the verbal abuse, but I think that's what you're saying. It . . . heartens me."

"It doesn't hearten me."

"I know. It scares you." He was rocking her back and forth. "If you'll just stop shaking, I promise I'll try to live forever."

No one lived forever. His heart pounded strong and steady beneath her ear, but it could have been stilled tonight. Her hands tightened on his shoulders. "Idiot."

"Hush."

"You'll do it again. I know it. You're a cop."

He was silent.

She was silent too. Moments passed and she sat there, listening to the beat of his heart. Lover. Best friend. Center.

She gradually stopped shaking.

He gently pressed his lips to her temple. "Someday will you tell me you love me?"

"Probably not." Her arms tightened around him. "You don't deserve it."

"True." He was silent again. "I won't take chances I don't have to, Eve. I've never wanted to live more than I do at this moment. Okay?"

"It has to be okay, doesn't it? I have to accept it. That's life."

"Yes, that's life. Welcome back." He brushed her hair away from her face. "You're a mess. I've gotten grease all over you."

"It will wash off." But what had happened that night could never be eradicated. Every one of her protective barriers had been stripped away and she'd been forced to face her true feelings for Joe. But they were too intense, almost unbearable. She pushed him away and slowly stood up. "We've got to leave to go to Professor

Dunkeil's lab. I'll use the powder room down here. You go upstairs and change. Those clothes are beyond hope."

"I'm on my way."

She watched him leave the room, not wanting to let him out of her sight. Get a grip. There were other things in life to worry about besides Joe Quinn. Two men had died tonight. Probably killed by Dom. He was getting nearer.

But so was she.

You haven't beaten us yet, Dom. I'll still find a way to see your face.

Eve and Joe were waiting across the street from the lab on Blue Mountain Drive when Spiro drove up.

"Professor Dunkeil's waiting for us. He was upset about Sung." Spiro studied Eve's face. "You look better."

"I'm fine. Did you reach Mrs. Cather?"

"Yes." His lips tightened. "I didn't talk to her very long. She broke down. She's only a kid herself."

"I know you were close to Charlie."

"I could have been closer. I thought I had to toughen him up." He shook his head. "Getting Dom is becoming very personal to me."

Eve started across the street. "Join the club."

She felt the tension rise as Joe rang the doorbell of the lab.

Please, don't let those young men have died for no reason. Don't let Dom win this one.

THE IMAGE OF Kevin Baldridge was still blurred. On the computer screen he was almost ghostlike, like a cadaver floating in a sea of light.

But his face was clear enough.

She couldn't breathe.

"Eve?"

"Tell me I'm crazy, Joe."

Joe was gazing at the screen and swore softly.

Spiro inhaled sharply. "Grunard."

Younger, thinner, but the charming, slightly cocky smile was the same.

Eve sank back in the chair, her mind whirling. "No."

"He's the right age. He's been close to you from the beginning," Spiro said slowly.

So close. "That guard at the welfare house . . ." She shuddered. "I told him to distract him if he ran across him."

Joe turned to Spiro. "He thinks he's safe. Pick him up before he learns what we've done here tonight."

"He may already know." Spiro took out his phone and punched in a number. "He's made some friends in the precinct the past few days."

Eve was thinking of the serial killer profile Spiro had given her in Joe's cottage.

*They usually are aware of police procedures and may even associate with the police.*

Joe had told her that Grunard hung out at the bar all the Atlanta police detectives frequented.

And a reporter could travel from place to place without suspicion. He had contacts and sources for finding out facts other people couldn't.

Mark had delayed going after Jane at the welfare house until eleven o'clock, giving him plenty of time to kill the security guard and make it to the alley where Mike had been. He would have had no trouble gaining access to Fraser all those years ago.

"No answer at Grunard's hotel." Spiro was punching in another number. "I'll send someone to the hotel."

Grunard. Dom.

He had wanted to stay at the lab last night. He had given Sung his phone number.

Spiro had finished his phone call and was heading for the front door. "I'll start a background check on

Grunard. I don't know how much good it will do. There's no telling how many times he's reinvented himself. Go back to the house and stay there."

Grunard.

All the way back to the house, Eve couldn't stop thinking about Grunard and Dom being the same person. It was crazy and yet it made perfect sense. He had been there all the time and she had not felt an ounce of suspicion. My God, she had even felt guilty for not keeping him more informed. And he had warned her not to let Dom see Eve and Jane together in Phoenix.

She felt as if she had been kicked in the stomach. "Jane."

She had left Jane alone.

"How far are we—"

"Shit." Joe pressed the accelerator. "Take it easy. We're only a block from the house."

They tore through the gates and she jumped out of the car and ran into the house.

"Eve." Joe was running after her.

Jane was safe. Jane had two guards to protect her, and Sarah and Monty.

But Dom had gotten to the porch of Joe's cottage at the lake.

She took the stairs two at a time.

She flung open Jane's door.

The bed was rumpled, the covers thrown back.

Jane was not in the bed.

"Let's try Sarah," Joe said behind her.

Sarah sat up groggily when they barged in her room. "What is it?"

"Jane. We can't find—" Eve sat on the bed in relief. "Thank God."

Jane was curled up beside Monty on a blanket on the floor beside Sarah's bed.

"She came in a couple of hours ago," Sarah said.

"She said she had a bad dream about Monty and asked if she could stay. It's okay, isn't it?"

Eve nodded, trying to quiet her pounding heart. "It's fine. I was just scared. Sorry I woke you."

"No problem."

Eve and Joe walked out. "God, I was afraid," she said.

"Me too." Joe put his arm around her. "Come on, let's go make some coffee. I could use a caffeine jolt."

SARAH CAME INTO the kitchen almost an hour later. "Okay. What's happening?" She yawned. "I tried to go back to sleep but couldn't because I got to thinking."

"We didn't want to bother you." Joe poured her a cup of coffee.

"Well, you didn't bother Jane and Monty. They're sleeping." She sipped her coffee. "The sleep of the innocent. It's a wonderful thing. Now, why were you scared about Jane?"

Sarah had finished her second cup of coffee by the time they'd filled her in. She leaned back in her chair. "So it's almost over."

"It's not over until he's dead or behind bars," Eve said.

"But you have a face and a name now. If he slips through the FBI's hands, put him on *America's Most Wanted* or some show like that. Someone's always finding murderers."

"You make it sound very simple," Joe said dryly.

"I have a very simple nature." Sarah smiled. "It comes from living with dogs. Everything's black and white, and you reach your goal by using the most direct path possible. That's why I work rescue instead of being a cop like you, Joe. I couldn't stand—"

The phone rang. Eve picked up the wall extension.

"Get out of there," Spiro said. "Tell Joe to get you and Jane away from there."

"Why? Dom?"

"No, there's no sign of Dom. But the Phoenix PD should be on your doorstep any minute."

"Why? Was I recognized at the wreck site?"

"They got an anonymous tip about where you could be found. Now, guess who would call that in?"

"Grunard."

"Right. He evidently wants to blast you out of your fortress."

"And he's doing it." She tried to think. "But if they put me in jail, he wouldn't be able to—"

"Jane won't be in jail. She'll go right back into Atlanta welfare custody."

If Jane was returned to welfare they'd be back to square one. "How much time do we have?"

"Zilch. Get out of there now."

She hung up. "The Phoenix PD is on their way here. They got a tip about Jane and me." She turned to Sarah. "You and Monty get out of here. Call Logan and tell him what's happened."

Sarah headed for the door. "I'm on my way."

Eve nodded. "I'll go get Jane. Throw some things into a suitcase, Joe."

THEY MADE IT only as far as the front gates. As the gates swung open, they saw the blinking lights of patrol cars just turning the corner onto the street.

Joe swore under his breath.

"Get out," Eve snapped at him.

"What?"

"Get out and hide in the bushes. It's Jane and me they want."

"And I'm supposed to leave you?"

"I'll be in jail. You're the one who'll have to keep an eye on Jane."

Joe muttered another curse but dove out the door and into the bushes beside the driveway. Eve slid behind the wheel and drove through the gates.

The headlights of the police car almost blinded her as it blocked her path.

"WELL, THIS IS a fine mess you've gotten us into," Logan said. "And that prison garb isn't at all becoming."

"You shouldn't have come here." Eve leaned forward to look at him through the glass. "And it's my mess, not yours."

"Not correct. Are they treating you okay?"

"As well as they treat any other felon. I've been in here only twenty-four hours, and that's enough to make me never want to even jaywalk. But there is a lot of time for thinking." Her folded hands clenched together in front of her. "I think that may be what Grunard wanted. He wanted to show me that even if he was on the run, he could still reach out and touch me. He wanted me to feel helpless and wonder what was happening to Jane. It worked. I nearly went crazy last night. Did Sarah call you?"

He nodded. "She gave me orders to make myself useful and bail you out."

"It's kidnapping, Logan. No one's going to bail me out."

"It might be possible. Extenuating circumstances. Barbara Eisley isn't being vindictive, and you're usually not a very dangerous character." He paused. "But it would be better if you told them where Quinn is. They want to question him about his involvement with you."

"I don't know where he is."

"And you wouldn't tell if you did." He stood up. "So I guess I'll see if I can find any judges in this town or in Atlanta I can influence."

"Logan, where's Jane?"

"She's being held in the local Family Services center. She's being returned to Atlanta as soon as a caseworker comes to pick her up. Spiro told me to tell you that he's got people watching her."

"That won't be enough."

"Grunard is on the run."

"He won't run far. It's getting too near the end of his game. If he ran away completely, it would mean he lost. He'll never admit that." She paused. "If he can't get to me, he'll kill Jane. It's the logical move for him. He wants both of us, but he'll take Jane because it will hurt me."

"Are you sure he knows it will hurt you?"

"Oh, yes." She smiled without mirth. "The bastard even warned me never to let Dom see us together."

"Nice." His gaze narrowed on her face. "I'm tempted to let you stay in here for a while. At least you're safe."

"And Jane becomes the target."

"I can surround her with protection."

"She was surrounded with protection in the welfare house and Dom could have gotten to her there." Her voice vibrated with desperation. "If you can get me out of here, do it, Logan. I don't know how fast he'll move."

He shook his head. "I don't like—"

*"Please."*

He muttered a curse and rose abruptly to his feet. "I'll see what I can do. It may not be today. It could be another twenty-four hours."

She stood up, and the guard moved forward to take her back to her cell. "Hurry."

*Another twenty-four hours.*

The words replayed in her mind as she walked down the long corridor to her cell. The idea of any delay scared her to death. How long would Grunard wait?

It could be all right. Joe would be watching over Jane. He would take care of her.

And Grunard would be watching Joe. He would know that Joe was guarding Jane. Which meant Grunard would try to take out Joe first.

Sheer terror went through her at the thought.

*I won't take chances if I don't have to. I've never wanted to live more than I do at this moment.*

But she'd sent him to take a terrible chance. She'd made Joe a target.

Panic seared through her as the door of her cell clanged shut behind her. She was trapped there, helpless to do anything.

Calm down. She closed her eyes and drew a deep breath. Panicking would be playing right into Grunard's hands. He was probably sitting somewhere now, picturing her in her cell, feeding on her fear and frustration.

Don't give him what he wants. He wants panic. Give him coolness. He wants mindless emotion. Give him logic.

Twenty-four hours.

Spend that time thinking about Grunard, going over every minute, every conversation of the last weeks. See if she could find a lead to him, a weakness that could be exploited. Pretend he was one of her skulls that had to be measured and then reconstructed. Use her mind, talents, and instinct.

She sat down on the bunk and leaned against the wall.

*Stay away from the people I love, Dom. Think of me shivering, brooding in this cell. Enjoy it.*

*Then maybe, just maybe, I'll have enough time to find a way to win your damn game.*

SHE WAS RELEASED on bail at one forty-five the next afternoon. Logan met her outside the jail. "The good news is that I think all the charges will be dropped. Spiro's been discreetly putting pressure on Eisley." He paused. "But until we get you cleared, you can't go near Jane. One of the terms of your release is that you're not seen within fifty city blocks of her. If you violate it, you get tossed right back in the slammer."

"I expected that. She's all right?"

"She's okay. I have a man watching the local facility."
He took her arm as they started down the steps. "The
caseworker from Atlanta is arriving today to take her
back."

"When?"

"Sometime this evening."

"Then they'll probably leave tomorrow morning."

His brows lifted as he held open the car door. "You're
very calm."

"No, I'm not." She got into the car. "I'm scared
shitless."

"Well, you're different from yesterday." He strode
around to the driver's seat.

She took out her phone and dialed Joe's digital number. God, his voiced sounded wonderful.

"I'm out," she said.

"Thank God."

"Things are going to be happening. Soon."

"If you're out, that goes without saying."

"I'll call you." She hung up.

"Quinn?"

She nodded.

He smiled sardonically. "But you had no idea where
he is."

"I still don't. I know only that he's guarding Jane."

He dropped the subject. "Where do you want to go?"

"Back to the house. I have some work to do."

"Work?"

"Telephone calls and then I need to get on the computer."

"You're not planning to hire a hit man to get Grunard,
I trust?"

"It's an appealing idea." She shook her head. "But
that's not what I had in mind."

"Am I allowed to help?"

"You bet you are."

•    •    •

SARAH PATRICK MET Eve as she walked into the foyer.
"Welcome home." She glanced at Logan. "You evidently
did something right."

"I didn't dare do anything else. I'm scared of Monty."
He turned to Eve. "You'll have what you need in a couple of hours. Okay?"

She nodded. "Thanks, Logan. I owe you."

"Friends never owe friends." He smiled. "Remember
that."

"Then is it okay if I'm grateful?"

"Same answer." He headed for the front door.

But she *did* owe him, she thought as she headed to
the office. And she'd owe him even more if he came
through with the information she needed.

Sarah trailed along with her. "You look a little jumpy.
Anything I can do?"

"You can check with the welfare office and make sure
Jane is all right."

Sarah nodded. "I've been calling a couple of times a
day. I tried to go see her, but they wouldn't let me and
Monty in the place."

"Too bad. Seeing Monty would have made her feel
better."

"That's what I thought. Have you had lunch?"

Eve shook her head. "But I'm not hungry. I've got
work to do."

"Really?" Sarah studied her face. "You're excited."

"Logan said I was very calm."

"On the surface. Beneath you're seething like a gey-
ser. Want to talk about it?"

Eve shook her head. "But I think I've found a way to
get him."


DONE.    Eve pushed her chair back from the computer
and covered her eyes with her shaking hand.

I've got you, Dom. I've got you.

Her phone rang.

"The caseworker from Atlanta, James Parkinson, and Jane just got into a squad car with two officers and are on their way to the airport," Joe said. "I'm following them."

"I didn't think they'd leave tonight."

"I didn't either. Parkinson was in and out of that welfare house in fifteen minutes. I'll call you when we get to the airport."

Eve tried to think. It was logical that the caseworker wanted Jane out of Phoenix now that Eve had been released. But Jane was more vulnerable outside the home and on the road.

*A twisted mass of metal at the bottom of the ravine.*

That couldn't happen twice. Besides, Joe was watching.

But so was Dom.

James Parkinson.

She called Joe back. "How do you know Parkinson is the social worker?"

"The squad car radioed the pickup back to the precinct, and I heard it on my radio."

"What does Parkinson look like?"

"He's black, heavyset, plump face. He would have had to show ID to both welfare administration and the officers in the squad car."

"IDs are easy to get, and Grunard's had time to plan." But she did feel a little better. "Watch closely, Joe."

"You know I will."

"I GUESS YOU'RE glad to be going home, young lady." Officer Rivera glanced back at Jane over his shoulder.

Jane didn't answer.

"I have a daughter about your age. She's on the softball team."

Jane gazed through the window, closing out Parkinson and the officers. She hadn't said a word since she'd gotten into the squad car. Poor kid, Rivera thought. He looked at Parkinson. "Is she going to be okay?"

Parkinson nodded, his white teeth flashing in his brown face as he smiled. "Just fine."

Jane suddenly stiffened, her gaze flying to Parkinson's face.

"There, honey, don't be scared." Parkinson patted her shoulder.

Jane went rigid and then slumped to one side.

"What's wrong with her?" Rivera said. "Pull over, Ken."

"Oh, no, don't do that," Parkinson said softly.

Then he shot Rivera in the head.

SHIT.

Joe's hands tightened on the steering wheel.

Something was wrong.

The squad car was weaving in and out of the city streets, even backtracking.

What the hell!

The squad car roared over railroad tracks, driving through the signal just as the train approached, leaving Joe stranded on the other side.

He radioed the precinct for backup as he waited for the train to pass. "I don't care who comes. Just get someone, anyone."

He wasn't getting through to them. He closed his eyes. "Okay, if you won't stop the squad car, come after me. This is Joe Quinn."

Joe gunned his car as the caboose rattled past.

It took Joe ten minutes to locate the squad car again.

But he lost it again in the traffic near the stadium.

There it was. Two blocks ahead, turning left.

He lost it again.

It took five minutes to locate the squad car this time.

It was pulled over to the side of a deserted street.

•    •    •

"I HAVE HER, Eve."

Dom.

"You're lying. She's on her way to the airport."

"No, you'll get a call soon. I just wanted you to know that the game is almost over. It's time for me to claim the stakes."

"I don't believe you."

"You believe me. I can hear it in your voice."

"Let me talk to her."

"No, she's not able to talk. I drugged the little angel. Just a little pinprick. A rather boring old trick but effective. It was such a wonderful disguise, but I think she recognized my voice. Besides, I have a distance to take her and I needed her quiet." He paused. "Shall I tell you what I'm going to do to her before I kill her, Eve?"

"No." She closed her eyes. "Don't hurt her."

"Not yet. She's no fun at the moment. She can't feel anything."

Rage seared through her.

"That made you angry, didn't it? I can almost feel the waves of emotion through the phone. It's quite wonderful, but you really shouldn't indulge me this way."

"You don't want her. You want me."

"That's right. I want you to die first, knowing what's in store for her. Come and get her."

"Where are you going?"

"A place you'll remember. Earth to earth. Salt to salt. I thought it fitting. My most satisfying kills were done there. But don't worry, I won't chop you into pieces as I did them. I respect you too much."

"Will she be there?"

"I'm not a fool. You might arrange a trap for me."

"I won't come up to the tent site until I know she's alive. Until I hear her voice."

"You'll hear it. Be there at nine tomorrow night." He hung up.

Christ.

She had thought she was so close, and Dom had still managed to pull the rug right from under her.

Joe called her. "He's got her. I found both officers dead in the squad car and Jane gone."

"I know. Dom called me."

"Shit. I screwed up."

"It's not your fault," she said dully. "He was disguised. Even Jane didn't recognize him right away."

"Is she alive?"

"He says she is. Right now."

"Don't you move a muscle. I'm on my way over there." He hung up.

Joe would come and some of the fear would go away. She didn't have to face this alone.

Yes, she did. From the beginning she'd known that she'd have to face Dom alone. He was planning on having her walk right into his trap and killing her and Jane. He would butcher Joe if he was anywhere around.

Then flip his plan. Catch the hunter before the trap was sprung.

"Sarah! Will you come in here?"

Sarah appeared in the doorway. "What?"

She held up a finger. "One minute." She dialed Spiro's digital number. He answered on the third ring.

"Dom has Jane, and I know where he's headed. I want you to meet me there." She had to stop to steady her voice. "You wanted to use me as bait. Okay, let's find a way to do it."

# EIGHTEEN

*The following night 8.45 P.M.*

Candles.

Everywhere.

Candelabras with tapers whose flames flickered in the wind. Lanterns. Oil lamps.

Eve parked her car at the bottom of the hill and looked up at the tent site.

Is this my welcome, Dom? Are you up there?

She dialed Spiro's number. "Where are you?"

"We're in a lay-by about two miles down the road to Jamison. We couldn't get any closer without risking him seeing us. That hill has a view for miles."

"I know. Can you see the candles?"

"Yes. Remember, press the radio signal as soon as you determine Dom's there, and we'll come in."

"You don't move until I'm sure Jane's alive and safe. He's supposed to call me."

"Stay locked in the car until you're sure. At least you're safe there. Do you have a weapon?"

"A revolver."

"Did Quinn give it to you?"

"No, I told you I didn't want him to know about this.

Sarah had one and lent it to me. It's in my jacket pocket."

"We could have used Quinn."

"And chance having Dom butcher him? He's done too much for me already."

"I should have known that protective streak would raise its head. Don't hesitate to use that gun." He hung up.

She sat in the car, staring up at the candles on the hill.

Five minutes.

Seven minutes.

The phone rang.

"Are you enjoying my candles?" Dom asked.

"I want to talk to Jane."

"Do you doubt me? I told you I wanted you to die first."

"Let me talk to Jane."

"Oh, very well."

"Eve, don't you do what he says," Jane yelled into the phone. "He's a slimy creep and I—"

Dom took the phone away. "Is that enough? It's all you'll get. I've been very patient with Jane since she woke, but she's really beginning to annoy me."

"It's enough."

"Then step into my parlor. I'll be there in ten minutes."

She pressed the off button and quickly dialed Sarah. "Ten-minute walk from here."

"That could cover a lot of territory."

"Find her. If he manages to kill me and escapes, you can't let him get back to Jane."

"We'll do our best."

Nine minutes.

Stay in the car. Be safe for just a little longer. Sit and watch the flickering lights on the hill.

•   •   •

SARAH PUT ON her utility belt and Monty tensed.

"That's right, boy. Time to get to work." She let Monty sniff Jane's T-shirt. "Find her." She started down the trail at a trot. She'd already scoped out the lay of the land and come up with the two most logical possibilities.

He wouldn't keep Jane out in the open. So there was the stand of woods near the base of the mountains to the west.

Or there was the brush-covered ravine to the east.

Either was a fast ten-minute walk to the hill.

Which direction?

She'd make the decision when she got closer.

Pray to God she'd make the right one.

Monty was stretched out, almost running.

*Child* . . .

TEN MINUTES.

Eve opened the door and got out of the car. The air was knife sharp, cutting her to the bone. It was a moonless night, icy cold with a promise of snow.

She started up the hill.

Candles.

Flames.

Are you there yet, Dom?

She reached the top.

No one.

Just the candles and the flames and the flickering shadows on the desolate earth. It wasn't as brightly lit as she'd thought from down below. There was a patch of deep shadow at the far corner of the site.

She moved farther into the circle of light.

Was he watching her, or was it her imagination?

She whirled around.

No one.

Or was there?

Something in those shadows . . .

She hesitated and then moved away from the light toward the patch of darkness.

"Dom? You wanted me here. Come and get me."

No sound.

DECISION TIME.

Sarah paused to catch her breath.

The woods or the ravine?

Monty had already made a decision. He was tearing across the ground toward the woods. He stopped, sniffed, and took off again.

He'd caught Jane's scent.

THE SUBSTANCE IN the shadow was no standing figure, Eve realized. Something on the ground . . .

She drew closer.

She still couldn't make it out.

A few steps closer.

It was taking on a vague shape.

She was almost on top of it.

A body?

Oh, God.

Jane?

She screamed.

The man's body was tied spread-eagled to four pegs, and his eyes were wide open. His features were contorted in a silent howl of agony.

Mark Grunard.

"That's how I staked out my father."

She whirled to see Spiro behind her.

He smiled. "A little welcome present. It was going to be the little girl, but I knew you wouldn't come unless you thought you had a chance of saving her."

"You," she whispered. "Dom?"

"Of course it was me."

*A man who stares at monsters.*

But he was the monster himself. "God, what a fool I

am. No trap. No FBI agents swarming in at the last minute to save me."

"Unfortunately not." He stepped closer and was almost lost in the shadows. "Don't put your hands in your pockets. I have a knife in my hand and I can reach you in a heartbeat, but I don't want it to end that soon. It's been a superb game, and I want to savor the win."

"You haven't won yet."

"That's what I admire about you. You never give up. But you should be more generous. I was very clever with every move. I deserve to win."

"You were clever. You set Grunard up perfectly. You even gave me the characteristics of the serial killer so I'd be able to associate them with Grunard later. It never occurred to me that they might also apply to you. You associate with the police as Grunard did, but even more, you're an FBI profiler. You could move from place to place. You liked to be in the field, you said. That means you were contacted by your digital phone and no one actually knew where you were at a given time. You could say you were in Talladega when you were in Atlanta."

"I do regard the digital phone as one of the most helpful inventions. And it was a real challenge to become an FBI agent. Background checks that had to be foolproof, psychological tests that had to show me as completely normal. I prepared for almost two years before I applied. Setting up the personal interviews with people from my supposed past was the most difficult. It took finesse, bribery, and a psychological sleight of hand that would fill you with admiration."

"No, it wouldn't."

"But it was all worth it. Who else would be in a better position to hide and change evidence? I had to keep an eye on where and when any of my kills surfaced so I could erase the records."

"But the VICAP report uncovered the Harding kills."

"Before I was able to sidetrack the search. Very annoying."

"But you led me here to find Debby Jordan."

"I'm a fatalist. I saw that everything was leading back to my roots. I wanted you here to help me start again, to revive that splendid surge of power." He smiled. "It did do that. When I killed Grunard, it was almost like the old days. But he wasn't you. It will be much better with you."

"Did you always plan to kill Grunard?"

"After I examined the situation and all the possibilities, I realized that his death would accomplish two ends, create a red herring and make our game more complicated. How could I resist? He would become Dom and disappear." He shook his head. "But that complication may cause me to have to move on and reinvent myself. Grunard's background is pretty solid. There may be questions." He shrugged. "Oh, well, I'll have plenty of warning and I've already set up an identity in Montana. It may be good for me. Being Robert Spiro made everything too easy for me. The kill, the cover-up . . . It may have been part of my problem."

"You'll move on and you'll kill again." Her voice was shaking. "Over and over."

"Of course, that's what I do."

"How many?"

"I really don't remember. I was drunk with the pleasure during those first years. I went out every night. Later everything blurred. More than thirty years . . . a thousand? I don't know. Maybe more."

"My God."

"But don't feel bad. You won't be like the others. I'll remember you."

"You have me. Let Jane go."

"You know I won't do that. She knows my face and the little bitch would try to find a way to hurt me. She's like you."

"But you were wrong about her being like Bonnie."

"But I set up an interesting scenario, didn't I? It pulled you in. The bones and then sweet little Jane."

"Whose bones were they?"

He was silent.

"*Tell* me. Were they Bonnie's bones?"

"I could let you go to the grave not knowing."

"Yes."

"But then you wouldn't realize how clever I've been. How wonderfully I'd set you up."

"They weren't Bonnie's bones."

He shook his head. "Doreen Parker's."

"Then everything you told me about your conversation with Fraser was a lie."

"Not entirely. I did talk to him. It was remarkably easy, since I was an FBI agent. He was a copycat and he was claiming some of my kills. We had a nice chat, and I told him to back off. Since he had the good sense to admire me enormously, he agreed."

"You knew about the ice cream. Did you find that out from the police records?"

"No, I told you, we had a nice chat. He told me a lot about Bonnie. Did you want to know how he did it?"

She clenched her fists as waves of pain washed over her. "No."

"Coward." His gaze narrowed on her face. "But you want to know where he buried her, don't you? You've always wanted to find her."

"I want to bring her home."

"It's too late. You're going to die without finding her. That hurts terribly, doesn't it? Your Bonnie is buried all alone in Chattahoochee National Park, and you're going to be buried here, hundreds of miles away from her. It cuts to the quick, doesn't it?"

"Yes."

"I can feel your pain."

"And you love it, you bastard."

"I have to squeeze as much as I can out of the moment. It's going to be over too soon." He paused. "You haven't asked me what color candle I'm going to give you."

"I don't care."

"It will be black. Black was the color of my candles, and I've decided to share it with you. I've never done that before. You should be honored. The candles are lying beside Grunard's head. Pick them up, Eve. Light them."

She didn't move.

"Pick them up or I promise you I'll make it very hard for Jane before I give her candle to her."

Eve hesitated and then walked over to Grunard.

How the man must have suffered. His expression . . .

"Pick them up and come back toward me."

He was standing in the shadow. There would be no chance if he stayed in the dark.

She picked up the black candles.

"Now come toward me."

She slowly started toward him.

One step.

Two.

Three.

"Hurry. I find I'm very eager for—"

She hurled the candles at his face.

"Eve!"

She took off running.

Out of the shadow into the candlelit center of the tent site.

"Stop running. The game's over, Eve."

She glanced over her shoulder. He was running after her.

Fast.

Closing on her.

Come on.

Faster.

Out of the darkness.

*Into the light.*

The single shot splintered the night.

Spiro jerked, stumbled, and collapsed to his knees.

The knife fell out of his hand.

He looked down in disbelief at his chest, which was bubbling with blood. "Eve?"

She turned to face him. "*Now* the game's over, you son of a bitch."

He touched his chest and brought his hand away. It was smeared with blood. "Who . . ."

"Joe."

"No, I—searched here before I lit the candles. There was nowhere he could hide . . ."

"He was a sniper in the SEALs. He told me once that he can hit a target from a thousand yards. It's not five hundred yards to that tree down the slope. I knew he could get you if he could see you, Spiro."

His eyes widened. "You knew . . ." He collapsed to the ground.

She walked over and knelt beside him. "Where's Jane?"

"Screw you."

"You're going to die, Spiro. What difference does it make?"

"It—makes a difference. How—did you know?"

"You made that anonymous telephone call and had me thrown in jail. I was there for forty-eight hours. For the first twenty-four hours I was a basket case. You would have loved seeing me. Then I realized I was letting you win. So I spent the second night thinking. I thought I was going to find a way to locate Grunard. I tried to divorce myself the way I do when I work on one of my skulls and just examine the facts and events. I started with something that bothered me at the time I learned about it, but I forgot about when I saw the photo. Charlie said that Sung was excited and talking about shifts and spectrums and that he made a phone call before he said he needed to see me. He could have called Grunard, but if he recognized Grunard as the killer, why call him? No, it had to be someone else. So I asked Logan to check phone records and find out who Sung called. It was to Multiplex, one of the digital imaging companies on the West Coast. Sung wanted to verify his findings on the photo. It was the middle of the night, but there's often a crew working at those big companies. You'd sent the photo out to Multiplex to have Grunard's image implanted in it so I could 'discover' it. That was why you stalled giving us the photo."

"Worked."

"But you didn't realize how sharp Sung was. State-of-the-art companies like Multiplex create their own software and the variance of the shifts in the light spectrums are almost like a fingerprint. Sung recognized that shift and he knew the picture had been doctored. Multiplex might not have been willing to confirm the specific job, but they would have no reason not to confirm the general technical aspects of the software. Did Charlie call you from the lab after he called me?"

"Of course. I trained him well."

"And then you killed him. What would you have done if Joe hadn't climbed down and retrieved that photo? Would that other picture you supposedly sent to Quantico surface?"

He didn't answer. He was having trouble breathing.

"But it was all guesswork, and I had to verify. Multiplex wouldn't talk to me. You'd probably told them to keep the job confidential, and everybody obeys the FBI. So I took the photo and did some work myself. I didn't have the equipment or expertise to do what Sung did, so I did a digital merge of the faces of your brothers." She smiled grimly. "And what to my surprise appeared? I came up with you."

"Lie. We look—nothing like each other."

"You're right and that was good. I was much more likely to pull up a completely distinctive face than if your brothers looked alike. I often use older family members' features for age progression for children. When I was studying at the National Center for Missing Children, I used to play with merging different familial faces and seeing what I could come up with. Even when the family members didn't look like one another, it was amazing how the similarities appeared when they were combined. The face I came up with didn't resemble you exactly, but it was close enough, and after I aged the image, it was even closer. It made me go over everything that had happened."

"I didn't make—mistakes. I didn't."

"No, you were almost perfect. But you were always there beside me or in the background."

"So was Grunard."

"Yes, and I stumbled over that conversation with Dom while you were in the same room with me at Joe's cottage. It was only later that I realized it wasn't really a conversation. Dom made a brief statement and hung up. A taped alibi set on a timer. Very effective." She shook her head. "There were so many things that became clear once I accepted that you were Dom. All the times you misdirected and lied to me and Joe. Why should we have suspected? You were Spiro of the FBI."

"You're so proud of yourself." His expression was full of malice. "You haven't won. I won't die. I'm feeling stronger all the time. I'll live and they'll say I'm insane."

"You won't live."

She looked up to see Joe standing beside her, staring down at Spiro.

"If there's even a chance of you living I'll put another bullet in you before the police get here," Joe said. "You'd be dead now if I hadn't decided not to risk a head shot. You were too close to her."

"Closer than you. Closer than anyone. She'll forget you. She'll never forget me." His gaze shifted to Eve. "The little girl will die. I've hidden her and it gets freezing cold up here at night. She doesn't have a coat and she's tied. You won't find her in time."

Fear rushed through her. "You lie. Sarah and Monty are looking for her now. They'll find her."

"What if I've laid a false trail? I knew you had Sarah and Monty at your disposal. You should know I never take anything for granted. Ah, I've scared you. You're not so—"

"Would you care to go down the hill and wait in the car?" Joe asked Eve. "I think it's time we said good-bye to the bastard."

"She won't let you. She's still too soft." Spiro raised himself up. "The girl will die, but I'll live forever. I'll live—" Blood gushed from his chest. "Stop the bleeding, Eve. You know you can't let me die."

"Screw you." She stood up and turned to Joe. "We have to call the local police and then ring Sarah and see if she's found Jane."

"I'll be right with you," Joe said.

"No." She looked down at Spiro. "I don't want it quick. Let the bastard bleed to death."

She turned and walked away.

"*Eve!*"

She stared straight ahead, ignoring Spiro's howl of disbelief and terror.

"WE HAVEN'T FOUND her, Eve," Sarah said.

"The temperature's falling."

"I know that. The bastard may have laid a false trail or even several."

"He wants her to die."

"Monty's moving in another direction. I have to go." She hung up.

Eve turned to Joe. "He has them running around in

circles." She shuddered as a sudden gust of wind knifed through her jacket. "It must be down to zero. If he has her tied, Jane can't even move to keep herself warm."

ANOTHER FALSE LEAD.

How many had the bastard laid? Sarah wondered.

*Child?*

Monty was bewildered too. He was running around in circles trying to find the scent.

He suddenly stopped short and turned toward the east.

*Child?*

"What is it, boy?"

His head lifted as if listening.

Jesus, he was trembling, and the hair was rising on his back.

What the hell was happening?

*Other child.*

He started at a dead run toward the east.

*Other child. Other child. Other child . . .*

"WE FOUND HER," Sarah said. "She was under some boulders on the slope of the ravine. We almost missed her."

"Is she okay?"

"She's cold but no hypothermia. Monty's lying beside her, keeping her warm. As soon as I get my breath, we'll start back."

"We'll come to you."

"No, I want her out of this cold. I gave her my jacket, and walking will be good for her."

Eve turned to Joe, who was coming down the hill. "She's okay."

"Thank God." He glanced back over his shoulder at the top of the hill. "Too bad Spiro isn't still alive so we could rub his nose in it."

"Did you . . . ?"

Joe shook his head. "Don't blame me. He was already dead when I went up to check on him."

"I wouldn't have blamed you if you had ended it for him. I would have killed him myself rather than chance having him go free."

"My, how you've changed."

"Yes, I've changed." She looked up at the hill still lit with candles. Dom had changed her. Not the way he had wanted to. He'd thought he could drag her down, close her away from life. He hadn't realized he'd caused her to reach out to life instead. How he would have hated knowing that.

"The police are coming." Joe's gaze was on the lights of two highway patrol cars coming up the road toward them. "There will be some tall explaining to do."

"Yes." She took his hand. His grasp was warm and strong and rock steady. See what you've given me, Dom? Life. Love. Light where there was darkness.

Burn in hell, you bastard.

She squeezed Joe's hand as they started down the road. "No problem. We'll manage to get through it together."

## E P I L O G U E

"You should go in. It may be March, but the lake breeze is still cool."

Eve turned to see Bonnie sitting on the porch steps, leaning against the rail. "I'm not cold. Who's the mother here?"

Bonnie giggled. "I'm making up for all the times you said things like that to me."

"Ungrateful child."

"Yep." She shaded her eyes as she looked out at the boat on the water. "Joe's got Jane all bundled up in his sweater. Why didn't you go fishing with them?"

"I was feeling lazy."

"And you wanted to give Joe the chance to bond with Jane."

"If you knew the answer, why did you ask?"

"You shouldn't worry. He really likes Jane. It's not easy for him to let anyone else into his life. It will take a little time for him to adjust."

"I'm not worried." She leaned her head back against the rail. "Life's pretty good, baby."

"It's about time. You've been very difficult, Mama." She looked back at the boat. "You haven't told Joe about me yet."

"I will soon."

"Are you afraid he'll think you're crazy? You should know better."

"Maybe I just want to keep you to myself for a little while longer. Is that so bad?"

"Not to me."

"Or maybe I'm afraid if I tell anyone, you won't come back."

"That's pretty dumb. Why would I leave you just when you're so much happier? I love to see you happy."

Contentment flowed through Eve in a golden tide. "We're going to find you, Bonnie. Sarah offered to come here with Monty next month and search the Chattahoochee park. I have a good feeling. We're going to bring you home, baby."

"You know that never meant anything to me, but it will make you happy." She leaned forward and linked her arms around her knees. "I like Monty. He's nice and smart too."

"And how do you know he's smart?"

Bonnie didn't answer.

"Sarah said something weird happened to Monty up in the mountains that night."

Bonnie's gaze shifted back to the boat. "Did she?"

"You wouldn't know anything about that, would you?"

"Don't be silly, Mama. How could I?" The teasing smile Bonnie turned on her was brimming with love and mischief. "When you know I'm only a dream."

# ABOUT THE AUTHOR

IRIS JOHANSEN, who has more than eight million copies of her books in print, has won many awards for her achievements in writing. The bestselling author of *The Face of Deception, And Then You Die, Long After Midnight,* and *The Ugly Duckling* lives near Atlanta, Georgia, where she is currently at work on a new novel.

Look for Iris Johansen's next novel of suspense

# THE SEARCH

Available in hardcover June 2000

As part of an elite search and rescue team, Sarah Patrick and her golden retriever, Monty, have a gift for finding what no one else can—whether it's a survivor buried alive by an earthquake or the skeleton of a murdered child. But their latest assignment is not like the others. This time Sarah is being forced to take part in a deadly mission by John Logan. He knows enough about her past to ensure her cooperation, and he won't take no for an answer. But Logan's promises that she and Monty will be safe may not be enough to protect them. Because a killer is devising a chilling vengeance . . . and he may soon find use for Sarah.

Turn the page for a sneak peek.

**Barat, Turkey**
**June 11**

"Get out of there, Sarah," Boyd yelled from outside the house. "That wall is going to tumble any minute."

"Monty's found something." Sarah carefully moved over to the pile of rubble where the golden retriever was standing. "Be still, boy. Be very still."

*Child?*

"How do I know?" Monty always hoped it would be a child. He loved kids and all these lost and hurt children nearly killed him. They nearly killed her too, Sarah thought wearily. Finding the children and the old people were always the most painful. So few survived these catastrophes. The earth trembled and the walls fell and life was snuffed out as if it had never been.

*Out.*

"You're sure?"

*Out.*

"Okay." She absently patted Monty's head as she gazed at the rubble. The second story of the small house had caved in, and chances of anyone being alive beneath the wreckage were minimal. She could hear no groans or weeping. It wouldn't be responsible of her to bring anyone else from the search and rescue team into the building. She should get out herself.

*Child?*

What the hell? Stop wasting time. She knew she wasn't going to leave until she investigated more closely. She reached for a stool and tossed it aside. "Go to Boyd, Monty."

The retriever sat down and looked at her.

"I keep telling you that you're supposed to be a professional. That means you obey orders, dammit."

*Wait.*

She tossed a cushion to one side and tugged at the easy chair. Jesus, it was heavy. "You can't help me now."

*Wait.*

"Get out of there, Sarah," Boyd yelled. "That's an order. It's been four days. You know you probably won't find anyone alive."

"We found that man in Tegucigalpa alive after twelve days. Call Monty, will you, Boyd?"

"Monty!"

Monty didn't move. She hadn't thought he would, but there was always a chance. "Stupid dog."

*Wait.*

"If you're going to stay there, I'm coming in to help you," Boyd said.

"No, I'll be out in a minute." Sarah glanced warily at the south wall, then tugged at the mattress until she got it to one side. "I'm just looking around."

"I'll give you three minutes."

Three minutes.

She pulled frantically at the carved headboard.

Monty whined.

"Shh." She finally heaved the headboard to one side.

And then she saw the hand.

Such a small, delicate hand, clutching a rosary . . .

"A SURVIVOR?" BOYD asked as Sarah walked out of the house. "Do we need to send in a team?"

She numbly shook her head. "Dead. A teenage girl. Two days, maybe. Don't risk anyone's neck. Just mark the site." She snapped on Monty's leash. "I'm going back to the trailer. I've got to get Monty out of here. You know how upset he gets. I'll be back in a couple of hours."

"Yeah, it's only your dog that's upset." Boyd's tone dripped sarcasm. "That's why you're shaking like a leaf."

"I'm fine."

"I don't want to see you take a step out of that trailer until tomorrow morning. You've gone without sleep for thirty-six hours. You know exhausted workers are a hazard to themselves and the people they're trying to help. You were incredibly stupid to run that risk. You're usually smarter than that."

"Monty was sure there was someone—" Why was she arguing? He was right. The only way to stay alive in situations like this was to stick to the rules and not act on impulse. She should have gone by the book. "I'm sorry, Boyd."

"You should be." He scowled. "You're one of my best people, and I won't have you thrown off the team because you're thinking with your heart instead of your head. You endangered not only yourself but your dog. What would you have done if that wall had fallen and killed Monty?"

"It wouldn't have killed Monty. I'd have thrown myself on top of him and let you dig the wall off me." She smiled faintly. "I know who's important around here."

"Very funny." He shook his head. "Except you're not joking."

"No." She rubbed her eyes. "She had a rosary in her hand, Boyd. She must have grabbed it when the quake started. But it didn't help her, did it?"

"I guess not."

"She couldn't have been over sixteen, and she was pregnant."

"Shit."

"Yeah." She gently tugged on Monty's leash. "We'll be back in a little while."

"You're not listening. I'm in charge of this search, Sarah. I want you to rest. We've probably found all the live ones. I'm expecting the order to pull out tomorrow. The Russian team can finish searching for the dead."

"All the more reason to work harder until the order comes. None of the Russians' dogs has Monty's nose. You know he's incredible."

"You're not so bad yourself. Do you know the other members of the team are making bets on whether or not you can actually read that dog's mind?"

"That's pretty dumb. They're all close to their own dogs. They know that when you live with an animal, you get to learn how to read them."

"Not like you."

"Why are we talking about this? The important thing is Monty is unique. He's found survivors before when everyone had given up hope. He may find more today."

"It's not likely."

She walked away.

"I mean it, Sarah."

She glanced back over her shoulder. "And how long has it been since you slept, Boyd?"

"That's none of your damn business."

"Do as I say and not as I do? I'll see you in a couple of hours." She could hear him swearing behind her as she picked her way through the rubble toward the line of mobile homes at the bottom of the hill. Boyd Medford was a good guy, a fine team leader, and everything he said made sense. But there were times when she couldn't be sensible. Too many dead. Too few survivors. Oh, God, too many bodies . . .

The rosary . . .

Did that poor girl have time to pray for her own life and the life of her child before she had been crushed? Probably not. Earthquakes took only a heartbeat to destroy.

Monty pressed against her legs. *Sad*.

"Me too." She opened the door of the mobile home for Monty. "It happens. Maybe next time it won't be that way."

*Sad*.

She filled up Monty's water dish. "Drink, boy."

*Sad*. He lay down in front of the metal dish.

He'd drink soon, but she'd wait for an hour or two before she tried to feed him. He was too upset to eat. He never got used to finding the dead.

Neither did she.

She sat down on the floor beside Monty and put her arms around him. "It will be okay," she whispered. "Maybe next time we'll find a little boy alive like we did yesterday." Was it yesterday? The days blurred together when they were on a search. "Remember the child, Monty?"

*Child*.

"He's alive because of you. That's why we have to go on. Even if it hurts." Jesus, it did hurt. It hurt seeing Monty this upset. It hurt remembering that girl clutching the rosary. It hurt knowing there would probably not be another person found alive.

But probably was not certainly. There was always hope as long as you kept trying.

She closed her eyes. She was tired and all her muscles ached. So what? She'd have time for a long rest later. All she needed right now was a few hours of sleep and she'd be ready to go on. "Come on, let's take a nap." She stretched out beside the retriever. "Then we'll go see if we can find anyone else alive in this hellhole."

Monty was whining softly as he put his head on his paws.

"Shh." She buried her face in his fur. "It's okay." It wasn't okay. Death was never okay. "We're together. We're doing our job. We just have to get through the next few days. Then we'll be back at the ranch." She began stroking his head. "You'll like that, won't you?"

*Sad.*

He was hurting, but it wasn't as bad as usual. Sometimes isolated cases were worse for him. It wasn't that he became callused to the massive loss of life he encountered in major disasters. Instead, they were working so constantly that the reaction was delayed. He'd be ready to go again in a few hours.

But would she?

She'd be fine. Just as she'd told Boyd. The last few days were always the worst. Hope was dimming, desperation growing, and the sadness lay in your heart and mind until you thought you couldn't bear it.

But she always did bear it. You had to bear it because there was always a chance someone was out there waiting. Someone who would be lost if she and Monty didn't find her.

Monty rolled over and lay on his side. *Sleep.*

"Yes, that's what we should do." Sleep, friend, and so will I. Let the memory of rosaries and unborn children fade away. Let death go. Let hope come back. "Just a little nap . . ."

●　　●　　●

"How many dead?" Logan asked.

"Four." Castleton's lips tightened grimly. "And two men are in the local hospital in serious condition. Can we leave now? The stench of this place makes me want to throw up. I feel guilty as hell. I'm the one who hired Bassett for this job. I liked him."

"In a minute." Logan's gaze wandered around the scorched ruins that had once been a state-of-the-art facility. It had been only three days, but the jungle was already reclaiming its own. Grass sprouted among the fallen timbers, vines reached toward the site in a macabre embrace from nearby trees. "Were you able to recover any of Bassett's work?"

"No."

Logan looked down at the dark red carnelian scarab in his hand. "And Rudzak sent this to me this morning?"

"I guess it was Rudzak. It was on my doorstep with your name on it."

"It was Rudzak."

Castleton's gaze shifted from the scarab to Logan's face. "Bassett has a wife and kid. What are you going to tell them?"

"Nothing."

"What do you mean, nothing? You have to tell them what happened to Bassett."

"And what am I supposed to tell them? We don't know what happened to him. Not yet." He turned away and headed back toward the jeep.

"Rudzak's going to kill him," Castleton said, following Logan.

"Maybe."

"You know it."

"I think he'll try to make a deal first."

"Ransom?"

"Possibly. He wants something, or he wouldn't have bothered to take Bassett."

"And you're going to deal with that bastard? After what he did to your people?"

"I'll deal with the devil himself if it will get me what I want."

It was the answer Castleton expected. John Logan had not gotten to be one of the foremost economic forces in the world by avoiding confrontation. He had made billions with his computer company and other enterprises before he'd reached forty.

And he had risked the lives of several scientists to realize the gigantic rewards the project offered. Some people would say that no man with a conscience would have set up this facility when he knew what consequences might—

"Say it." Logan was staring at him. "Let it out."

"You shouldn't have done it."

"Everyone in this facility chose to be here. I never lied to them about what they were facing. They believed it was worth it."

"I wonder how they felt when the bullets hit them. Do you think they still thought it was worth it?"

Logan didn't flinch. "Who the hell knows what's important enough to die for? Do you want out, Castleton?"

Yes, he wanted out. The situation was becoming too deadly and complicated. He didn't deal well with either, and he cursed the day he'd become involved in it. "Are you firing me?"

"No way. I need you. You know how things work down here. That's why I hired you in the first place. But I'll understand if you want out. I'll pay you and let you walk away."

"Let me?"

"I could find a way to keep you on the job," Logan said wearily. "There's always a way to do anything you want to do. You just have to decide how far you want to commit yourself. But you've done a good job for me and I'm not willing to force you to stay on. I'll try to find someone else."

"No one could force me to do anything I don't want to do."

"Have it your way." Logan got into the jeep. "Take me back to the airport. I've got to get busy. Am I going to have trouble with the local police?"

"You know better than that. These hills are deep in drug country. It's not safe to ask questions. The police just look the other way." He smiled bitterly as he started the jeep. "Isn't that why you built the facility here?"

"Yes."

"And they won't help you get Bassett away from Rudzak. He's a dead man."

"If he's not dead now, I'll get him back."

"How? Money?"

"Whatever it takes."

"It's impossible. Even if you pay a ransom, Rudzak may kill him anyway. You can't expect to—"

"I'll get him back." Logan's voice suddenly vibrated with harshness. "Listen to me, Castleton. You may think I'm a son of a bitch, but I don't shrug off my responsibilities. Those were my employees who died and I want the men who did it. And if you think I'm going to let them kill or use Bassett to get at me, you're wrong. I'll find him."

"In the middle of the jungle?"

"In the middle of hell." Logan's voice was flint sharp. "Now you've been telling me how sorry you are and how guilty I should feel. Well, I don't have time for guilt. I've always found it counterproductive. You do what you have to do, but don't tell me anything's impossible until you've tried and failed and tried again. I won't buy it."

"You don't have to buy it. I'm not asking you to—" His gaze narrowed on Logan's face. "You're trying to manipulate me."

"Am I?"

"You know damn well you are."

"Smart man. You should have expected it. I'm just as ruthless as you think I am, and I told you I needed you."

Castleton was silent for a moment. "Do you really think you have a chance of saving Bassett?"

"If he's alive, I'll bring him back. Will you help me?"

"What do you want me to do?"

"What you've been doing all along. Grease palms and take care of my people. By the way, I want them out of that hospital and on their way home as soon as possible. They're too vulnerable here."

"I was going to take care of that for you anyway."

"And keep your ears open and your mouth shut. If I'm not in the area, Rudzak will probably contact you first." He smiled crookedly. "Don't worry, I'm not going to ask you to put your neck on the block. You're much too valuable to me in other ways."

"I'm not a coward, Logan."

"No, but this is out of your area of expertise. I always get the right person for the right job. I assure you I wouldn't hesitate to rope you into it if I thought it necessary."

Castleton believed him. He had never seen Logan like this. Most of the time he kept that streak of hard ruthlessness buried beneath a layer of easy charisma. He suddenly recalled the many stories about Logan's shady associations in the early years, the years he had spent in Asia. Gazing at Logan now, he could believe there was more truth than fiction in those wild tales of smuggling and violent power struggles with local gangs who had tried to sell him "protection."

"Well?"

"Okay." Castleton moistened his lips. "I'll stay."

"Good."

"But not because of anything you've said. I just feel guilty as hell that I was in town and not here when it happened. Maybe I could have done something, anything to prevent—"

"Don't be an idiot. You'd have been dead too. Now, do you know of any contact Rudzak might have that we can tap?"

"The talk is there's a dealer named Ricardo Sanchez in Bogotá who's been acting as a go-between for the Mendez cartel and Rudzak."

"Find him. Do anything you have to do. I want to know where Rudzak's camp is located."

"I'm not a thug, Logan."

"Then would it hurt your delicate sense of ethics to hire a thug?"

"You don't have to be sarcastic."

"No, I don't," he said wearily. "If I weren't pressed for time, I'd go to Bogotá and pressure Sanchez myself. Never mind, I have a man who can find out what I need to know."

"I hope you succeed."

"So do I. But even if Sanchez proves useless, I'll still find Bassett."

Castleton shook his head. "No one around here is going to tell you where he is or go into that jungle to look for him."

"Then I'll find him on my own."

"How?"

Logan said grimly, "I know someone who might be able to help me."

"The right person for the right job?"

"Exactly."

"Then God help him."

"It's not a man." Logan glanced back over his shoulder at the ruins. "It's a woman."

# IRIS JOHANSEN

| | | |
|---|---|---|
| LIONS BRIDE | \_\_\_\_56990-2 | $6.99/$8.99 in Canada |
| DARK RIDER | \_\_\_\_29947-6 | $6.99/$8.99 |
| MIDNIGHT WARRIOR | \_\_\_\_29946-8 | $6.99/$8.99 |
| THE BELOVED SCOUNDREL | \_\_\_\_29945-X | $6.99/$8.99 |
| THE TIGER PRINCE | \_\_\_\_29968-9 | $6.99/$8.99 |
| THE MAGNIFICENT ROGUE | \_\_\_\_29944-1 | $6.99/$8.99 |
| THE GOLDEN BARBARIAN | \_\_\_\_26604-3 | $6.99/$8.99 |
| LAST BRIDGE HOME | \_\_\_\_29871-2 | $5.99/$8.99 |
| THE UGLY DUCKLING | \_\_\_\_56991-0 | $6.99/$8.99 |
| LONG AFTER MIDNIGHT | \_\_\_\_57181-8 | $6.99/$8.99 |
| AND THEN YOU DIE | \_\_\_\_57998-3 | $6.99/$8.99 |
| THE FACE OF DECEPTION | \_\_\_\_57802-2 | $6.99/$9.99 |
| THE KILLING GAME | \_\_\_\_58155-4 | $6.99/$9.99 |
| THE SEARCH | \_\_\_\_80091-4 | $24.95/35.95 |

❧    THE WIND DANCER TRILOGY    ❧

| | | |
|---|---|---|
| THE WIND DANCER | \_\_\_\_28855-5 | $6.99/$9.99 |
| STORM WINDS | \_\_\_\_29032-0 | $6.99/$8.99 |
| REAP THE WIND | \_\_\_\_29244-7 | $6.99/$9.99 |

---

Ask for these books at your local bookstore or use this page to order.

Please send me the books I have checked above. I am enclosing $\_\_\_\_ (add $2.50 to cover postage and handling). Send check or money order, no cash or C.O.D.'s, please.

Name _____

Address _____

City/State/Zip _____

Send order to: Bantam Books, Dept. FN37, 2451 S. Wolf Rd., Des Plaines, IL 60018
Allow four to six weeks for delivery.
Prices and availability subject to change without notice.          FN 37 5/00